TIME HEALS ALL WOUNDS...

Her cheeks reddened, making her unbelievably beautiful. She lowered her gaze and slanted her eyes back up at him in a manner that seemed almost provocative. "Again, I apologize. But, Zacharias, I know you still feel something for me. That kiss the other day—"

"Was a mistake," he finished gruffly, more to convince himself than her.

She shook her head and smiled slowly. "I don't think so."

"Are you telling me you *enjoyed* it?"

"Are you telling me you didn't?"

Good Lord, the woman was flirting with him. *Flirting.* Agatha! If he didn't know better, he'd swear he was dreaming. And worse, he liked it. There'd been a time when he'd have given anything to have her look at him as she did now. When he'd have sold his soul to have her touch him.

"Perhaps you'd like another," he said, inching closer, hoping she'd say yes but expecting her to scurry away.

"Perhaps I would." Her gaze didn't even falter. Instead, he saw a gleam of anticipation in the dark eyes. Her lips parted slightly. Her breath grew shallow. He could see her pulse in the hollow of her throat.

Urgent need wiped away the last of his reservations. Without giving himself a chance to think again, he pulled her into his embrace and lowered his lips to hers . . .

A Time to Dream

Sherry Lewis

JOVE BOOKS, NEW YORK

TIME PASSAGES is a trademark of Penguin Putnam Inc.

A TIME TO DREAM

A Jove Book / published by arrangement with
the author

PRINTING HISTORY
Jove edition / December 1999

The Penguin Putnam Inc. World Wide Web site address is
http://www.penguinputnam.com

ISBN: 0-515-12729-9

A JOVE BOOK®
Jove Books are published by The Berkley Publishing Group,
a division of Penguin Putnam Inc.,
375 Hudson Street, New York, New York 10014.
JOVE and the "J" design
are trademarks belonging to Penguin Putnam Inc.

PRINTED IN THE UNITED STATES OF AMERICA

10 9 8 7 6 5 4 3 2 1

With grateful thanks . . .

*to the original Coal Dancers
Heather Horrocks, Joann Jones, Sherry Leach,
Sherry Mathewson, and Alice Trego.
Here's to crossing barriers, slaying dragons,
and spinning straw into gold.
Here's to hippos in tutus,
high tea and unshaved legs,
and dancing the cha-cha-cha.*

*And to Susette and Robert Williams,
who took time from their romantic anniversary getaway
to pick up research material for a stranger.*

*And to my editor and friend,
Gail Fortune, whose faith in me leaves me speechless,
whose assistance and guidance is priceless,
and whose phone calls always lift my spirit.*

Chapter 1

HEART THUDDING, HEAD fuzzy, and eyes still blurry from sleep, Shelby Miller tried not to trip over the hem of her robe as she raced down the grand staircase. She'd been in the middle of a perfectly lovely dream when someone had started pounding on the door and jerked her mercilessly awake. Whoever it was, she thought as she stumbled past the landing, they'd better have a good reason for waking her.

Early-morning sunlight spilled down the staircase from the huge window on the landing and into the foyer through the full-length windows flanking the door. Even this early—surely not later than seven o'clock—the temperature and the dense Missouri humidity made her long for central air-conditioning.

Clutching the collar of her robe, she ran her free hand through the curls she could feel bobbing wildly with every step—the hated curls that had earned her the nickname Medusa as a child. She'd probably scare whoever was so rudely—and insistently—banging on the door. Well, if she did, it served them right. Maybe it would teach them a lesson in manners.

Before she could make it to the bottom of the staircase, the pounding started up again. "Hold on," she shouted impatiently. "I'm coming." Shelby had never been at her best in the morning, which was one of the reasons she loved her position at Winterhill. She didn't have to look perky, dress for success, or even be coherent before noon if she didn't want to be.

Slipping a little as she crossed the polished wood floor, she skidded to a stop in front of the massive door and yanked it open. When she saw Jon Davenport, her dearest friend in Hannibal—her *only* real friend anywhere—on the porch, backed by the rising sun, his hand raised to knock again, she let out an annoyed sigh. "What are you doing?"

Jon lowered his arm quickly and ignored her question. "It's about time you answered. Where were you?"

"In bed. *Asleep.*" She stepped aside to let him enter and closed the door behind him. "Why aren't you at work? And why are you banging on my door like the world's coming to an end?"

"You might think it has ended when I tell you what I just heard on the morning news." Jon's eyes were dark and uncharacteristically solemn, his mouth nothing more than a thin slash cut into his tanned face.

Shelby made another vain attempt to tame her curls. "Okay. What did you hear?"

"Evan McDonald has put Winterhill up for sale."

It took a moment for the words to sink in completely, but when they did, the old, familiar anxiety began to pulse through Shelby's veins. "He's done *what*?"

"He's listed this house on the market."

Hoping she'd heard wrong, Shelby shook her head. "But he can't do that."

"He can," Jon said, "and, according to the news, he has."

"But *why*?" Her voice came out sharp, but she made no effort to soften it. "I thought he'd decided to restore Winterhill."

"Apparently he's decided not to."

Time slowed, ice water flowed through her veins, and

a steady pounding started somewhere behind her eyes. "But—" Working as caretaker at Winterhill for the past six months had given her the first security she'd ever known. She'd even started to believe it would last. She should have known better. "But why didn't Evan tell me first?"

"Who knows?" Jon moved to stand behind her and put a hand on her shoulder. The weight of his hand and the depth of his concern bore down on her.

She tried to step away from both. She'd spent most of her twenty-eight years on her own. Jon's friendship was the first real tie she'd ever had to anyone or anything, and it still left her slightly off-balance.

Jon didn't let her escape. "Even when Evan's mother was alive, he didn't like this house, Shelby. And to tell you the truth, everyone at the historical society was surprised when he hired you after she died instead of selling it."

She couldn't bear the gentleness in his voice. It made the pain worse somehow. She'd grown to love Winterhill, and she'd even let herself dream of staying here in Hannibal. Its history appealed to her and made her long to be a part of it.

Pacing to the front window, she glanced outside and let her gaze linger on the crumbling turrets of the neighboring house barely visible above the rows of trees that separated the two properties. "What about Summervale?" she asked softly, turning back to face him. "What about the movement to save the twin houses?"

"There *is* no movement," Jon admitted reluctantly. "I haven't been able to whip up much excitement about saving Summervale. Most people think it's already too dilapidated to save. And without Winterhill—" He broke off and shrugged helplessly.

"But the twin houses are a piece of Hannibal's history."

"A piece nobody's much interested in," Jon reminded her.

Shelby pushed a curl away from her forehead.

"Maybe whoever buys Winterhill will be interested in restoring both houses."

"I doubt it," Jon said, shaking his head slowly. "People are speculating that Evan will sell this place to some industry or developer."

Shelby's heart twisted painfully. "And they'll tear it down. And Summervale will follow."

"Probably."

Tears stung her eyes, but she refused to give in to them. Crying had never solved a problem for her, not even once in her life. "I won't let that happen," she said, lifting her chin.

A shadow flitted behind his eyes. "You can't stop it, Shel. The only real selling point we've ever had in trying to save the houses was that they're less than two miles apart, built by the same man within only a few years of each other, and virtually identical in every respect."

"Yes. Exactly!" She paced a few steps away ignoring the pity she saw on his face, fighting her sudden flash of resentment. "And the mystery, of course."

"There *is* no mystery." Jon's voice sharpened slightly as it always did when she raised the subject. "Summervale belonged to a crazy woman who lived as a recluse most of her life. . . ."

"Yes, and Winterhill belonged to her husband and children who lived within spitting distance of her and never saw her." Shelby let the fear building inside her come out as anger. "And nobody knows why. You can't tell me that's not fascinating stuff."

"It's not fascinating stuff," Jon said, his voice slightly more gentle. "Not fascinating enough to convince anyone to shell out the fortune it would take to restore Summervale. Not enough to save Winterhill." The pity in his eyes deepened. "Nobody cares, Shelby."

"*I* care." Desperation made the pounding in her head worse. If she couldn't even convince Jon to fight for the houses, how could she convince anyone else? She waved a jerky hand toward the window and Summervale and tried again. "There was no hint of insanity before Agatha married Zacharias Logan."

"So, her husband drove her crazy," Jon said with a lazy shrug. "The point is—"

"The point *is*," Shelby interrupted, growing angrier and more hurt by the minute, "if we could find out what happened to her, maybe we could generate public interest in the houses."

"We've tried to find out what happened," Jon reminded her, "over and over again. Zacharias's papers hardly mention Agatha at all, and we can't find any of her letters or journals."

"That doesn't mean they don't exist. There *has* to be some record somewhere. Some explanation for why Agatha turned her back on her children."

Jon's eyes roamed her face, searching, probing, and making her distinctly uncomfortable. "Is *that* why you're so obsessed with the Logans?"

"I'm not obsessed," she insisted. "I'm interested. There's a difference."

"Aw, Shelby." Jon touched her shoulder again. "Finding out why some woman—a woman who's been dead for more than a hundred years—turned her back on *her* children isn't going to explain why your mother abandoned you."

Shelby jerked away, wishing she'd kept that part of her past secret from him, as she had from everyone else. "My mother *didn't* abandon me, she put me up for adoption. The fact that nobody ever wanted to adopt me wasn't her fault."

Pity filled his entire expression now. "Why do you stick up for your mother, Shel?"

"I'm not sticking up for her," Shelby said quickly. She hated thinking anyone felt sorry for her. She might not have any idea who her mother was, she might have bounced from one foster home to another as a child, she might even have moved from one city to the next as an adult, but many people had difficult childhoods, and she'd long ago adjusted to hers.

She forced a laugh and tried to change the subject. "We're not talking about me, we're talking about the twin houses." She paced to the other side of the foyer and trailed her fingers across the gleaming wood of the bannister. "If Agatha hadn't died so young. Or if Zacharias had stayed in Hannibal . . . If they'd stayed together, there'd probably still be Logans living in both of these houses, and they wouldn't be in danger now."

"Maybe," Jon said without conviction. "But Agatha did die, and Zacharias didn't stay. And the houses have brought bad luck to every family who's tried to live in them since."

"That's nothing but superstition."

"Maybe." Jon glanced at a scowling portrait of Zacharias hanging on the wall of the landing. "But wishing things had turned out differently won't change anything."

"I know that." And she did. Only too well. She dropped onto one of the steps and stretched out her legs in front of her. "But I can't stand by and let these houses be destroyed, Jon. I just *can't*."

Jon sat beside her, his shoulder barely grazing hers. "What do you have in mind?"

"Nothing, unfortunately. Not yet, anyway."

Jon put a hand over hers and rested his cheek on the top of her head. "If I thought you had a chance, I'd help you in whatever way I could." He let out a sigh that spoke of tested patience. "Why don't I ask around and see if I can find you another job somewhere?"

Shelby fought the urge to draw away. "I don't want another job. I want to save the twin houses."

"I know. And I wish I knew of a way for you to do that. But I just don't want you to get your hopes up. You can't rewrite history."

"Well, I wish I could," she muttered as a wave of futility crashed over her.

Maybe she *should* know better than to get her hopes up. Maybe she should have learned her lesson after watching her dreams vaporize one by one over the years.

But everything had seemed so different here in Hannibal, and the longer she stayed the more she loved it.

She took a deep breath and tried to pull herself together. But she couldn't face losing another home and having to start all over again. After the last time, she'd vowed it wouldn't happen again. And that was a promise she intended to keep—no matter what it took.

Clutching a hammer in one hand and a crowbar in the other, Shelby checked behind her one last time to make sure no one had watched her cross the boundary between Winterhill and Summervale. Even with the deep shade of oak and willow trees to block the sun, the heat was vicious and unrelenting.

Far below, at the bottom of Union Street Hill, she could see the Mississippi River curving lazily toward the bluff below town as it made its way toward the ocean. But only the hum of insects and the slight rustling of a much-needed breeze in the branches overhead broke the stillness.

She moved on, down one short hill and up another toward the gardens, pushing through waist-high weeds and overgrown hedges until she came to a stop in Summervale's neglected front garden. Weeds filled what once must have been beautifully tended beds of flowers, hedges, and ornamental shrubs. More weeds grew unchecked along the circular drive and wrapped around the trunks of the trees that formed a canopy over it.

The sun beat down upon her unmercifully while she stared at the house in front of her. Sheets of weathered plywood covered the windows and doors. Paint peeled in strips from the trim. Bricks crumbled. Shutters sagged at the plywood windows. Branches from an overgrown willow clawed at the roof of the grand porte cochere and second-floor windows above it.

Shelby ran her arm across her forehead, wiping away the dirt and perspiration that trickled into her eyes. Somewhere inside, she'd find Agatha's papers and journals. She just *knew* she would. And somewhere inside them she'd find the means to save the twin houses.

Slowly, carefully, she made her way through the overgrown garden and up the front steps. The boards creaked and groaned under her weight and made her wish she wasn't still packing that extra ten pounds from last winter.

What if she fell through one of these rotting boards and broke a leg? Who would find her? And if someone *did* find her, what possible explanation would she give for being here?

Well, she told herself firmly, that just wouldn't happen. She wouldn't get hurt and she wouldn't get caught. Period. End of story.

Working quickly, she pried the nails from the plywood over the door and hefted the unwieldy board to one side. Then, dusting her hands on her jeans, she turned to face the door itself. She hesitated at the threshold with one hand on the heavy brass knob. She'd waited so long to see inside Summervale, she almost hated to spoil the moment. But success never came to the faint of heart.

Squaring her shoulders, she opened the door and plunged into the near-darkness. Musty air rushed to fill her nostrils. Cobwebs trailed from light fixtures to doorways to the few pieces of heavy furniture that hadn't been removed. Deep shadows filled the broad foyer, relieved only by the sunlight that crept in through the doorway behind her and snuck around the boards covering the window on the landing.

A grand staircase rose to a broad landing then on to the second floor, just as it did at Winterhill. An identical window seat, made of the same rich, dark wood, graced a bay window that she knew overlooked the back gardens and the rows of trees that separated the two houses. At least she wouldn't have trouble finding her way around. That was a plus. The two houses did, indeed, appear to be identical. Except that Summervale was somehow *more*.

She turned slowly, marveling at everything. Winterhill

was beautiful, of course, but it paled by comparison to the original—not in its current state, but in Shelby's imagination.

Sighing softly, she whispered to the empty house: "You must have been absolutely breathtaking. How could Agatha bear to keep you hidden away?" There were no answers, of course. And Shelby gave herself a stern warning to stop daydreaming and get down to business.

Abandoning the crowbar near the bottom of the stairs, she pulled a flashlight from the back pocket of her jeans and started up the stairs. Instinct told her Agatha must have occupied the large turret room overlooking the front drive. It was the largest bedroom in the twin houses and at Winterhill it was graced by a massive fireplace with an ornately carved mantel. It was the room *she* would have chosen, anyway, and as good a place as any to start her search.

She followed the flashlight's pale beam up the stairs to the second-floor landing. Without even a slight breeze to stir the air, the heat inside was suffocating. But the bedroom was everything she'd imagined, even with the cobwebs, several floorboards missing, and a dressing table with a cracked and broken mirror listing precariously to one side.

Shelby gave her imagination free rein for a moment, picturing the room as it might have been once. Agatha's bed would have rested against the short wall, she thought, and chairs would have flanked the fireplace. Perhaps a frame had held Agatha's needlework in front of the hearth and a writing table might have stood near the windows to catch the sun.

Candlelight would have danced across the room and softened Agatha's stern face—the face Shelby had seen only once in an old photograph in the library's archives, but had never forgotten. Agatha had been a formidable woman. An unhappy woman. But she hadn't been crazy. Shelby just *knew* it.

Shaking off the imagery, Shelby tiptoed to the dressing table and carefully worked open the drawers, one at a time. But she found nothing except rotting wood and spiderwebs, and a few other moldy objects she didn't want to look at too closely. She checked for hidden compartments, careful not to break anything, or worse, disturb slumbering insects. When her fingers brushed a web hidden in one darkened corner, she let out a muffled shriek that echoed throughout the empty house.

She clamped her lips shut and felt along the wall on the off chance she'd find a secret passageway or hidden alcove. She even used the flashlight to look into the gaping holes in the floor. But if Agatha's papers were still inside Summervale, they weren't in this room.

Sighing softly, she looked into the broken mirror. The heat had become almost insufferable, but she scarcely noticed it. Instead, she stared into the murky depths of the glass at her wildly curling hair and dirt-smudged face and neck.

"What happened here?" she whispered.

Perspiration soaked her T-shirt and trickled between her breasts, but she ignored her discomfort and kept her attention riveted on the mirror, as if it might actually answer. "You know all the secrets," she said, a little louder now. "Why don't you tell me what they are?"

The mirror caught a stray beam of light from somewhere and reflected it back at her.

"Not telling, eh?" She shifted position slightly, marveling at the way the glass made her eyes look so different. Darker, somehow. Almost brown. And narrower. Shadows drifted across the room and distorted her reflection. For a moment, she imagined two faces there—hers and Agatha's.

"I'd give anything to know what really happened to you," she told the flickering reflection. "You know that, don't you? I'd give anything to save this house of yours."

A faint breeze stirred the dust around her. The second reflection faded for a moment, then reappeared. Its eyes widened almost imperceptibly, as if it had seen something that surprised it. Laughing softly, mocking her vivid imagination, Shelby tried to look away, but the eyes in the mirror held hers.

The heat intensified, and the room seemed to tilt beneath her feet. She gripped the table, praying she wouldn't pass out up here, alone in a deserted house.

The dust swirled again, filling her throat and nostrils. She coughed, gasping for breath, and told herself she should leave. But she'd barely begun to search. If she could just pry the wood from the windows and get some fresh air, she'd be fine.

Still holding on to the dressing table, she took two steps toward the barricaded windows, but dizziness overwhelmed her again. Groaning softly, she leaned forward, put her head between her knees, and willed the dizziness to pass. But it grew steadily worse and the air seemed to grow heavier, more oppressive.

Again, the room tilted, whirled, swayed as if she'd had too much to drink. She couldn't seem to focus on anything. Pictures darted in and out of her mind, delirious pictures of a large poster bed, a blaze in the fireplace, a brocade chair. Of sunlight spilling across the wooden floor and framed paintings on walls.

Sounds came next. Birds. A dog barking. The soft clop of a horse's hooves. A man's voice somewhere close by. Scent came last. A sharp pungent aroma she couldn't identify mixed with—unbelievably—coffee and bacon.

Shelby tried to take deep, steadying breaths, but she couldn't seem to get any air to her lungs. She reached out instinctively toward the imaginary bed, knowing even as she did there was nothing there.

Amazingly, her fingers brushed something soft and warm—like fabric. Her eyes flew open again and she focused slowly. The shadows faded, and she could see the dressing table, highly polished instead of old and rotting, complete with a set of silver-backed brushes on its surface.

She let out a disbelieving, frantic laugh and stepped

away from it. Her foot caught on the corner of a rug and sent her sprawling into the velvet curtains at the window.

Curtains?

She touched them hesitantly. Yep . . . deep burgundy velvet curtains. She was hallucinating, no doubt about that. And if she had an ounce of brains in her head, she'd get out of this room before she *did* pass out . . . or worse.

"Madame?" A woman's voice cut through the silence.

Startled, Shelby whirled around and found herself staring at a short, gray-haired woman with a pleasant, round face.

Embarrassed at having been caught, Shelby stammered, "I'm . . . I'm sorry." Her voice sounded odd. Lower, perhaps. Almost hoarse. "I didn't realize anyone was here."

"Well, of course I'm here." The woman bustled into the room carrying a silver tray loaded with food. It looked incredibly heavy and *real*. "Where else would I be?"

Shelby backed a step away, and heard the distinctive swish of skirts and petticoats as she moved. She looked at her legs, stunned to see deep gray broadcloth instead of faded denim. She touched it gingerly, then pulled her hand away as if the material had scorched her. "Where did this come from?"

"Where did what come from, madame?"

"This . . . this *dress*. Why am I wearing this?"

The woman stopped walking and a quick scowl marred her features. "It's the morning frock you asked me to lay out for you, madame. You specifically said—"

Shelby cut her off with a quick shake of her head. "No. No, this isn't real. I didn't ask for this."

"Excuse me, madame." The woman's scowl deepened and Shelby caught an almost imperceptible flash of irritation in her eye. "Perhaps I made a mistake."

"Or I did." Shelby took another step backward, certain that she'd made a *big* mistake and wondering how long it would be before a real person found her.

The woman's gaze grew solemn. Worried, even. "Forgive me for asking, madame, but are you quite all right?"

Shelby massaged her temples slowly. "I don't think so. I think maybe I passed out from the heat."

"Then perhaps you should rest awhile."

Give in to the delirium? Not on her life. "I can't. I have to find the papers."

"Papers?"

"Journals. Letters. I'm not sure. But I have to find them or I can't save the house. *Both* houses."

"Which houses, madame?"

"Summervale," Shelby explained impatiently. "And Winterhill, of course."

The woman studied her closely for a long moment, then slowly carried the tray toward a small round mahogany table. "Are you certain you're all right?"

"Yes. Yes." Shelby rubbed her temples a bit more frantically and gave a thin laugh. "I'm just having a dream. A hallucination. All this furniture . . . and *you.*" She closed her eyes then opened them again, but the woman hadn't disappeared. "Other than talking to a figment of my imagination, I'm fine."

The woman stepped away from the table and gave the lace on her collar a twitch. "You think you're imagining me?"

"You and the furniture and the food . . . everything."

"But surely you recognize me, madame. Meg." She glanced around the room as if she were seeing it for the first time. "And most of the furnishings in this room were left to you by your mother."

"My *mother*?" Shelby gave herself a mental kick for coming up with *that* one. Obviously Jon's comment had planted that idea in her mind. Aloud, she said, "That's not funny. I don't have a mother."

Meg nodded slowly. "To be sure, your mother has passed on, but I didn't intend to make light of that, madame."

"Will you please stop calling me that?" Shelby took a steadying breath and another long look around. The room, from the heavily draped windows to the smallest table, looked exactly like the few old photographs she'd seen of Summervale. What a strange trick for her imagination to play. "Or maybe it's not so strange," she muttered.

Meg pulled her bottom lip between her teeth. "Something's strange," she said firmly. "Perhaps I should help you back to bed."

Shelby put a chair between them, nearly falling as she tried to maneuver in the long gown. Her imagination had gone into elaborate detail with it, from the draped skirt to the fitted bodice to the pagoda sleeves. She lifted her arm and stared at the complex embroidery, then laughed softly.

Meg took a hesitant step toward her. "Madame, are you *quite* all right?"

Shelby didn't answer immediately. She ran her fingers along the gleaming wood of the dresser and touched the silver-backed brush set. She turned to the bed and fingered the bedcover, then crossed to the round table and touched a gilt-edged plate on the tray. "Everything seems so *real*. I can even smell the breakfast."

She laughed again when she realized how hungry she was. Jon's visit had taken away her appetite for breakfast, and the light dinner she'd eaten the night before was nothing more than a distant memory. She'd probably passed out from heat and hunger.

But even realizing that didn't make Meg disappear. The imaginary woman started toward the tray, keeping a wary eye on Shelby as she walked. "You'll feel better after breakfast, I'm sure."

Shelby laughed again, more relaxed this time. To be perfectly honest, she hadn't had such a fun dream in ages. Walking slowly—*demurely,* she thought with a silent chuckle—she rounded the end of the bed and started to sit in the rose-colored brocade chair near the table.

Halfway into her seat, something gave her such a sharp jab in the ribs, she let out a cry of surprise and jerked upright again.

Of course, that brought Meg's head up with a snap

and deepened her scowl. Shelby sent her a reassuring smile and tried again to sit, but another sharp jab pulled her to her feet once more.

What on earth . . . ?

She touched her ribs and realized in disbelief she was imagining a corset. She didn't mind a little realism in her dreams, but couldn't she have left out the cage? She couldn't even breathe, much less sit.

Meg watched her uncertainly. "I mentioned the roses to Colin this morning, madame. He said he should be able to prune them by midweek."

Shelby perched carefully on the foot of the bed and decided to play along. "Thank you, Meg."

Meg's hand froze and an odd expression crossed her face.

"What's wrong?" Shelby asked. "Was it something I said?"

"No, madame," Meg assured her, but she backed a step away and looked as if something was very wrong, indeed. "Will you be needing my assistance this morning?"

Shelby picked up a thick slice of toast and took a huge bite. Heaven. Pure heaven. "Your assistance with what?"

"With your breakfast, madame."

Shelby glanced at the eggs, toast, and bacon and bit back a smile. "No, thanks. I think I can manage on my own."

Another flicker crossed Meg's face. "Then if there's nothing else . . ." She backed another step toward the door as if she couldn't get away fast enough.

Shelby took another bite and sighed with pleasure. "No, there's nothing else."

Meg made tracks across the room as fast as her short legs could carry her and closed the door behind her with a firm click. Shelby waited until she heard her footsteps fade away, then let out the closest thing to a sigh she could manage in her confining dream clothes.

She ate half of the eggs and a slice of bacon, but the restraints of the corset made her stop there. How had women in this day ever survived when only a few bites made her uncomfortably full?

She pushed the tray aside and tried to decide what to do while she waited to wake up again. Curious to see what she looked like in this getup, she stood again and crossed to the dresser. As she had only minutes before, she bent to study her reflection in the glass, now sparkling in the bright spring sunlight. But when she saw herself, she froze.

Gone was her curly hair and the ski-jump nose she hated. Gone were the clear blue eyes she'd inherited from some relative she'd never know and the slightly rounded cheeks she detested. Instead, she found herself staring at a woman with thick, dark hair pulled severely away from her face. A face with high cheekbones and deep brown eyes.

She dropped to the chair in front of the table, touched her cheek, and traced a finger across the full lips. Her dream was really out of whack. Instead of her own reflection, she was looking at the severe, disapproving face of Agatha Logan.

Chapter 2

"I'M TELLING YOU, Colin, there's something wrong with the missus."

Meg's husband leaned back in his chair and laughed. His husky frame filled the poor chair to overflowing and his teasing smile irritated her no end. "There's always been something wrong with the missus. Are you just now figuring that out?"

Meg sent him a look. *The* look. The one that let him know she meant business. "I don't mean *that* kind of wrong," she whispered, just in case the missus decided to prowl around as she often did. "She's acting odd, even for her."

Colin laughed again and tried to capture her hand. "And what would be makin' you think that, m'dear?"

Meg avoided him with the ease of long practice and slapped his feet away from the chair he'd perched them on. "She seems disoriented. Strange, like. She acted like she didn't know who I was when I took in her breakfast."

Colin's lips twitched and his pale blue eyes sparkled. "Maybe she had you confused with one of the thousands of callers she has."

Meg glared at him. No one joked about the missus, and no one ever alluded to the Unfortunate Incident or its aftermath. No one but Colin, that is. She put two biscuits on a plate and handed it to him. "She thanked me for bringing in her breakfast."

That got his attention. His smile faded and a concerned frown replaced it. "She *thanked* you?"

"She thanked me." Meg sniffed and pushed a crock of butter toward him. " 'Thank you,' she said, plain as day."

Colin scowled thoughtfully as he spread butter on his first biscuit. "Maybe someone coshed her on the head and it's put her off."

"I'd almost think so," Meg hissed, "if there had been anyone but the three of us in the house. Something's not right." She plunked a biscuit onto her own plate. "I tried to convince her to have a lie down, but she wouldn't hear of it."

Colin's scowl deepened and put crags in his weathered face. "Maybe we should have the doctor in."

Meg shook her head and dusted her hands on her apron. "She would never allow it. And you and I would be out on our ears for even suggesting such a thing."

"True enough. But one of these days, she'll have to let someone in." Colin wedged half a biscuit into his mouth and spoke around it. "She can't hide from the world forever."

"She can," Meg said harshly, "and she will. 'I'll let the gossips in when I lay dying,' she's told me time and again, 'Not a minute before.' "

Colin washed down his biscuit with coffee and wiped his mouth. "Well, maybe that's it. Maybe she's—" He broke off abruptly, lurching to his feet and dropping his fork to the table with a clang.

Meg knew what that meant. She turned slowly to face the missus who stood in the doorway. Lord Almighty, how much had she heard? Holding her breath, she waited for the explosion.

But the missus crossed the threshold and stared

around at the kitchen as if she'd never seen it before. As if she didn't rule it and every other room in the house with an iron fist. Instead of anger, she turned a girlish smile on them. "Oh, this is spectacular. Absolutely spectacular."

Meg let out her breath slowly. "Pardon me, madame. But what is spectacular?"

"This." She spread her arms and gestured around the monstrous room, at the rafters on the ceiling, the bundles of drying herbs, the scrubbed pine table and ladder-back chairs. "It's incredible. Is this really how it was?"

Meg sent another pointed look in Colin's direction just to make sure he'd learned a lesson about doubting her, then wiped her expression clean and turned back to the missus. "How what was?"

"The kitchen. Is it authentic?"

"It's as it's always been, madame."

Agatha came closer. Her eyes sparkled with a light Meg had never seen in them before—even when the missus was a lass. "You'll have to excuse me. I'm dreaming, you know."

Dreaming? Meg thought. Saints above.

Meg tried to remain calm. She didn't want to frighten the missus—even though the missus was scaring the very devil out of her. "Perhaps I should help you back up to your room."

The missus danced—*danced!*—a step away. "Oh, no. I can't. I might wake up any minute, and I want to see as much as I can before I do." She pivoted toward the back stairway so quickly Meg caught a glimpse of ankle. "The ballroom. Tell me, is that in the dream, too? And the music room?" She whirled back again. "And what about the gardens and the stables?"

The stables? Meg barely held back a gasp. Lord help them all, the poor thing *had* lost her mind. She caught Colin's attention and whispered, "Do something."

He spoke out of the corner of his mouth. "What do you suggest?"

"Something. *Anything.* We cannot let her roam about like this."

Colin flicked an annoyed glance at her. "And what would you have me do, woman? Hog-tie her?"

She swatted his arm impatiently. "Of course not. But we have to do *something,* that's plain as day."

Colin hesitated for another second or two. He watched the missus warily. Then slowly, hesitantly, sketched a bow toward Meg. "As you wish, m'dear. As you wish." With shoulders squared like a soldier marching to certain death, he crossed to the missus and held out his arm. "Would you like me to show you around?"

Meg nearly groaned aloud. *That's* not what she had in mind.

The missus grinned up at him. "Yes. Please. I want to see absolutely everything."

Please? Meg shook her head in wonder.

"Where would ye like to start?" Colin asked gently.

The missus gave that a moment's thought. "Outside, I think. I want to see the gardens. I love the gardens."

Except for an occasional foray onto the covered porch, the missus hadn't left the house since . . . well, since before the master left—not even to stroll through the gardens. She'd always claimed the gardens made her sneeze.

Stunned, Meg watched as Colin led the missus toward the outside door, shook her head again, and collapsed on the chair he'd vacated only moments earlier. Something had happened to the missus this morning—something Meg couldn't understand.

Not that she didn't like the missus better this way. Who wouldn't? But Meg didn't trust the change. Life had been tough enough at Summervale these past five years with only herself and Colin left to do for the missus. They didn't need this.

When the missus became herself again, what would happen then? *Lordy.* Meg sighed heavily. It wouldn't be good, she knew that for certain.

• • •

Stifling a yawn, Zacharias Logan leaned against the mantel and pretended an interest in the conversation between his mother and Patricia Starling. Their voices blended together, rising and falling with an unsteady rhythm that made his head ache.

The truth was, he'd rather be almost anywhere but in this room at this particular moment. But his mother had insisted that he be present, and so he was. Life was infinitely easier for anyone wise enough not to buck Victoria Logan's edicts.

The voices halted for a moment and pulled his eyes back toward the two women. His mother, thin and sharp-edged, settled her cup in its saucer and smiled—or as close to a smile as he'd ever seen on his mother's lips. "Naturally, Patricia, you will help Zacharias receive his guests."

Naturally. Zacharias wondered again just why he had to be present when between them, the two women had his life well in hand. He had only to appear on schedule and conduct himself with a dignified air.

A pleased smile curved Patricia's lips and a gleam of triumph sparkled in her clear blue eyes. She turned a jubilant look in Zacharias's direction, even though she spoke to his mother. "Thank you, Victoria. It would be an honor."

Another twitch of his mother's lips signaled her pleasure at the compliment. But when she looked at Zacharias, the smile evaporated like morning dew in a strong sun. "It is an unpleasant necessity that we are reduced to asking you to receive Zacharias's guests this way again." She let out a sigh designed, he knew, to make her seem wistful. "Perhaps before our next entertainment, Zacharias will have managed to clear up these irritating loose ends."

He forced an unconcerned smile. "Agatha is still my wife," he reminded them both. "And I foresee no change in the immediate future."

Victoria worked her fan a little harder and her mouth turned down at the corners. "I am aware of the circumstances, Zacharias. But I consider your stubbornness on the subject unfortunate, to say the least."

"And unlikely to change," he said, "no matter how much you might like it to." Absent Agatha's death—and the likelihood of that happening was highly remote—Zacharias was chained to her as surely as if someone had wrapped shackles around his legs. At times he cursed the bond. At others, he blessed it.

Patricia rose in a wave of pink cotton and crossed the room to him. Tucking her arm beneath his, she tilted her chin just so and smiled up at him. "Don't begrudge Zacharias his honor, Victoria. It is his precious honor that makes him who he is."

Zacharias wondered if he'd actually heard the slight inflection on the word "precious" or if he'd only imagined it. Patricia was, as she always had been, willing to fill his most public and private needs. But her position in his house and at his side would never be secure as long as Agatha was alive, and he was well aware that it made her unhappy.

He often wondered if his mother accepted Patricia so willingly as a way of rubbing salt into the wound caused by his decision to marry Agatha in the first place. He loved his mother—she was his mother, after all—but he harbored no delusions about her. She'd always believed Patricia more suitable to be his wife and the mistress of his estate than Agatha. And she'd never failed to make her displeasure felt over the choice he'd made.

Now, she smiled sweetly at Patricia. "Yes, of course. We all admire Zacharias for his honor."

Zacharias stifled another yawn and moved away from Patricia, crossing casually to the sideboard for a cup of coffee, so as not to offend her. "Perhaps I should leave the planning of this grand event to the two of you. I only seem to be in the way."

"I'm sure there are pressing matters that require your attention," his mother said with false hesitation, "but we really must decide on the details while Patricia's here."

More pressing matters, indeed. They all knew he had

nothing urgent on his agenda. He never did. Though he'd been raised to the role, being a gentleman of leisure didn't suit him. Talk of flowers and music, the nuances of social position and seating arrangements didn't interest him. He'd have been far happier up to his elbows in a task that mattered to someone somewhere. But any task that appealed to him would require him to soil his hands. That would have distressed his mother to no end. And when his mother was distressed, the entire household felt it.

Before he could frame a response, a soft cough sounded from the doorway behind him. Zacharias turned toward it eagerly and found Abraham, the man who served him as butler and valet, wearing an odd expression. For Abraham to wear any expression at all was unusual, but Zacharias only recognized a way out of his current situation.

As if he could read Zacharias's mind, Abraham bowed slightly, let his gaze travel to the women, then snapped it back to Zacharias again. "Begging your pardon, sir, but there is a person here asking to see you."

Impatient to be away on any task, Zacharias abandoned his cup and saucer on the sideboard and strode toward the door.

But Abraham didn't move to let him pass. "Before you go, sir, I feel I should warn you that the person is from Summervale."

Zacharias stopped in his tracks. He heard his mother's soft intake of breath and sensed more than saw Patricia's quick scowl. And no wonder. In the five years since Agatha had banished him from her presence, he'd never once received word from anyone in her household.

He tried not to show his sudden apprehension. "From Summervale? Interesting. Who is it?"

Abraham darted another worried glance at Victoria. "I believe it is Mrs. Logan's man, sir."

"Colin?" Zacharias's apprehension grew. Colin was usually levelheaded and even-keeled. For him to come to Winterhill must mean a serious problem. He took another step toward the door. "What does he want?"

His mother's skirts rustled as she stood behind him, and her voice cut through the room. "Surely you don't intend to speak with him."

Zacharias nodded back at her. "I'm afraid I must, Mother. Something is obviously wrong."

His mother's expression didn't alter, but he saw the soft gleam of hope spring into Patricia's eyes. "Of course, he must speak with the man," she said, moving quickly to his mother's side. "Perhaps Agatha is ill."

Apprehension turned to dread, but Zacharias forced it aside along with irritation at his mother's sudden, pleased smile. If Agatha was ill, so be it. He'd long ago abandoned the feelings he'd once had for her.

"Yes, of course." Victoria waved him toward the door and started across the room as if she intended to accompany him.

But Zacharias didn't want her with him. "Stay with Patricia," he said quickly. "I'll see to Colin." To prevent her from arguing, he hurried past Abraham into the foyer and motioned for him to close the door.

But the sick feeling in his stomach grew as he followed Abraham toward the kitchen where Colin had been left cooling his heels and formed a solid knot when he took in the man's broad, worried face and the way he twisted his cap round and round in his huge, work-worn hands.

There was definitely something wrong.

Zacharias nodded for Abraham to leave them. "Yes, Colin. What is it?"

"I wouldn't have come, sir, but there's trouble at Summervale."

"What sort of trouble?"

"It's the missus." Colin twisted his cap a little harder. "She's been taken bad, sir."

As always, thinking about Agatha brought up the bitterness, hurt, and anger he preferred to keep locked away. "Explain."

"Meg and I . . . well, we don't know what happened

to her, sir, but she's acting different-like this morning."

Zacharias ignored the flash of relief that came with the realization that she wasn't lying dead in her sanctuary. "Mrs. Logan is free to act in whatever way she pleases, without permission from me."

"True enough, sir." Shadows drifted across Colin's eyes. He twisted his cap even more frantically. "And that's just what I said to Meg. But now I'm thinkin' maybe there's something to worry about." He took a deep breath, as if he needed courage. "She thanked Meg for serving her breakfast, sir."

Zacharias made sure the surprise didn't show on his face. Colin was, after all, a servant. A trusted man to be sure, but still a servant. "I see." He toyed casually with the chain on his pocket watch as he crossed to the window. "Is that all?"

"No, sir." Colin moved a step closer and lowered his voice. "She asked me to show her the gardens, sir. And the stables. Which I did, despite me own misgivings. And she laughed. Right out loud."

Agatha laughed? Impossible. Scowling to show his displeasure, Zacharias leveled the man with his gaze. "If you're having a joke at my expense—"

Colin interrupted, too agitated to consider the implications. "She told me she's having a dream, sir. She thinks she's fast asleep."

Zacharias didn't care about Agatha, not anymore, anyway. But Patricia was right about the sense of duty he felt toward her. She was his wife after all, though it had been a long while since she'd been his wife in anything but name only.

"And what would you have *me* do about her dream?"

"That I don't know, sir. Meg is showing her around the house even now. It's as if she's never seen it before." Colin stopped twisting his cap and squared his shoulders. "Meg and I thought you should know, that's all."

"Well, now I know."

Colin began twisting again. "We thought maybe you should also know that she asked to see the ballroom."

He paused and added, "And I heard her humming, sir."

Zacharias deepened his scowl to make sure Colin understood how much that news displeased him. "Humming?"

"Yes, sir."

"You must have been mistaken."

"Begging your pardon, sir, but I heard her with me own two ears. And so did Meg. That's when Meg told me I should bring myself over here and let you know."

There had been a time when Zacharias would have welcomed that piece of information. A time when it might have given him hope. But he'd been young and foolish then. He was older and wiser now.

Still, if Agatha was humming, walking out to the stables, and thanking the servants, something was definitely wrong. Much as he'd like to leave her to her dream, he couldn't. Much as he'd like to leave the dealing with her to someone else, he wouldn't.

She'd already caused enough scandal to last a lifetime. For the sake of his sons, he couldn't allow her to cause more. But that didn't mean the thought of seeing her again pleased him.

Blast the woman.

Blast her to hell and back again.

He spent a moment adjusting his cravat as if he hadn't a care in the world. "I suppose I am obligated to see what is wrong with her."

Colin let out a sigh, heavy with relief. "Yes, sir."

Zacharias flicked a hand toward the doorway. "You may go, Colin. I'll be along shortly."

"Thank you, sir. Meg'll be much relieved."

No doubt, Zacharias thought bitterly. He just wished he could say the same for himself.

Shelby followed Meg along the corridor, taking in everything as she walked. The deep, rich, gleaming wood; the heavy crystal chandeliers; the portraits hanging on the walls; the thickly woven Oriental rugs. She'd always known she had a vivid imagination, but this really was incredible.

Meg glanced over her shoulder, as if she wanted to be sure she was all right. "You don't remember the yellow bedroom?"

"I didn't even know there *was* a yellow bedroom," Shelby said with a soft laugh. "But I'd love to see it. I want to see everything—even if it isn't real."

"It's quite real," Meg said firmly as she stopped outside a thick wooden door. She swept another worried glance over Shelby, then pushed open the door and stepped aside.

Shelby's breath caught. She clasped her hands and let out a sigh. A magnificent poster bed with beige candlewicked coverlet and matching tassled canopy dominated the room. Chairs upholstered in a yellow-backed floral pattern surrounded a brightly colored woven rug. Pale yellow walls sported a green border sprigged with rose and yellow flowers. "Oh," she said softly. "Just *look* at it."

Meg followed her gaze as she took in the room. "It is a lovely room, that's for sure."

"Oh, it's more than that. It's . . . it's . . . ." Shelby broke off and laughed. "I don't know how to describe it," she said at last, "but it's incredible. I just can't imagine why anyone would want to tear it down."

Meg scowled deeply. "Tear down Summervale? Why would you want to do that, madame?"

"*I* don't want to." Shelby wheeled to face her. "Evan does. But I don't want to think about that now. Not while I'm dreaming. I can deal with that when I wake up again."

Meg took a hesitant step toward her. "Forgive me for overstepping my bounds, madame, but why do you think you're dreaming?"

"I'm here, aren't I? The house is completely furnished. I'm dressed in this ridiculously uncomfortable gown. And look at *you*."

"Me?" Meg glanced at her own clothing. "What about me?"

"Well, your clothes are just so quaint. So old-fashioned. So completely authentic. You look as if you belong here."

"I have been with your family since before you were born," Meg said sharply. "And I came to Summervale when you did."

Shelby didn't want to offend anyone—even in a dream. "That's not what I mean," she said quickly. "I mean *here* and *now*. Tell me, what day is it?"

"Monday, madame."

"No, no, no. I mean, what is the date?"

"The first of May."

"What year?"

"Eighteen and seventy-one."

"Eighteen seventy-one. Amazing." Shelby laughed again and hurried across the parquet floor toward the far windows. "That means Winterhill is there, doesn't it? Can I see it from here?"

"You want to look at it?" Meg's frown cut deep into her face. "Are you quite certain, madame?"

"Yes, of course."

"You can still see it," Meg said with obvious reluctance. "The trees haven't grown in yet."

"The trees?" Shelby wheeled back to face her. For some reason, she'd always assumed the trees had grown there naturally, and she'd always wondered why someone didn't thin them to make the view better from each of the houses. "You mean someone planted them there on purpose?"

"Yes, madame."

"But why?"

Meg took a deep breath and squared her shoulders. "Because you instructed us to."

"*I* did?" Shelby was stunned for a moment until she realized Meg was talking about Agatha. "Why did I do that?"

"Because, madame, you've made it quite clear you

don't want Winterhill visible from anywhere on the estate."

Shelby thought about that for a moment. Yes, she knew this was a dream, but maybe her subconscious had retained something about Agatha and Zacharias, Winterhill and Summervale, something that her conscious mind had skipped over. She decided to see where her subconscious would take her. "And why have I done that?"

Meg shifted her weight and looked as if she were arguing with herself about answering.

"It's all right, Meg." Shelby put a hand on her arm and smiled into her eyes. "It's only a dream." Meg stiffened beneath her touch and looked so uncomfortable, Shelby drew her hand away again. "You can tell me," she urged. "Why have I tried to hide Winterhill from view?"

"Because of the Unfortunate Incident, madame." Meg's voice sounded soft and hesitant.

Shelby thought about pressing further, but the concern in the older woman's eyes stopped her. Even in a dream, she didn't want to hurt someone else. She peered out the window and smiled slowly. She could see the red-brick turrets from here, the massive gardens surrounding Winterhill and even those stretching away from Summervale. If Jon could see the houses like this, surely he'd move heaven and earth to save them. But Jon wasn't likely to join her in her dream.

Sighing softly, she tore herself away from the view. "Lead on, Meg. I'm ready to see the rest."

"Perhaps it would be best if we continued your tour later."

"Oh, but I can't wait. I need to see everything now." She closed some of the distance between them again, but stopped at Meg's sudden frown. "Have I offended you?"

"No, madame." Meg's cheeks flushed so brightly, Shelby knew it was a lie. "But I do have chores to finish before the end of the day and your luncheon and dinner to prepare."

"Don't worry about meals. I won't be around that long." Surely she'd wake up any minute and find the house deserted, dusty, and disheveled once again. "I wonder if Winterhill is as grand as this place," she said, more to herself than to Meg. "I'd like to see it while I'm still asleep."

That seemed to cause Meg even more distress. "You want to see Winterhill?"

Shelby laughed at her stricken expression. "Is that bad? Out of character? I'm sorry, Meg. It's just that I'm not used to being Agatha Logan. I'm not certain how she'd act." She settled herself on the edge of the bed and arranged her skirts carefully. "Why don't you tell me how she'd behave."

"You are a fine lady, madame. From one of the best families in Hannibal."

"I know that," Shelby assured her. "That's in all the books. But what about Agatha? What makes her tick?"

"*Tick,* madame?"

"What drives her? What pushes her buttons?"

Meg's brows knit and her cheeks flamed again. "I'm afraid I don't understand."

"What motivates her, Meg? I assume she has reasons for what she does."

"I'm quite certain of that, madame."

"Well? What are they?"

Meg's fingers flew nervously across the lace on her collar. "You would know that better than I would."

"Well, I don't. And I want to know what you think they are."

Meg studied her for a long moment. "I think," she said at last, "that she is lonely."

"*Now* we're getting somewhere. Why do you suppose she's lonely?"

"Because . . ." Meg's eyes locked onto hers. "Because she has been hurt."

Shelby held back a shout of triumph. She was right.

Agatha *wasn't* crazy. "How was she hurt? What happened?"

"We never speak of that time, madame."

Shelby smoothed the fabric of her skirts and wondered why her dream characters were so stubbornly tight-lipped. She made a conscious effort to loosen Meg's tongue. "I want to speak of that time," she insisted.

"I am only following your instructions, madame."

"That's nice, but I'm changing my instructions. Do you think she's . . . *I'm* . . . crazy?"

Meg's gaze danced around the room, but it never lit on anything for long. "No."

Shelby ran out of breath and stood again. "Neither do I. But I wish I knew how to prove that."

"To whom, madame?"

"To everyone. To Zacharias, and the people in town, and to people who'll live a hundred and thirty years from now."

"Yes, madame."

"You don't have to keep calling me madame, you know."

"No, madame."

"I'm serious." She stood to face Meg. "Until I leave, I'd rather have you call me . . ." If she asked Meg to call her Shelby, Meg *would* think she was crazy. "Call me Agatha."

"As I did when you were a child, madame?"

"Exactly." Impulsively she grabbed Meg's hand and tugged her from the room. "Come on. Show me the rest of the house before I wake up."

Meg went along for a few steps, then ground to a halt and looked at her with such worry, Shelby felt a pang of guilt. "I don't care what anyone says, madame, I think we should have the doctor in. You aren't yourself."

Shelby laughed, surprised at the way the sound echoed in the cavernous house. She'd never had a dream that seemed so utterly real before. "You're right about that," she said. "But I don't want to waste even a moment of the time I have here worrying about doctors."

"Still—"

"No." She moved away again toward the magnificent staircase that cut through the middle of the house. "If you won't show me the rest, I'll explore on my own."

To her surprise, Meg stood her ground. "I won't show you the rest, madame. Not until you've seen the doctor."

"Why not?"

"Because there is something wrong, madame. You aren't acting like yourself at all. And when you become yourself again and think back on this experience, you will not be happy."

"It won't matter, Meg. This isn't real. None of this is real. *You're* not even real."

"*Please*, madame."

Shelby wanted to refuse again, but Meg looked so worried she finally relented. "Oh, all right. I'll lie down for a while. Will that make you happy?"

Meg nodded hesitantly.

"But *no* doctor."

"If you say so, madame."

"I do." She followed Meg back to the large bedroom and stepped inside. She allowed Meg to help her lie on the bed and even closed her eyes just to wipe some of the concern from Meg's kind face. But when she heard Meg walk away and close the door, she also heard the unmistakable sound of a key turning in a lock.

Her breath came in shallow gasps. Her heart thundered. It had been such a lovely dream. Such a lovely, lovely dream, but now it had turned into one of her nightmares. She tried to sit up but the damned corset made her flop backward again. Feeling like a grounded seal, she rolled to her side and lowered her feet to the floor, then pushed herself up from the bed.

Any minute now she'd wake up, drenched in sweat, exhausted from the effort. Any minute now. But that didn't stop her from racing across the room and trying the door. Or from pounding on it with her fists when it refused to respond to her efforts.

She hated being locked up. Hated being constrained. And she couldn't seem to rid herself of the nightmares where it happened.

Shouting, she pounded again, but Meg didn't come back. Shelby didn't expect her to. Nobody ever came back in her dreams. She pounded until shafts of pain zinged through her arms and shouted until her throat began to hurt.

It was the pain that finally made her start to wonder. She never felt physical pain in her dreams. Never. Fear, yes. Pain, no.

She took a calming breath, then pinched her arm hard enough to jolt anyone out of a dream. It did nothing except hurt. She bit her lip, then released it quickly.

If this wasn't a dream, what was it?

She crossed to the mirror and studied her reflection— or, rather, Agatha's. She couldn't actually *be* Agatha, could she? No. That was ridiculous. Impossible.

Crazy.

She pinched her cheek and winced at the sudden sharp pain. Okay . . . This was almost like an episode of *Quantum Leap*, one of her favorite old television shows. It was almost as if she'd been transported through time and dumped into Agatha Logan's stiff, prim body.

But that was impossible . . . *wasn't* it?

She ran her fingers across Agatha's face and stared into her eyes. She looked at the breakfast tray, listened to the sound of a tugboat whistle, and the sound of a train clacking across rails in the distance. Then she suddenly came to the soul-shattering conclusion that not only could it happen, but it had.

She didn't know how and she couldn't imagine why, but she was Agatha Logan.

Chapter 3

SHELBY PACED FROM one end of the bedroom to the other, pausing occasionally to look out one of the windows gazing at the shaded lane, the broad circular drive, the rolling expanse of lawn and formal gardens that separated Summervale from the main road. A train whistle shattered the stillness and set her nerves jangling. Far below, she could see the river through the trees and the river traffic that only made her more convinced she'd really made a gigantic leap through time.

The familiar panic she'd felt as a child when she was ripped from one foster home and dropped into another sang through her veins and no amount of positive self-talk made her feel better.

Then, as now, she'd had no idea what behavior her new "family" would consider appropriate, no idea how to think or act or behave, no idea whether tears would meet with hugs or anger. She'd learned to school her expressions and hide her emotions, and that's exactly what she wanted to do now. Nothing else would be quite safe.

She felt marginally better for a few seconds, then reality came crashing down around her again. Meg had

locked her in the bedroom, which probably meant she'd
sent for the doctor, after all. But how would Shelby ever
pass herself off as Agatha to the physician's probing
eyes? If the doctor knew Agatha well, Shelby would fail
miserably. She could only hope that Agatha had already
cut herself off so completely from the outside world that
no one other than Meg and Colin really knew her.

Pacing again, her mind raced, trying to remember
everything she'd ever read about life in the 1870s. But
even that wouldn't tell her how Agatha had occupied
her days, or what she'd done in the evenings, or what
she liked to eat, or how she reacted to stress, or . . . or
any one of a zillion other things.

The only bright spots Shelby could find were that
Agatha hadn't been fond of entertaining, so her audience
would be limited. And that Agatha and Zacharias were
estranged, so she wouldn't have to pretend to be some
strange man's loving wife. If Shelby only had to fool
Meg and Colin and the occasional stray doctor, she
might be able to pull off the deception for a little while.

A pang of sympathy tore through her when she
thought of Agatha cooped up in this house—lovely
though it was—without anyone but Meg and Colin for
company. Without telephones. Without television. Without friends. Really, the poor woman had a miserable
existence. And that existence, at least for the time being,
was Shelby's.

What a depressing thought.

She started to turn away from the window, but the
sight of a massive brown horse and an equally massive
rider making their way up the drive caught her eye. As
he drew closer to the house, his gleaming black top hat
kept his face shielded from view, but she recognized the
quality of his pearl-gray coat, the breeches that stretched
taut across his thighs, and the polished boots that
gleamed in the late-morning sun.

Obviously the doctor had arrived. It was time for
Shelby to give the performance of her life.

While Meg admitted the doctor to the house, she tried

to decide which Agatha was most likely to do—lie on the bed to wait, or remain standing. She decided on the latter. Agatha had survived many years alone in this house. She'd endured gossip and scorn. She must have been a strong woman. But Shelby certainly didn't feel strong when she heard the heavy tread of footsteps on the stairs. And when the key turned in the lock a moment later, her heart began to pound with dread.

Pasting on a mask of courage, she turned toward the door.

Meg, flushed and anxious, appeared first. "I'm sorry, madame. I—"

Before she could finish, a tall blond man with angular features and chiseled jawbone pushed past her into the room. "What kind of nonsense are you pulling this time?"

The attack caught Shelby off-guard. She took an involuntary step backward, caught herself, and forced herself to stand up to him. He looked vaguely familiar, but Shelby figured she'd probably come across his picture in the historical society's archives. While most of the old pictures she'd seen were flat, faded gray or yellowed images of stern, unyielding faces, this man was very much alive. So alive she could almost feel the energy radiating from him.

It didn't take much effort to keep her voice cool and haughty. The attack was totally unwarranted and completely unprofessional. "I beg your pardon."

"I'm sorry, madame," Meg said again, twisting her hands together in front of her. "I asked Colin to fetch the doctor. I had no idea he would do this."

Then this *wasn't* the doctor? Shelby let her gaze travel over the man again, more slowly this time. She took in the broad forehead, the slightly patrician nose, the clenched jaw and thin lips.

"Zacharias?" The name escaped her before she had a chance to stop herself.

She seemed to catch him by surprise and that put them on more equal footing for a moment. But no more than that. He stared at her and curled his lip in disdain. "You're actually speaking to me? To what do I owe this pleasure?"

The venom in his voice surprised her. Whatever drove Agatha and Zacharias apart had certainly left him angry. Perhaps Agatha was angry, as well, but Shelby didn't have a lot of anger in her. "I haven't been myself this morning," she said honestly.

"So I hear." He took a step further into the room. "I wouldn't have disturbed you, but Colin seemed inordinately worried." He let his gaze roam her face for a second or two. "I suppose now I can understand why."

"I seem different, then?"

He laughed harshly, one bitter note that tore a gasp from Meg, who still hovered near the door. It brought him around to face her. "What do you think, Meg? Does she seem different to you?"

Meg nodded slowly. "I'm afraid so, sir."

"Well," he said, turning back toward Shelby, his movements outwardly languid but rife with tension below the surface. "There you have it. I suppose it's too much to hope for an explanation."

Shelby did her best not to look nervous, not to clutch the fabric of her skirts or reach for a lock of hair to twist around her finger as she'd always done when something frightened her. "If I had an explanation," she assured him, "I'd certainly give it to you."

"Would you? How interesting." Zacharias motioned for Meg to leave them alone, which sent another wave of panic through Shelby. Meg closed the door slowly, almost as if she was reluctant to do so. When they were alone, Zacharias smiled coldly. "What is your game, Agatha?"

"Game?"

"Ho! She speaks again. Tell me, how am I expected to react to this sudden change?" He began to pace and spoke to the walls and furniture as if she wasn't there. "Am I to be flattered? No, I think not. She would have me believe that she's confused, perhaps even unwell.

But Agatha would not allow herself to be unwell. It would be a"—he glanced at her from beneath furrowed brows, and the hatred she saw in his eyes shocked her— "a weakness of the flesh. Isn't that right, my dear?"

"I—"

He cut her off before she could stammer anything more. "Furthermore," he said to the mantel, "I know Agatha does nothing without reason. A cold, calculated reason. So, what do you suppose she has up her sleeve?" He stopped pacing and faced her squarely. "You have noticed, I presume, that I have been allowed to invade the sacred bedchamber and am still alive to tell the tale."

His sarcasm made her angry and she lashed back without thinking. "If this is so distasteful to you, why did you bother coming?"

"I came," he said carefully, "because Colin convinced me that you were ill. But now that I see you looking quite healthy, indeed, I wonder why you sent for me."

"I didn't send for you," she protested. "I had no idea Colin would fetch you."

"No?" His brows knit a bit further.

"No. And if I'd had any idea you were going to be so thoroughly disagreeable, I never would have let you in."

His mouth twisted bitterly. "*That* is one threat that no longer has any power over me, my dear."

Shelby didn't miss the nuances behind that statement, and it gave her a bit of courage. "But it did once?"

"As you know only too well."

She let her eyes stay locked with his for a moment. Who would ever have imagined that his eyes would be so blue or full of fire. The portrait on the wall at Winterhill certainly hadn't done him justice. It had captured the likeness, but not the essence. And the essence charged the air between them.

He looked away quickly, but not before she saw the flicker of something unexpected beneath the anger.

Thinking quickly, she decided to offer an explanation for her seeming confusion. "I'm afraid I don't remember," she said with a weak smile. "I seem to have lost my memory."

Concern darted across his face, but it disappeared almost immediately. "Indeed?"

"Yes."

"How did that unfortunate circumstance come about?"

"I really don't know. I awoke feeling weak and disoriented, and unable to remember anything at all. Maybe we should talk about this . . . situation . . . between us."

He stiffened his shoulders and plunged his hands into his pockets. "Is that why you've lured me here? So you can see me humble myself to you?"

Shelby held up a hand in protest. "No, of course not."

"Well, that's good. Because it won't happen. I've humbled myself for the last time, Agatha. I told you that years ago."

"I just think it might be wise to talk about it."

"It is *wise*," he snarled, "to continue as we have been." He reached for the door handle as if he intended to walk out without telling her anything.

She bit her lip and thought quickly. "What about the children? We do have to consider them."

Zacharias froze with his hand in midair. A dozen different emotions flashed across his face and through his eyes. "The children?"

"Mordechai and Andrew."

"I am aware of their names." His voice was harsh and angry. "However, I'm surprised that *you* remember."

That was a low blow, Shelby thought. She crossed to the windows to give herself a moment. "Can't we at least be civil?"

"I *am* being civil," he snapped. "As civil as I care to be. Now if there's nothing more, I'll take my leave. It's obvious you don't need me here."

She stole another peek at his lean face, but the pain had disappeared again. She knew instinctively that if something didn't change soon, it would probably vanish forever.

"I'll not humble myself to you, Agatha," Zacharias

said, yanking open the door. "Not again." And without missing a beat, he left, slamming the door shut behind him.

Shelby stared at the door for a moment, trying to decide whether to go after him or let him go. Agatha wouldn't have gone after him, but history proved that Agatha hadn't always made the smartest choices.

On the other hand, Zacharias wasn't exactly open to discussion. If Shelby chased after him, she might make the situation worse.

Not that it could get much worse, she thought with a scowl. Other than a few foster parents, she didn't remember ever encountering such hostility in her life. She didn't harbor any delusions about marriage—she'd seen her share of bad ones as she'd bounced from house to house—but the depth of his anger toward Agatha shocked and saddened her.

Why had she been zapped back into the past and dropped into Agatha's place? Why did she have to take the brunt of his hostility? She knew the eventual outcome for these two people if they continued along the path they were on and for the first time she thought maybe things had worked out for the best, after all.

Or had they?

Maybe she'd been brought here to nudge them in a different direction. Maybe if she brought these two people back together again, she could alter the future and save the twin houses. After all, she *had* seen those two lightning-quick glimpses of pain behind Zacharias's anger.

And maybe not, a warning voice whispered.

She pushed it aside and smiled slowly. Surely she hadn't been brought here by mistake. There had to be some reason. Maybe she'd been brought here to save Agatha from dying so young. In doing so, she might even save the houses. And what better reason than to rewrite history?

●　　●　　●

Seething, Zacharias rode Goliath along the road separating the two houses. *His* houses, he thought, and let the familiar twinge of bitterness dance in his chest. The midday sun beat down upon his shoulders, perspiration dampened his shirt and collar, but he welcomed the discomfort.

He had forgotten how beautiful Summervale was. How magnificent she'd made it with her one-of-a-kind treasures. Or maybe he'd simply refused to let himself remember. Walking back into the home he loved had been at once soothing and painful.

He hated Agatha for banishing him from the home he'd paid for, the home he'd lovingly built—maybe not with his own two hands, but certainly with his heart. He hated her for that and so much more.

So why had the confusion he'd seen in her eyes touched him? And why had he nearly given in to her request to talk?

Talk. He thought with a bitter laugh. Agatha didn't talk. If she'd been open to discussion even once, they wouldn't be in this mess now.

Well, he wouldn't allow himself to weaken. Only an idiot would forget what she'd done. Only a fool would believe such a ludicrous story as the one she'd told and succumb to the charms of a woman who'd burned him so badly.

Scowling at the niggling reminder that what she'd done had been a reaction to his own mistake, he reminded himself that he'd tried to make amends. He truly had. No one could have expected him to do more. Most men—men less thoughtful than he—would have done far less. Why, he'd even let her stay at Summervale. How many men would have allowed that?

Very few.

He let out a heavy sigh and turned his thoughts to his real home. He'd done his best to re-create Summervale, but time had been of the essence then, and patience had been at a premium. He hadn't had the luxury of waiting two years for hand-carved mantels or imported Italian floor tiles.

Scowling darkly, he reined Goliath and shifted in the saddle to look behind him. Summervale rose majestically amid the trees and the deep-red brick of its turrets gleamed in the sunlight. Outwardly, Winterhill was its twin. Ah, but inside . . .

Inside, Summervale was truly a masterpiece. And *she* locked it away from its rightful owner, away from the admiring eyes of his peers, away from the small boys who would one day inherit it.

At least he had that, Zacharias thought, straightening in his saddle again and touching his heels lightly to Goliath's flanks. Agatha might rule Summervale now, but the title to the house still belonged to him. And one day, his sons would inherit.

One of them would live where he could not. It wasn't much, but it was something. He had to content himself with that.

He tried to hold on to the anger instead of the melancholy. Whiskey would help. A good, stiff whiskey to wash the taste of argument from his mouth and remove the image of Agatha's dark eyes from his memory.

He tilted back the brim of his hat and let his gaze follow the road as he rode slowly toward home. He had no desire or inclination to discuss the morning's bizarre events with his mother. A man should be master of his domain, after all.

But Zacharias had never been master of his. If his current living arrangements and the estrangement from his wife weren't proof enough, the very fact that his mother ruled Winterhill with the same iron thumb she'd once used on his boyhood home ought to convince even the most skeptical.

Obedience had been the watchword in his parents' home. Until his father's death, he'd associated the rule with the old man. It wasn't until his father wasn't around any longer to take the responsibility for his mother's actions that Zacharias began to understand the truth.

She was a clever woman, he'd grant her that. And he loved her. One should love one's mother and so, of course, Zacharias did. But he no longer suffered any delusions about her. She might appear to be a lady, but she'd been forged of iron.

She wanted a life for him that he didn't want for himself, and she wouldn't listen to anything he had to say on the subject. Only his sense of duty and the respect had been drilled into him from earliest memory kept him from speaking his mind more often.

Duty. Respect. Love.

Zacharias's mouth twisted bitterly. Those words were the bane of his existence. Duty kept him locked in a sham of marriage. Respect kept him tied to his mother. Love had eluded him all his life.

There was Patricia, of course. Patricia Starling, in whose willing arms he'd found welcome when there was none anywhere else. In whose lips he sought solace. In whose soft body he found occasional release. And in whose mind he found . . . nothing.

Ah, for a woman with something between her ears. A woman with a wit quick enough to hold him spellbound. With a mind sharp enough to grasp world events and enjoy fine literature. But even Agatha hadn't given him that. She'd been too concerned with propriety and appearances to flaunt convention.

Perhaps he should listen to his mother and seek divorce. Perhaps he should move on with his life and provide Andrew and Mordechai with the mother they needed. Lord only knew, things weren't ever going to get better between himself and Agatha. So why did he keep hanging on?

Divorce wasn't common but it wasn't unheard of, either. No one would fault him. Hell, most of the county already thought she was crazy. And there were times when Zacharias thought they might be right.

But there were other times—times when he remembered the pain on her face that horrible morning—that he *knew* it wasn't true. Agatha might be bitter and angry.

She might be hostile and even cruel. But she wasn't crazy.

In his most candid moments, when he lifted the veil on his heartache and looked at himself with brutal honesty, he admitted he had only himself to blame. That's why, in spite of every argument his mother presented, in spite of Patricia's disappointment, in spite of Agatha's bitter hatred, he didn't set her aside.

Once again, it boiled down to duty.

But to hell with duty. To hell with introspection. And to hell and back again with women. If he lived to be a thousand, he'd never understand them. Not a single, living one of them. The world would be a perfect place if God had simply never created them.

Zacharias sat with his back against a tree and a book propped open on his knees. Shaded from the worst of the hot morning sun, he let out a sigh of contentment. Much as he wanted to believe he'd separated himself emotionally from Agatha, her strange behavior yesterday had left him tied up in knots. And his mother's foul temper at breakfast hadn't done anything to make his mood better.

He'd climbed to the nursery to spend time with Mordechai and Andrew, only to have his mother follow him upstairs and begin another argument. And he'd distinctly heard her say something about expecting Patricia to call.

That was all Zacharias needed to drive him outside. If he couldn't find a moment's respite from women *inside*, surely he'd find it here. No one ever came to the copse of trees that separated the two pieces of his property. Agatha stubbornly pretended that Winterhill didn't exist. His mother pretended that Summervale and Agatha didn't exist. And Patricia didn't like to be outdoors.

This was the perfect hideaway. Abraham might know where to find him, but Abraham understood his frustrations, though he'd never overstep his bounds far enough to say so, and he respected Zacharias's need for privacy.

He tried reading again, but the printed words couldn't

hold his attention. He kept seeing Agatha's face as it had been yesterday, so much softer than he'd ever seen it, so full of life and hope and confusion. In truth, it had left him confused and unable to sleep most of the night.

Growing frustrated, he set the book aside and turned his thoughts toward other matters. He wished he could say "more pressing" matters, but nothing in his life was even slightly pressing.

One day stretched endlessly like the one before it, with nothing vital demanding his attention, nothing particularly important crossing his path. Building Summervale had occupied his days for a time. Trying to salvage his souring marriage had once kept him busy. Later, the construction of Winterhill had filled his days. But now . . .

Now, the endless round of social calls and dinner parties just wasn't enough to make him happy. Suddenly too agitated to sit still, he pushed to his feet and silently cursed the twist of fate that seemed to hand him everything a man could want, but which robbed him of that which he wanted most. Muttering under his breath, he started away from the clearing. But when he glimpsed the lone figure of a woman strolling beneath the trees along the edge of Summervale's property, he froze in his tracks.

Who would dare to trespass on private property—especially at Summervale? Or did Agatha have a caller? He laughed at that idea and moved stealthily into the shadows where he could watch her.

She wore a gown of dark blue, one of Agatha's favorite colors, but he knew she wasn't Agatha. The idea was preposterous enough to be laughable. Hadn't she told him she never wanted to *see* Winterhill? Hadn't she ordered these very trees planted to help her forget he and the twins even existed?

Never, not once in five years, had she come near the boundary between the two properties. In fact, if he could believe what Colin and Meg told him, she rarely set foot outside. Even as she'd been yesterday, he couldn't imagine her coming here.

Maybe he should warn the poor woman to leave before Agatha learned of her presence. Facing Agatha in a temper was an experience he wouldn't wish on anyone—not even a trespasser. Convinced he needed to make himself known to prevent trouble, he stepped to the edge of the clearing and waited until she drew closer. But when she did, he got the surprise of his life.

"Agatha?" The instant her name left his lips, he wished he could call it back. He had no wish to argue with her this morning. But for the life of him, he couldn't imagine what she was doing here.

She glanced toward him quickly, but instead of the hateful scowl he expected, she smiled. "Zacharias."

That set him back a pace. Perhaps Meg and Colin were right to be concerned. "Forgive me," he said, sketching a small bow and preparing to leave her alone. "I didn't mean to intrude."

"Oh, but you're not." She moved quickly, hand outstretched as if she might actually *touch* him. "Actually, I was hoping I would run into you. Colin told me you often come here."

Thoroughly confused, Zacharias nodded. "I do."

"I can see why. It's always been one of my favorite spots."

Zacharias nearly laughed. And he might have if she hadn't robbed him of the ability to make a sound. When he found his voice again, he demanded, "*This* spot?"

"Yes."

"I wasn't aware you'd ever been here before."

Her cheeks burned red and she lowered her gaze. "No, you wouldn't be, I suppose."

He studied her silently, carefully, and argued with himself about the wisdom of pursuing a conversation. But boredom and curiosity mingled with a gnawing irritation with his mother got the best of him. "Why did you hope to run into me?"

"Because I wanted to talk to you."

"Why?"

She tugged on one of her gloves as if it felt strange on her hand. "You *are* my husband, aren't you?"

He nodded once, wondering at the lack of animosity in her voice, marveling at the way she looked into his eyes again today. "I am."

She smoothed her hands along the folds of her skirt. "You're looking at me strangely. Am I behaving so differently?"

"Quite."

"You seem suspicious of me."

"With good reason," he pointed out. "You haven't spoken a word to me in five years. Now, suddenly, you seek me out."

"Yes, so I understand." She sighed softly. "Will you tell me why?"

"Why?"

"Why I haven't spoken to you."

He studied her carefully, but her face was as innocent of guile as a baby's. "You truly don't remember?"

"I truly don't." A fleeting smile crossed her lips and the breeze lifted a lock of hair from her face. "It's as if I've stepped into someone else's life."

He tried to keep his scowl in place so she wouldn't mistakenly think he was concerned about her. "Perhaps you should allow the doctor to see you, then."

"No." The word came quickly, vehemently. "It's nothing a doctor could help me with. What I need is for you to help me understand."

Zacharias rubbed the back of his neck and studied her carefully. She looked completely serious and one small part of him wanted to believe her. "Unfortunately for you," he said after a lengthy pause, "I have no desire to rehash that particular ugliness."

"So you said yesterday." She took a shallow breath and smoothed her hair back into place. "Maybe we could put it behind us and try to mend our marriage."

That was the second time she'd made that ludicrous suggestion, and Zacharias was growing more confused by her behavior by the moment. "Surely you can't be serious."

"Oh, but I am."

"After everything that's passed between us, all the ugly words and accusations, all the anger and hatred—"

"But don't you see?" she interrupted, "I don't remember any of it. So what does it matter?"

"Ah, but you will," he predicted, and bitterness twisted his mouth. "And I'm not about to let myself think things can get better between us, only to go through that hell all over again."

To his surprise she lifted one hand and touched his chest. To his dismay, his heart began to thunder in his chest as if he'd never been touched by a woman before. He jerked away and tried to glare, when all he really wanted to do was gather her in his arms.

She moved toward him again. "Was it really so awful?"

"Worse."

"Why won't you tell me what went wrong?"

"And have you begin again right here?" He laughed sharply and put some distance between them. "Not on your life." Disappointment darkened her eyes and it looked so genuine, Zacharias felt like a cad. He forced himself to remember all the hateful things she'd said to him the last time she'd deigned to speak to him. When his resolve still refused to form, he remembered the things she'd said about Andrew and Mordechai.

That, at last, was enough to shake him out of his stupor. Beneath all the softness, she was the same viper she'd always been. For the sake of his sons, he had to stay away from her.

Ignoring the pleading look in her eyes, he turned away. "Enjoy your stroll, my dear. I'll leave you to it." And with that, he hurried back across the clearing, scooped up his book, and headed back to the house.

Chapter 4

WITH A SINKING heart, Shelby watched Zacharias storm across the clearing and push through the trees toward Winterhill. Her corset was killing her, the yards of blue Irish linen of her elaborate walking dress nearly suffocated her, and all the curls and loops Meg had worked into her hair that morning were giving her a headache.

How was she supposed to fix things if he was going to be so damned stubborn? How would she save Agatha and zap back through the mirror to the days of running water and flush toilets if he refused to bend even a little? How would she ever return to the convenience of hot showers and antiperspirant if he wouldn't give Agatha a chance?

Summoning all her courage, she lifted the pesky skirts and followed him. He'd set a rapid pace and she had trouble keeping up, so she called after him. "You said you don't want to think things could get better between us. But that sounds like you *want* to believe it."

He shot an angry glance over his shoulder, but she could swear his step slowed. "A moment of weakness."

So he *did* feel something for Agatha. Shelby tried to

walk a little faster but her skirts hampered her. "Why must you be so stubborn?" she shouted.

"Me?" He wheeled about to face her. "*You're* calling *me* stubborn?"

"Yes. Stubborn. Or should I say bullheaded. Obstinate. Mulish. Take your pick." Her skirt snagged on a piece of undergrowth and brought her to a screeching halt. Frantic to catch him, she bent to loosen it. But the twig held fast.

"Perhaps you recognize the quality because you're so intractable," he called back.

It was a little thing, but Shelby took heart from the fact that he'd indulge in the volley of name-calling. She tugged harder on her skirt, but the thicket held fast and she nearly lost her footing on the slippery leaves underfoot.

Frustrated, she gave another yank and at the same time let loose with, "Oh, this *stupid*, damned dress."

Zacharias had turned away again, but he stopped as if she'd jerked on a chain, and turned slowly to face her. "What did you say?"

She bit her tongue and the slow flush of embarrassment crept up her neck and into her cheeks. She'd tried so hard to sound like a woman of the 1870s, and now she'd blown it. "I—I'm stuck."

"So I see." He started back toward her, his movements almost lazy now. "But I want to know what you said."

"I don't remember," she hedged.

"You said *damned*."

"Okay. Maybe I did. . . ."

"You. Agatha Carruthers Logan." To her surprise, he tilted back his head and laughed aloud. "Now I *know* you're telling me the truth."

His reaction stunned her. "Why would hearing me say a little thing like that convince you?"

"Because as long as I've known you, you've very nearly expired of apoplexy every time I said anything remotely similar."

"Oh." She bit back a smile and cast a longing glance

at her skirts. "Then, would you please help me get loose? I can't believe you'd go back to Winterhill and leave me stuck out here."

He sketched a bow and closed the distance between them, hunkering down so he could see her skirts and petticoats. "Will you tell me what happened to rob you of your memory?"

"I don't know." She watched as his huge fingers struggled with the delicate fabric. "One minute I was myself, and the next . . ." She left the rest unsaid. She certainly couldn't tell him the truth.

He glanced up at her with eyes the color of the sky and all the anger and bitterness seemed to have vanished. "You don't remember being ill, or getting hurt?"

Heat tore through Shelby—heat that had nothing to do with the temperature or humidity. "No."

"You don't remember *anything*?" He managed to extricate her from the annoying bush and dropped his hands onto his thighs.

Shelby let her gaze follow them and noticed the swell of muscles beneath the finely woven fabric. Her mouth dried and her pulse picked up a notch. Horrified by her reaction, she tore her gaze away again and forced herself to respond to his question. "I don't remember anything."

"What about your life before you married me?"

"Nothing."

"Our wedding?"

"Nothing." She longed to sit on the ground beside him, but the stupid corset she wore wouldn't let her.

He stood slowly, brushing off his pant legs. "But you remember who you are?"

"Yes." She kept her gaze locked on his. Big mistake. Big, *big* mistake. A shattering awareness of him shot through her and left her off-balance and confused.

His lips curved ever so slightly. "And you obviously remember who *I* am."

His smile gave Shelby another jolt. She reminded herself that she was here to salvage his marriage to another woman. "Yes, but I don't remember anything about our life together, and I certainly don't remember why we no longer have one."

He rubbed his chin thoughtfully. "Most interesting."

"Most *upsetting*. So? Will you help me?"

He shrugged and turned away. "Perhaps it would be best simply to let that time in our lives fade away."

"And take up where we left off?" she asked hopefully.

"No."

"But *why*?" Shelby wondered if a man more bull-headed had ever been created. If so, she'd never met him. "Maybe you don't want to discuss what happened between us, but you can help me fill in some of the blanks I'm carrying around with me."

"No."

She bit her lip and tugged a loop of hair loose from its pins. "Why not? What's so horrible that you won't tell me about it?"

"No."

Thoroughly frustrated, she propped her hands on her hips. "Fine. Then I'll just ask someone else."

He stiffened and all the anger and bitterness came flooding back. "Are you blackmailing me?"

Oops. Too far. "Blackmail? No, of course not." Shelby managed a thin laugh. "I just want to know what happened, that's all. But if you don't want to talk about it, I'm sure someone else will fill me in."

"Ah," he said, and his eyes gleamed with satisfaction. "That's where you're wrong."

She lifted her chin and stared back at him. "I doubt it."

"Oh, but you are. No one will tell you anything at all, my dear, because you and I are the only two people alive who know the entire story."

Still frustrated by her earlier meeting with Zacharias, Shelby carefully descended the staircase and tried not to trip over the hem of her gown. She could smell something cooking, something rich and wonderful and beefy. Though she rarely ate red meat anymore, she had a feeling she'd wolf down anything Meg placed in front of her.

Meg's cooking was definitely one of the bright sides of this whole experience. It was hands-down better than the salads or frozen microwave dishes Shelby usually fixed for herself. If she had to stay for a few days, at least she'd eat well.

She stopped partway down the stairs and sighed softly. Candlelight flickered from the chandelier high overhead and danced off the rich wood. It threw the corners into stark relief, revealing, then hiding again. But in spite of the beauty, something was missing.

A pall hung over everything at Summervale. Sadness where there should have been laughter. Melancholy where there should have been an air of joy and contentment. Of generations linked together. Of continuity.

But there was none of that. Only a yawning emptiness.

Shivering in spite of the oppressive humidity, Shelby walked into the dining room. There, too, candles lit everything and reflected off the china and crystal and silver. Eight chairs flanked the long mahogany table, but only one place had been laid for dinner. One lonely place, where there should have been countless more.

Shelby closed her eyes and pictured the room as it should have been, with Zacharias at the head of the table and a dozen smiling friends and relatives anticipating a night's entertainment and a spectacular meal. She imagined soft chamber music and laughter and the muted clink of silver against china.

"Madame?"

Meg's worried voice brought her eyes open again. She folded her hands in front of her and smiled. "Just thinking, Meg. Wishing things were different."

Meg ignored that and bustled into the room to light the candles in the centerpiece. "I didn't know whether you would come downstairs again or take a tray in your room as usual."

"Down here, please." How could Agatha stand to isolate herself that completely? Shelby smoothed the folds of her skirt and tried to set Meg's mind at ease. "In fact, unless I tell you differently, I'll eat all my meals down here."

Meg sent her a sidelong glance. "If I may say so, madame, that's good to hear. Shall I serve now?"

"In a minute." Shelby crossed to the huge windows that ran from the floor to the high ceiling overhead and let her fingers linger on the rich gold fabric. "First, I'd like to ask you a couple of questions."

"Questions?" Meg sounded nervous.

"About Zacharias."

"I hope . . ." Meg broke off, gave an anxious cough, and started again. "I hope you're not angry over what happened yesterday. Colin and I were worried—"

"Don't worry about it," Shelby said with a quick smile. "I'm not mad at you. But I need to know why Zacharias is so angry with me."

Uncertainty darted across Meg's face. What *was* it that had everyone acting like she'd poked them with a cattle prod whenever she brought up the subject of Agatha's estrangement from Zacharias?

Meg straightened the flower arrangement in the middle of the table. "I would think Mr. Logan is still upset over the Unfortunate Incident, madame."

Well, duh! Shelby bit back her instinctive response and tried again. "Probably. But what *was* the Unfortunate Incident?"

There went that cattle-prod look again. Meg pulled back stiffly. "I'm sorry, madame, but I daren't discuss it with you."

"Why not?"

"Because, madame." Meg busied herself with the linen napkin and readjusted the silver. "You have made it quite clear that you will dismiss us if we discuss it."

"Even with me?"

"Especially with you."

Well, that was certainly healthy. Shelby scowled

lightly. "I see. Well, I've changed my mind. I want to talk about it."

Meg pulled a cloth from her apron and vigorously attacked an imaginary spot on the sideboard. "You might think you want to talk about it, madame, but what will happen when you are feeling more like yourself?"

Shelby couldn't make any guarantees, of course, so she didn't offer any.

"I wouldn't dare to speak of it," Meg went on. "I value my position at Summervale. Besides, Colin would never forgive me if I were to do something foolish and land us both out on our ears."

"But Colin raced off to Winterhill and brought back Zacharias without checking with you," Shelby pointed out. "That doesn't seem fair."

"Colin did what he thought was best, madame. I doubt very much he'll be quick to repeat that performance."

"But if you won't talk to me, and Zacharias won't talk to me, who will?"

The cloth fluttered from Meg's hand and her mouth rounded in shock. "Surely you don't mean to talk to someone else."

"Why not? I know I haven't wanted to speak of it in the past, but I want to now."

Meg gripped the sideboard as if she needed something to hold her up. "Madame—"

"Agatha," Shelby reminded her.

Meg nodded and hurried on. "You cannot discuss the Unfortunate Incident. Believe me, it would be the worst thing you could do."

"Why? If I can save my marriage—"

"Your marriage?" Meg shook her head frantically. "You can't . . . you mustn't . . ." She took a deep breath and finally managed to string a few more words together. "Madame, you can't be serious. With Mrs. Starling at Winterhill so often, you'd only stir up talk."

"Who's Mrs. Starling?"

"Patricia Starling, madame. *Surely* you remember her."

"But I don't." Though the look on Meg's face was starting to give her a few clues. "Is she a friend of the family?"

A dozen emotions darted across Meg's round face, all too quickly for Shelby to read. "If you want to call it that."

"Then maybe I'll go talk to her."

Meg took a step toward Shelby and lowered her voice as if she worried about someone overhearing them. "Madame, you *must* not call on Mrs. Starling."

"Why not?"

"Because . . ." Meg shook her head as if she couldn't find the right words to explain. "Because."

"But if she's a friend of ours, perhaps Zacharias has confided in her."

"Patricia Starling is no friend of *yours*," Meg blurted, and immediately looked contrite for letting it slip.

"I see." And Shelby had a sudden flash of understanding. So, Zacharias had already moved on to someone else, had he? Well, that only made it even more imperative that she figure out what had happened between him and Agatha. "Are you saying that she's a friend of Zacharias's but not of mine?"

"Almost certainly, madame." This was only a low mutter from Meg as she turned her back.

Shelby hurried after her. "You can't say that and then walk away, Meg. It isn't fair."

"I'm sorry, madame." Meg turned back to face her again.

"So, tell me."

Meg hesitated for a long moment, then her shoulders slumped and she gave in. "If you must know, Mr. Logan has been . . . friendly . . . with Mrs. Starling since the death of her husband."

"By friendly, I assume you mean they're having an affair?"

Meg's eyes widened slightly. "I'm sure I don't know *that*, madame."

Shelby suspected she did know, and probably half the

town knew it, too. "Before I lost my memory, did I know about this?"

Meg's gaze faltered. "Yes."

"And did I mind?"

"Mind?"

Meg was stalling for time, but Shelby pressed harder. "Tell me the truth, Meg. Do I care that Zacharias has started seeing Mrs. Starling?"

"I wouldn't know, madame. We never discuss it."

Shelby had no idea how Agatha felt about it, but for some strange reason *she* minded very much. "There seems to be a lot that we don't discuss," she said, trying to push aside the ridiculous feeling that Zacharias had betrayed her in some way. "But I think it's time for that to change." She sat on one of the chairs and patted the one beside it for Meg. "Sit down, Meg. Let's talk."

Meg backed a step away. "I don't think that would be appropriate."

"Well, I do." She patted the chair again and waited.

Meg glanced nervously at the chair.

"I won't bite you, Meg. Sit down. Please."

The older woman gave in so reluctantly, Shelby's heart went out to her.

She kept her voice gentle, but firm. "Tell me about Zacharias and Patricia Starling."

"I only know what I hear, madame. And you know how people talk. That's why you mustn't even think of talking to Mrs. Starling."

"So I'm just supposed to turn my back and pretend that my husband isn't seeing another woman?"

"I think it might be best."

Shelby propped her chin in her hand. "Well, I don't. Why should I pretend that I don't care?"

Meg held her gaze steadily for the first time. "But madame, you *don't* care. You've made that quite clear."

Shelby lifted her head slowly. "I don't?"

"No, madame."

"But—"

"For the past five years, you've forbidden us even to

speak of Mr. Logan, madame. You've wanted absolutely
nothing to do with him. You've resisted every effort he's
ever made to reconcile with you. You've even said he's
dead in your eyes."

"So he's turned to another woman." Shelby supposed
she could understand that, even if it did disturb her in
ways she didn't want to think about. She thought for a
moment and clutched at the only straw she could find.
"So, why doesn't he just divorce me? I mean, he could
get a divorce, couldn't he?"

"Probably."

"Why doesn't he?"

"I don't know." Meg stood slowly, obviously uncomfortable with the conversation. "Only he could answer
that."

"But he won't."

"If you really want to know," Meg said, crossing to
the door to escape, "I suggest you ask him again."

Zacharias's heart twisted painfully as he watched Mordechai and Andrew playing contentedly on the nursery
floor, surrounded by a staggering number of toys. He'd
given them everything he could, more than he should,
perhaps, in an effort to make up for the loss of their
mother. They didn't seem to notice the lack of maternal
care now.

Their nurse, Jada, gave them time and attention and
even a certain amount of affection. But every so often
the thought crossed his mind that perhaps he'd made the
wrong decision.

Scowling, he forced that thought away. He'd made
the right decision, dammit. The only decision he *could*
have made under the circumstances. And he wouldn't
start second-guessing himself now.

It was Agatha's fault, he thought as he stood abruptly.
Entirely Agatha's fault. He'd never harbored a moment's
doubt until two days ago. Until she'd changed so dras-
tically. Until she'd sought him out and talked of reconciliation. Until she'd laid her hand so gently on his

chest and he'd imagined an invitation in her touch.

Invitation, indeed.

He scowled a bit harder and forced the memory away with a harsh, silent laugh. Imagining an invitation from Agatha was like imagining the wooden soldiers in Mordechai's chubby hands suddenly coming to life. Or the carved horse Andrew rode sprouting wings.

Utterly impossible.

"Look, Papa." Mordechai held out a wooden soldier for his inspection. "I think he's been killed."

Zacharias pushed Agatha out of his mind and took the soldier carefully. "I don't think so, son. I think he's just asleep."

"No." Mordechai shook his head and thrust out his lip in a gesture so reminiscent of his mother, Zacharias had to look away. "He's killed, all right, and now we'll have to bury him in the garden."

"Not killed," Andrew sang out from his speeding rocking horse. "Papa said so."

Mordechai whirled around to glare at him. "Is so."

"Is not."

"Is *so*." Mordechai's face reddened and he looked as if he might cry.

"Honestly, Zacharias," his mother's voice from the doorway behind him caught him off-guard. "How can you allow these children to be so morbid?"

"Not killed not killed not killed," Andrew sang again. As the elder, by less than five minutes, he took great delight in keeping Mordechai in his place.

Zacharias put an arm around Mordechai's shoulders and spoke softly. "Keep a careful eye on your soldier for now. If he truly is killed, we'll bury him this afternoon."

Mordechai sent him a brave smile. "Okay."

Andrew rolled his eyes and rode his horse a bit faster. "Not killed," he warned.

Victoria took a step into the nursery and folded her arms, which had the effect of dropping a hush over both boys.

Zacharias resented the intrusion. He remembered only too well being their age and feeling the same disquiet during his mother's rare visits. He stood and crossed the room to her. "Grandmama and I will leave you two alone," he said to the boys and guided her firmly from the room.

She wasn't happy, but that came as no surprise. She rarely was. "You're entirely too lax with those children. You spoil them horribly."

"Perhaps." He linked his hands behind his back and set a pace away from the nursery. "But at least they're mine to spoil."

"Indeed." Her face puckered with disapproval, but she dropped the subject and launched into another. "What are your plans this morning?"

Whenever she asked about his plans, that meant she had something in mind for him—usually something he'd rather avoid. A lie sprang easily to his lips. "I'm riding into town to take care of some business."

"Not today, Zacharias. We're expecting a guest for luncheon and I'll expect you to join us."

A guest could only mean Patricia, and Zacharias didn't feel up to facing the two of them today. "Unfortunately, that won't be possible."

"And why not? What could you possibly have to do in town?"

"I'm meeting Philip at my club." Another lie, but a necessary one.

His mother's lip curled as it always did whenever his friend's name came up. "You made it sound as if you had something important on your schedule. Since that's obviously not the case, I'll expect you for luncheon."

"My apologies, Mother, but I won't be there."

She stopped walking abruptly and turned to glare at him. "I don't like your tone, Zacharias."

"There's nothing wrong with my tone," he argued mildly. "What you don't like is me saying no to you."

"I have no trouble accepting no for an answer"—her eyes flashed and her mouth thinned—"if there's a justifiable reason for it. But to put an afternoon with an acquaintance before your duties as a host is the height of rudeness."

"Philip is a friend, not an acquaintance," Zacharias said firmly. "And your luncheon guest is your responsibility, not mine. I don't recall issuing any invitations."

His mother's eyes flashed again. "What has gotten into you, Zacharias? You're behaving so strangely the past few days." She studied him for only a second, then went on. "It's that woman's fault, isn't it?"

"Agatha's?" He said the name purposely, knowing how much his mother hated to hear it.

Victoria's nostrils flared slightly. "Surely you haven't let one case of the vapors wipe everything she's done from your mind."

Zacharias sent his mother a thin smile. "I believe it was more serious than the vapors."

"She's mad, Zacharias. For her to summon you, after five long years—"

"She didn't summon me," he snapped. Making an attempt to soften his tone, he went on. "If you'll recall, Colin came to inform me of the trouble."

"At her bequest."

"Not at all. She assured me—"

"She *spoke* to you?" Shock registered on his mother's face. "You must be joking."

"Not at all."

"She's up to something."

"Actually, she seemed quite genuine."

"Genuine?" His mother let out an acid laugh. "Surely you don't believe that. Not after everything she's done."

"Our estrangement isn't entirely her fault," Zacharias reminded her softly.

His mother glared at him. "It most assuredly is. You did nothing wrong."

"I hurt her. And I'm not particularly proud of it."

"Nonsense." Victoria met his gaze levelly. "You did nothing your father didn't do. Or his father before him.

She behaved in a most unreasonable fashion about the whole episode."

"Perhaps," he admitted grudgingly. "But—"

"Listen to me, Zacharias. I will not have you behaving like an adolescent over her. Not again."

"She *is* my wife."

"In name only. You allowed her to make a mockery of you and of the entire family once. You cannot allow her to do it again."

"Perhaps not," he admitted grudgingly. He hated gossip passionately, and hated being the subject of it even more.

Victoria started walking again, slowly. "I know you don't want to discuss this, but in light of your attitude, I feel I must bring it up again."

"Divorce?" He sent her a smile twisted with bitterness. "No."

"You *must* divorce her, Zacharias. You really have no choice."

"No divorce." They'd been over this subject a thousand times, yet he could make no headway with his mother. "Divorce would only subject Andrew and Mordechai to more scandal. I won't do that to them."

His mother started down the staircase. "Do you really think you're protecting them from scandal by remaining married? You *must* think of your children, of the Logan name, of the dynasty your father left in your hands."

"I do think of them," he assured her, following more slowly. "Almost exclusively."

"And you still intend to spend your life chained to a madwoman?"

"I intend to spend the rest of my life chained to *no* woman. And that would be the only purpose for divorcing Agatha, wouldn't it? So I could marry again."

"To a woman more suitable, yes."

"To Patricia."

"Patricia would be a far more suitable wife, a far better representative of the Logan name. You know that as well as I do."

"Perhaps. But I don't love her."

"Love?" Victoria pushed away his argument with a brisk wave her hand. "Love is for the lower classes. For servants. For people who have no land or fortune to preserve, or who have no standing to think about. You can't afford to concern yourself with love."

"I won't marry without it," he insisted.

Victoria let out a sigh heavy with impatience. "Then fall in love with Patricia. Considering your history, it shouldn't be difficult to do."

Zacharias would have protested that unfair remark had Abraham not stepped into view at precisely that moment. "Pardon me, sir, but there is someone here to see you."

Victoria leveled the man with a glance. "Mr. Logan is occupied, Abraham. Tell whoever it is—"

Irritated, Zacharias cut her off before she could finish. "Mr. Logan is not occupied, Abraham. My mother and I have just finished our conversation." He abandoned her without ceremony and motioned for Abraham to lead on.

When they'd put some distance between them, Abraham slowed his step. "I've shown the caller into the library, sir. I hope I've done the right thing. It seemed to be the best thing—"

"I'm not in the habit of turning away guests, Abraham. You know that." He took a deep breath, tried to rid himself of the lingering aftertaste of disagreement, and matched Abraham's pace. "So, who is my mysterious visitor?"

Abraham slowed his step and glanced over his shoulder to make sure Victoria hadn't followed. Then he turned back to Zacharias and nearly whispered.

"It is Mrs. Logan, sir. Mrs. *Agatha* Logan."

Chapter 5

ZACHARIAS STOPPED WALKING entirely and the echo of his footsteps died away. He eyed Abraham suspiciously. "Agatha? *Here?*"

"Yes, sir." Even Abraham couldn't manage to keep his normally inscrutable expression in place.

"You're absolutely certain it's her?" It was a fool's question. Abraham had known Agatha as long as Zacharias had. Perhaps not as well, but certainly as long.

"It is Mrs. Logan, sir. I ought to know her when I see her."

Zacharias stole a glance over his shoulder. Good Lord, if his mother knew Agatha was here . . . He shuddered at the thought. "I believe it would be best if we don't tell my mother about this."

"My thoughts exactly, sir."

Zacharias paced a few steps away and scrubbed his face with his palm. "Did she say what she wants?"

"Not to me, sir."

"No. No, of course she wouldn't." He laughed harshly, a lifetime of schooling his expressions and keeping his thoughts hidden from the servants forgotten.

"Forgive me, Abraham. It's just that this comes as quite a surprise."

"Of course it would, sir." Abraham sent a pointed look toward the library door. "If I may make a suggestion, sir, perhaps you should see Mrs. Logan before your mother comes to see who your caller is."

It was the furthest Abraham had ever stepped over the line between servant and employer, but Zacharias didn't intend to question him. Instead, he was grateful to the man for snapping him out of his daze.

"Yes. Yes. Good idea, Abraham. Of course I'll see her." Zacharias took a steadying breath and darted one last glance behind him. "Yes," he said, more to himself than to Abraham. "I *will* see her."

Abraham's usual inscrutable expression dropped back into place as he opened the library door. Zacharias stepped inside, but when he didn't immediately see Agatha, he thought surely Abraham had brought him to the wrong room. He started to turn back to the door and caught sight of her standing in front of the bookshelves that flanked the window.

She'd always tolerated his love of books, but only just, and only because she considered it proper for a gentleman to read. As for herself, she'd never shown any interest. But this morning, she traced one finger across the spines of the volumes and studied them with rapt interest.

She turned quickly when she heard him, but she didn't drop her hands at once. "You have some wonderful books here. Do you have anything by Mark Twain?"

"Twain?" Zacharias laughed in spite of his confusion. "*Mark* Twain? The man's a quick wit, but hardly worth granting shelf space."

She laughed softly. "You might be surprised. His wit hides some caustic social commentary." She tilted her head and looked him over slowly. "Do you know him?"

"Twain?" He shook his head and moved toward his favorite leather wing chair. "I know of him, certainly. He's garnered a small amount of fame."

"That's too bad," she said with a soft smile. "I'd like to meet him."

He lowered himself into his chair and gripped the armrests. "How is it that you know of Clemens, but you don't remember your own life?"

Her smile faded and a faint stain tinted her cheeks. "Good question. I can't explain it."

He ignored the sudden appeal of Agatha flustered and crossed his legs with studied indifference. "And is that why you've come? To admire my library?"

"No." She pulled her hands away from the leather-bound books reluctantly and clutched the fabric of her skirt. "I came so I could talk to you."

"I thought we'd decided yesterday that we had nothing to say."

"But we do have something to say. Beginning with why you're so angry with me."

"Angry? I think perhaps you could find another word that would better describe it, don't you?"

"Could I?" She took a hesitant step toward him, looking so confused, Zacharias felt an unexpected twinge of compassion.

He forced it away. "Why are you so determined to discuss what happened between us?"

"Because you're my husband." She seemed to hesitate over the word, but she smiled again and went on. "And, as I told you yesterday, I have no recollection of what went wrong between us."

Grudgingly, he admitted she must be telling the truth. Why else would she come to Winterhill? Why else would she risk meeting his mother or making herself an object of whispered speculation? Why else would she even speak to him when she'd remained stubbornly, spitefully silent these past five years?

But he refused to let his doubts weaken him. Nor would he let her beauty cloud his judgment. "Perhaps it's selfish of me, but if what you say is true I have no wish to remind you."

"Don't you think you're being unfair?"

"Perhaps. But I still think the past is a subject better left alone."

Her brows knit, not with the anger he was used to seeing, but with confusion and even a little frustration. "If we don't talk about it, how can we ever hope to fix it?"

"Fix it?" He laughed sharply. "Perhaps it has escaped your attention, my dear, but there is nothing left to fix."

"Oh, but there is." She closed the distance between them. "There must be. We are still married. . . ."

"Unfortunately." He kept his voice gruff and put some distance between them. He could not, *would* not, allow her to bewitch him.

She let out a sigh so soft it might have been a baby's breath. "You must really hate me."

"On the contrary. I feel absolutely nothing for you." He had to lie through his teeth to get the words out, but he did it. At the moment, he didn't know what he felt. But whatever it was, it nearly overpowered him.

"You loved me once."

"Yes." He turned away to avoid looking at her. "Yes, I did. Once. Many years ago."

She put a hand on his arm and her touch ignited a flame he'd thought long dead. "Then surely there's something of those old feelings left."

Giving himself a stern mental shake, he stepped away again. All the anger and hurt threatened to evaporate when she touched him, and he couldn't allow that to happen. He forced a cold smile. "I'm afraid not."

"When did you stop loving me?" Soft words to match the sadness in her eyes.

Scowling, he put half the room between them. "I see no purpose in talking about this, Agatha. No possible good can come from it."

"There is a purpose if it mends the rift between us. If the four of us can be together again—"

"The *four* of us?"

"Yes. You and me . . . and our sons."

As it had yesterday, her mention of the twins cleared

away his confusion and brought him back to solid ground. Difficult as it was to believe she wanted to mend their marriage, it was a thousand times more difficult to believe she suddenly wanted to be a mother to Morde-chai and Andrew. And her behavior toward them was a thousand times more difficult to forgive.

With sinking heart, Shelby watched the color flood Zacharias's face and the fury fill his eyes. Obviously she'd said the wrong thing . . . and just when she thought she might actually be reaching him.

He gripped the back of a chair so hard his knuckles turned white and a muscle in his jaw jumped. "Leave."

There was so much anger in that single word, Shelby took an involuntary step backward. "What?"

"Leave here now," he said, his voice low and cold. "And don't come back."

Shelby thought back over the last few exchanges in their conversation, trying to figure out what she'd said wrong. It didn't take a genius to figure out that he got angry with her every time she mentioned the twins.

She admired him for caring so deeply for his children. She couldn't fault him for wanting to protect them. She'd have given anything to have had someone care about her that way when she was young and alone. But if she was here to mend this rift, she couldn't back down.

"I won't leave," she said. "Not until you talk to me."

"I don't know what kind of game you're playing, Agatha, but I want no part of it."

He looked as if he could cheerfully wring her neck, and Shelby's stomach lurched. She tried to look strong and brave. "Zacharias, please . . . At least let me see the children."

His face reddened dangerously. He released the chair, threw open a humidor on the desk, and pulled out a cigar. But instead of lighting it, he tossed it back inside and slammed the lid. "Never."

"Why not?"

His eyes turned to blue flame, his face to granite. "Until this moment, you've refused even to look at them."

Shelby's heart ached for all four people involved. She took a deep breath and blinked back the unexpected tears that stung her eyes. "But they're my sons."

Zacharias backed away from her slowly but his eyes never left her face. "You really have gone mad, haven't you?"

Great. She was making this worse, not better. "Is it so difficult for you to believe I've changed?"

"Not difficult. Impossible. You're a dangerous woman, Agatha. I don't want you anywhere near my sons."

"They're my sons, too," she reminded him.

"As God is my witness," he said slowly, as if he thought she might have trouble understanding, "you'll never see those children."

"At least tell me why."

Zacharias's hands curled into fists at his side. "Are you going to pretend you don't know?"

"I'm not pretending," Shelby assured him, "and I'm not mad. I'm asking you for help. You're my husband, and I'd like to understand what happened between us." When he didn't respond, she straightened her shoulders and decided to fight fire with fire. "Is it your relationship with Patricia Starling that makes you unwilling to talk to me?"

He didn't say a word, but his face looked as if it had been carved of cold, gray marble.

"At least tell me why you prefer her to me," Shelby insisted.

If someone had told her Zacharias could look more formidable than he had a moment ago, she wouldn't have believed them. But the evidence presented itself right before her eyes. "There is a simple answer to that, *my dear*. Patricia has a heart."

So much poison filled the words, Shelby had to work hard to remember they weren't directed at her. She rested her hand on the back of a chair and hoped he wouldn't notice the trembling of her fingers. "So do I, Zacharias."

"Is that so?" The frigid smile curved Zacharias's lips again. "Could it be that you have decided to become a woman, at long last?"

Shelby lifted her chin a bit higher. "I have always been a woman."

"Have you?" He dragged his gaze along her, leaving no doubt about the direction his thoughts had taken.

Shelby still refused to run. She forced herself to stare back into his eyes. "Yes."

"Patricia *enjoys* my attention."

What a jerk, she thought. Aloud, she said, "Maybe I would, too, if you gave me a chance."

"Is that so?" he said again. His eyes narrowed into slits as they roamed across her face. His nostrils flared slightly.

Without warning, he closed the distance between them and gripped her shoulders, pulling her slightly off-balance. "Have you decided you like this, then?"

Before she could make a sound, he settled his lips on hers. His arms slid around her, solid, firm, and as unyielding as steel bands. She tried to protest, but she couldn't draw a breath. She tried to push him away, but he held her too tightly.

Without warning, his anger seemed to evaporate. He deepened the kiss slowly, tentatively, and Shelby's anger and fear vaporized. All at once, he didn't seem huge and threatening. Still huge, but now almost gentle.

He probed her lips gently with his tongue. Shelby knew she shouldn't respond, but it had been so long since anyone had kissed her, and he did it so well, she couldn't seem to help herself. She parted her lips slightly inviting more even while her brain shouted at her to pull away.

She'd been kissed before, but never like this. From somewhere far away, she imagined a slight moan of pleasure. Was it from him? Or her?

"Agatha." It was more a sigh than a word, but it

brought reality back with a resounding crash.

Zacharias wasn't kissing her, he was kissing Agatha. And Shelby had no business responding to another woman's husband. Planting both hands against his chest, she shoved him away. But his mask had slipped and she saw the man behind it fully. His eyes were soft and clear and even vulnerable. His chest heaved as he struggled to catch his breath.

In the next second the mask came crashing down again, the vulnerability she'd glimpsed disappeared, and the cynical expression returned.

"You still don't like it," he drawled. "Do you?"

On the contrary, she'd liked it very much. *Too* much. But apparently Agatha hadn't. Shelby didn't know what to say or how to react. Her biggest question of the moment was, what kind of woman could stay unaffected by a kiss like that?

She tried to maintain her dignity, to keep her chin up and her hands steady. "I don't like being manhandled against my will, if that's what you mean."

"That was always the trouble," he said, wrenching open the door and making to step through. "It was always against your will. And I'm no more interested in marriage to a block of ice than I ever was. I'm tired of trying to find a welcome in your bed, Agatha. If I ever take a wife to my bed again, it will be one who knows how to behave like a woman."

"Like Patricia Starling?" It was petty and spiteful, but it popped out before she could stop it.

Zacharias's face hardened, his eyes turned to fire, but instead of arguing with her he sketched a mocking bow. "Good-bye, Agatha. Abraham will see you out."

"I think that went well," Shelby said to the walls when the door slammed behind him. "You'll have him eating out of the palm of your hand in no time." Sighing, she picked up her gloves from the table where she'd dropped them and started to pull them on. From the corner of her eye, she saw someone step into the room.

Abraham, no doubt, come to give her the boot.

Trying to look as if nothing had happened, she glanced up . . . and straight into the cold hard eyes of a woman whose thin, patrician face was made severe by lines of stern disapproval. She might have been any age from thirty to sixty, Shelby couldn't tell. Her honey-colored hair might have been flecked with gray and the skin around her eyes might have sported a few wrinkles, but Shelby couldn't be certain. She seemed ageless.

While Shelby watched, disturbed by the coiling fingers of unnamed apprehension, the woman closed the door and gave Shelby a slow once-over, assessing every lock of hair, every cell on her face, every inch of fabric.

"Well. Agatha." Her voice was heavy with distaste. "To what do we owe this honor?"

Strangely, a line from a deodorant commercial popped into Shelby's head. *Never let 'em see you sweat.* But this was one scenario she'd never seen portrayed in the advertisement and she wondered if any modern antiperspirant could have stopped the clammy feeling that came over her.

She tried desperately to look unaffected while she pulled on her gloves. "I came to see Zacharias."

"I see. And what, pray tell, could you have possibly had to say to him?"

"That is between Zacharias and me."

The woman laughed, one harsh note that seemed to reverberate from the walls. "I see." She walked slowly toward a green brocade chair, perched on it like a queen taking her throne, and motioned Shelby toward another. "I suppose it's time for the two of us to have a little chat."

The encounter with Zacharias had left Shelby shaken, and another confrontation—with a woman who looked as if she could freeze fire—didn't sound very appealing. But her years of bouncing from one foster home to another had taught her to begin as she meant to go on. If she showed weakness now, she'd never be able to face this woman from a position of strength.

She sat carefully and forced herself to meet the woman's gaze. "What do we need to talk about?"

"Perhaps you'll be kind enough to explain what brings you to Winterhill after all this time?" It wasn't a request, it was a command, and Shelby resented the woman's imperious manner.

But she also realized she might learn something from this hateful woman, so she lifted her chin and answered. "That's very simple," she said. "My family is here."

"Your family."

"My husband and children."

The woman's eyebrows arched. "The husband and children you turned your back on five years ago? The husband and children you have refused to speak to or even set eyes upon? The husband and children you have consistently treated as if they were dead? Is that the family you speak of?"

Shelby's mouth dried and an ache started in the back of her neck and shot into her head, but she held her ground. "I don't understand what concern this is of yours."

"Don't you?" The woman's face clouded and hatred sparked in her eyes. "Perhaps you don't. A woman capable of turning her back on her own children might not understand a mother's concern for her son and grandchildren."

This was Zacharias's mother? Shelby had read about Victoria Logan, of course. The archives were full of stories about her. But how on earth had this cold, granite-skinned woman given birth to the man whose passionate nature attracted her and whose kiss had just rocked the world beneath her feet?

She tempered her tone before she spoke again. "I can understand your concern, Victoria, better than you can imagine. But I assure you I'm not here to hurt Zacharias or the children."

"No?" Her eyebrows arched even higher. "Well, that makes me feel so much better. Perhaps I am worrying needlessly."

If the words hadn't been heavily laced with sarcasm, Shelby might have believed her.

"Nevertheless," Victoria went on, "I do worry. I shall not sit idly by and watch you destroy my son again."

The words were delivered with the brutality of a sword thrust. Shelby rested her hands on the arms of the chair and visualized a verbal fencing match.

She parried. "I didn't come here to destroy your son. I came to make things right."

Victoria's lip curled. "I see."

"Circumstances have changed," Shelby said, "and I very much want to put my family back together. I want to be a mother to my children."

Victoria pulled a fan from the folds of her skirt and waved it languidly in front of her face. "And you want my blessing?"

Shelby hesitated over her response. Victoria's animosity was so strong she could feel it across the room. Shelby didn't want anything from her, and the likelihood that she'd give her blessing was virtually nonexistent. But it would be nice not to have to wage war against the dragon lady sitting across from her.

"I would very much like your blessing," she said at last.

A satisfied smile curved Victoria's mouth. "Of course you would. But that's one thing you'll never get from me." *Vicious thrust.*

What a thoroughly nasty woman, Shelby thought. She reminded her of the foster mother she'd had the year she turned twelve—bitter, angry, full of hate, and determined to prove to the world that no one could be nastier than she. Then, Shelby had been young and easily intimidated, and her life had been pure hell for eight long months. Now, she didn't have to tolerate cruelty.

"I'm sorry to hear that," she said, "but it won't make any difference. I still intend to put my family back together."

"Surely you can't think I'll believe you've suddenly had a change of heart, or that I've forgotten the humiliation you have brought upon this family. For all your upbringing, Agatha, you have behaved abominably."

Shelby wanted desperately to ask how, but she knew Victoria would view her questions as a sign of weakness. "Whether or not you believe that I've changed, that doesn't make it any less true. Even you can't change truth into falsehood." *Take that, you old bat.*

"Perhaps not." Victoria waved her fan a little faster. "Let's not pretend with one another any longer. I never did approve of you as a wife for Zacharias. If he'd listened to me and married Patricia Starling in the first place, none of this would have happened." *Ouch. Deep thrust.*

"But he didn't marry Patricia Starling," Shelby pointed out reasonably. "He married me." *Right back at you.*

"Unfortunately. But he has the chance to rectify that mistake, and I intend to see that he does."

They weren't fencing any longer, Shelby realized. Victoria had issued a declaration of war as clearly as if she'd drawn a gun and fired it. It might not be Shelby's war, but she was the one in the trenches and she wouldn't retreat from the battle for Agatha's life and sanity.

She stood quickly. "You've made your position clear, Victoria. Now I'll do the same. Zacharias is my husband, Andrew and Mordechai are my children. I'll fight to the death to put my family back together, and no one—not even you—will stop me."

Victoria's smile grew even more satisfied, like a cat with a dish of cream. "We all know what a pretense that is, Agatha. And I've agreed to it for the sake of the children. But make no mistake. If you persist in trying to put your marriage back together, I'll expose everything."

Shelby didn't let her uncertainty show, though she wished desperately she knew *what* Victoria could expose. "If you were going to do that," she said, keeping her voice tightly controlled, "you'd have done it already.

No matter what threats you make to me, you won't expose anything that might harm the children."

Victoria's eyes widened almost imperceptibly, then narrowed again. She dipped her head in acquiescence. "Perhaps you're right. Perhaps I won't expose the truth. But I will do everything in my power to make sure that Zacharias divorces you." She rose to her feet and leveled Shelby with an acid glare. "Rest assured of that." Without waiting for a response, she swept from the room and left Shelby trembling in her wake.

What a perfectly dreadful woman Victoria Logan was. And what a frighteningly powerful one. But with her blessing or without it, Shelby still had a job to do.

Zacharias stood well back from the window in his second-floor sitting room, determined to make certain Agatha wouldn't see him there. That kiss had shaken him to his core and left him confused. Who would have ever imagined Agatha capable of such surrender?

No, he amended quickly, not surrender. Not capitulation. Not Agatha. Not ever. She'd responded with a passion stronger than he would ever have believed. The kind of passion he'd once dreamed of awakening in her, but never had.

If only she'd responded that way during their marriage. If only she'd welcomed his embrace, even once. If only she hadn't stiffened each time he touched her, and looked upon their lovemaking as a distasteful duty to be endured with tight lips and closed eyes. If only he had been the kind of man for whom that would be enough.

His scowl deepened. The man didn't exist for whom that would have been enough. Zacharias's needs weren't the problem. The problem was that Agatha had expected everything from him and had been willing to give nothing.

He kept his eyes riveted on her as the carriage lurched away from the mounting block and rolled down the drive. And he saw, unbelievably, her shoulders slump when she thought no one could see her.

That, in itself, was enough to make him wonder. She'd been behaving like a different woman these past two days. Even he couldn't deny that. But after everything that had passed between them, how could he believe it was genuine? How could he trust it to last?

If only he could, he just might agree to make another attempt at their marriage. But two days out of a lifetime weren't enough to convince him she'd truly changed. Sooner or later, she'd go back to being the same stone-hearted woman she'd always been and Zacharias would be a damned fool if he let himself believe her.

He stepped away from the window, snatched up his hat and coat, and stormed out of the room, bellowing for Abraham to call for his horse. And he promised himself that, difficult though it might be to resist her until she tired of her game, that's exactly what he'd do.

Chapter 6

ZACHARIAS STRODE INTO his gentleman's club determined to spend some time in the company of men where he could forget about Agatha and put the feel of her lips out of his mind. Divested of his hat and coat, he made his way into the dimly lit room where strategically placed leather chairs and tables made private conversation possible, and listened to the muted buzz of male voices.

There'd be no talk of dinner parties and flower arrangements here. No one asking him to reconcile or divorce. No one making demands of any kind. He wanted only stimulating conversation about subjects that mattered.

He signaled for a brandy and moved toward a small knot of men standing near one of the room's gigantic fireplaces. Smiling in anticipation, he clapped a hand to Judge Beaming's shoulder, took his place in the circle, and nodded a greeting to Orville Englund, Nathan Fullmer, and Gregory McDonald. "Gentlemen. Do you mind if I join you?"

"Not at all." Judge Beaming turned his watery blue

eyes on Zacharias and followed with a quick smile.
"Good to see you again, my boy."

"As a matter of fact," Nathan Fullmer said, making a
vain attempt to tug the edges of his waistcoat across his
expanding middle, "we were just talking about you."

Flattered, Zacharias accepted his brandy from a silent-
footed waiter. Did they seek his thoughts on politics?
Business? Finances? Industry? No matter. He could discuss them all with equal confidence. He sipped and lowered his snifter again, prepared to delve into something
of merit. "In what context?"

"Prudence informs me that we've been invited to
Winterhill for one of your famous dinner parties, and
I've just learned that these fine gentlemen will also be
in attendance." The judge's jowls wobbled slightly as he
talked, evidence that he'd enjoyed a great many dinner
parties in his time. "We were wondering what culinary
delights your Emmaline will have in store for us."

They wanted to discuss his cook? Zacharias's smile
chilled. He stared from one face to the other in stunned
disbelief. "I'm afraid I have no idea. My mother has all
those decisions well in hand." He made an effort to shift
the conversation to something more substantial. "I was
noting the progress on the bridge as I rode into town—"

"How is your mother?" the judge interrupted.

Zacharias broke off to answer. "She's well, thank you.
And Prudence?"

The judge's thick lips pursed. "Well. She occupies
herself with good works these days—and with trying to
find a suitable husband for Gloria."

Zacharias ignored the reference to the judge's avail-
able daughter. The last thing he needed was another
zealous mother nipping at his heels. He allowed a suitable moment to lapse, then tried again. "I'm beginning
to wonder if the railroad will finish the bridge on schedule."

Nathan Fullmer waved a hand as if the project were
of no import. His thin lips puckered and his deep-set
eyes gleamed. "Perhaps not. My main concern at the

moment is catching the eye of that waiter so he can bring me another brandy. Of course even this brandy can't compare to the one you served at your last dinner party, Zacharias. Will you have more on hand?"

Gregory McDonald turned a hungry smile in his direction. "If you ever decide to rid yourself of one of those houses, old man, you know where to come. Just be sure you include the contents of the wine cellar in your asking price."

"I have no plans to sell either house," Zacharias assured him as he had at least a dozen times in the past, "or to part with the contents of my wine cellar." He slung back the rest of his own drink and cast about for an excuse to escape.

Just when he thought he was stuck in a dismal discussion that could have taken place around his own dining table, he heard a familiar laugh and his spirits climbed. He followed the sound and caught a glimpse of his boyhood friend, Philip Clayton, engaged in conversation with several men on the opposite side of the room.

Offering his apologies, he motioned for a second brandy and made his way toward Philip. But even then, he had to stop occasionally to answer a greeting or an inquiry about his mother's health.

At long last, he drew abreast of his friend. Philip, as dark as Zacharias was fair, as husky as Zacharias was lean, had been his closest friend since childhood even though Victoria had never approved of the bond between the boys. She hadn't approved of his father's friendship with Isaiah Clayton, either. Isaiah Clayton had toiled for his fortune, and his wife, Eleanor, had come from Savannah, which had always made her suspect in Victoria's uncompromising Yankee eyes.

But even her stern disapproval hadn't stopped the boys from becoming fast friends, nor the men from continuing their association. Philip knew more about Zacharias than any other living soul, and of course the reverse held true as well. But even Philip didn't know every-thing.

Smiling broadly, Zacharias waited for a break in the conversation, then clapped a hand to his friend's shoulder. "Fancy meeting you here in the middle of the day. Won't the sawmill suffer without you there to oversee it?"

"Undoubtedly," Philip said with a laugh. "But it was too fine a day to stay cooped up with logs and invoices and bills of lading."

"So instead, you coop yourself up with brandy and cigars." Zacharias accepted his glass from a black-coated waiter and sipped eagerly. "The workings of your mind remain a mystery to me, my friend."

"No more than yours are a mystery to me." Philip nodded toward his companions and stepped away for a private word. "What brings you here?"

Zacharias waited until they'd put some distance between them and the nearest set of ears. "Same as you. The need to escape."

Philip laughed again. "And speaking of escape . . . How *is* dear Victoria?"

"As ever." Zacharias felt some of his tension slipping away, but, then, Philip's company always had that effect on him. "I seem to have given her new cause for alarm."

"Really?" Philip's eyebrows winged upward, two dark caterpillars on his broad face. "What have you done now, served the wrong port to guests? Chosen the wrong cravat?"

"Worse. Much worse." Zacharias downed his brandy, welcoming the burn as it traced a path through him. "I've been in contact with Agatha."

Philip rocked back on his heels and stared at him. "You're joking."

"Not at all."

"Why would you want to put yourself through that torture again?"

Zacharias sometimes thought his friend was angrier with her than he was himself. But of course, without all the facts at his disposal, he would be. "She seems to have undergone a complete change of personality."

Philip studied him for a moment, no doubt searching for a hidden smile or flash of mischief in his eyes. "It's a trick."

"I thought so at first," Zacharias admitted. "But it seems she's suffered a loss of memory. She remembers nothing about the events that led to our estrangement."

Philip smoothed his fingers over his moustache. "Nothing?"

"Nothing."

"Are you certain?"

The memory of her lips beneath his returned to haunt him. The look in her eyes and the soft sound of her voice wound their way through him. "I'm certain."

Philip shook his head emphatically. "It's a trick, Zacharias. She wants something from you. Don't be fooled by it."

Until that moment, Zacharias hadn't realized that he'd hoped Philip might encourage him. But the strong shaft of disappointment that accompanied Philip's warning made him take stock of himself and acknowledge the truth.

In spite of everything, he wanted very much to believe her.

Maybe it was foolish. Dangerous. Even downright irrational. But that didn't change the way he felt, it didn't dampen his hopes or douse his enthusiasm. It didn't make the memory of her kiss distasteful or convince him to keep a safe distance from her. He was intrigued by the changes in her and he wanted very much to explore the differences.

God help him.

He signaled for another brandy and argued his case. "She has asked me to resume our marriage."

Philip's eyebrows hitched a bit higher. "*All* of it?"

The question brought on a surge of heat that had nothing to do with the brandy. "All of it."

"You said no, of course."

"Of course." Zacharias led Philip toward two chairs far enough removed from the others to give them some privacy. "But she's behaving so differently, I wish you could see for yourself."

"We both know that's not likely to happen. Even before she became a recluse, she didn't like me."

"Don't feel bad," Zacharias said with a wry grin. "She didn't like me, either."

"True enough." Philip pulled a cigar from his pocket, snipped the tip, and lowered it again without lighting it. "Then why does she want to resume the marriage?"

"I suppose it's because she can't remember *why* she didn't like me."

"And you didn't remind her."

"Of course I didn't. She'll remember soon enough. In the meantime—"

Philip's brows knit. "You're not considering it."

"Absolutely not." Zacharias sipped carefully, hoping he looked and sounded convincing.

Some of the tension left Philip's shoulders. "What does our dear Victoria have to say about this latest turn of events?"

The question dropped a pall over Zacharias's mood. "She's not happy, I can tell you that. She still insists that I divorce Agatha at last and marry Patricia."

Philip turned his cigar slowly between his fingers. "But you're not going to, are you?"

"I have no desire to marry Patricia," Zacharias reminded him. "I have no desire to marry anyone. Remaining legally bound to Agatha is convenient. It prevents my mother from pushing matrimony at me too enthusiastically."

"The woman made your life a living hell," Philip said, lowering his voice. "Why are you even considering reconciling with her?"

"I'm not," Zacharias said tersely. "Haven't you been listening? I'm telling you all the reasons I *won't* let myself get caught in that trap again."

Philip let out a disbelieving laugh. "Okay, if you say

so. Personally, I hope never to see you that miserable again."

"And I hope never to *be* that miserable again." Zacharias scowled at the memories of the life he'd shared with Agatha, the things she'd said, and of the hatred he'd seen in her eyes before they separated.

Philip lit his cigar and smoked thoughtfully for a moment or two. "Does Patricia know?"

"No doubt my mother has told her."

"But you haven't?"

"I've seen no need to tell her."

Philip lowered his cigar again and leaned closer. "The woman is obviously in love with you."

Zacharias sent him a thin smile. "Perhaps she is. But my heart doesn't belong to any woman, nor is it likely to any time soon."

"You could do a sight worse than to have Patricia on your arm and running your household."

Zacharias sent him a sidelong glance. "What are you doing, playing devil's advocate? As I recall, you've never been overly fond of Patricia, either."

Philip chuckled softly. "Only because she's not the right woman for you, no matter what your mother thinks."

Zacharias set his brandy aside. "No," he said thoughtfully, "she's not. I've always thought I might enjoy the companionship of a woman who could, occasionally, discuss something relevant."

"Then divorce Agatha quickly but for hell's sake, don't marry Patricia. Save your serious talk for your fellows and leave women to what they do best."

"What they do best," Zacharias muttered, "is to make my life miserable." He let his gaze trail slowly over the room. "I envy you, Philip. At least you have something to escape to."

Philip waved his words away. "So you say. But your father cared enough to leave you financially secure, so why do you complain?"

"Yours left you with an occupation," Zacharias countered. "That to me would have been a far greater gift."

Philip studied him with eyes narrowed in doubt. "You'd trade your life for mine?"

"In a heartbeat."

Philip shifted his weight in his chair, paid attention to his cigar for a moment, then ran his fingers over his moustache once more. "I wouldn't have brought this up, but as luck would have it I'm somewhat in need of a cash infusion at the moment. The expansion we undertook last year has left me short on the books."

Zacharias didn't like the sound of that. He'd always thought Philip financially secure. "Is there cause for alarm?"

"No," Philip assured him quickly . . . perhaps a bit too quickly. "But I've been thinking for the past month of finding an investor . . . or a partner." He smiled weakly. "If I must, I'd rather have you in that position than anyone else."

Zacharias didn't know whether to worry or be offended. Whether Philip really needed an investor, or if he extended the offer out of pity. "Don't toy with me," he warned. "I'm in no mood—"

"Who's toying?" Philip sloshed his brandy. "If you're serious about wanting an occupation, I can offer you one. If not you, I'll have to take on someone else. And, as I said, I'd rather see your face every day than any other." He sobered before he went on. "Trust is a valuable commodity, my friend, and at the moment I'm in as great a need of trust as I am of money." He held up a hand to keep Zacharias from responding. "Don't worry. Your investment would be perfectly safe."

Zacharias nodded slowly, running the pros and cons through his mind rapidly. "How involved in the day-to-day business would I be?"

"As involved as you want to be."

"I wouldn't want to jeopardize our friendship."

"Neither would I," Philip agreed. "But I trust that if we did have a disagreement, we could resolve it as quickly as we used to settle our boyhood skirmishes."

"But not in the same manner, I hope," Zacharias said with a laugh.

"Bloody noses?" Philip's laughter joined his. "I would hope not—for your sake. I'm quite sure I could still best you."

"You have a faulty memory," Zacharias said with a laugh. "You never bested me." His smile faded slowly. "It's a tempting proposition, I'll say that."

"On both sides." Philip's manner became even more serious and the concern in his eyes tipped the scales. "To tell you the truth, I'm at a loss to explain how I find myself in this position. I thought finances were secure, but the books indicate that the mill is creeping closer to the red every month."

Even if Zacharias hadn't been close to desperation for something to occupy his time, he would have considered the partnership for Philip's sake.

Philip's moment of seriousness evaporated. "If you accept, your mother will want to have me shot. You realize that."

"And me along with you," Zacharias agreed.

"Good thing the old gal doesn't frighten me, isn't it? What will Patricia think of this?"

"I don't care."

"And Agatha?"

Zacharias downed the last of his brandy and shoved his glass away. "I know exactly how she'll react. When it comes to what's expected of a gentleman, she's even less forgiving than my mother." He extended a hand to Philip. "You've got yourself a partner. Shall we take care of the details on Monday? I can ask Arthur Williams to draw up the paperwork—if that's agreeable to you."

Philip held back for a moment. "Don't you want to think about it?"

"I have thought," Zacharias assured him. "You have no idea how much I long for something substantial to occupy my time."

He just hoped it would work. If he didn't do something to take his mind off Agatha, he just might make the biggest mistake of his life.

Victoria didn't give any indication of her distress as she rode through the streets of Hannibal. She'd long ago learned how to behave like a lady under any circumstances, and she'd been taught from earliest childhood that there was nothing more important than maintaining the proper appearance, regardless of the circumstances that may cross one's path.

But inside . . .

Inside, Victoria was tied in knots. For the past four days, Zacharias had been behaving abominably. First the strange turn of events with Agatha, then his decision to go into business with Philip. The embarrassment was almost too much to bear.

She blamed Zacharias's father for this horrible turn of events. She'd always been a willing and pliable woman, bowing first to her father's will, then to Hugh's, though with Hugh, she'd had to exert an ever-so-mild influence from time to time to counteract his utter disregard for decorum.

It was Hugh's insistence that Zacharias be allowed to marry that woman—in spite of Victoria's objections—that had brought them to the brink of disaster now. And perhaps a small share of blame lay at her own feet. She'd always been the most agreeable of persons—too agreeable, perhaps. Too pliant. If she hadn't bowed to Hugh's will, they wouldn't have been brought to this.

Agatha—Victoria could hardly bear to think of that woman by name—had come from the most unfortunate of circumstances. She'd been born to a wholly inappropriate mother who'd obviously neglected her training. Though it pained Victoria to admit it, Zacharias was too much his father's son to recognize how inappropriate the marriage was. She had hoped that Agatha's behavior over the Unfortunate Incident would bring Zacharias to his senses. And for a time, it seemed that it had.

But Zacharias had always been too softhearted, and his reaction to Agatha's odd behavior over the previous four days only bore that out. Though he was thirty years old, he still needed his mother's gentle guidance to keep him on the right path—a path that did not include the former Agatha Carruthers.

When her carriage drew up in front of Avondale, Victoria alit and swept up the front stairs. And within minutes, she was seated in the sunny drawing room with Patricia. She let her gaze linger with satisfaction on the Chinese Export pieces on the mantel, the exquisite heirloom mirror over the fireplace, and the muted floral fabric covering the chairs. Though her own tastes ran to more substantial furniture and stately colors, the care Patricia lavished on her family pieces gave her great comfort. This was a woman she could trust with the Logan heirlooms when she could no longer care for them herself.

"I'll get straight to the point," Victoria said when the maid finished serving tea and left them alone. "I've come to ask for your help."

"Of course, Victoria." Patricia settled her cup and saucer on her knee. "What is it?"

"Zacharias." Victoria didn't miss the slight softening of Patricia's expression. What mother could resist a woman who so obviously loved her son? She set aside her cup and folded her hands in her lap. "Or perhaps, I should say the trouble is that woman."

"Agatha?" The softness disappeared immediately and the name hung between them like a storm cloud.

Victoria inclined her head a fraction of an inch. "I thought you might like to know that she paid a visit on Zacharias yesterday."

"A visit?" Patricia's face revealed nothing—she was too well-bred for that—but her eyes said everything. "She left Summervale?"

"Indeed."

"Did he receive her?"

"Unfortunately."

"I see." Patricia stood quickly, her agitation obvious in every movement.

Victoria indulged in a private smile. Patricia was everything she'd ever hoped for in a daughter, and Victoria knew that in Patricia she had an ally. "I have long known that you have a . . . shall I say . . . a particular fondness for Zacharias."

"I am fond of him." Patricia smiled softly. "But, of course, circumstances being what they are . . ."

Victoria waved her words away. "I am not interested in circumstances. I have allowed my family to be a victim to them for entirely too long. I intend to manage the circumstances in which we presently find ourselves." Victoria smoothed the folds of her skirt and allowed herself a sip of Patricia's excellent tea before she went on. "It seems that Agatha wishes to resume her relationship with Zacharias."

Color flooded Patricia's face and a cloud darted across her eyes. "How does Zacharias feel about that?"

"Feelings are highly overrated, Patricia. Zacharias's emotions have put us in this unfortunate situation to begin with. I shall not allow him to compound his mistake by resuming his relationship with that woman."

"I see."

Victoria smiled slowly at the almost indiscernible gleam of approval in Patricia's eyes. "It would, of course, be best for everyone concerned if Zacharias were to obtain a divorce."

"But he will not." Patricia sighed softly and let her gaze travel to the window. "He has made his intentions clear on that score."

"Which is why I've come to you," Victoria explained. "Zacharias is not immune to your charms, Patricia. Surely you must know that."

Patricia's lips curved into a pleased smile. She lowered her gaze becomingly. "I do believe he is fond of me."

"If I may speak honestly. . . ." Victoria lifted her brows and waited for Patricia's nod. "You would be a far more appropriate wife for him, and better as a mother for Andrew and Mordechai. I believe you would take the proper interest in their upbringing and raise them as they should be raised—with an eye tuned toward their future."

Patricia nodded slowly. "They are delightful children, of course, and I do understand how important it is for children to receive the proper upbringing and attend the appropriate schools. But I have no say as long as Zacharias remains married to Agatha."

"That is precisely what we must change. That marriage is an unfortunate circumstance. One I will not tolerate any longer. Zacharias's one weakness is the softness of his heart, and Agatha is playing on that weakness."

"Most unfortunate."

"Most inappropriate," Victoria corrected archly. "There is one way I believe I can convince Zacharias to take action. He must be made to realize that Agatha has lost her mind."

Patricia's cup rattled softly against the saucer. She stilled it quickly and set it aside. "Surely he is not trying to deny that. The evidence is irrefutable."

"He does deny it. Worse, he is under the impression that she has undergone some change that has rendered her sane."

Two bright spots of color sprang into Patricia's cheeks. "And has she changed?"

"She *is* behaving differently." Just thinking about the way Agatha had spoken to her the previous afternoon made Victoria's blood boil. "But I do not believe she has truly changed at all. Perhaps she is dismayed over Zacharias's growing attachment to you and seeks to come between you."

Patricia tilted her head to one side. "But *does* he grow more attached to me? At times, it seems he is growing further removed."

"Never doubt his affection," Victoria snapped, then tempered her voice and repeated it more gently. "Never doubt it." If he didn't love her now, he soon would. Victoria would make certain of that.

Patricia glanced at her hands. "You said you needed something from me. What would you have me do?"

"Zacharias must be made to realize that Agatha is a danger, not only to himself but to the children. He must be made to see that the only way to protect the children is to set her aside, once and for all."

"But she has refused even to acknowledge them these past five years," Patricia pointed out. "Do you really think she would hurt them now?"

"I think it entirely possible. Even probable. The circumstances surrounding their birth . . ."

Patricia looked away quickly. "Yes, of course." She sighed softly and took a bracing sip of tea.

Victoria smiled to herself. She'd made her point. She wouldn't belabor it unless it became necessary. "You are surprised that I would speak of it."

"Yes."

"I shan't do it again. There is no need. As long as we understand one another—"

"Perfectly."

Victoria sighed with satisfaction and lifted her teacup. "As for your marriage to Zacharias, don't worry about appearances. Everyone knows that Agatha is insane and how deeply you mourned the loss of your dear husband."

Patricia's fingers trembled slightly. "I was fond of Steven."

"Of course you were. Your period of seclusion after his death gave ample evidence of your devotion. But you are a young and remarkably beautiful woman. And no one will dare to question whether your marriage to Zacharias is appropriate. I will see to that personally."

Patricia lifted her eyes slightly. "Then I shall do whatever I can to see that he realizes the truth about Agatha."

"Wonderful." Victoria set aside her cup and stood. "We shall not discuss this again. I am not anxious for anyone to think we are"—she cast about for the right word, then sent Patricia a thin smile—"that we are in collusion—especially not Zacharias."

"I won't give him reason to wonder."

"If I had any doubt of that, my dear, I never would have come to you." Completely satisfied, Victoria swept toward the door. "Your presence at Zacharias's side in two days at the dinner party will not go unnoticed. And you will further cement your position as the future mistress of Winterhill by calling on us often in the days following. Together, we will right this wrong. I promise you, I will let nothing stand in your way."

Chapter 7

STEALING A GLANCE over his shoulder to make certain no one was watching, Zacharias slipped out of the ballroom, took refuge behind a trellis of climbing roses, and let out a sigh of relief. He'd been cooped up inside with guests all evening, smiling, laughing, dancing, and playing the perfect host. He'd made his mother happy and done his best to treat Patricia with the deference she deserved as his hostess. But even surrounded by friends, he couldn't seem to stop thinking of Agatha.

When he'd watched Patricia receiving his guests, he'd imagined Agatha in her rightful place at his side. While he'd swept Patricia across the dance floor, he'd pictured his wife's hand in his, her face upturned and slightly flushed. Her image had grown so persistent, a dull ache had started behind his eyes and it now felt like an iron band coiled around his head.

He needed a few minutes of solitude before he had to go back inside to face the music. Tilting his head, he studied the starlit sky, the three-quarter moon, the soft clouds gliding above the trees. He closed his eyes and took a deep breath full of scents from the garden—roses, wisteria, night-scented stock, clematis. But when Agatha's image floated into his head, strolling through the gardens and smiling softly, he opened his eyes again and blinked it away.

At that moment, the sound of approaching footsteps drove him further into the shadows, and when he recognized his mother's voice, he congratulated himself on his decision. Until tonight, his mother had been circumspect about her hopes for his future with Patricia, but this evening Zacharias had caught her in several careless mistakes. He had no wish to tempt fate by putting himself in front of her.

"I'm so glad you're enjoying the evening," he heard her say as the footsteps drew closer. "But I must confess that I had little to do with the preparations. Our dear Patricia really deserves the credit."

Zacharias barely restrained a laugh. His mother had never let anyone else handle anything important, and he very much doubted she ever would.

Now, she let out a wistful sigh. "She's such a dear. Like a daughter to me already."

Zacharias glowered at the back of the trellis and vowed to discuss her slips of the tongue over breakfast.

Her companion spoke for the first time, and Zacharias recognized the voice of Anne Lamott, his mother's friend. "I'm sure you look forward to the time when Patricia's presence here is not a temporary arrangement."

"I do, indeed."

"Do you think it will be soon?"

"I believe so." His mother's voice cut out when she turned away, then rose again. "That fiasco will soon be over. Much as it pains me to say it, Agatha simply isn't well."

Zacharias's pulse slowed ominously.

"It's such an unfortunate situation," Anne said, her voice dripping with false sympathy. "Do you often hear from her?"

"Never." Victoria's voice drifted away again. "Not surprising considering her upbringing."

Anne sniffed with disapproval. "You're right, of course. Her mother simply was not the kind of woman one would have expected Jacob Carruthers to marry." The two women moved away together and Zacharias lost the remainder of their conversation.

But he'd heard enough. More than enough. And none of it true.

Agatha's mother had been a lovely woman, far more kind and gracious than his own mother could ever hope to be, and a slow-burning fury built in his chest at his mother's blatant attempts to manipulate his future. He waited, seething, until he was certain the two women had returned to the ballroom, then started to leave his hiding place.

But a movement in the distance, behind a sprawling pyracantha, caught his attention. He ignored it at first, assuming some of his guests had wandered out into the gardens for privacy, but when the figure moved again— quickly, furtively, darting behind a Japanese yew, running to hide behind a stand of juniper, he had second thoughts.

Intrigued, he held his place in the shadows and watched. Even in the moonlight, he could tell it was a woman. But who? One of the servants? Jada, perhaps, sneaking out through the gardens to meet a lover after the twins went to sleep.

Zacharias supposed he didn't mind that, as long as the twins were safely abed. Smiling slightly, he peered over the balcony to see what she intended to do next. A cloud drifted away from the moon and soft light spilled into the garden illuminating everything in its path.

The woman ducked behind the juniper again, but not before Zacharias got a better look. And what he saw wiped the smile from his face and rooted him to the spot.

Agatha?

Surely he was mistaken. He pulled back sharply, rubbed his eyes, and leaned forward again, convinced that this time he'd see Jada or another of the servants. He moved slowly, carefully, chiding himself for letting his imagination get the best of him. Agatha *had* been behaving oddly the past few days, but even so, she wouldn't risk running into anyone from the society she'd shunned.

Would she?

He held onto the cool iron railing and waited while a couple strolled past the bush where his furtive wife hid. When they disappeared again, she poked her head out again. This time he saw her so clearly even he could no longer believe he'd made a mistake.

While he watched, utterly dumbfounded, Agatha craned her neck to see inside the parlor, glanced anxiously around to make sure she hadn't been discovered, and moved a little closer as if the sights and sounds of the gathering enticed her.

Zacharias went numb all over. If he'd still harbored doubts about the changes in her, this dispelled them all. And when she closed her eyes and began to sway in time to the music of the string quartet, he staggered backward into the rose trellis.

Agatha's eyes flew open and her gaze flashed to the balcony. Zacharias held his breath, half hoping she couldn't see him, half hoping she could. He had no idea whether he should reveal himself to her or remain hidden. But since he hadn't the foggiest idea what he'd say to her, he opted for the latter.

Quickly, like a frightened deer, she backed out of sight, and a moment later he saw her making her way back across the garden again. Zacharias stayed rooted to his spot and watched her, wondering what she'd hoped to accomplish by sneaking over here in the middle of his evening's entertainment.

In the next breath, he realized there was only one way to find out. Determined to catch her, he slipped out from behind the trellis and started toward the gardens. But before he could step off the terrace onto the lawn, a hand grabbed his arm from behind.

He whirled to offer his excuse for not stopping, and found himself looking into Patricia's distressed eyes.

She forced a tremulous smile. "*There* you are. I've been looking everywhere for you."

"I've been busy with guests." The lie came easily. Perhaps too easily. "And now I must see to something quite urgent, so if you'll excuse me—"

Patricia slid her hand around his arm and tightened her grip. "There's no need for you to see to any details, Zacharias. You have a house full of servants who can see to everything our guests need."

Our guests? She didn't seem to notice the slip, but Zacharias certainly did. And it sent a cold shiver of apprehension through him. He darted a glance over his shoulder, but if Agatha was still out there, she'd hidden herself completely.

"Come." Patricia's voice was too close to his ear, her breasts brushed against him provocatively. "I believe you owe me the next waltz. How would it look if you were in the gardens instead of on the dance floor with me?"

He wanted to tell her he didn't give a damn for appearances. That he wanted to talk to his wife and find out what was going on inside her mind. That he could offer Patricia no hope for the future. But tonight, with guests spilling out of every door, filling every room, watching every move he made, was not the time to deal with either problem.

Forcing a smile, he turned toward the ballroom doors. He gritted his teeth and steeled himself to endure the rest of the evening. But he didn't relish the idea of dancing with one woman while another occupied all his thoughts.

Growing more dismayed by the minute, Shelby stood in front of the dressing table while Meg pulled dress after dress after ugly, dowdy dress from a trunk on the floor. Sunlight splashed into the room, a light breeze kept the temperature balmy, and Shelby loved every moment she could spend not wearing her corset. But the inventory of the clothes in Agatha's wardrobe made her feel worse by the minute.

"These gowns are no better than the ones I wear every day," she said with a scowl at the dark blue bombazine with high neck and long sleeves that Meg held aloft. "Don't I own anything colorful?"

"Colorful, madame?"

"Something other than navy blue, brown, or gray. Every gown I've seen will make me look old and frumpy." How could she hope to win Zacharias's affection if she looked like someone's grandmother?

Meg's face puckered with confusion. "Frumpy?"

"Dowdy. Drab. Stodgy." Sighing heavily, Shelby sat at the dressing table and studied Agatha's dark hair and eyes and her clear, pale complexion in the mirror. "Definitely a winter complexion. I think I'd look nice in royal blue, or red, or a deep forest green. Don't I own anything like that?"

"No, madame."

"Nothing pastel? Lavender, or peach, or baby blue?"

Meg lowered the gown and shook her head. "No. You prefer more sedate colors."

"Well, not anymore." Standing, Shelby adjusted the ties of her wrapper more securely. "I've changed. And these styles . . ." She ran her fingers along the collar of one of the gowns heaped on the bed. "Is everything I own high-necked and long-sleeved?"

Meg sent her a sidelong glance. "I'm afraid so, madame."

"I *like* looking like an old lady?"

Meg's lips twitched an instant before she ducked her head. "You do not approve of women who reveal too many of their charms, madame."

"Apparently not." Shelby gave the collar another twitch. "But there's a difference between revealing too many of your charms and dressing like a nun. Tell me how I go about ordering some new dresses."

Meg gathered an armful of linen, bombazine, broadcloth, and satin from the bed. "I can have Colin drive me in to town. There are several fine seamstresses with broad selections of fabric. If you'll tell me which colors you would prefer, I'll make the purchases for you."

"Oh, but . . ." Shelby dropped to the foot of the bed and crossed her legs. "What if I want to choose for myself?"

Meg glanced back at her, obviously surprised by the question. "I always purchase the fabric you desire, madame."

"And I suppose you also make all my clothes."

"Yes, madame. I have for several years."

"In addition to everything else you have to do?" Shelby shook her head slowly, amazed by the ever-growing list of demands Agatha made of Meg and Colin.

Meg's expression remained carefully schooled, revealing nothing. "It is as you wish, madame."

"Yes, I'm sure." Shelby kicked one foot slowly. "So, I overwork you because I don't want to see anyone? Am I really so selfish?"

Meg turned away quickly to hide her sudden smile. "Colin and I are happy to do as you wish, madame."

Happy? Shelby doubted that. The only sounds of happiness she'd heard in the past week had come from the kitchen when Meg and Colin thought she'd retired for the night. And much as she longed to join them, she'd never interrupted the few minutes they had each evening to relax.

"You and Colin are wonderful," she admitted aloud, which earned another surprised glance from Meg. "But I think I'd like to go in to town myself."

Meg dropped the bundle of gowns she held, then bent to retrieve them. "Perhaps you should wait, madame . . . until you're fully recovered and feeling yourself again."

She looked so flustered, Shelby's heart went out to her. "Perhaps," she said slowly. "And perhaps not. Tell me, Meg, why are you so anxious to keep me here?"

"Anxious?" Meg flushed a deep red as she scooped the last of the gowns from the floor. "Do I seem anxious?"

"Very. What do the people in town think of me?"

Meg stood quickly and turned toward the wardrobe. "They think nothing, madame. They wouldn't dare."

Laughing, Shelby stood again and began gathering an armful of gowns. "Surely you don't expect me to believe that. People always think, and I'm quite sure they talk as well."

"Perhaps they do, madame, but not when Colin and I can hear."

Shelby grimaced at a particularly ugly brown Irish poplin. "Only because they're afraid you'll tell me what they say. Am I really so formidable?"

"You are highly respected, madame."

"Highly suspect is more like it. They think I'm crazy, don't they?"

Meg's lips thinned. "I don't know what they think, madame."

Shelby handed Meg the gowns and bent to gather more. "Don't worry, Meg. I'm not going to get angry. But how can I fix anything if I don't know exactly what's wrong?"

Meg's gaze flew to hers again. "What is it you wish to fix, madame?"

"Everything, beginning with my marriage to Zacharias." Shelby turned back and smiled at her. "I wish you'd tell me what's going on around here, Meg. I wish someone would tell me why Zacharias and I are estranged, why he left me alone here and built Winterhill for Mordechai and Andrew, why his mother hates me so."

Meg's expression changed subtly. She hesitated for a moment before she spoke. "Victoria Logan is a vicious woman."

"So I gathered when I spoke with her the other day."

"You *spoke* with her?" Meg's face paled. "When? Did she dare to come here?"

"No. I saw her when I went to Winterhill."

"I knew that was a mistake," Meg said under her breath. "What did she say to you?"

Shelby held back her pleased smile at the sign that Meg was starting to relax a bit. She picked up the silver-handled brush and began to run it through her hair. "She warned me not to attempt a reconciliation with Zacharias. So . . . ? Why does she dislike me so much?"

Meg spent a moment or two hanging gowns, then gave a resigned sigh. "She dislikes you, madame, because you are so much like her."

"Like *her*?" Shelby made a face. "Yuck."

Meg laughed softly. "I think she dislikes strong-willed people because she can't boss them around. And you, madame, are quite strong-willed."

"I must be if I can stay cooped up alone all the time." She caught Meg's gaze in the mirror and smiled. "And Zacharias? Is he strong-willed?"

"Very much so, madame."

"He doesn't seem strong-willed when it comes to his mother."

"Oh, but he is in his own way," Meg said with a secretive smile. "He married you, didn't he?"

Shelby lowered the brush to the table. "She opposed our marriage?"

"Vehemently."

"But he married me, anyway?"

"Yes."

The strangest sensation of joy darted through Shelby, almost as if they were really talking about her instead of Agatha. "Then he must have loved me once."

"Indeed he did, madame."

Shelby turned in her seat to face Meg. "Tell me the truth, Meg. Do you think there's hope? Do you think I can win his love again?"

Meg's eyes sparkled. "I do, madame."

Yes! The first hint of encouragement she'd had yet. "Will you help me?"

Meg nodded slowly. "Yes, madame."

"Great! Then, let's get started. I want you to tell me everything you know about him, about me, about his obnoxious mother . . . *and* about Patricia Starling."

The sparkle in Meg's eyes died. "Patricia Starling? I—"

Shelby cut off the protest she sensed coming. "If I'm to win back Zacharias's heart, I need to know my competition."

Meg's lips curved slightly. "Yes, madame."

"So, tell me everything. Tell me what kind of woman she is, what Zacharias sees in her, and what she gives him that I don't."

Meg folded away the last of the gowns. "She is a rather self-centered woman, I think. I have always believed she sees Zacharias as the means to a fortune."

Great. A gold digger. Still, that would be easier to fight than a woman who was honestly in love with him. "And how do you think *I* see him?"

Meg closed the trunk and latched it. "I think, madame, you have always seen him as the means to respectability."

"Ugh." Shelby shook her head slowly. "Do you think I loved him?"

"Love?" Meg tilted her head to one side and gave that some thought. "I think you loved him as much as it's possible for you to love anyone."

"That doesn't sound very promising," Shelby said with a grimace. "Why aren't I capable of loving?"

"You are . . ." Meg hesitated, then blurted, "You are uncomfortable with physical affection."

"Not exactly cuddly, eh?" Shelby couldn't say that surprised her. Cuddly women didn't lock themselves away from other people for years at a time.

Meg went on as if she hadn't spoken. "And Mr. Logan has, if I may say so, a very passionate nature."

Shelby glanced at her quickly, but told herself she shouldn't be surprised that Meg knew about that. It was impossible to live in the same house and not pick up on the vibrations between people, even if they never said a word. "I see. And I was uncomfortable with his nature?"

"Quite, madame."

"I didn't welcome his affection?"

"You preferred to maintain separate bedchambers."

Good grief! How could Agatha live with him, be the object of his affection, and *not* share a bedroom with him? Not only was he devastatingly handsome, but Shelby suspected he was actually quite nice—if she could believe the rare glimpses she'd had of the man behind his anger.

She scowled slightly. "I take it he didn't like that."

"No, he didn't. Though he did tolerate it for several years. I believe he thought he could win you over. He certainly tried everything he knew of to do it. But after that last time, he gave up."

Now they were getting somewhere. "What happened that last time?"

"I believe, madame, you called him a rutting pig."

Shelby could just imagine how Zacharias had reacted to that. "Did he tell you that, or did I?"

"No one told us, madame. Colin and I could hear quite clearly. You were in the parlor, madame, on Christmas Day. He presented you with a diamond and emerald necklace and matching earbobs, and then attempted to kiss your cheek."

"I called him a pig because he tried to kiss my cheek?"

"A *rutting* pig, madame."

Shelby leaned her head against the bedpost and tried to imagine anyone being that frigid. Poor Agatha. Poor frustrated Zacharias. His male ego must have taken a terrible bashing. "Do I still have the necklace and earbobs?"

"I believe so, madame, but you have never worn them."

"Well, maybe it's time I did." Shelby stood quickly and paced toward the mirror. "First, I'll get a new dress made in emerald green, and then I'll stroll over to Winterhill so that Zacharias can see me wearing his gift. Maybe that will convince him that I've changed."

"I certainly hope so." Meg hurried to the closet, disappeared inside, and reappeared a few seconds later holding a heavy wooden box. "I know it's not my place to say so, but I would love to see you give Patricia Starling some competition."

"Competition?" Shelby laughed. "I'm going to blow her right out of the water. Do you think one of the seamstresses from town would come here? I don't want Patricia or Victoria Logan to guess what I'm up to."

Meg beamed. "I do, indeed. And I know just the dressmaker we can trust. I'll send Colin after her. But first—" She opened the box and held it out toward Shelby.

Shelby peeked inside and sucked in a surprised breath when she saw the magnificent necklace and earrings inside. Two ropes of glittering diamonds were held together by three evenly spaced, very large emeralds rimmed with even more diamonds. She'd never seen anything so incredible in her life, and she couldn't imagine being loved enough to warrant such an amazing gift.

Holding her breath, she touched one emerald almost reverently. "It's beautiful."

"He did love you very much," Meg said softly. "And he will again."

"I hope you're right." Shelby lifted the necklace carefully and draped it across one hand. It wasn't the price of the gift that awed her, but the realization that Zacharias would give Agatha something so beautiful after repeatedly being turned away. It spoke volumes about the depth of his love for her.

"I am right," Meg said firmly. "You'll see. I'll send Colin to town at once."

Shelby waited until she'd disappeared again, then returned the necklace to its velvet bed. She cast another glance at the reflection in the mirror and whispered, "I'm sorry to do this to you, old girl, but you really do need to start acting like a normal woman."

A flash of light answered her, and slowly, unbelievably, her own image formed like a hologram. Blue eyes, curly blond hair, stupid ski-jump nose.

Heart pounding, Shelby shot to her feet so quickly

she knocked over her chair. But she couldn't tear her gaze from the glass. Her throat constricted, her heart set up an erratic pulse, and her limbs grew weak and limp.

"No!" She backed away, nearly tripping over the toppled chair. "No."

The image pulsed for a moment and static electricity charged the air around her. Then, miraculously, it faded away almost as quickly as it had formed.

Weak with relief, Shelby turned away from the mirror and reached for the bedpost to steady herself. But she couldn't shake the sense of urgency that hummed through her veins.

Did Agatha want her life back? Could she come back if she wanted to? And where was she? If prudish Agatha had been tossed into the sexually unrepressed future, it was no wonder she wanted to come back.

But Shelby wasn't finished here. She couldn't go back. She didn't want to go back.

She gripped the bedpost tighter and fought a rush of panic she didn't completely understand. If Agatha came back now, she'd die. According to the calendar, she had less than a month to live. Shelby *had* to prevent this poor, misguided woman from dying a miserable, lonely, untimely death. She had to save her marriage to Zacharias. She had to reunite those two innocent boys with their mother.

But she'd have to work fast. Time was running out.

Hoping to get away before his mother could stop him, Zacharias strode quickly toward the stables. His mind raced with possibilities about his new venture as Philip's business partner. He'd listened to his mother's dour predictions and tolerated her sour mood for four long days. He'd put up with her attempts to secure his future with Patricia. He'd even resisted the never-ending urge to confront Agatha about her odd behavior—all because he wanted to keep a clear head for this morning.

This was the beginning of a new life for him. Exactly the kind of change he'd been needing for a long time.

Let his mother rant and rave to her heart's content. Let her throw Patricia at him if she wanted. Let Patricia scowl and pout. Let Agatha creep around in gardens or revert to her old, cold self. Today, he didn't care.

If he could teach his sons nothing else, he'd teach them pride. Pride in themselves and their accomplishments. Pride in their ability to *do* something important. Pride in their family name and in their father. He couldn't think of a better gift to give them, and he wouldn't let anything distract him from it.

"Zacharias."

The whisper of his name, so unexpected in the silence of the early morning, brought him up short. He glanced around quickly, but the path stood empty on either side of him. Convinced it had been nothing more than the breeze whispering through the trees, he started on his way again.

"Zacharias." The voice came louder this time.

And this time, he recognized it. "Agatha?"

She stepped out from behind a flowering dogwood wearing a gown of such vivid green it made his breath catch. He hadn't seen her looking so . . . so *womanly* . . . in a long time. If ever.

She moved toward him, so compellingly soft and feminine, he had to remind himself sternly why he wanted to stay away from her. "I'm sorry if I startled you," she said. "But I need to talk to you."

"Talk?" His voice came out gruff, but not entirely with anger. There was, he admitted reluctantly, a measure of longing in it, as well. He tried valiantly to hide it. "I thought we'd established that we have nothing to discuss."

"*You* established that." She moved closer, close enough for the deep brown of her eyes to hold him captivated. "But I don't agree."

"Nevertheless . . ." His voice caught in his throat.

"Please, Zacharias."

He scowled darkly, his best sort of scowl, the kind that should have made her think twice. "Forgive me if

I'm wary, madame, but you have refused to acknowledge my existence for the past five years. I find it hard to believe we suddenly have so much to talk about."

"You have every right to be wary." Her hand flickered to her throat and drew his attention to the necklace that encircled her neck and lay gleaming against her pale skin in the sunlight. It was most inappropriate for the middle of the morning, yet seeing it there touched him deeply.

To hide his reaction, he stiffened his shoulders and turned away from her. "Why have you suddenly taken to skulking about Winterhill's gardens?"

She bit her lip and her eyes rounded slightly as if she worried that he might have seen her the other night. In the next breath, she pulled herself together and tossed a question back at him. "Where else am I going to find you?"

The pleading in her eyes, the glitter of emeralds and diamonds at her throat, and the soft curve of her lips all took their toll on him. "Very well. Pray, madame, tell me what you wish to talk about."

"First, I'd like you to stop calling me madame and start calling me by my name."

He could feel the shock revealing itself on his face, his brows arching with surprise. That *was* a change of heart. "Very well," he said again. "What else?"

"I'd like to know more about you. About your likes and dislikes, your hopes and dreams—all the things a wife should know about her husband."

He resisted the pull of her soft voice. "Now I *know* this is a trap. Since when have you cared a jot about what I like or dislike?"

She actually looked sad. "Have I really been so unkind?"

"Unkind is perhaps too gentle a word." He stepped away but kept his gaze riveted on hers, trying to decipher any signs of trickery.

"Then, please, accept my apology."

She sounded earnest, but he still didn't want to trust her. "I shall note your apology, madame. Whether or not

I can accept it remains to be seen. Perhaps in time . . ."

She sighed softly, a mere whisper of sound. "Unfortunately, time is one luxury I don't have."

"Really?" He quirked his brows a bit further. "And why not?"

"I can't explain," she said hesitantly. "I wish I could. It would make everything so much easier."

"Undoubtedly." He tipped his hat and made to step around her. "If you will excuse me, I must be on my way."

Her smile faded. "You're going somewhere?" He could think of no reason to hide the truth from her other than to avoid a repeat of the arguments he'd had with his mother. Still, some rebellious part of him wanted to test her reaction. "Actually, I've started a new business venture with Philip."

"Philip?" Her brows knit as if she were struggling to remember. To his surprise, he didn't see the flash of distaste he'd expected.

"Clayton," Zacharias supplied, baiting her. "You remember him, certainly."

She gave that some more thought, then nodded slowly. "The name sounds vaguely familiar. Is he a friend of ours?"

"Of *ours*?" Zacharias laughed outright. "No, Agatha. Not of ours. He has been a friend of mine since we were boys. You find him coarse and ill-bred."

"Oh." She tilted her head to one side. "Do *I* have any friends?"

Odd question. One the old Agatha would never have asked. Zacharias felt another doubt crumble. "I believe you feel no use for friends."

She made a face, but he had the distinct impression it was directed at herself. She fingered the necklace for a moment while she thought some more. "Philip Clayton. Is he, by chance, connected with a sawmill?"

"As a matter of fact, he is. And as of today, so am I."

"You've become his partner."

The accuracy of her guess set Zacharias back a step. "As usual, news travels fast, I see. But pray tell me, madame. Where did *you* hear of it?"

She flicked her gaze to his, then looked away again without answering the question. Instead she countered with one of her own. "Why have you decided to do this? Are you in need of money?"

"Most assuredly not." He sent her a deep frown to show how much he disliked that suggestion. "I've simply had enough of spending my days in frivolous pursuits."

"So, it's just something to occupy your time?"

"Indeed."

"And is it something that interests you?"

"Lumber?" He studied her carefully. Could it really be that she didn't remember how much he'd enjoyed the building of Summervale or her objections to his involvement? Could her memory loss be *that* complete? Apparently so. And her reaction—or perhaps he should say her complete *lack* of reaction—robbed him of the satisfaction he'd expected to get from making the announcement. "You have no argument against my decision?"

"It's something you want to do?"

"It is."

"Well, then, why should I argue?"

Disconcerted, he sat on the stone bench, but he tried like hell to look casual and unaffected. "You might argue that I'm a gentleman and that, as such, my pursuing an occupation would bring embarrassment to you."

"But I won't. If it will make you happy, then do it."

He tried desperately to keep his scowl in place. "You might argue that I have no skills."

"And I might also argue that you can learn some."

"You might argue—" he began.

She cut him off with a wave of her hand. "The point is, Zacharias, I'm not *going* to argue." She smiled teasingly, and his heart skipped a beat. "For heaven's sake, the idea of an able-bodied man like you sitting around here and twiddling your thumbs while you watch your money pile up is silly." She sat beside him on the bench, just close enough to make him nervous.

He resisted the urge to move away. "Am I to understand that you *approve* of me pursuing an occupation?"

"One hundred percent." She brushed her hand against his knee, so softly he knew it must have been accidental, but it sent a flash of longing through him that left him distinctly uneasy.

"You had a purpose for seeking me out," he said. "What was it?"

"You know what it is. I want to put an end to our estrangement. I want you to believe that I've changed."

Zacharias let his gaze drift over her again. "I can see that, madame."

"Agatha."

"Agatha." He jerked to his feet and paced a step or two away. "You *are* behaving differently, there is no doubt about that. But I have no interest in putting an end to our estrangement."

"Why not?"

"As I've told you repeatedly, too much has passed between us—"

"But I don't know what happened." She stood to face him, rested one hand on his chest, and looked deep into his eyes. "Please, Zacharias. Tell me."

Another flash of yearning shot through him and he wanted desperately to believe her. He almost wanted to clear away her confusion. But memories stilled his tongue. "I am many things, my dear, but a fool is not one of them. And I'd be a fool to expose myself and my sons to you again. Now, if you'll excuse me, I really must be on my way."

She clutched his arm as if her life depended on it. "Okay. Tell me about you and Patricia Starling instead."

He turned to face her again and drew his arm away slowly. "That is one subject I won't discuss with you. Not now. Not ever again."

"You'll have to," she warned, "because I'm not going

to give up. Meg tells me you turned to Patricia because I wasn't exactly a loving wife—"

"Loving?" He cut her off with a curl of his lip. "No, Agatha, *loving* has never been a word I'd use to describe you."

Her cheeks reddened, making her unbelievably beautiful. She lowered her gaze and slanted her eyes back up at him in a manner that seemed almost provocative. "Again, I apologize. But, Zacharias, I know you still feel something for me. That kiss the other day—"

"Was a mistake," he finished gruffly, more to convince himself than her.

She shook her head and smiled slowly. "I don't think so."

"Are you telling me you *enjoyed* it?"

"Are you telling me you didn't?"

Good Lord, the woman was flirting with him. *Flirting.* Agatha! If he didn't know better, he'd swear he was dreaming. And worse, he liked it. There'd been a time when he'd have given anything to have her look at him as she did now. When he'd have sold his soul to have her touch him.

"Perhaps you'd like another," he said, inching closer, hoping she'd say yes but expecting her to scurry away.

"Perhaps I would." Her gaze didn't even falter. Instead, he saw a gleam of anticipation in the dark eyes. Her lips parted slightly. Her breath grew shallow. He could see her pulse in the hollow of her throat.

Urgent need wiped away the last of his reservations. Without giving himself a chance to think again, he pulled her into his embrace and lowered his lips to hers.

Chapter 8

AGATHA MELTED AGAINST him eagerly and opened her mouth to him, inviting, teasing, pulling him even deeper beneath her spell. He tried like the devil to keep his wits about him, but her total acquiescence and the impatience of her response wiped everything but need from his mind.

Tightening his embrace, he deepened the kiss, plundering her mouth with his tongue, pouring all his frustrations into the contact, seeking what he never thought he'd find, finding what he'd only dreamed of.

He moved his hands to her hips tentatively and when she didn't pull away, he crushed her against him. She moaned with pleasure and let one hand stray across his shoulder while the other found its way into his hair. Fire coiled in his belly, need pulsed through his veins, desire pushed all rational thought from his mind.

When he could no longer breathe, he reluctantly ended the kiss but instead of pulling his mouth away, he trailed it along the curve of her neck. She arched closer and moaned again, and the sound nearly drove him wild.

God in heaven, he wanted her. He wanted to pull her

into the hedges and make love to her right then and there. He ached to hear her cry out with pleasure, yearned to give in to her request and forget all that had passed between them.

But remembering cooled his ardor and brought back his sanity. He released her as suddenly as he'd embraced her. "Forgive me, Agatha. Your charms made me forget myself."

"Good."

"No." He barked the word with a harshness that surprised him and made Agatha's eyes widen in surprise. "It shan't happen again. It *can't* happen again."

Her eyes clouded, but the clouds were gentle. "Why can't it happen again? We are still married, aren't we? There isn't anything illegal about kissing your wife in the garden, is there?"

"Certainly not. But it's been a long time since I thought of you in that way."

"In what way? As your wife?"

Stunned by the flirtatious curve of her lip, the almost sultry gleam in her eye, he could only give a curt nod.

"Well, then . . ." She touched her hand to his chest again and he thought his heart might well burst from it. "Maybe you should start."

Had he not had such control, his mouth would have fallen open. As it was, he could only stare at her. He couldn't deny that something had brought about a miraculous change in her. It made no sense at all, but neither did his reaction to her. She seemed so different—almost as if some other woman had taken her place.

He'd satisfied his urges with Patricia over the years, but none of her kisses had been as satisfying as Agatha's in the past few days. None of them had made his blood rush quite so fast or his pulse thunder through him with such fury. He took a deep, steadying breath, argued with himself for half a heartbeat, then captured her hand with his.

Whether it made sense or not, this was the Agatha he'd always dreamed of. This was the woman he'd fallen in love with, and he didn't have the strength to fight his attraction for her. It had always been there, just waiting for her to respond to him as a woman—as a *wife*—should.

"Perhaps you're right," he said softly, giving in to the temptation to lift her hand to his lips. "But God help you if you're toying with me, Agatha."

Her eyes darkened even further and her lips parted ever so slightly, but he resisted the urge to capture them again. She turned her hand over and laced her fingers through his. "Believe me, Zacharias, I'm not playing a game. Can we put our marriage back together and give our sons the family they need?"

God help *him*, he thought, for weakening. Once again, he'd been swayed by a woman's charms. Once again, he'd nearly let reason suffer because of the soft touch of a hand. He'd thought himself well over that particular weakness. He'd learned to watch for women who used their feminine charms to get what they wanted. The problem was, he'd never expected *Agatha* to employ them.

"As tempting as your offer is," he whispered, "I cannot do it."

Without giving her a chance to respond or himself an opportunity to change his mind, he hurried away and put as much distance between them as he could. But as God was his witness, he thought as he strode away, he'd have to keep a better guard over himself in the future.

With a sinking heart, Shelby watched Zacharias storm away. She hadn't expected to try to seduce him. She wasn't *supposed* to seduce him. He was a married man, for heaven's sake, and he only *thought* he was married to her. She was supposed to be doing this for Agatha, but she'd completely forgotten whose body she was inhabiting until he'd pulled away.

She took a ragged breath and tried to still the hammering of her heart. What had come over her? Why had she let him affect her that way? She'd had relationships in the past, though never anything remotely serious. But she'd never met a man whose slightest touch took away her ability to think or whose kiss left her little more than a bundle of nerve endings the way Zacharias's did.

She stood there, trembling, until Zacharias disappeared from view. Then, slowly, she turned toward home.

The word checked her step and she sighed softly. Not home. Summervale. Agatha's home. Even though the lines between Shelby Miller and Agatha Logan were blurring a little more every day, she had to remember who she was and why she was here. There were too many lives at stake to forget herself for even a moment.

Thoroughly exhausted, Zacharias descended the grand staircase. He'd dressed for dinner, but he sincerely hoped his mother had planned a quiet meal for a change. He didn't have the energy to entertain guests, nor did he have the stamina for another argument. He wanted only to enjoy his evening meal in peace, spend a few minutes with the twins before bed, and then escape to his study with a bottle of port and a fine cigar.

Philip had kept him busy from the moment he arrived at the lumberyard until the time he left, and his body ached from the unaccustomed exertion. But even hard work hadn't wiped the encounter with Agatha from his mind or removed the eagerness of her kiss from his senses. Every time he blinked, the woman's face floated in front of him, smiling, beckoning, pulling him deeper into a morass from which he might never escape.

He needed some time to himself. Time to think. Time to put everything in perspective. And tonight he'd have it. No matter what his mother might do or say, he wouldn't allow her to drag him into another argument about the sawmill, about Patricia, and especially not about Agatha.

He reached the bottom of the stairs and turned toward the sitting room, nodding at Abraham, who stood at the ready outside the door. But when he heard voices coming from inside, he held up a hand as a signal to wait. "Do we have dinner guests?"

"Yes, sir, you do."

Zacharias held back a groan of dismay and leaned closer to listen. Patricia's voice rose and fell. His mother's wove through it like a discordant note. He turned a weary glance at Abraham. "Mrs. Starling?"

"Yes, sir. And Dr. Mensing, too."

"Dr. Mensing?" Zacharias did groan this time. He couldn't help it. His mother might hold the old windbag in high regard, but Zacharias had always considered him self-important, smug, and boring as hell. An evening in his company would ruin even the best of days.

Letting out a deep, resigned breath, he nodded for Abraham to open the door, then put on his best smile and plunged inside. He turned to the doctor first and forced a heartiness he didn't feel. "Mensing. Good to see you." He shook the older man's gnarled hand, then bowed toward Patricia. She wore a deep, rose-colored silk gown that revealed enough of her shoulders and bosom to tempt a saint.

But for the first time in recent memory, the sight left Zacharias unaffected.

"Say hello to our darling Patricia," Victoria said, sailing across the room toward him. "Doesn't she look lovely?"

Zacharias gave the expected response—the only possible response under the circumstances. "Of course. Lovely as usual." He bowed over her hand but refrained from passing his lips across her fingertips. "I'm sorry I'm late joining you. I've recently gone into partnership with Philip Clayton at his sawmill and business prevented me from arriving home until just now." He poured a sherry and handed it to Mensing. "You know Clayton, don't you, Doctor?"

Mensing accepted the glass and nodded. "Of course. Isaiah's son."

Victoria's smile faded immediately. "Zacharias thinks he wants to get involved with industry."

"Zacharias is *certain* he wants to get involved in industry," he corrected with a tight smile. "And he has." He lifted his own glass and took a good, stiff drink. The liquor traced a pattern of warmth down his throat and settled in his stomach.

Victoria waved away his response as if it was of no consequence. "Perhaps I'm too indulgent, but I shan't let myself worry about what is surely only a passing interest." Her lips curved into a frigid smile. "There are, as I was just explaining to Dr. Mensing, more important things to concern ourselves with."

Her patronizing tone set Zacharias's teeth on edge. "Oh? And what might they be?"

"You know very well what concerns me." Victoria smoothed her skirt with one hand and sent Mensing a look full of meaning. "I am most disturbed by this recent business with Agatha."

Zacharias carefully lowered his glass to the table. "Am I to understand you've been discussing Agatha with Dr. Mensing?"

"Of course I have. Her recent behavior concerns me deeply and, since the doctor has attended her in the past, I thought it expedient to consult him."

"I see." Forcing himself to maintain control, Zacharias turned toward Mensing. "I'm sorry my mother has taken up your valuable time, Doctor. There's really nothing to worry about."

"I'm afraid I don't agree." Mensing settled a hand on his ample stomach and leaned back in his chair. "Victoria tells me that Agatha claims to have suffered a loss of memory."

"Yes. And I'm convinced she's telling the truth."

"After one or two brief conversations with her?" Victoria laughed sharply. "Have you suddenly become an expert on the workings of the human mind?"

"Of course not." Zacharias paced toward the windows and looked out at the city below and the moonlight on the river. "But I do know Agatha."

"Indeed." He could see his mother's reflection in the

glass and the glance she shared with Patricia.

His palms grew frigid and his pulse slowed. "Yes, Mother. Indeed. Regardless of what you may think of her, she *is* my wife."

"I'm aware of that," Victoria said, rising slowly. "*Painfully* aware of that. And that's precisely why I asked Patricia and Dr. Mensing to join us this evening." The rustle of her skirts as she moved toward him sounded ominous. "Perhaps you aren't interested in protecting this family from that woman, but I am. I have not devoted my entire life to building the Logan reputation only to have some madwoman dash it to the ground while I stand idly by."

Zacharias clenched his fists and met her gaze. "Ah, but you see, Mother, that's where you and I disagree. I don't believe she's mad."

Mensing shifted in his seat and leaned into the conversation. "Tell me, my boy, has she given you any indication how this memory loss came about?"

"I don't believe she knows."

Patricia and Victoria shared another long glance.

Mensing twitched his moustache and tugged his coat across his stomach. "It is my considered opinion that a complete loss of memory would be impossible without a severe head injury to bring it about."

"Then perhaps she had an injury."

"*Really*, Zacharias." Victoria's voice prickled with irritation. "She didn't appear injured to me."

"No," he admitted slowly, "she didn't. But that means nothing. Even you must admit she is not the same woman."

"Which only proves my point." Victoria bobbed her head and her earrings caught the glow of the candles, shooting sparks of light onto the wall. "You seem determined not to listen to me, but I had hoped you would pay attention to Dr. Mensing."

"Please, Zacharias." Patricia's distress sounded clearly in her voice. "Listen to them."

He turned his back on all of them, angry, frustrated,

even strangely, unbelievably protective of Agatha.

"My best advice," the doctor said, "is to avoid her when at all possible. If you must speak with her, watch for signs of disorientation and odd behavior. With sufficient proof, you can commit her to an asylum."

Zacharias looked at each of them in turn. "Out of the question."

"My dear boy," the doctor said patiently, "that is precisely the question. If Agatha is behaving strangely, she could be a danger—not only to you and your sons, but to herself, as well."

"I don't believe that's the case."

"Ah!" Mensing smiled triumphantly. "But can you be certain?"

The question brought him up short. He wanted to say yes, but hadn't he asked a similar question earlier? And hadn't Agatha expressed her own doubts? Not about her sanity, to be sure, but the effect was the same.

"Can you be certain?" Mensing asked again.

Zacharias shook his head reluctantly. "No."

A triumphant smile crossed Mensing's lips. A victorious gleam lit his mother's eyes. A relieved sigh escaped Patricia's lips. And Zacharias felt like a traitor.

"Then you must keep an eye on her," Mensing insisted. "And under *no* circumstances should you allow her near your children."

Zacharias hadn't thought of letting Agatha see the boys yet, but hearing Mensing's warning made him realize that he'd been hoping that day would come. Clenching his teeth in frustration, he glared at his reflection in the glass.

It was time to admit the truth. He'd created this mess, no one else. He'd hurt Agatha, taken advantage of Patricia, angered his mother, and put his sons' futures in jeopardy. Only he could set things right. The trouble was, he couldn't set anything right without hurting someone further in the process.

●   ●   ●

Meg stood in the doorway to catch a breeze while she waited for the dishwater to heat on the stove. At this time of afternoon, the fire made the kitchen almost unbearable, and while she'd forced herself to suffer it in the past, the last ten days had brought about such a change in Agatha, she no longer feared reprisal if she took a moment or two's respite from her workload.

Nor did the load seem quite so heavy these days.

A shout of laughter brought her head around and Colin's voice reached her a second later. "Be careful, madame. Watch yerself on them stones. They can be slick."

Agatha laughed again. "Just promise that if I fall, you'll help me back up again."

Meg shook her head in wonder when Colin's laughter filled the silence. Much as they'd both tried to maintain their distance, Agatha's cheerful attitude and her laughter had touched them both.

Who'd ever have imagined Agatha mucking about in the gardens with Colin? Who'd ever have imagined her carrying dishes into the kitchen after she finished a meal, or asking if she could eat in the kitchen with them instead of alone in the dining room?

Meg turned back to check the water on the stove. A head of steam drifted lazily to the ceiling. If she worked quickly, she could snip the beans Colin had picked for dinner on the back porch while the kitchen cooled down again.

She hoisted the heavy cast-iron pot from the stove and started toward the sink with it. But the unmistakable— and wholly unexpected—sound of the knocker at the front door startled her, and she nearly dropped the scalding water.

It had been so long since anyone had come calling, Meg thought for a moment she was hearing things. But after the second time, she found a safe place to leave the pot and hurried through the dining room, wiping her hands on her apron as she walked.

For anyone to call at Summervale was such an unusual event, Meg couldn't even begin to guess who she might find on the other side of the door. She gripped the door handle, smoothed her apron with her free hand, and pulled the door open warily. And when she found Victoria Logan waiting with barely concealed impatience, a thick knot of dread landed like a boulder on her heart.

Victoria looked her over slowly, then stepped inside without so much as a by-your-leave. "Good afternoon, Meg."

Meg prayed that Colin and Agatha would stay in the kitchen garden so the old dragon wouldn't hear their laughter. She wasn't about to let Victoria see Agatha in her current disheveled state.

She pointedly left the door open so as not to give Victoria any ideas about being welcome here. "I'm afraid the missus isn't at home."

Surprise darted across Victoria's face, but she hid it well. "I didn't expect her to receive me, Meg." She pulled off her gloves slowly. "I came to speak with you."

Meg couldn't hide her surprise. "With me? Whatever for?"

Victoria smiled slowly, a vicious sort of smile that turned Meg's blood cold. "As you can probably imagine, I'm deeply concerned about the way Agatha has been behaving lately."

Meg reminded herself sharply to keep her place and bit back the immediate reply that rose to her lips. Though she didn't consider herself in Victoria Logan's employ, she knew only too well where the money came from that kept Summervale going and provided a roof over her head and Colin's.

She gripped the door handle a bit tighter and waited for Victoria to go on.

The old harridan took a few more steps inside and looked around as if she was taking mental inventory of Agatha's things and calculating their worth. "Dr. Mensing shares my concerns."

Meg didn't like the sound of that at all. She wouldn't trust that old drunk as far as she could throw him. "Dr.

Mensing hasn't seen Mrs. Logan in years. How could he have any opinion at all?"

Victoria's lips curved into a semblance of a smile. "Surely you must realize the recent changes in Agatha haven't gone unnoticed in town. Dr. Mensing is quite aware of her recent erratic behavior."

"Anyone who considers Mrs. Logan's recent behavior erratic has been misinformed." And she had a pretty good idea who'd done the misinforming.

Victoria arched her eyebrows. "Indeed?" She strolled casually toward the console table, ran her fingers along it, and checked the tips of them as if she expected to find a coating of dust. "If you feel that way, perhaps you've been locked away with her for too long."

Once, Meg might have agreed with her. Now, she only wanted to pop the old biddy in her blue-blooded nose and send her on her way before Agatha and Colin came back into the house.

Victoria turned back to face her. "I came here today to enlist your help, Meg."

"Mine?" Meg took an involuntary step backward. "What possible help could *I* be to *you*?"

"Dr. Mensing is understandably concerned that Agatha might pose a threat to my grandsons."

"She'd never harm those boys," Meg assured her. At least, not the way she was the past ten days.

Victoria looked like a snake ready to strike. "To that end, the doctor suggests we keep a watchful eye on her behavior. Since you and Colin are the ones closest to her, the ones most likely to observe any aberrant behavior, I give you the charge of keeping me informed. I, in turn, will take that information to Dr. Mensing."

"And use it to put Agatha away somewhere." Meg couldn't believe the woman's gall. Asking her to spy, of all things. She drew herself up to her full height and faced Victoria squarely, knowing that she could be putting her position on the line. "There is no abnormal behavior to report, madame. Mrs. Logan is quite well."

At that moment, laughter rang through the house and

the sound of running feet pulled Victoria around just as Agatha burst through the kitchen door, mud-draped, barefoot, hair straggling about her shoulders, and holding a cluster of lavender sprigs in one hand. "Look, Meg. Isn't this beautiful?"

She broke off the very instant she saw Victoria standing there, and Meg's heart sank. Holding her breath, she willed Agatha to say nothing Victoria could use against her. Her appearance was damning enough.

Agatha did a good job of pulling herself together—considering that she looked like a scullery maid who'd been tossed into a pigpen—and walked slowly into the foyer.

"Victoria. I wasn't aware that you'd come to call. Please, Meg, fetch my mother-in-law some tea. I'll freshen up and rejoin you in a minute."

Victoria gave her a slow once-over, taking in every tiny detail of her appearance, every flaw, every possible imperfection as if they alone would prove her case. "There is no need, Agatha. I was merely having a word with Meg."

Agatha's gaze darted to Meg's face. "Oh. I see." She forced a smile and turned back to the old witch. "But surely you can stay long enough to have tea."

"I'm afraid not." Victoria tugged on her gloves, crossed to the front door, and yanked it open. "I'm late for an engagement in town."

With Dr. Mensing, unless Meg missed her guess. She followed Victoria to the door, unwilling to take the chance of her changing her mind. The less Agatha had to do with her, the better.

Victoria met Meg's gaze with a meaningful one of her own. "I shall speak with you again soon, Meg."

"I'm afraid that would be no use, madame. I won't have the information you want."

Victoria's lips curved into a semblance of a smile, but her eyes remained frosty. "No matter. There may not be the need for further information." And with that, she swept down the front steps toward her waiting carriage.

Meg closed the door firmly and turned back to face Agatha. But she kept her mouth shut and Victoria's request to herself. She didn't want to worry the missus, didn't want to cause trouble, and she certainly didn't want to risk changing her back to the way she had been for so long.

But she knew one thing for certain—she and Colin would have to be on their guard as never before if they hoped to protect the missus.

Sawdust filled the air and stung Zacharias's eyes as he stared at the figures that floated on the ledgers in front of him. Sweat plastered his shirt to his back and dampened his hair. He'd run the figures several times, compared invoices against inventory, checked bills of lading, and double-checked dates to make sure he wasn't including a shipment that belonged in last quarter's accounting, but the bottom line was always the same.

Philip was losing money—and quickly. And now, so might he.

Mopping his face with his hand, he leaned back in his chair and glanced at Philip who stood near the room's only dirt-covered window. "Well, you're right," he said reluctantly. "I don't know how you've managed to hang on this long."

Philip ran a hand through his hair and tried to smile. "It's pretty grim, isn't it?"

Far more grim than Zacharias had imagined. But he'd never felt quite so useful or alive. "Nothing we can't turn around if we both put our minds to it," he said.

Philip's smile grew a bit stronger. "I'm glad to hear you say that."

Zacharias brushed a few flakes of sawdust from his shirtsleeve. After his first day at the mill the grit, grime, sawdust, and rough pine plank walls had convinced him to leave his best trousers, vests, and topcoats hanging at Winterhill, and to trade his usual silk shirts for cotton. "We'll be showing a healthy profit by the end of the year," he predicted.

"I hope you're right, or I'll be making some big changes in my lifestyle."

"We're in a boom," Zacharias reminded him. "The entire industry is at an all-time high, and once the railroad finishes the bridge across the river, we're going to be sitting pretty. First, though, we need to clear the outstanding debt and then we can think about buying some new equipment. . . ."

Philip had been looking out the window as Zacharias talked, but he suddenly stiffened, shot a glance at Zacharias over his shoulder, and turned back to the window again. "I'll pull out the accounts receivable in a minute, but first I think you need to come and take a look at this."

Mild curiosity piqued his interest, but he was far too deep into the books to want a distraction now. "Can't it wait?"

"I don't think so." Philip darted another glance at him. "I have the feeling you're going to want to see this."

The look on Philip's face convinced him. He strode toward the window and followed the direction of Philip's gaze. From their position backing the river, they had a reasonably unobstructed view up Church Street. But as he bent to look, a carriage rolling slowly past the window blocked his view. "What is it?"

"Just wait. You'll see." When the carriage moved out of the way, Philip nudged him with a sharp elbow and pointed at something in the distance. "Look. There."

Zacharias bent to look again, his eyes locked on a woman partway up Church Street wearing a gown of deep peach and carrying a matching parasol.

"Is that who I think it is?" Philip asked.

Zacharias's pulse slowed, his throat dried, his head buzzed as if he'd had one too many glasses of wine. All his senses told him who she was, but he shook his head quickly. "Certainly not. Agatha hasn't been to town in well over five years."

Philip wiped a spot on the window with his shirtsleeve and looked closer. "Are you sure?"

"Positive." Zacharias started to turn away, but he couldn't seem to tear his gaze from her. She walked slowly, taking in the town as if she'd never seen it before. But it was the stunned reactions of the few people who passed her that convinced him. He pulled away sharply and wiped his brow with a shaky hand, and he tried once more to convince himself. "It isn't her."

"I think you're wrong," Philip said, still unable to take his eyes off her. "Maybe you ought to check."

Zacharias scowled at him. "If it is her—which it isn't—then I'm glad she's chosen to end her life of solitude. But I'm not about to start tongues wagging by going out there and talking to her."

"You're just going to let her roam about town, then?"

"What would you have me do?" Zacharias stole another glance out of the window.

"I figured you might want to find out what she's doing."

"Obviously, she's taking a stroll through town," Zacharias snapped.

"And earning some pretty curious stares in the process."

Zacharias swore under his breath. Once again, that urge to protect her reared its ugly head. Once again, he tried to tamp it down.

"I'll bet your mother receives a few visitors this afternoon," Philip predicted.

Zacharias swore again—aloud, this time. "I suppose I *should* see what she's about."

"I suppose you should." Philip's lips twitched as if he found the predicament amusing, scooped up Zacharias's topcoat, and held it out for him. "Besides, I'm curious as hell to know and I can't very well approach her."

Zacharias rolled down his shirtsleeves and snatched his coat away from his friend's eager hand. "The way she's been acting the past ten days, she'd probably give you a big, friendly hug."

Philip backed a step away and laughed in disbelief.

"She couldn't have changed *that* much. I'll leave this to you."

Zacharias slipped into his coat and strode outside into the warm spring afternoon, trying not to look apprehensive, which would only stir up more gossip. Agatha strolled so slowly, he had no difficulty catching up to her. When he did, he spoke her name softly, half hoping the woman was her, half praying she wasn't.

She turned to face him. When she recognized him, a pleased smile curved her mouth. "Zacharias? I didn't expect to run into you."

He clasped his hands behind his back and began to stroll casually, as if they walked through town together every day. "May I ask what you're doing?"

She fell into step beside him. "I'm taking a walk."

"So I see. But to what end?"

"So I can see the city. It's quite something, isn't it? Everything looks so new." Excitement sparkled in her eyes—or was it the feverish glint of insanity? "I was planning to walk past Mark Twain's boyhood home. Would you like to join me?"

"Twain again?" He shook his head, impatient on the one hand, intrigued on the other. "You'd do a sight better to see some of the important buildings in town."

"Such as?"

"The lending library, for one." He slanted a glance at her upturned face. "Since you're so interested in Clemens, maybe you'll be interested to know that his father, John Clemens, helped organize it."

"I know. I think that's great."

"You know?" He studied her face carefully. "What else do you know?"

Her smile faded and her gaze faltered. She bit her lip and took a deep breath. "Nothing."

"Nothing except a few odd facts about John Clemens and his son."

She looked thoughtful for a second or two, then turned a smile as bright as the sun on him. "I don't remember anything until something happens to jog my memory. So I may have a few odd bits of information here and there, but no real memory."

"I see." Disappointment slowed his step. What a cad he was to wish that her memory would never return. "Is that all you're doing? Taking a tour of the city?"

"Not entirely. I thought I might pay a few calls while I'm here."

"Calls?" He stopped walking abruptly. "Why?"

"Because I want to," she said, matching his tone. "If you won't tell me what I want to know, I'll find someone who will."

"There is nothing to tell," he lied.

"I don't believe you."

"That comes as no surprise. You rarely do." He made an effort to control the sudden disquiet, but the thought of Agatha calling on people willy-nilly—on anyone at all—disturbed him greatly. Hannibal society would chew her up and spit her out again. But he could tell by the stubborn lift of her chin and the dangerous gleam in her eye that he'd get nowhere by arguing. This situation called for mild persuasion. "And pray tell," he said evenly, "on whom do you plan to call?"

She smiled up at him, a bright, sunny smile, then doused him with cold water. "Who else but Patricia Starling?"

Chapter 9

SHELBY WATCHED ZACHARIAS recoil, his eyes widen in horror, and his mouth twist into a bitter scowl.

"You will not," he ordered.

"Oh, but I have to," she said with false bravado. "If you won't tell me what I want to know, I'll ask her."

His face became even more rigid, his eyes even more angry. "Indeed, madame, you must not. I forbid it."

"Forbid?" Shelby laughed aloud. "You *forbid* it?" She knew things were different for women in this day and age, but it was hard to believe this man truly thought he could control her actions. "You can't do that."

"I can, and I do. I am still your husband."

"Yes, so I hear." Shelby tightened her grip on her parasol and took a steadying breath for courage in the face of his anger. "But you're so unwilling to act like one, it's hard to believe. And even that doesn't give you the right to forbid me anything."

He took her arm in a way that looked casual, but was anything but. "You took a vow to obey me, Agatha, and I insist that you honor it."

"Do you?" She tried unsuccessfully to tug her arm

away. "And what vows did *you* take, Zacharias? Do you honor them?"

His eyes narrowed suddenly. She knew she'd scored a direct hit. "Any vows I've broken have been at your request, madame."

"Really?" She lowered her parasol and met his gaze fully. "Why on earth would I request that you do that?"

"Because you prefer it this way."

"Why?"

He glared down at her, so angry she shivered in spite of the sun's warmth. "Must we get into that?"

"I'm afraid we must," she said with false bravado. "I've already told you, if you don't explain our situation to me, I'll find answers from other people—like Patricia Starling. And maybe you'd also like to explain why you're so eager to protect her from me."

A muscle in his jaw twitched and he glanced away quickly. "It's not Mrs. Starling I seek to protect."

"Then who do you seek to protect?"

Zacharias sighed heavily. She thought for a moment he'd refuse to answer again, but his next words surprised her. "Very well. Obviously, you are determined to know and I suppose it will be best to hear it from me. Do you want the truth, or the reasons you gave me?"

"I'd like both."

"Fine." He looked over his shoulder again, making sure no one could hear them. "The truth is, Agatha, you care very little for me or for my company but you do care about your reputation and appearances. If you insist upon calling on Patricia Starling, you will put the things you care about most in jeopardy."

"My reputation? How would a simple social call put that in jeopardy?"

"By prompting people to begin speculating about the nature of my relationship with Patricia."

"I see. And just what *is* the nature of your relationship with Patricia?"

"Exactly what you suspect."

Her sudden surge of anger surprised her as much as

the sting of jealousy that accompanied it. "So you *have* started seeing another woman already. And that *is* why you refuse to reconcile with me."

"Our marriage has been nonexistent for five long years," he said sharply. "That hardly qualifies as 'already.' "

She refused to acknowledge his point, valid though it might be. "How long have you been carrying on with her?"

His gaze faltered and his cheeks burned red, and Shelby had her answer.

She stared at him in disbelief. "Do you mean to tell me this whole sordid mess came about because you couldn't keep your . . . your . . . fly buttoned?" She resisted the urge to belt him in the head with her parasol and waved her hand toward the object in question instead.

The color in Zacharias's face deepened. "Can we discuss this somewhere else? I'd prefer not to air our differences in front of the entire town."

Shelby didn't care who heard them, but a flicker of common sense warned her not to give the town gossips more fuel. "Do they know?"

"No one knows the entire story," Zacharias whispered harshly. "We agreed to keep it quiet to spare you embarrassment."

"To spare *me*?" Shelby gripped her parasol a little tighter. "I suppose *your* reputation wasn't even a minor consideration."

"My reputation wasn't in question," Zacharias said tightly.

"And Patricia's?" The woman's name tasted bitter as she said it.

"If you destroy her reputation, you only destroy your own."

Shelby lost all the air in her lungs, as if someone had cinched her corset several inches too far. "Is that what you told me to keep me quiet? Because if it is—"

He cut her off. "Silence was your choice, Agatha."

She tried to take a steadying breath, but her lungs refused to work. Poor Agatha. And damn Zacharias.

"If you wish to discuss this," he said softly, "I suggest we go somewhere more private. Otherwise, I'm taking you home."

"I don't want to go anywhere with you." She spat the words at him.

"Nevertheless, I must insist." He waited while an elderly woman strolled past, then went on. "You insisted upon knowing. Don't be angry with me if you don't like what you heard."

"I'm not angry over what I heard," she whispered through clenched teeth. "I'm angry over what you *did*."

His eyebrows arched as if she'd shocked him. "You're angry that I turned to another woman?"

"Don't tell me that surprises you."

"As a matter of fact, it does." He glanced around quickly, tipped his hat to a passing gentleman, then turned back to her. "Can we *please* continue this conversation elsewhere?"

Dimly she became aware of people watching them. Slowly she remembered her responsibility to Agatha. Once again, she'd let the line between them blur. "All right," she said reluctantly. "I'll speak with you in private. Where would you suggest we go?"

He cast about quickly and his gaze landed on the buggy Colin had left standing only a few feet away. "We can take a ride out of town—away from prying eyes and curious ears."

"And from anyone who might tell Patricia you've been spending time with your wife?"

"If I wanted to prevent that," he said as he guided her toward the buggy Colin had driven her to town in, "it would already be too late." He sent her a mocking smile. "And if you're worried about your virtue, you needn't be. Compromising that precious commodity is the *last* thing on my mind."

"You really are obnoxious, aren't you?" Shelby made

another vain attempt to pull away from him. "Must you be so hateful all the time?"

Pain flashed through his eyes, but it disappeared almost immediately. "I return what I'm dealt, madame. Surely you remember that." He helped her into the buggy and stepped back.

"Shouldn't we tell Colin that we're leaving?" she asked, searching the streets for him.

Zacharias rounded the buggy and climbed onto the seat beside her. "Someone will be sure to tell him."

He didn't speak again until they'd ridden to the edge of town and started north along the narrow road toward Cardiff Hill. The river lapped gently along its banks and fields studded with goldenrod, wild hollyhocks, and bloodroot tossed in the gentle breeze.

At long last, he sent her a sidelong glance and resumed their conversation. "You really have lost your memory, haven't you?"

Shelby scowled at him. "What do you think I've been trying to tell you? Did you think I was making it up?"

"To be honest, I didn't know what to think. Our relationship hasn't exactly been amicable for a long time."

"So I hear." She settled her skirts more comfortably. "And all because you had an affair."

He sent her another long glance. "That's not entirely true."

"No? There's more?"

His gaze shifted back to the road. "It wasn't my relationship with Patricia that drove us apart."

"Wasn't it? It seems to me any woman would be hurt by infidelity—even me."

"Hurt?" He laughed bitterly. "You weren't hurt by it, Agatha. As I said, I only did what you bid me to do."

Shelby glared at him. "You expect me to believe that I *told* you to sleep with another woman?"

"I'm afraid you found my attentions distasteful."

"So I sent you off to another woman's bed?" The buggy hit a rut and sent Shelby sprawling against him.

She pulled back quickly and clutched the seat to keep herself in place. "You're lying."

"Not at all. Actually, you were quite happy to be relieved of that particular duty."

Shelby felt her cheeks redden and she found it impossible to meet his gaze. Having such an intimate discussion with him suddenly seemed dangerous. What if she was successful in rekindling the romance between them? Would she be expected to make love to him? Or would Agatha return in time for that?

Her pulse quickened, then slowed. She tried to concentrate on what Agatha would think about what she'd done instead of the possibility that she might have to take Agatha's place in Zacharias's bed. "Perhaps you misunderstood me."

He laughed aloud. "I don't think so, my dear. You left little room for misunderstanding."

"And my lack of interest wounded your male pride so deeply you rushed out and slept with someone else?"

His smile faded. "Indeed not. I always slept at home under your roof. *Sleep* was one thing we got very little of."

"How lovely for both of you," she said, barely controlling the urge to slap him. "And how very gentlemanly of you to tell me about it."

He looked immediately contrite.

Shelby didn't back down. "I must have tolerated your attention occasionally. We have two children to show for it."

"Indeed." His gaze faltered and he turned his attention back to the road in front of them. "Indeed," he said again, softer this time.

Silence yawned between them for a long moment, and only the sound of the horse, the creak of buggy wheels, and the soft lapping of the river against the shore broke it. She forced herself to look at him. At least he'd finally had the decency to be honest with her. She supposed that was something.

"You know the whole story now," he said at last. "I'd prefer not to discuss it further."

Shelby had no intention of letting him off the hook that easily. "Oh, but I would. I'd like to know why you're so damned smug—"

"Smug?" Anger flared in his eyes. "I've hardly been smug, Agatha. I've been more sorry than you know. I've begged your forgiveness for my actions and my decisions. I've done my best to make amends by giving you Summervale and the solitude you demand. Beyond that, I don't know what I can do." As he spoke, the anger in his eyes faded and a deep sadness took its place.

Some of Shelby's anger evaporated along with it. "Maybe I didn't believe you were truly sorry."

"If I could believe that . . ." He let his voice trail away and flicked the reins. "I swore I'd never beg you for anything else, but I was wrong. For Mordechai and Andrew's sakes, I'm begging you now. Leave the matter alone. Let things lie as they are . . . *please.*"

He'd put his heart into the request and it shook Shelby to the core. Any parent who cared so deeply about his children deserved some credit. And though she sensed that he hadn't told her the complete truth, she couldn't make herself ask him for the rest. At least not now.

She only hoped her time wouldn't run out before she had the answers.

Shelby tiptoed down the third-floor corridor holding a candle aloft to light her way. Since Zacharias wouldn't tell her the rest of the story, and nobody else knew, she had only one remaining source of information. She'd made such progress without Agatha's journals and letters, she'd all but forgotten that's how she'd landed up here. But now she had no other choice.

That evening she'd searched Agatha's sitting room, writing desk, and bedroom from floor to ceiling, but she hadn't found a single helpful piece of paper. Though she couldn't imagine why Agatha would move her journals to the attic while she was still alive, she just *knew* there

must be some record of her breakup with Zacharias
somewhere.

But where?

She approached the attic stairs cautiously, moving
soundlessly past the door to the bedroom Meg and Colin
shared under the rafters, then inched open the attic door
and started up the steps. The air was surprisingly clean
and fresh, as if Meg had recently aired it.

Holding fast to the handrail, Shelby tested each stair
to make sure it wouldn't creak before she put her full
weight on it. Meg and Colin had both been so concerned
after she'd abandoned Colin in town, they'd spent the
entire evening watching her, clucking over her, worrying
about what she'd do next. She could just imagine what
they'd think if they found her creeping around in the
attic in the middle of the night.

Dear Meg. Kind, gentle Colin. If anyone had told her
that she'd grow so fond of them in such a short time,
Shelby would have laughed aloud. She'd grown adept
at keeping her heart in check and remaining one step
removed from the people around her. But Meg and Colin
had somehow managed to sneak past her defenses.

And Zacharias . . . She shook her head and tried not
to think of him. In spite of his confession that afternoon,
her feelings hadn't changed. She'd spent a good portion
of her life watching other people, observing instead of
participating, but she knew that there were always two
sides to every broken marriage.

But the more she'd thought about all of them, the
more deeply she realized she was becoming involved,
the more determined she was to keep some distance between them and her heart. She knew how dangerous it
was to grow attached, especially since she could be
ripped away without notice.

If Zacharias hadn't been so obstinate, so recalcitrant,
so . . . so . . . *pigheaded*, she'd probably be gone already.
But his damned stubbornness kept her here, and she fell
more in love with him each time she saw him.

That thought brought her to a stumbling halt on the

top step. *In love?* No. She'd used the wrong word. She admired his devotion to Mordechai and Andrew, of course. But she wasn't in love with him. She might be attracted to him. What woman wouldn't be? But she *wasn't* in love with him.

With that firmly settled, she climbed the final step and stood in the center of the huge attic. Turning slowly, she took in the trunks and crates, old wardrobes and other objects buried so deep in the shadows she couldn't immediately identify them.

The sheer size of the attic and the number of possible hiding places overwhelmed her. If Agatha had brought her journals up here, it might take weeks to find them. But she didn't have weeks to look. The date of Agatha's death crept closer with alarming steadiness.

Biting her lip, she picked the corner as far from Meg and Colin's bedroom as possible and got to work. The first few crates yielded nothing but old clothing that the Historical Society in Shelby's own time would have given their eyeteeth to get hold of. She found shoes, boots, brogans, capes, shawls, beeches, abandoned hoops from skirts only recently out of fashion, gloves, pantalets, and even a collection of old pipes. But not a single journal or letter.

Dust rose from the crates and tickled her nose. She could feel the grime under her fingernails and on her cheeks. With each new treasure, her imagination ran wild for a few minutes, but each time she drew herself resolutely back to her task.

Agatha *must* have kept some written record, and once Shelby found it, she'd find the answers to all her questions. And then, hopefully, she'd go home—before she lost her heart and her head completely.

It must have been an hour later when she felt her determination falter and the need for sleep begin to tug at her eyelids. She opened a trunk, hopeful that it would yield something of value. But she found only another folded stack of clothes in styles she calculated to be at least twenty years old. Exhausted, she sank to the floor and tried to blink away tears of frustration. If she couldn't find Agatha's journals, how would she ever get home again?

Slowly, she replaced the lid on the crate, picked up the candle, and started back toward the staircase. But instead of descending, she changed direction and crossed to the window where she could look out at the slumbering city and the river curving softly between the bluffs.

Only a few flickering lights dotted the landscape and she lost herself in imagination as she'd done so often as a child, trying to imagine life in someone else's house. Life with a loving family and friends. Houses filled with laughter and security.

Sighing softly, she leaned an elbow on the windowsill and listened to the hum of insects in the dark. Maybe she'd never leave here. Maybe she was doomed to stay and live out the rest of Agatha's short life alone. And what did it matter? Who would miss her?

There was nothing waiting there for her in the future, nobody who wanted her here. Zacharias had already moved on. The twins didn't even know her. Meg and Colin seemed to like her, but she doubted even they'd grieve when she died.

She lifted her head again and stared out the window again while conflicting emotions chased through her. Fear, hope, worry, peace, longing, and satisfaction all tied together, each almost undistinguishable from the next. But she'd never been one to indulge in self-pity for long, and tonight was no exception. Somewhere, from deep at the bottom of her emotional well, one nagging thought kept rising, gaining strength, pushing away everything else as it grew.

There were children involved. Agatha, Shelby, and Zacharias didn't matter, but the children did. She'd been focusing on the wrong thing all this time. She was here not to bring Agatha and Zacharias back together, but to make sure those children had what they needed—the security of knowing that someone loved them.

· And she'd give that to them if she did nothing else. She wouldn't let anyone stand in her way. Not Zacharias. Not Victoria.

Not even Agatha.

Shelby took a steadying breath and slipped through the last of the trees separating Summervale from Winterhill. She wished she had the courage to march up to Winterhill's front door and demand to see Agatha's children. But after the way Zacharias had pleaded with her the day before, she didn't dare chance running into him. And she certainly didn't want to risk another encounter with that viper who called herself a mother-in-law.

She had to find some other way to make contact with Mordechai and Andrew. Some way to convince Zacharias that the twins needed their mother.

Keeping one eye on the house as she walked, she hurried into the sculptured garden, then moved furtively toward the pond on the far side of the house. Meg assured her that the twins spent mornings there with their nurse, and the thought of seeing the pond again and sitting beneath the shade of the summer house filled her with excitement.

She hurried past the library windows and when no one shouted at her to stop, she breathed a sigh of relief. The scent of roses filled the air, but she didn't let herself stop to enjoy it. As she drew closer to the pond, the sound of voices and childish laughter caught her ear and made her walk faster.

She tiptoed beneath the arbor into the clearing, then stopped to watch. The nurse sat with her back to Shelby, shielding her eyes from the sun while she kept watch. The twins were so caught up in their game, they didn't notice her. Just as well, she thought. She didn't want to startle them.

Both towheaded like their father, they ran after each other along the gently rolling hill that led down to the water's edge. The sun winked off their hair, and their laughter echoed in the stillness. They didn't appear to be identical. Other than sharing Zacharias's coloring, they bore little resemblance to one another. One boy was tall and lanky, the other shorter and husky. One narrow-faced, the other broad.

Shelby's heart skipped a beat. Their sheer pleasure in each other, their joy in the morning, their exuberance, their energy held her spellbound.

Oh, Agatha, how can you bear being separated from them?

She didn't know how long she watched before some-one grabbed her arm and tugged her around on the path. Holding back a cry of dismay, she found herself looking into Zacharias's very unhappy eyes.

"What are you doing here?"

Shelby pulled away from his grasp and tried not to show her uncertainty. "I came to see the children."

"After I specifically asked you to leave them in peace?"

"Whether or not you agree, those children need a mother."

Zacharias clenched his jaw tightly as if he were mak-ing an effort to control himself, then wheeled around and pulled her back into the gardens and away from the children and their nurse. He set such a rapid pace, she stumbled in her efforts to keep up, but he didn't slow his step.

Once safely away, he released her and lashed out again verbally. "Are you still so angry with me that you'd purposely try to hurt them?"

"I don't want to hurt them," Shelby insisted, rubbing her arm gently. "I just want to see them. And since you're so determined to keep me away, I decided to take matters into my own hands."

He clamped his mouth shut and studied her intently for several long seconds. His eyes, a clear, icy blue, seemed to bore into her and his mouth became nothing more than a thin slash in his bronzed face. "I forbid you to do this again, Agatha. I forbid it, absolutely."

"Haven't we been over this already? You have no right to forbid me anything."

"I most certainly do," he snapped. "Especially when it concerns Andrew and Mordechai."

"Why?" She put a little distance between them and kept his hands in view. He had a grip like a steel trap and she wasn't interested in suffering it again. "I'm sorry, but I can't accept this notion that you can order me about simply because you're a man and I'm a woman. It's absolutely archaic."

"That would be reason enough," he said, his voice tightly controlled, "even if there weren't other considerations to keep in mind."

"*What* other considerations? Obviously there's something I don't know, so why won't you tell me?"

"Because I won't discuss it again, even with you." He paced a step away, rubbed his face, and let out a heavy sigh. "I've humbled myself to you in the past, Agatha. I've apologized as many times as I'm going to. Maybe you truly don't remember, but you will eventually. Dr. Mensing assures me of that and, God help me, I believe him. I can't take the chance that you'll hurt the boys when your memory returns."

"But why would I hurt them?"

"Because you hate them, Agatha."

Shelby recoiled as if he'd slapped her. If that were true, maybe Agatha *was* crazy. How could any sane woman hate two innocent children? "How could I possibly hate them?"

"Shall I quote you?"

She nodded slowly, not at all certain she wanted to hear his answer.

"As you told me many times," Zacharias said with a bitter twist of his mouth, "the sins of the fathers shall be visited upon the children."

Shelby's shoulders sagged, her eyes filled with tears of frustration and hopelessness. How could Agatha have been so hateful, so wrong, no matter what Zacharias had done? "I said that?"

"Indeed."

She tried frantically to hide the tears, but all her efforts were in vain. "I'm sorry, Zacharias. Truly, truly sorry. I don't know how I could have said such a horrible thing."

Silence stretched between them for a long time. Shelby watched him, holding her breath, waiting for him to respond. He shook his head in disbelief and sent her a thin smile. "I don't know what's going on with you, Agatha, but in all the years I've known you, I don't think I've ever heard you apologize for anything."

She took a hesitant step toward him. "Then doesn't that prove that I'm not the woman I used to be?"

"I knew that the first time I kissed you." His smile warmed slightly and something she couldn't read darted across his eyes. "If I thought there was a chance that you'd remain as you are . . ." He let his voice trail away for a moment, then turned to face her. "Can you assure me that you'll stay this way? Can you guarantee that you won't go back to the woman you were?"

Shelby longed to give him what he asked for. She ached to promise that things wouldn't change once Agatha returned. But she couldn't give him that promise, and she wouldn't lie. That would only make things worse in the long run. She might stay here forever, but she might just as easily zap back to her own time. And Agatha's fate was still uncertain.

She shook her head slowly. "I can't promise anything."

Zacharias straightened his shoulders and the coolness returned. "I thought not."

"But neither can I say that I *won't* stay exactly as I am. And maybe—just maybe—letting me spend time with the children will make a difference once my memory returns." She held out a hand toward him, pleading with him silently to give Agatha another chance.

For a moment, she thought he might actually agree. But in the next breath she saw that she'd lost again. "I'm sorry, Agatha. It's too late to make amends—for either of us."

"I don't believe that."

"Nevertheless." He sketched a mocking bow. "I must insist that you stay away from Winterhill and from the children."

"And if I don't?"

"If you don't," he warned, his voice ominous, "I'll take steps to see that you do." With that, he pivoted, and walked away.

Shelby stood there for a moment, rubbing her arm even though she could no longer feel the pressure of his fingers. She toyed with the idea of ignoring Zacharias's warning and returning to the pond. But he'd meant what he said. And the laws of 1871 would probably be on Zacharias's side, even if Agatha hadn't deserted her children. Shelby couldn't risk goading Zacharias into taking legal measures—especially when he was half convinced she was crazy.

Even so, she couldn't give up the fight. Her life—and Agatha's—depended on it.

Chapter 10

MEG CARRIED THE tray carefully up the stairs, wondering if today was the day the missus would be back to her old self. She'd wondered the same thing every morning for the past two weeks, yet every morning the missus greeted her with a smile and tried to engage her in idle chitchat. Perhaps someday Meg would trust this change. Perhaps someday she'd be able to accept that this new Agatha was here to stay.

But not yet.

Balancing the tray on one hip, she knocked softly on the door and prepared herself for the worst. But again, the missus called out a cheery "come in."

Smiling to herself, Meg pushed open the door and let her gaze travel around the bedroom. Sure enough, the new Agatha was propped up in the bed, hair tousled as if she didn't care who saw her that way.

She smiled when Meg entered. "Good morning, Meg."

"Good morning, madame."

"Mmmm, that smells delicious." Agatha stretched carelessly and rubbed her eyes. "What have you brought me?"

Meg watched her, amazed at the changes in her. Agatha never rubbed her eyes. It caused wrinkles. And she never allowed Meg or anyone else to see her in such a disheveled state. The missus had always been tightly controlled and pulled together.

Now, she tossed back the bedcovers and swung her legs over the side. "I need your help with something, Meg."

"Of course, madame."

"I've decided I'm going to invite guests for dinner."

Under other circumstances, Meg might have thought that wonderful news, but she knew only too well what the vultures of Hannibal society would do to Agatha. She carefully lowered the tray to the drop-leaf table and framed her reply with equal care. "Maybe you should think about it awhile first."

Agatha waved away her suggestion. "I have thought about it, Meg. I've been locked away for far too long as it is."

"But . . ." Meg thought quickly, frantically. "But you can't *do* that, madame."

"Why not?"

"Because people will talk, madame. And you hate gossip."

"Let them talk," Agatha said with a wave of her hand. "They do anyway."

"Well, yes, madame. But . . ."

But it would be ever so much worse, Meg thought in despair.

"I've realized that there's only one way I'm going to convince Zacharias to trust me, and that's to show him how much I've changed. And what better way than to come out of hiding?"

"It's a terrible chance you'd be taking," Meg warned.

Agatha stood quickly and crossed to the hearth. "I've tried everything else, Meg. Nothing's working. He's not mellowing at all."

"I still think you should reconsider."

"You think I should give up." Agatha scowled deeply,

a ridge forming between her eyes. "But I can't do that, Meg. I just can't. Those children need me."

Meg couldn't understand what had suddenly made the missus care so deeply about someone besides herself. Not that she didn't like seeing it, mind you. But it was such a change, she didn't know what to make of it. "Is it really so important to you, then?"

"Important?" Agatha laughed softly and let her fingers linger on the brass candlesticks on the mantel. "You might say my life depends on it. If he still doesn't believe that I've changed, I'll simply have to change more."

Lord above. Meg took a hesitant step toward her. "Do you really think this is wise?"

Agatha glanced back over her shoulder. "I don't know if it's wise or not, but I don't know what else to do. Please don't argue with me. I don't need you against me, too."

"I'm not against you," Meg assured her quickly.

"Then help me."

"I'm trying to, madame. But laying yourself open for gossip won't help."

"It seems to me that I've been far too concerned about gossip in the past," Agatha said firmly. "I've been more concerned with appearances than anything or anyone else. It's cost me my husband and my children."

True enough, Meg thought, but she'd never expected to hear Agatha admit it.

"If I have to subject myself to gossip to win them back," Agatha went on, "then so be it."

Meg darted an anxious glance over her shoulder and thought about Victoria. What would she make of this? She voiced her concerns aloud, but Agatha didn't seem convinced.

"They already think I'm crazy, Meg. Even if I don't rejoin society, that won't change. Believe me."

"But—"

"But nothing." Agatha turned toward her quickly. "I have to do this, Meg. Please."

Sighing softly, Meg resigned herself to the inevitable. "If you insist, I will help you. But it will be against my better judgment."

Agatha beamed, oblivious to what lay in store for her. "Good. Then tell me who I should invite."

"In God's truth, madame, I don't know."

"Patricia Starling?"

Meg tried to pour Agatha's tea, but succeeded only in sloshing it onto the saucer and tray. "Good Lord, no. If you must do this, do *not* invite that woman."

"Why not?"

"Surely, madame . . ."

Agatha laughed as if Meg's distress delighted her. "I know. I know. But if you don't tell me, I may make a mistake."

"Then perhaps Orville and Lydia Englund."

"Englund?"

"Orville Englund owns the largest bank in Hannibal," Meg explained, "and Lydia is one of the undisputed queens of society. But they are kind people. You should be safe in their company."

Agatha nodded quickly and made a note of their names. "Who else?"

"Is it necessary to invite anyone else? Perhaps you should start with a small party."

"And I will," Agatha assured her. "But I want more than one couple here. Come on, Meg. Help me."

"You could invite John and Caroline Baxter, I suppose."

"Okay. Who are they?"

Meg tried once more to discourage her. "If you don't remember these people, why are you doing this?"

"To win back my family." Grim determination darkened Agatha's eyes.

Meg abandoned the fight. She knew a lost cause when she saw one. "Caroline Baxter was your closest friend when you were a young woman. Before your marriage to Zacharias."

Agatha smiled slowly. "*My* friend? Really?" She

wrapped her arms around her waist and hugged herself. "Do you think she'd come?"

"Of course she would." Meg let down her guard for a moment. "Anyone in town would give their eyeteeth to get inside this house. That's what worries me."

Agatha laughed as if her fears were groundless. "Then that should make my dinner party an unqualified success."

Meg only wished that were true. She wished she could stop there, but the missus would bear the brunt of much speculation if the table wasn't balanced. "You'll need one more," she said hesitantly. "A man."

Agatha nodded. "Zacharias, of course."

"Of course." Would he come? Perhaps. But the potential for disaster was frightening. Meg tried once more to push aside her misgivings. "When do you want to hold this dinner party?"

"Soon. Very soon. How much advance notice do I need to give?"

"You could probably give an hour's notice and everyone would still come." Meg tried to ignore the sinking sensation in her stomach and the mounting apprehension in her heart. "But I'd give it a week if I were you."

"A week." Agatha sighed softly, but she nodded in agreement. "You'll help me plan the menu, won't you? And will Colin deliver the invitations when I've got them ready?"

Meg smiled sadly. "Of course, madame." Colin would do as he was bid. And so would she. It was how they'd held on to their positions as long as they had. But she couldn't lie to herself. This new Agatha worried her almost as much as the old one had.

"A dinner party?" Victoria stared at Prudence Beaming's benign face in disbelief. She kept her posture rigid and her face impassive, but her heart thumped ominously in her chest and anger began to boil just below the surface. "Surely, you're mistaken."

"Not at all." Prudence took an irritatingly slow sip of

tea and smiled as if she enjoyed upsetting Victoria. "I believe the invitations are for Friday evening." She fluttered a hand and pretended concern. "Oh, dear. Have I upset you? I thought surely you knew."

Victoria patted the back of her hair carefully. "Which unlucky souls has she invited?"

"I believe she asked Orville and Lydia Englund."

"Lydia Englund?" The name escaped before she could stop it. The idea of Agatha trying to get Lydia Englund on her side was simply too much to bear.

Prudence smiled knowingly, which only made Victoria angrier. "I believe the others are John and Caroline Baxter. At least, that's what Gloria understood from Emma White."

Victoria bit back a scathing comment about Prudence's unfortunate daughter and her penchant for gossip. At least Agatha hadn't compounded her error by inviting someone else of the Englunds' social stature. She should be glad of that. "Orville and Lydia will refuse, of course."

"On the contrary." Prudence's smile grew almost vicious. "I believe they have sent her an acceptance, as have the Baxters. But, then, Caroline always was fond of Agatha, as you know."

"Indeed."

"It presents a problem for the rest of us." Prudence flipped open her fan and waved it in front of her face. "Gloria wonders if we'll be expected to include her on the guest list for our ball at the end of the month."

"I shouldn't think it will be necessary to include Agatha in future entertainments," Victoria assured her. "I doubt very much she is seriously interested in rejoining society. You know how difficult it always was for her."

Prudence nodded slowly. "Yes, it was, wasn't it? You'll pardon me for saying so, Victoria, but she simply doesn't have the breeding. Not that I blame her, of course. One simply can't make a silk purse out of a sow's ear."

No one believed that more deeply than Victoria, but

she loathed Prudence Beaming for saying it aloud. It was, she thought with a scowl, quite a tactless jab against Zacharias—against *all* the Logans, for that matter. "There is nothing you can say about Agatha that I haven't said myself. Zacharias is well aware of the error he made by marrying her, but he is making plans to rectify it at once."

"Surely you don't mean he would divorce her?" Prudence pretended shock, but Victoria could see the gleam of anticipation in her eye.

"I mean exactly that." Victoria picked up her teacup again and watched Prudence over its rim. "Zacharias has been more patient with her than most men would have been, but he has finally admitted that it's pointless to continue this way. He's thrown enough of his life away on a woman who, though I hate to say it, isn't mentally stable."

Prudence lowered her fan to her lap. "Do you really believe she is unstable?"

"Do you really believe she is not? Why would someone who *wasn't* unstable lock themselves away as she has?"

"Well . . ." Prudence tilted her head to one side and gave that some thought. "There was talk at the time that Zacharias's . . . friendship . . . with Patricia Starling was at the root of her decision."

This was exactly what Victoria feared most. That Agatha's presence in society would stir up all that ugliness again. "Zacharias's friendship with Patricia Starling is far more acceptable than his marriage ever was," she pointed out. "And even if there *was* some truth to that particular rumor, what man's eye doesn't wander from time to time? Any woman with breeding would have turned a blind eye to it."

Prudence sighed softly. "You're right, of course."

Of course, she was. Hadn't Victoria turned a blind eye on Hugh's philandering? Didn't every woman with class and breeding do the same thing? Of course, Zacharias had been the worst kind of fool to confess. What need had there been of that? But Agatha's reaction had been the ultimate mortification and Victoria wouldn't suffer anything remotely similar again. She wouldn't sit idly by while Agatha thoughtlessly brought more shame upon the Logan name.

She forced a smile. "When did you say this dinner party was?"

"Friday evening."

Victoria thought quickly, trying to decide the best way to minimize the damage. If only she could prevent Agatha from having her dinner party. If only she could convince Dr. Mensing to do what he should have done long ago.

Yes, she thought with a satisfied smile, that was the best thing. She hated to resort to such unseemly measures, but she'd do anything necessary to protect Zacharias's reputation from that woman's thoughtless actions.

Anything at all.

Zacharias turned over the envelope in his hand and shot a glance at Philip. A missive from Agatha had to be bad news, especially after the way he'd shouted at her in the gardens. Not that he'd been wrong to vent his anger. But a niggling guilt had been eating at him since he'd stormed away from her. And now she'd found a way to extract her revenge.

"Well?" Philip demanded. "What is it?"

Zacharias tossed the envelope onto his cluttered desk and willed it to disappear.

Philip watched it land. "You're not going to open it?"

"Not yet."

"What if it's an emergency?"

"It's not," Zacharias said firmly. "Colin would have said so."

Philip crossed to the desk and picked up the envelope. "It looks like an invitation to me."

Zacharias laughed aloud. "From Agatha? Do you forget who you're talking about?"

"I haven't forgotten anything," Philip said, sniffing

the envelope experimentally. He grinned broadly and shoved it back at Zacharias. "Lavender."

"You're mistaken. Agatha doesn't use scent. She never has." Soap and water was more her style—strong lye soap capable of killing romantic notions before they could start. She sure as hell wouldn't scent an envelope before sending it to him.

He perched on the corner of Philip's desk, pointedly ignoring the small scrap of white paper in his friend's hand. "Do you mind if we get back to the matter of our livelihoods?"

"We can get back to that after you read your letter. I'm too curious to wait."

Irritated, Zacharias tore the damn thing open and pulled out the missive. He expected venom. Spite. Hatred. Instead, he found himself looking at an invitation to join Agatha for dinner. He lowered it to his desk in stunned disbelief.

"Well? What is it?"

"She's invited me to dinner."

Philip laughed, obviously delighted by the turn of events.

But Zacharias suspected a trick. What in the hell was she doing? What was she thinking? Why would she invite guests to Summervale? Why would she invite him after the way he'd shouted at her in the garden? "She's gone too far this time," he muttered, swiping a hand across his face. "Definitely too far."

"Maybe she's finally come to her senses."

"Or lost them completely." Zacharias pushed to his feet and paced toward the window. "I tell you, Philip, I don't know what to think anymore."

"Nor do I." Philip tipped back in his chair and rested his feet on the corner of his desk. "You'll accept the invitation, won't you?"

"Not on your life." Zacharias wheeled to face him, trying to ignore the sudden image of a laughing Agatha that formed in his mind. "I won't tolerate being manipulated. Maybe the nuances of it escape you, but this invitation forces my hand. If I accept, I'll be making a public statement that our marriage is intact. If I decline, I'll be admitting that I wish it to be over."

"The nuances don't escape me at all," Philip drawled. "But maybe it's time for you to finally make that decision."

Zacharias glared at him. "Thank you for your show of support."

"You've been estranged for five years, and your life has been stagnant the entire time."

"I *like* my life the way it is," Zacharias insisted, though if he'd been forced to tell the truth, he'd have to admit how untrue that was. Again, the image of Agatha as she'd been in Winterhill's gardens drifted in front of his eyes. The wistfulness of her expression as she watched the twins at play had touched him deeply and frightened him at the same time. How could he allow her to see the twins when there was still one remaining secret between them? How could he allow her to step into their lives unless he told her the truth first? And how could he tell her and risk losing her again? The first time had cut, but to lose her now would devastate him.

Philip's soft laugh dragged him back to the moment. "Ah, yes. I can see why you're so happy. You're married to a woman who refuses to acknowledge that you even exist. And—pardon my bluntness—but you're carrying on a discreet but highly unsatisfactory affair with a woman who'd as soon own your soul as bed you. Your mother has assumed control over your home and your life. Your children are growing up without the benefit of a mother." He broke off and tapped his chin thoughtfully. "Let me see . . . have I forgotten anything?"

"I think you've managed to hit all the fine points," Zacharias snarled. "But I'm still not interested in changing. My life works for me."

"Does it?"

"Perfectly."

"I see." Disbelief shaded Philip's voice. "You're perfectly content sneaking off to visit Patricia whenever you feel the need."

Zacharias glared a little harder. "I'm content *not* dealing with a wife. I had my fill of that particular pleasure."

"Then your decision is made, isn't it?" Philip linked his hands behind his head. "If you truly desire to live out the rest of your life without a wife, take your mother's advice and divorce Agatha."

For some reason the suggestion made Zacharias even angrier. He turned away and stared out the window. "I don't want to be pressured into making *any* decision."

"The thought crosses my mind that perhaps you're avoiding the decision because you don't want a divorce."

"Exactly."

"No. I mean, maybe you want to stay married to Agatha."

"Precisely."

Philip rolled his eyes and tried again. "Maybe you're still in love with her."

"It isn't a question of *love*," Zacharias snapped. "I merely feel responsibility toward her."

"You needn't remain married to satisfy any financial obligation you may feel. You can always make a generous settlement—"

"No." The word exploded from his mouth before he could stop it.

Philip studied him too intently for comfort. "Why do you feel so responsible? She's the one who demanded that you leave Summervale, isn't she?"

"She is."

"And she resisted every attempt you made to save your marriage . . ."

"She did."

"Then why?"

Talking it over with Philip might help clear some of his confusion, but Zacharias had vowed never to reveal the entire truth, and he couldn't go back on his word. "She is my wife," he said after a long pause.

"Ah-h-h. That explains everything." Philip tucked his hands into his pockets and crossed one foot over the other. "Why don't you tell me the truth? There's something more, isn't there?"

"No."

"Listen, old man, I understand why you'd hesitate to divorce the mother of your children. But she's refused to acknowledge you *or* them for five long years."

"I know. I know." Zacharias rubbed the back of his neck but he couldn't relieve the tension there. "And she is behaving strangely—even more strangely than ever. Still . . ."

"If you hesitate, my friend, maybe you should ask yourself if you truly feel nothing for her. Maybe you should accept her invitation and see what happens."

Zacharias shook his head quickly. "And what if I decide later to divorce her? Won't I have made everything worse?" He picked up a paperweight and hefted it in his hand for a moment, wishing he could relieve his frustration by throwing it against the wall. Instead he kept his emotions in check, just as he'd been taught all his life. "I can't subject my sons, my mother, *or* Agatha to any more gossip."

Philip's eyes clouded. "What you can't do is to worry so much about everyone else that you suffer."

Zacharias laughed bitterly. "That, I'm afraid, is the nature of my position."

"To hell with your position," Philip snapped. "If this kind of agony is what a rich man has to endure, I'd much rather teeter on the brink of disaster."

"And well you should."

"I'm serious, Zacharias. For you to make yourself miserable just so that everyone around you is pleased . . . well, that's utter nonsense."

"And to do anything less would be utterly irresponsible."

Philip grabbed his shoulders and pulled him around until they stood face-to-face. "Your sons would benefit a sight more from seeing you happy and contented than they would from watching you live a miserable, lonely life."

Zacharias pulled away from his friend's grasp. "This is not a matter I will discuss with my sons."

"No, of course you won't. What man would? But tell me, Zacharias, were your parents happy?"

"What kind of question is that?"

"An honest one." Philip shrugged lightly. "You say you'd rather spend the rest of your life in limbo than to spend it with Agatha or marry again. I'm just trying to figure out why."

"Because marriage is an unendurable state. Believe me, I know."

Philip pushed away from the wall. "Based on your vast experience?"

"Only a fool keeps putting his hand back into the flame once he learns that it's hot. If I must be unhappy, I'd prefer to do it alone."

"Only a fool refuses to allow himself to walk toward the warmth. What if you could be happy?"

"I'm far too old to believe in such nonsense."

"You sound more like your father every day."

Only Philip knew how deeply that comment cut, and Zacharias resented him for making it. "Perhaps that's all I can hope for."

"And perhaps not." Philip waved a hand through the air, his own agitation growing more obvious by the moment. "Your parents lived like virtual strangers in the same house. Now, you're taking it one step further by living alone."

"You can't compare the two situations," Zacharias argued. "It's not the same thing at all."

"Isn't it?" Philip propped a hand against the wall and held his gaze. "Or are you leaving your sons the same legacy your parents gave to you?"

The suggestion was a preposterous one, and Zacharias had no intention of entertaining it for an instant. He pushed past Philip, snagged up his topcoat, and began to shove his arms into the sleeves.

Philip straightened quickly and narrowed his eyes. "Where are you going?"

"Out. There's no reason for me to stay since you're supremely uninterested in business, and I'm equally uninterested in discussing my personal life."

"Will you be back?"

"Yes." Zacharias jammed his hat on his head and flung open the door. "When you're ready to concentrate on figuring out who's robbing you blind." Without giving Philip a chance to respond, he slammed the door hard enough to make the glass rattle.

But giving in to his temper gave him no satisfaction whatsoever. Muttering under his breath, he stormed down the walk toward the center of town. The humidity was high this morning, high enough to make him uncomfortable beneath his starched collar and coat. But he ignored his discomfort and increased his pace in an effort to work off some of his frustration.

His thoughts held his attention so completely, he paid no attention to anything around him until the door to a shop opened as he passed and Patricia stepped directly into his path.

Cursing his bad luck silently, he ground to a halt and narrowly missed plowing into her.

She smiled, revealing the dimples that had once charmed him, but today only set his teeth on edge. Her complete lack of surprise made him wonder if she'd seen him coming and orchestrated this meeting.

But the idea seemed so preposterous, so disloyal, he forced it away and did his best to hide his agitation. Obviously, Agatha's recent behavior was making him paranoid.

"What an unexpected pleasure this is," Patricia said, taking his arm gently. "I didn't expect to see you out and about in the middle of the day. Dare I hope that you're growing disillusioned with your little business venture?"

His *little* venture? The word rankled. "As a matter of

fact," he said stiffly, "I find myself more fascinated with it every day."

Patricia's eyes flashed but they softened again almost immediately. "Really, Zacharias." She laughed lightly and slipped her hand further beneath his arm. "I suppose there's no harm in allowing you to amuse yourself for a while, but you look positively disreputable."

"Do I?" He glanced at his suit, even though he knew full well how he looked. "Does it embarrass you to be seen with me?"

"Of course not." She flashed her dimples again. "If it amuses you, I have no real objection to your new pastime."

"It doesn't *amuse* me," he said, struggling to keep the anger from his voice. "And it's more than a pastime."

Patricia laughed as if he'd said something wildly amusing. "Of course it is. I have no head for business anyway, and it's much too nice a day to ruin with a disagreement." She glanced behind her at the shop. "I've just had the final fitting on a new ballgown. It's quite daring." She nestled against his shoulder as if she belonged there. "Are you too busy to see me home? It's so pleasant, I'd rather walk than ride."

Zacharias glanced at the waiting carriage only a few feet away. He had no desire to dally with her, but to refuse would be rude. "Of course."

"I'll be wearing my new gown at the Beamings' ball." She lowered her voice and added, "I think you'll like it."

Zacharias forced out the expected answer, knowing even as he spoke how Patricia would interpret his response. "If you're wearing it, I have no doubt that I will."

She glanced around to make sure no one could see them and brushed against him more provocatively. "I'd be happy to wear it for you . . . privately."

Every instinct inside him urged him to say no, but again his training tore the expected response from him. "Would you?"

"With pleasure." Patricia dropped her voice so that it was little more than a whisper. "All you have to do is say the word."

The only word that came to mind was adultery, and Zacharias didn't think that was the one she had in mind. "Perhaps another time," he said, hoping to let her down gently. "I really must attend to business."

Patricia's flirtatious manner evaporated. "Why are you so distant today?"

"Am I?"

"Yes you are, and this isn't the first time, either."

"I have a lot on my mind," he hedged.

"Yes, I know, and Agatha has put it there."

He shot a surprised glance at her. "In part."

"In part? She's driving us apart, Zacharias. Whenever I touch you, you look as if you find it distasteful."

A denial sprang to his lips, but he suspected there was more than a little truth in her observation. He owed Patricia honesty if not much more.

"You aren't considering reconciling with her, are you?"

"I don't know."

"She's a troubled woman, Zacharias. But you aren't responsible for that."

"Aren't I?"

"No. And neither am I." Patricia drew her hand away slowly. "She's making herself look foolish, and you'll look foolish right along with her if you condone her actions."

"Right or wrong, I *am* still her husband."

"There is no need to remind me of *that*." Patricia's voice sharpened, her expression hardened. "But that doesn't mean you have to turn yourself into a comic figure for her. Don't you see? She's a curiosity. An oddity. No one will accept her back into society. And you'll only ostracize yourself if you have anything to do with her."

Zacharias let the impact of her words swirl around inside his head for a few minutes. But instead of convincing him to turn his back on Agatha, the warning had the opposite effect. Something inside of him snapped. The wall he'd so carefully constructed came tumbling down.

Good or bad, right or wrong, Agatha was his wife. Maybe she was mad. Maybe she was more sane than she'd ever been. Maybe he would make himself a laughingstock if he chose to stand beside her. And maybe Philip was right. Maybe he'd be truly happy for the first time in his life.

Chapter 11

EVERYTHING WAS READY. Candles gleamed in chandeliers, china, silver, and crystal sparkled on the table, the scent of fresh jasmine filled the air. Even the weather had cooperated. The humidity had abated slightly, and a soft breeze blew in through the open windows.

Shelby ran her fingers along the gleaming sideboard and smiled. Everyone, including Zacharias, had accepted her invitations. While receiving the other acceptances had relieved some of her worry, hearing that he planned to attend had made her positively giddy with relief.

She'd been trying for days not to read too much into it—after all, it was only dinner. But at least he wasn't turning his back on her—on *Agatha*—completely. And that was a very good sign.

Humming softly, she pushed open the door to the kitchen and watched Meg for a moment as she made last-minute dinner preparations.

When Meg saw her standing there, she lowered the spoon she held to the table and sighed dreamily. "Oh, my dear. Look at you." She held out her hands, beckoning Shelby closer. "You look positively radiant."

Shelby laughed with delight. Had she been in her own body, she might have brushed aside the compliment, but she could look at Agatha with enough detachment to know Meg spoke the truth. The deep green silk brought out the best in Agatha's coloring and set off the jewels in Zacharias's necklace and earrings to perfection. Her eyes looked even darker and larger than usual, her cheeks were faintly brushed with color, and her hair, thanks to Meg, was nothing short of a masterpiece.

"I have you to thank," she said honestly.

Meg waved the compliment away. "Nonsense, Agatha. You have always been a beautiful woman." She let her voice trail away, as if she had something more to say.

Shelby took a step closer. "But?"

"But . . ." Meg brushed her hands on her apron and thought for a second or two. "Well, if I may be blunt, you haven't always been interested in looking beautiful."

"I know," Shelby said with a soft laugh. "I've seen the pictures." When Meg's smile faded and confusion darted across her eyes, she added quickly, "What I mean is, I've seen the gowns in my wardrobe and I know how I've worn my hair in years past. I'll admit it wasn't exactly becoming."

"Well, all that's behind you," Meg said with a bob of her head. "And tonight, Zacharias will fall in love with you all over again."

"I hope you're right," Shelby said softly, but the idea brought an unexpected pang with it. If Zacharias did fall in love with Agatha again, Shelby's time here might be over. By the end of the evening, she might be back in her own body wearing jeans and a T-shirt instead of this incredible gown. She might be back at Winterhill as nothing more than a caretaker instead of mistress of this amazing house. She might be alone again, without Meg and Colin, without Zacharias—without anyone.

How odd that she would envy Agatha her life, when just three short weeks ago she'd pitied her.

Meg picked up her spoon then lowered it again

slowly. "Oh, dear. Now you look sad. Did I say something wrong?"

"No," Shelby assured her. "Not at all. I'm just nervous, I suppose."

"Of course you are. But the evening will be a success, madame. I have no doubt of that. As long as the food turns out, that is."

"That's the *one* thing I have no worries about." Shelby crossed the room and put a hand on her shoulder, then bent down and kissed the older woman's cheek. "Thank you, Meg."

Meg's startled eyes flew to her face and a soft smile curved her mouth. She patted Shelby's cheek with a gentle hand. "The change in you is a miracle, Agatha. I hope you stay exactly as you are tonight forever."

Shelby laughed around the sudden lump that formed in her throat. "Then, you don't think I'm crazy any longer?"

Meg's cheeks turned a deep shade of red. "I never thought you were. And if you are, I hope you never regain your senses."

Shelby laughed again, but the sound of the door opening behind her kept her from saying anything else. Colin appeared in the doorway; a stiff white collar framed his ruddy face and an elegant suit encased his husky body. "Begging your pardon, madame," he said with a formal bow, "but the first of your guests has arrived."

Everything else faded and nervousness engulfed Shelby. The moment had arrived, but could she really pull off this deception in front of others? What would she talk to her guests about? She clasped her hands in front of her, reminded herself that she'd already fooled those who knew Agatha best, and tried to tamp down the rising panic. "Who is it? The Englunds or the Baxters?"

"Neither, madame." Colin's eyes glinted with mischief and his mouth twitched. "Master Zacharias is waiting for you in the library."

"Zacharias." A sigh of relief escaped her lips. A rush

of anticipation followed it. "How does he look? Is he . . . is he in a good mood?"

Colin grinned at her. "He looks quite dashing, if I may say so. And I'd say he's a wee bit nervous."

It was exactly what Shelby needed to hear. She could have kissed Colin for saying it. In fact, as she started across the room, she gave in to the urge and brushed a light kiss to his weathered cheek.

Colin looked every bit as startled as Meg had, but he recovered quickly. "Ye'll do fine, lass. Meg'n I are with ye all the way. Remember that."

Shelby hugged that thought to her as she crossed the entry and stepped into the parlor. Here, too, Meg had outdone herself. Crystal vases of white flowers filled the room with their perfume. The chandelier sparkled on the high ceiling and the antique brass candlesticks gleamed.

Zacharias stood near the fire, his face bare of the mask of impatience and frustration he usually wore. Shelby's heart skipped a beat and her hands grew damp.

The instant he saw her, the shield slipped back into place and covered everything but his eyes. They roamed her face and body, lingering on the necklace at her throat and the jewels in her ears. They devoured her with a hunger that surprised and pleased her and filled her with a deep, answering warmth.

Somehow she managed to find her voice. "Thank you for coming."

"I felt it prudent."

She tried not to laugh at the stiffness of his tone that seemed at such odds with the softness in his eyes. If he still needed to hold back, that was fine with her. At least she was making progress.

She crossed the room to him, enjoying the way his eyes darkened to a deep cobalt, the way his pulse jumped at his temple, the way his jaw clenched and un-clenched as he tried not to show his feelings.

She lifted her gaze to his and held it, trying to still the rapid beating of her own heart. "I'm glad you're here, for whatever reason."

He smiled hesitantly and let his gaze drop to her neck, her bosom, then dragged it back to meet hers. "You look lovely, Agatha."

As always, hearing him speak his wife's name brought Shelby crashing back to earth in a hurry. Even that didn't stop her mouth from drying, her skin from tingling, and her pulse from racing. It didn't take away the slowly coiling heat inside her or make him any less attractive. But it did fill her with guilt for lying to him, for making him believe Agatha had changed, for giving him hope for a future she couldn't guarantee.

The unthinkable had happened. She'd come here to save Agatha's marriage, but she didn't *want* to save it. She wanted Zacharias to fall in love with her, just as she'd fallen in love with him.

Finally relaxing slightly, Shelby led the women from the dining room into the drawing room. Dinner had gone without a hitch—at least without a hitch Zacharias couldn't smooth over. Each time she'd faltered during conversation, he'd stepped in to save her, and she was more grateful than ever that he'd accepted her invitation.

Unfortunately, his kindness only made her feel worse about loving him. His tenderness toward Agatha, though sometimes well hidden, only proved how deeply he loved her. And the more apparent his love for Agatha became, the more confused Shelby grew. The softness in his eyes made her insides feel like melted butter at the same time it cut like a dagger in her heart. The touch of his hand sent sparks shooting through her at the same time it filled her with despair.

Caroline Baxter, a thin, dark-haired woman of about Agatha's age with a soft voice and friendly smile, touched her sleeve and brought her back to the moment. "Will you play for us, Agatha?"

Shelby froze halfway to her seat, but the yards of silk and all the padding of her bustle pulled her the rest of the way with a *whoosh*. "Play?"

"The piano." Caroline gestured toward the baby grand

near the back windows. "You still play, don't you?"

Sure, if you counted a rousing two-fingered rendition of "Chopsticks" Shelby shook her head quickly. "No, I uh . . . I haven't played in some time."

"But you were always so talented," Caroline protested. "Surely you could play a simple piece when the men rejoin us. I know how much Zacharias loves to hear you perform."

Shelby laughed nervously. "No, really. I . . . I've forgotten—"

"Nonsense," Lydia Englund said with a wave of her hand. "I don't think one ever truly forgets. Something of Mozart's, perhaps. Or Beethoven."

Shelby shook her head again, harder this time. "I can't. I"—she forced a weak smile—"I can't. I'm afraid I don't remember." She watched the other women carefully. "I've recently suffered a loss of memory."

Lydia's green eyes filled with sympathy. "I didn't want to say anything about it, but that's what I hear. How on earth did it happen?"

"Yes, do tell us." Caroline leaned forward slightly. "I must admit I've been worried as well. If I'd thought you'd welcome a visitor, I'd have rushed here to be with you."

Another set of conflicting emotions tore through Shelby. Unexpected tears filled her eyes. Their concern touched her deeply even as it made her angry with Agatha for turning her back on her friends. And the lies Shelby had to tell tasted bitter on her tongue. "I don't know what happened," she said softly. "I don't remember."

Lydia put a hand on top of hers. "Have you forgotten everything?"

"Everything."

"But you know who you are?"

"Well, yes. But . . ."

Caroline's eyes looked suspiciously moist as well. "Do you remember anything of your childhood or of your parents?"

"No." That was at least partially true.

Lydia waved her fan to stir the warm air. "It's just so very sad. Dr. Mensing said it didn't seem that you'd had any injuries."

"None that I know of," Shelby admitted, then, as Lydia's words hit her, she scowled and added, "But I haven't even seen Dr. Mensing, so how would he know?"

Caroline sat back in her seat, her smile suddenly gone and a slight frown in its place. "I would imagine Dr. Mensing has been consulting with Victoria."

"With Victoria?" Shelby looked from one to the other in disbelief. "But isn't it unethical to discuss someone's medical condition with others?"

"Victoria gets whatever she wants," Lydia told her. "And if she wants to involve Dr. Mensing, she will."

"Involve him in what?"

Caroline glanced toward the doors as if she worried someone might overhear. "I hate to tell you this, but she visited me after I received your invitation."

"Victoria did?" *The dreadful old cow!* Blood rushed to Shelby's face and anger thumped heavily in her chest.

"She tried to convince me not to come tonight. She insinuated that you might be . . . dangerous."

"Dangerous?" Shelby couldn't believe even Victoria would stoop so low. "In what way?"

"I believe she is trying to prove that you are unstable," Lydia said gently. "I don't want to upset you, Agatha, but if you aren't careful, she may succeed."

Shelby's ears rang and the room tilted in front of her. "But I'm not crazy, and I'm certainly not dangerous." Her fingers curled into fists in her lap. How was she expected to fix Agatha's life if she had to battle her mother-in-law every step of the way? "Believe me, you're perfectly safe."

Caroline smiled slowly. "We know that. If either of us were even slightly worried, we wouldn't be here. But, my dear, you must be on your guard at all times. Others

won't be so quick to agree with us. Victoria is a powerful woman in this town."

"Maybe so, but I'm not about to let her railroad me
into an insane asylum just so she can hand-pick Zacharias's next wife."

Lydia laughed, then clamped her lips together and
glanced at the door. "I must say I'm glad to hear you
say that. So, the first thing we must do to fight her is
make certain that you're at our ball next week. The more
you hide away, the easier it will be for her to convince
others."

"She's right." Caroline said, tapping her fingers on the
arm of her chair in agitation. "Your best defense is to
return to society and let other people see you for themselves."

Return to society? Face everyone at once? The
thought nearly did Shelby in. She bit her lip and argued
with herself for a moment. But she had no real choice.
Frightening as it might be to walk into Hannibal society
as Agatha, it would be worse to spend the rest of her
life locked away.

She dragged up every ounce of courage she could find
and nodded. "I'll do it. And thank you . . . both of you.
You have no idea how much your friendship means."

Lydia beamed approval and her eyes sparkled as if
she looked forward to the battle. "You're not alone,
Agatha. Remember that."

Caroline gave Shelby's hand a reassuring squeeze.
"You do have friends."

Shelby clutched her hand tightly. "I'm beginning to
realize that. Please accept my apology for being so distant in the past."

"No apology necessary," Caroline said. "All I want is
for you to finally stand up to Victoria."

Shelby took courage from their support, but she had
the sick feeling she'd need all that and more. Seeing yet
another portion of the life Agatha had turned away from
left her even more determined to continue the battle. But

she had just a little over a week left in which to win the war.

While Agatha bid good night to her guests, Zacharias leaned against the mantel and watched her. She looked incredible. More than incredible, if the truth be told, and with every passing moment the scales tipped a bit further in favor of a complete reconciliation.

It wasn't only the way she looked. She'd behaved perfectly all evening, smiling at her guests, listening to their stories as if nothing interested her more, treating each one as if they were the center of the universe. If his mother could see her now, even she'd have to relent.

Her laughter floated toward him, the soft sound of her voice wrapped itself around him, and her scent lingered in the parlor. He resisted the urge to join her at the door and contented himself with waiting. He'd made a statement just by being here. He needn't go overboard. But it took a considerable amount of effort to keep himself in place.

When the last of the guests departed and Colin closed the door behind them, she turned back to face Zacharias wearing a smile so genuine, another piece of reluctance fell away. At this rate, *he'd* be on his knees to her within the week, begging her once again to forgive him.

While he watched in amazement, she lifted the hem of her skirt, kicked off the slippers she wore, and wriggled her toes, sighing as if nothing had ever felt so good.

Stunned, he averted his gaze away from her ankles, away from the simple gesture of pleasure the old Agatha would have abhorred. But the pull was too strong and he found himself watching her again.

She kicked the slippers out of the way, sending one beneath a chair, and lowered her skirt to the floor again. "I think tonight went well. What did you think?"

He cleared his throat and took a deep breath. "I think it went quite well."

Her smile grew even wider and her eyes sparkled with delight. "I can't tell you how much I appreciate everything you did for me during the evening. Without you, I would have fallen flat on my face."

He battled a smile. "As I said before, it seemed prudent for me to be here."

"Prudent?" She tilted her head and grinned at him. "Is that all, Zacharias? Is that the only reason you came?"

He tried like hell not to respond to her teasing smile. "What other reason would you like me to give?"

His stiff tone seemed to have no effect at all. Her smile grew even more coquettish. "I'd like you to say you're here because you still feel something for me."

He was reluctant to admit that, no matter how true it was. "I feel a tremendous sense of responsibility."

She moved closer and held his gaze. Her skirts rustled and the breeze carried her scent the rest of the way. "Nothing else?"

In spite of his efforts to maintain his dignity, his voice came out gruff with longing. But he would not give in to the temptation to kiss her again. "What else would you like me to feel?"

"I'd like you to say you still care for me." She touched his sleeve, a gentle touch that made him weak in the knees.

He closed his eyes, as if he could block out the rest of his senses that way. "Agatha—"

"Zacharias. Look at me."

He did as she asked—not because he wanted to, but because he was powerless to resist.

"It's time for this madness between us to stop."

He tried quirking an eyebrow. Tried to keep his wits about him. "By that, I assume you mean this madness of your design."

She scowled, but there was no anger in her expression. "Would you stop being so tough? Can't we just put the past behind us and move on?"

He'd give anything to do that, but there was still no guarantee that she wouldn't remember everything some day, that she wouldn't hate him again, that the twins wouldn't suffer as a result.

"I came to your dinner party," he said, "but I can't promise anything beyond that."

She let out a sigh of resignation and turned away. "Speaking of my dinner party, did you know that your mother tried to talk my guests into refusing my invitation tonight?"

The abrupt change of subject caught him unaware. "How do you know that?"

"Lydia and Caroline told me." Agatha looked over her shoulder and held his gaze for a heart-stopping moment. "Did you know she's trying to have the doctor declare me insane?"

Zacharias shook his head quickly, trying to convince himself, perhaps, more than Agatha. "She talks about it, but she wouldn't dare try."

"She *is* trying," Agatha insisted, and the sadness in her eyes tugged at his heart and conscience. "She told Lydia and Caroline not to accept my invitation because I might be dangerous."

Zacharias closed his eyes for a moment, disheartened by this latest bit of news. "I thought she'd confined her outbursts to me."

"Apparently not." Agatha moved a step closer and her scent threatened what was left of his self-control. "So, you knew she felt this way?"

"She has expressed doubts."

"Doubts? She wants to have me committed, Zacharias. She's already trying to convince people that I'm crazy. I think that qualifies as more than a doubt."

He bit back an angry oath and ran a hand over his face. "If you're angry, Agatha, be angry with me. I've ignored her destructive nature for too long."

"I don't want to be angry with you, but I do want you to stand up for me."

She had no idea how often he'd done that already, and he had no intention of telling her.

She searched his eyes carefully. "Do you think I'm insane?"

"No," he said honestly. "I do not."

"Thank you." Her sudden smile lit the room as if a thousand candles burned and a suspicious glitter in her eyes made him wonder if she might be crying.

He pushed that idea away immediately. Still the joy on her face told him he'd made the right decision—for once in his life. "I won't let my mother have you committed, Agatha. I promise you that."

"Will you also help me take my place in society again?"

"Your place—?" He broke off, uncertain just what her place might be.

"I can fight your mother best by letting people see for themselves that I'm perfectly sane. But you saw what a mess I might have made of tonight. I'll do much better if you'll stand beside me. And I don't want to wait for your mother to strike again. If I do that, I'll only be reacting, running around after her and putting out the fires she starts."

Her phrasing was a bit odd, but her point well-taken. "Unfortunately, she can start a great many fires."

"So, will you acknowledge me as your wife again?"

He told himself not to ask the next question, but he had to know how far she intended to go if she was asking him to participate in a charade. "In name only?"

She bit her bottom lip and looked up at him, but she didn't look repulsed by the question. In fact, the quick blush on her cheeks made his heart lighter than anything had for a long time. Her eyes drew him into their depths, her smile touched something deep inside him.

He told himself to turn away. He warned himself to proceed cautiously. He argued with himself that he couldn't afford to let her get under his skin.

But all the logic in the world couldn't affect him now. He gathered her into his arms and kissed her, groaning low in his throat when she opened her mouth beneath his, nearly losing his self-control when she ran her hands down his back. Sensation after sensation flamed through him. Desire, need, and passion went to war with caution—and caution lost.

He plundered her mouth with his, ravaged her with his tongue, let his hands roam along her shoulders, her arms, her back, let his fingertips brush against the soft swell of her breasts. She melted against him and when a whimper of pleasure escaped her throat, he thought he'd lose control right then and there.

He longed to sweep her into his arms and carry her up the stairs to her bedroom. He wanted desperately to toss aside all the pain and anger and bitterness of the past and make love to her right now.

But he wouldn't be responsible for taking *that* step. If they were ever truly man and wife again, it would have to be at her request. Reluctantly, he ended the kiss, but he allowed himself one last, lingering brush of his lips against her forehead.

"For now," he said slowly, "I think it would be best to proceed as we have been. I shall acknowledge you publicly as my wife—but I won't move back into Summervale. Nor will I expect you to perform your wifely duties."

This time, he knew what he saw in her eyes. She was disappointed. And he couldn't help the surge of elation that worked its way through him.

"What about the children?" The question came out so softly, he had to strain to hear it.

Again, the voice in his head urged caution. Again, he shoved it aside. "You really want to spend time with them?"

"I really want to."

The warning voice grew louder. He shook it away. "I see no reason to say no. I will let you see them—as long as I'm there to supervise when you do."

The voice practically deafened him. He was walking on thin ice, taking a dangerous risk, but he'd fallen head over heels in love with her all over again. Or perhaps it would be more accurate to say he'd fallen truly in love with her for the first time. And he wasn't at all certain he had the strength to deny her anything.

If she knew what she did to him with her eyes, if she

had any idea how rickety his resolve became, she'd also realize she could pretty much do anything she damn well wanted to do. And, though Zacharias no longer distrusted her, he wasn't willing to confess everything. Not yet.

He kissed her once more and forced himself to walk away—but it was the hardest thing he'd ever done in his life.

Chapter 12

ZACHARIAS LOWERED HIS fork to his plate and let out a sigh of contentment. "The roast beef was perfect, as usual."

His mother worked up a halfhearted smile. "I'll let Emmaline know you were pleased."

He tossed aside his napkin and reached for his coffee. "None of the servants care one whit whether I'm pleased or not, as long as *you* have no complaints."

His mother's mouth pursed in disapproval. "At least Emmaline's efforts weren't in vain this evening."

"Emmaline's efforts weren't in vain yesterday evening, either. You were here to enjoy the meal, weren't you? And I believe you had a guest."

"Patricia joined me." His mother took another bite and chewed slowly. "It was most kind of her not to leave me alone."

"Then I'm glad you have her friendship." He kept his voice stern, refusing to give in to her attempts to make him feel guilty for dining with his own wife. Leaning back in his chair, he took a steadying breath and decided to broach the subject they'd been avoiding all evening.

"You might as well know, Mother, that I came to a decision last night."

"Did you?" Her eyes turned to flint, but her smile didn't waver. "I'm glad to hear you've come to your senses at last. You don't belong at the sawmill—"

He cut her off before she could go further. "Not about the mill. About Agatha. I made a public statement last night by attending her dinner party."

"I'm well aware of that, Zacharias. I only hope it's not too late to undo the damage."

"The point is, Mother, I don't want to undo it." He sipped his coffee slowly, keeping his movements unhurried. "I've decided to reconcile with Agatha."

All the blood left his mother's face. It came rushing back a moment later and turned her cheeks a deep shade of crimson. "You cannot do that."

"Of course I can. I reached my majority a good many years ago. I'm old enough to make decisions without your assistance."

"You do not need to destroy your life to make that point."

"I'm not destroying my life," he said evenly. "I'm taking charge of it for the first time." He set his cup aside and tossed out the next bombshell. "You should also know that I've agreed to let her see Andrew and Mordechai."

That brought his mother to her feet and earned him a hostile glare. "I forbid it."

"I'm not asking permission, Mother. The decision has been made."

"The decision has *not* been made." Her voice rose with each word. "You will send her a note and tell her you've changed your mind."

"No."

Victoria tossed aside her napkin in agitation. "You can *not* allow that woman near the boys."

"*That woman*," he said, straining to keep his voice level, "is my wife."

"Don't remind me." Victoria stood in a whoosh of

silk and satin, of lace and ribbons, and glared down at him. "If you give in to her now, if you allow her to behave like a mother to those boys, you'll destroy everything I've worked for these past five years."

"And just what is that, Mother? What have you been working for?"

"For you to take your rightful place in society with the proper sort of woman at your side."

"The proper sort of woman . . . or Patricia?"

"They're one and the same, Zacharias. One and the same. Patricia is everything Agatha is not. Agatha is an embarrassment—"

"To whom, Mother? To you?" Gritting his teeth in anger, Zacharias stood to face her. "She's not an embarrassment to me."

"Well, she should be. You should be mortified to have anything at all to do with her. You never should have married her."

"So you've said time and time again." He crumpled his own napkin into a ball and threw it to the table. "But why not, Mother? Because she isn't the sort of woman who'll try to control my every move? Is that the kind of wife you wish for me?"

"I wish you a proper wife." His mother's voice came out clipped and tight. "I wish you the kind of wife who will hold her head up when things get tough, not slink into the shadows to hide. And I wish you the kind of wife who'll react to difficult situations as a lady should—with taste and decorum. You aren't the first man to look elsewhere for your pleasures, but a lady should always pretend not to notice."

"Perhaps ladies should notice," Zacharias muttered, surprising himself with the comment as much as he did his mother.

"A lady would never stoop to discussing something so vile."

Zacharias couldn't resist the urge to bait her. "Perhaps if fewer ladies considered it vile, fewer gentlemen would feel the need to look elsewhere."

The crimson flush returned to her neck and cheeks. "I will remind you who you're speaking to, Zacharias. Kindly refrain from discussing something of that nature in my presence."

"You raised the subject," he reminded her. "And you'll remember something of *that nature* destroyed my marriage. Or more accurately, I destroyed my marriage because I believed the notion that I was right to indulge myself. Agatha and I have discussed it—"

"Which only *proves* she isn't a lady," his mother interrupted.

"On the contrary," Zacharias said with a smile, knowing his mother would consider him insolent. "Agatha is very much a lady, and I've let the opinions of others keep me from my marriage long enough."

"You can't seriously be considering reconciling with her."

"Indeed I can."

"I forbid it," she said again.

"You have no right to forbid me anything, Mother. I'm no longer a boy."

"Then stop behaving like one."

"That's exactly what I plan to do." He took several steps toward her. "I ask you to remember that this is my house, and I am master of it. You are here at my request, but circumstances have changed. If you can't accept my decision to reconcile with my wife, you're free to leave."

His mother's face became horrible in her anger, but it didn't affect him as it once had. "You would throw me out?"

Zacharias stood his ground. "I hope you decide to stay, but only if you can support my decision."

His mother's lip curled. "This is what comes of associating with someone like that woman."

"All the more reason for me to thank her."

"Don't be crass, Zacharias. It doesn't suit you." His mother gathered her skirts and started toward the door. "Perhaps I should ask Dr. Mensing to examine *you*." And with that, she swept from the room.

Zacharias watched her go, alternately enjoying the sensation of standing up to her and worrying about her next move. Because he didn't for one minute think that she'd take this lying down.

Now that Zacharias had agreed to let her see Andrew and Mordechai, the reality made Shelby almost sick with fear. The possibility of seeing Victoria again filled her with dread. The idea of spending more time with Zacharias left her foolishly giddy. If she didn't watch out, she'd pass out from the heat and emotions right here in the buggy. Wouldn't that make a delightful scene as she rode up the lane toward Winterhill?

A trickle of perspiration ran from the back of her damp hair and down her neck. Maybe she should have let Meg style it on top of her head instead of insisting on pulling it back at her nape and securing it with a ribbon, but she'd been almost desperate for a day free of pins and ribbons and loops and curls.

Snapping open her fan, she worked it in front of her face. The air dragged at her, so heavy and humid, it felt as if someone had loaded it with lead pellets. This was the kind of day when Shelby would have cranked the cooler in her car to high and gulped the refrigerated air gratefully.

The buggy hit a deep rut and Colin tossed an apology over his shoulder as he fought with the reins. Shelby worked the fan a little harder, hoping she could keep herself cool, calm, and collected for her arrival at Winterhill. She didn't want to look like a wild woman when the twins saw her for the first time.

This meeting could very well be the final unturned stone that kept her here. Every inch she traveled on the road between Summervale and Winterhill might be bringing her closer to the moment when she had to leave. And every passing second made her long to stay even more than she had the one before.

She'd been a fool to fall in love with Zacharias, but telling herself that repeatedly didn't change the way she felt. She'd have to be on guard against her emotions when she met the children. She'd be an even bigger fool if she allowed herself to grow attached to them as well. She'd simply do what she had to do to put Agatha's family back together and leave. She'd stay focused, she'd ignore Zacharias's smile, his eyes, his shoulders, hands, and arms. She'd forget the way those arms felt around her, put the touch of his lips completely out of her mind. . . .

As if she could actually do that. Shivering with re-membered pleasure, she closed her eyes. He wasn't even here and she was ready to fling herself into his embrace again. She forced her eyes open again and told herself to be strong.

But as Colin turned into the drive leading to Winter-hill, doubt and fear crashed over her again like a tidal wave. What would she say to the twins? How would they react to seeing her? What did they know of Agatha?

Strong, she reminded herself. *Be strong.*

She squared her shoulders as the door flew open and Zacharias came out onto the porch to greet her. She tried desperately to ignore the immediate racing of her pulse and the slowly curling heat that started deep within her when he helped her from the buggy and the rubbery feel of her limbs when he smiled down at her.

"Are you ready?"

She tried to ignore the way his voice, deep and rich and warm, filled every inch of her and managed an an-swering smile and a weak nod. "I am."

He took her arm gently, but he didn't move toward the door. "Before we go up, there's one thing we should discuss. I don't want to tell them who you are. Not yet, anyway."

Knowing it would be much easier to stay detached if they didn't call her "Mama," she nodded. "I don't have any problem with that. They'll probably need time to adjust to me."

"No argument?"

"None."

He smiled slowly. "Will I ever get used to this?"

His reaction soothed her jangled nerves. "You're re-silient," she said with a laugh. "I'm sure you will."

His answering laugh surprised her and the change in his face took her breath away. She'd thought him handsome before, but now . . . How *could* Agatha have resisted him?

She took a ragged breath and smiled brightly. "Is there anything else?"

"Nothing." He touched her back gently and guided her toward the door. "I've told them you're coming, so your visit won't be a complete surprise."

"Who have you told them I am?"

"A friend. There will be time enough later to tell them the truth."

She followed Zacharias's lead through the house, noting details with rapt attention until they finally drew to a halt in front of a door on the third floor.

"This is it," he said, searching her eyes with such compassion she lost another piece of her heart to him. "Are you nervous?"

"Very."

He put an arm around her in a gesture so tender it almost brought tears to her eyes. "Don't worry. You'll be fine. They'll love you."

But her own inadequacy suddenly welled in front of her like a huge gully. "You won't leave?"

"I won't leave."

Forcing a trembling smile, she nodded for him to open the door and stepped inside. The nursery looked different than what she'd expected. Instead of the muted pastels she was used to, the room was bright and cheerful, warm and inviting.

The boys looked up from a game of war they were playing on a braided rug in the center of the room and watched her warily. Two sets of wide cornflower eyes followed her every move. Two heads of pale blond hair caught the sunlight and turned the color of wheat. The stocky one—Mordechai, she thought—shared so many of Zacharias's features, her heart melted. But Andrew must have inherited his features from some other relative. She saw little of either Zacharias or Agatha in him.

Mordechai stood quickly and eyed her as if he suspected her of being an ax murderer. "Who are you?"

Zacharias hunkered down to his son's level. "This is the friend I told you about. Her name is Agatha."

Andrew tilted his head to one side as if he needed to give that some thought. "Is she the mean lady we're not 'posed to talk to?"

Victoria had obviously struck again. Shelby glanced at Zacharias whose face had turned a dangerous shade of red.

"She's not a mean lady," he assured the boy. "She's actually quite nice."

Mordechai gave her another once-over. "Are we 'posed to talk to her?"

"I think it would be nice if you did. She's come here just to see you."

Shelby smiled reassurance at both boys. "Your father has told me a lot about you."

Mordechai twisted his wooden horse in his hands for a moment while he studied her. He looked so serious, Shelby had to fight the urge to laugh. But the urge faded when he shook his head and scowled at her. "I don't want to talk to her. She talks funny."

"Nei'ver do I," Andrew said, turning his back on her firmly.

Zacharias tugged them both back around to face him. "Now, listen here, you two. I insist that you show some manners."

Shelby put a hand on his shoulder to stop him. Much as she longed for them to accept her, she wasn't surprised by their reaction. Not only did they have abandonment issues—which nobody in this century probably understood—but with Victoria setting examples for them, their reactions didn't surprise her in the least.

"Don't force them," she said softly.

Zacharias scowled up at her. "I'll not tolerate rudeness."

"They're not rude, they're babies."

"*I'm* not a baby," Mordechai protested, obviously deeply offended. "I'm five."

"I didn't mean real babies," Shelby assured him quickly. "Of course you're not babies. Look how big you are."

That seemed to mollify him a little. "Andrew's a bigger baby than I am."

Andrew's eyes flew wide in horror at that. "Am not."

"Are too." Mordechai dropped to the floor and walked his horse onto the rug. "Even Grandmama says so."

Shelby chalked up another reason to dislike Victoria. She didn't believe in making those kinds of sweeping negative statements to children, and she resented Victoria for making them about Mordechai and Andrew—especially when they could hear.

When tears pooled in Andrew's eyes, Shelby did her best to reassure him. "Well, I don't think you're a baby. In fact, I'm amazed that you're so grown up for five years old."

Andrew dashed away his tears angrily. "I *am*, too."

"That's perfectly obvious for anyone to see," Shelby assured him. "And I'll say it to everyone I know." That made for a very short list, but Andrew didn't need to know that. She crossed to the carved wooden box that held their toys and perched on the corner. "Do you mind if I sit here for a while and watch you play?"

Andrew sniffed loudly and worked up a shrug. "I 'pose it would be all right."

Mordechai scowled deeply, exactly like a miniature Zacharias. "You won't touch anything, will you?"

Shelby bit back a smile and held up both hands. "I wouldn't think of it."

"Promise?"

She sketched an X over her heart. "Promise."

Mordechai pondered some more. "I guess so," he said at last. "All right, then." He turned his attention back to his horse, whinnied, and made the wooden figure rear on its hind legs. Within seconds, they both seemed to forget about her. But Shelby didn't mind. She enjoyed watching and loved listening to their chatter.

As always, the question of how Agatha could have deserted them nagged at her. No matter what happened between her and Zacharias, how could she have walked away from these two boys? How could any mother walk away from a child?

Jon's accusation came rushing through 130 years to torment her. Maybe she was obsessed with Agatha's decision because of the choice her own mother made. She hadn't thought so when he first suggested it, but she wasn't so certain now.

Zacharias stood again and crossed to stand beside her. "I don't approve of being too permissive."

"I don't approve of being too strict."

"I want them to grow up well-mannered."

She held his gaze steadily. "I want them to grow up loved and happy."

Something flickered in his eyes, but it disappeared too quickly for her to read it. "So do I," he said, his voice soft. "More than anything."

"I want them to live out their lives in Winterhill and Summervale. And to have lots of children and grandchildren so that there's always someone to inherit, and I want the halls of both houses to ring with laughter."

Zacharias glanced away as if he didn't want her to read his expression. "These houses haven't heard much laughter in recent years. But perhaps, together, we can change that."

"Together?"

He turned those incredible blue eyes to look at her and took her hands in his. "If you're still willing."

Tears burned her eyes. Hope filled her heart. Joy sang through her veins. In the next breath, everything inside her froze. That future didn't include her. Zacharias and *Agatha* would change their lives . . . together. It was at once the most beautiful and most horrible word she'd heard in her life.

Whistling under his breath, Zacharias led the boys up the front steps of Winterhill. Every morning for the past three, he'd gone with the boys to meet Agatha. Every morning for the past three, she'd been warm and caring, kind and loving toward them—certainly kinder than Patricia had ever been—and their reservations were fading as quickly as his own had.

The change in her mystified him even as it pleased him, and he congratulated himself on making the right decision. And he was rapidly drawing closer to approaching her about a total reconciliation.

The boys darted in and out of his path, nearly tripping him several times. He laughed at their antics, then wagged a finger at them. "Behave now. Grandmama's probably waiting for us inside."

Just as it had when he was a boy, the threat of Victoria's disapproval wiped the joy from their faces. Andrew straightened his posture; Mordechai frowned. Zacharias gave himself a mental kick for opening his mouth and took pity on them.

Resting a hand on each of their shoulders, he guided them up the front steps. "Why don't you two run upstairs and have tea with Jada. I'll make your excuses to Grandmama."

That earned him two eager smiles and put a matching one back on his own face.

"Really, Papa?" Andrew asked.

"Really. Tell Jada I sent you so she doesn't think you're trying to avoid tea. I'll take care of the rest."

Mordechai threw his arms around Zacharias's legs and nearly knocked him off-balance. Andrew ran up two steps, then caught himself and walked the rest of the way more slowly.

Zacharias grinned after them, watching them tussle up the stairs, listening to their excited whispers. But when he turned back toward the sitting room, his smile faded.

His mother wouldn't be happy with his decision, but it was time she accepted the new order of things.

He straightened his cravat and took a deep breath to steel himself, then opened the door. To his surprise, Patricia sat with his mother near the tea table. She sent him a smile so tremulous, an internal warning bell sounded.

His mother inclined her head slightly. "There you are, Zacharias. You've kept us waiting."

"I've been with the boys," he said, carefully leaving out any mention of Agatha. "I sent them to the nursery to have tea with Jada."

"That's just as well." His mother motioned toward a chair. "There are matters we need to discuss."

The knot in his stomach twisted a bit tighter. He sat where he could easily see both of them and nodded. "Go ahead."

"As you know," his mother said, her voice stiff, "I am disturbed by your recent behavior."

"I'm aware of that. And you are aware that I have no intention of changing."

Patricia studied her fingers intently, as if meeting his gaze might damage her somehow.

His mother's lips thinned. "I'm afraid, under the circumstances, you will have to."

"And what circumstances would those be?"

"Patricia has come to me this morning with some rather distressing news." His mother poured tea into a cup and handed it to Patricia with a smile that sent a chill up Zacharias's spine. "It seems you have again managed to put us all in a difficult situation."

The gleam in her eye made him nervous and Patricia's refusal to look at him made his pulse crawl. "What situation would that be?"

"Patricia is with child."

Everything inside him turned to stone. The room seemed to sweep backward and leave him dangling over a precipice. He tried to tell himself he'd heard wrong, but Patricia's almost bashful glance at that moment warned him he'd heard right.

He caught her gaze. "Is this true?"

"Yes."

He flinched as if someone had landed a blow to his stomach, his heart sank as if someone had tied boulders to it, and his mind raced in a thousand directions at once. Agatha's image formed in his mind, smiling softly, faith shining in her eyes. Faith in him, in their future together, in his love.

He stood and took a couple of jerky steps toward the fireplace. This wasn't a discussion he wanted to have with his mother present. He glanced at her and the triumph shining in her eyes made him stomach pitch and roll. "Would you leave us alone, Mother?"

She hesitated, and for a moment he thought she might refuse. But when Patricia sent her a tight-lipped smile, she relented. "Very well. But I expect you to do what's right this time, Zacharias."

What *was* right? He was married to Agatha. All his hopes for the future centered on putting their marriage back together. But he'd callously, selfishly endangered everything. He couldn't turn his back on Patricia. He *wouldn't* turn from his unborn child. But how could he face Agatha with this news?

When the door clicked shut behind his mother, he let out a long breath. "It's true?" he asked again, hoping against hope that she'd deny it this time.

Patricia's gaze flicked over him quickly, then away. "Yes."

"But how? We haven't been together in months."

"It must have happened the last time we were together."

He thought back quickly. "But that was three months ago. Why are you only now telling me?"

"I wasn't certain until now." She clasped her hands together on her lap and twisted her fingers. Tears filled her eyes and a wave of sympathy mixed with guilt washed over him.

"Of course not." He ground his teeth together and finished his trek to the fireplace. He heard the rustle of

her skirts and knew she'd come to stand behind him.
"May I ask why you brought the news to my mother
instead of to me?"

"Because I knew you'd be angry."

"I'm not angry," he said, turning to face her. "And I
don't blame you. But I can't pretend that I'm happy."
He rubbed his forehead and tried to think. "When will
the child arrive?"

"Around Christmas."

He closed his eyes and tried desperately to think, but
Agatha's face, her smile, her laugh, haunted him. What
a mess he'd made of everything.

Patricia touched his shoulder lightly. "What will we
do, Zacharias?"

"I don't know," he admitted.

"You won't leave me to have this child out of wed-
lock, will you?"

He didn't answer. He couldn't. How could he ask that
of her? But how could he put Agatha aside now? "What
do you want me to do?"

"I want you to keep your promises."

"That seems to be my downfall, doesn't it?" He met
her gaze again, but the look in her eyes hurt him. "If I'd
kept the vows I made to Agatha, none of this would
have happened." He spoke more to himself than to Patricia, but she heard him, of course.

She stiffened and drew her hand away. "You can't
expect me to care about your vows to Agatha."

"No. Of course not."

"And it's not as if you love her or she you. It would
take so little for you to divorce her and make everything
right."

A protest so vehement rose to his lips and the truth
hit him so squarely, Zacharias could do nothing more
than draw a ragged breath. The truth was, he *did* love
Agatha. Try as he might to deny it, the truth remained.
And he'd seen love shining in Agatha's eyes as well.
Just as he saw it now in Patricia's. But he didn't return
Patricia's feelings. In truth, he'd never loved her, though

he'd certainly pretended to, and his lack of honesty had brought them to this pass.

Patricia's eyes narrowed. "You don't love her," she said again, and he could hear an almost desperate note in her voice.

He had only himself to blame for this situation. Only he could make things right. "Yes," he admitted. "I do."

Tears spilled down onto her cheeks. He watched them tracing delicate silver patterns but resisted the urge to wipe them away. "I know that hurts you—"

"*Hurts* me?" She took a jerky step away. "You've destroyed me, Zacharias. You've ruined me." She waved a hand toward her stomach and made a face. "Can you be so callous that you'd take advantage of me and then turn your back on the consequences?"

Her anger didn't surprise him. He'd seen it flare before. "Let's be honest, Patricia. You were as anxious for our association as I was."

"Yes, but only because I believed that you loved me."

"We never spoke of love," Zacharias reminded her, but the fire in her eyes warned him to tread carefully.

"I didn't think we had to *speak* of it." She turned away and put some distance between them. "I love you, Zacharias, and I believed you returned my affection."

"I do care for you—"

She cut him off before he could finish. "*Care?*" Her voice caught and the fire in her eyes flamed hotter. "You *care* for me? You came to my bed and took your comfort when you only cared for me?"

He took a step toward her. "Please, try to understand."

She backed away as if he had a contagious disease. "I understand completely, Zacharias. And now it's time for you to understand. I expect you to keep your promises to me. I expect you to behave like a gentleman and do right by me. I expect you to set aside that crazy woman you've been shackled to and marry me as you should have done in the first place."

"She's not crazy."

Patricia laughed bitterly. "Isn't she? You said yourself that she'd lost her mind."

"Yes, because I was angry. But she did nothing wrong, Patricia. We were wrong, not her. Never her."

"Don't speak to me of her," Patricia warned. "Don't *dare* use her as an excuse for your ill-bred behavior."

"If I could turn back time," he said wearily, "I'd do it. I'd leave you your integrity and I'd keep my own. But that's not possible, and the only thing I can do now is move forward and try to make something of the mess I've created. For what it's worth, I have no intention of damaging your reputation now."

"*My* reputation isn't the one at stake." Her voice rose higher. "If you turn your back on me and reconcile with that . . . that demented shrew, I'll see that you're both ruined."

Utterly defeated, Zacharias watched her sail toward the door and slam it shut behind her. He didn't give a damn about his own reputation, but he cared deeply about Agatha's. And the worst part of it was that if Patricia brought him down, she'd ruin the twins in the process.

Chapter 13

LIFTING HER SKIRTS carefully, Shelby hurried down the rolling hill toward the boundary between Summervale and Winterhill. She looked forward to the time she spent with them each morning, clung to the moments almost frantically, delighted in the stories the boys shared with her and their tiny masculine antics as they battled for her attention and affection.

No matter how many times she'd warned herself to remain detached, she was fighting a losing battle. Or maybe it would be more honest to say that she'd already lost.

The boys had won her heart completely, and Zacharias already held it firmly in his grasp. She alternated between fear that she'd be yanked back to the future at any moment and the growing hope that she might actually be here to stay.

Smiling at the thought, she slipped between the rows of trees and took care to keep her skirts from trailing in the dirt. Once on Winterhill's grounds, she made her way up the short hill and into the sculpted garden. But before she could reach the footpath that would take her to the pond, a dark-clad figure stepped out from behind a hedge and blocked her way.

Victoria.

Shelby slowed her step. She had no choice.

Victoria raked her gaze over her. "I assume you are aware that you're trespassing on private property."

Good morning to you, too, you old bat. Shelby kept her chin high and smiled. "Apparently, you aren't aware that I'm here at Zacharias's invitation."

Victoria made a noise of derision. "I'm afraid you're mistaken. Zacharias doesn't want you here."

"He seems to want me here very much."

Victoria waved a hand in dismissal. "He has always been softhearted, always taken pity on those less fortunate. Surely, you remember that, if nothing else."

Shelby tried to step around Victoria. "I know what you're trying to do, but it won't work. You might as well save your breath."

Victoria held firm. "What I'm trying to do," she said with an icy smile, "is to spare you further embarrassment. Zacharias will never make you his wife again."

"Really?" Shelby laughed softly. "Perhaps you should ask him about that before you say more."

Victoria's eyes narrowed. "He might find it mildly amusing to toy with you for a while, but it will never last. In fact, he has been making plans this morning to end your marriage."

Shelby's heart stopped. She swore it did. She willed it to start beating again and clenched her hands hard enough to make her nails bite into her palms through her gloves. She wanted to shout that Victoria was lying. She longed to force the creepy old woman to admit the truth. But she couldn't make herself speak.

What if Victoria was telling the truth? What if Zacharias was pretending, hoping to throw her off-balance long enough to secure a divorce? She didn't want to believe it of him, but she'd seen the anger in his eyes in the beginning. Though it had faded over the past three weeks, she couldn't be certain that what she saw now was genuine.

She shook her head, slowly at first, then with more conviction. "I don't believe you."

Victoria seized on her uncertainty like a dog with a bone. "Spare yourself further humiliation, Agatha. Go back to Summervale and stay there."

"Zacharias wouldn't humiliate me," Shelby insisted. "Whether you like it or not, he loves me."

Victoria laughed, and the sound sent chills up Shelby's spine. "Zacharias doesn't love you, you foolish woman. How could he?"

"I'm his wife."

"Yes, and it's such a pity. He realized almost immediately after the wedding that he'd made a mistake, and he's rued the day ever since. If you care for him at all, you'll leave him alone and let him find happiness with the woman he truly loves."

"Patricia Starling?" Shelby forced the name out of her swollen throat.

"She's the one he loves, Agatha. She's the one he's always loved. He should have married her in the first place. I know it, you know it . . . and most importantly, *he* knows it."

"I am well aware of their relationship, Victoria. Zacharias has been completely honest with me."

"Has he?" Victoria pretended to be relieved.

"Absolutely."

"Then you know about Patricia."

"Yes."

"And you know why they must marry."

"Maybe I should remind you that he's already married."

Deep red splotches stained Victoria's cheeks. "You're a foolish woman, Agatha. You always have been."

And you're a meddlesome old cow, Shelby thought. Aloud, she said, "I'm a wife and mother, and putting my family back together is the only thing I care about."

"Your family." Victoria's mouth twisted. "You *have* no family, you stupid, *stupid* woman."

Okay, *that* did it. No more Mrs. Nice Guy. No more game playing. Shelby could tolerate a lot of things, but she *hated* being called stupid. "I have nothing more to say to you, Victoria. Now, if you'll excuse me . . ." She tried again to step around the Wicked Witch of the West.

"I don't know why you're pretending not to remember. Nor do I understand what made you change your mind about being a mother to Mordechai and Andrew."

"I am their mother," Shelby reminded her.

"You are *not* their mother."

"You might be a powerful woman, Victoria, but even you can't change the facts."

"Nor can you." Victoria's eyes gleamed and the look of triumph on her face filled Shelby with icy dread. "I don't know why Zacharias ever asked you to raise those children in the first place. I told him he'd rue the day he brought them to you."

Shelby's heart gave a sickening lurch. Her stomach felt as if someone had turned it over. "What do you mean, he brought them to me?"

"Exactly what I said." Victoria smiled coldly. "If he'd listened to me, none of this would have happened."

"When did he bring them to me?"

"When they were born, of course. Are you trying to pretend you don't remember that, either?"

Shelby's hands trembled, her knees buckled, and the day darkened as if the sun had slipped behind a cloud. "Are you saying that I'm not the boys' natural mother?"

"That is precisely what I'm saying."

"Then, who . . . ?" Her voice cracked, and she broke off to catch her breath. She didn't want to believe it, but it made a horrible kind of sense.

"Who is their mother?" Victoria's lips curved into a smug smile. "Why, Patricia Starling, of course. Since you were unable to provide Zacharias with an heir, you can hardly fault him for turning to someone who could."

Shelby had never fainted in her life, but she could feel

the ground rise up toward her and the gardens begin to tilt.

"And now that a third child is on the way," Victoria went on, her voice unrelenting, "Zacharias is understandably anxious to put an end to this charade between the two of you."

Shelby stumbled toward a stone bench on the edge of the path and sat. A third child? Bile rose in her throat and she thought for a moment she might be sick. She reminded herself over and over again that Zacharias hadn't betrayed *her*, but it didn't help. Apparently, Agatha had no place in Zacharias's life or in the lives of the twins.

And neither did Shelby.

"Where is she, Papa?" Andrew tugged on Zacharias's coat and frowned up at him. "Where's Agatha?"

Zacharias glanced toward the path but tried not to let the boys see his mounting concern. "I don't know, son. Perhaps something happened at Summervale to keep her from meeting us."

Mordechai's little face puckered into a tight scowl. "Doesn't she like us anymore?"

"Of course she does." Zacharias hunkered to their level and put an arm around each of their shoulders. "Didn't she kiss your knee better yesterday after you fell?" he asked Mordechai, then gave Andrew's shoulders a gentle shake. "And didn't she let *you* tie her to the tree?"

Andrew nodded slowly. "But then, why isn't she here?"

"I don't know." Zacharias let his gaze travel to the arbor again, hoping against hope she'd be there this time. "I'll stop by Summervale on my way to the sawmill and make certain everything's all right."

"Can we go with you?" Mordechai's eyes lit up with hope. "Can we?"

Zacharias smiled at each of them in turn, hoped he

looked less worried than he felt, and shook his head.
"Not this time."

"Please?" Andrew could hardly contain his enthusiasm over the idea. He bounced up and down, jostling
Zacharias's arm from his shoulders. "Please, Papa. We'd
be good, wouldn't we, Mordechai?"

"Very good," Mordechai said solemnly. " 'Specially
good. We wouldn't even break nuthin'."

Zacharias laughed softly, but he couldn't let himself
give in. With the specter of Patricia's news hanging over
him, yet another confession to make to Agatha, and the
very real threat that she might easily send him packing
casting a giant shadow across his path, he didn't think
it wise to let the boys accompany him.

"Another time, perhaps." He stood again and smoothed
the legs of his trousers. "For now, let's—"

"There she is!" Andrew interrupted. He darted away
and raced across the lawn toward the arbor.

Weak with relief, Zacharias turned to look. But it
wasn't Agatha who strolled through the arbor to meet
them. And seeing Patricia there turned his relief into
quick, sudden anger. For five long years she'd acknowledged the boys only in passing. She'd never once sought
out their company or tried to spend time with them.
Now, apparently, she'd been overcome with maternal
urges.

Clutching Mordechai's hand, he started across the
lawn and watched as Andrew realized belatedly that he
wasn't running toward Agatha. His little legs stopped
churning and he ground to a halt several feet in front of
Patricia who approached him cautiously, one hand extended.

"*That* isn't Agatha," Mordechai said with a scowl.

"No, it's not." Zacharias swung the boy into his arms
and increased his pace. "It's Mrs. Starling. You remember her, don't you?"

Mordechai nodded solemnly. "I don't like her."

Zacharias's step faltered, but he picked it up again.
"Why not?"

" 'Cause she don't like us." Mordechai sent another glare in her direction.

"Of course she does," Zacharias assured him, chucking him under the chin. "What's not to like?"

"No, she don't. She wants us to go 'way."

This time Zacharias made no effort to keep going. He stopped walking and shifted Mordechai so he could see his eyes. "Go away? Where?"

"Dunno, but she told Grandmama we should go 'way soon."

To a damned boarding school, no doubt. Exactly the kind of school his mother had banished him to as a child, the kind of place he'd vowed never to send his sons. "Don't worry about it, son. I don't want you to go anywhere."

Mordechai sent him a fleeting smile. "Nei'ver does Agatha."

No, Zacharias thought, she wouldn't. Not now. He took an unsteady breath and sent up a silent prayer that he hadn't destroyed everything through his dalliance with Patricia. He added another that Agatha would forgive him, but he held out scant hope.

Whatever price he had to pay was just and fair. If he had to spend the rest of his life alone, he'd earned every miserable minute. But it didn't seem right that his sons should have to live without a mother—or that they should have to suffer because he'd chosen the wrong mother for them.

Shelby stared at the spot of blood seeping into the linen in front of her. She stuck the finger she'd pricked into her mouth and swore under her breath. She should have left Agatha's embroidery alone, but she'd been nervous and agitated ever since she ran back to Summervale after her encounter with Victoria, and she'd convinced herself she could manage a few of the simple stitches one of her foster mothers had tried to teach her.

Now, she'd ruined the intricate sampler, just as she'd ruined everything else she'd touched since she arrived.

She stood quickly and searched through Agatha's dresser for an old piece of cloth she could use to scrub out the stain. And she tried to ignore the heavy weight that dragged at her heart. She'd expected Zacharias to come searching for her when she didn't meet him. But the day had nearly slipped away, and he still hadn't arrived.

Logically, she knew it was for the best. But the thought of him married to Patricia tore at her like the claws of some wild beast, and the pain was as real, as physical as the sting of her pricked finger—only a million times worse.

She tried to force it away and to pull herself together. She'd been the worst kind of fool to let herself fall in love with him. She should be angry with him, not hurt and sad. She should be furious that he'd omitted that one important detail when he told her about his relationship with Patricia. But all the shoulds in the world didn't change a thing.

Loneliness filled her. Melancholy dogged her steps. Pain weighted her heart. And fear rendered her almost unable to function. She wasn't certain which she feared most—dying as Agatha in a few short days, staying here and living alone for the rest of her life while Zacharias made a life with Patricia and the twins, or returning to her own time where she would never see any of them again.

Tears filled her eyes and blurred her vision. She tried to dash them away, but they came harder and faster than she could fight. Lowering her face to her hands, she gave in to the pain, to the fear, to the anger, to the hurt of Zacharias's betrayal. Her sorrow began with losing Zacharias, moved to the twins, then shifted to encompass her whole pathetic, lonely life.

She'd been foolish to dream that she could have the family she'd always wanted. She'd always known that family and security weren't in the cards for her. Yet the minute Zacharias looked at her with those incredible eyes of his, the first time he'd wrapped his arms around her, she'd willingly tossed logic aside and rushed head-long into a situation that could only bring her pain.

Maybe she could forgive herself that, but she'd also endangered the twins' family and security. She'd come frighteningly close to keeping them from their mother. And that was unforgivable.

Still battling tears, she crossed to the window and stared out at the rooftops of the town and the river crawl-ing in the distance. Somewhere down there, Patricia Starling was carrying Zacharias's child and waiting to be a mother to her boys. Shelby had nearly destroyed her chance.

She caught her reflection in the glass and glared at her-self for a long moment. Victoria's words danced in her memory, the viciousness of her voice made her feel even worse. No wonder Victoria hated her. No wonder—

Her brain came to a screeching halt and eyes widened as that last thought took hold. Victoria hated her. She'd vowed to do anything she could to drive Agatha and Zacharias apart. And she'd very nearly succeeded.

But what if it wasn't true? Shelby had accepted Vic-toria's news without question. She'd tried and convicted Zacharias without batting an eye. But what if Patricia *wasn't* the twins' birth mother? What if she wasn't now pregnant? What if it was all a horrible lie?

The least she could do was ask Zacharias and give him a chance to deny it. He might be angry with her for not meeting him that morning, but surely he'd under-stand after she explained.

She turned away from the window and ran to the dressing table to pull herself together. She looked even worse than she'd expected—puffy, red eyes; swollen cheeks; and blotchy skin. Lovely. That ought to win Zacharias's heart.

Wishing for a little makeup—foundation and con-cealer, if nothing else—she splashed her face with tepid water left over from her morning toilette. But it didn't make a difference. She still looked like something the cat dragged home from a fight.

Sighing with resignation, she bent forward to take a closer look. Without warning, the reflection changed. The blue eyes and ski-jump nose that were growing less familiar with every passing day formed in front of her. Masses of blond "medusa" curls took the place of the smooth brown chignon.

She froze with her hands on her hair, and a wave of dizziness crashed over her. "No," she whispered. "Not now."

The reflection grew stronger, luring her closer, drawing her toward it.

"No!" She closed her eyes and struggled to resist the mirror's pull. "Not yet. *Please* . . . "

Dizzy with fear, Shelby spun away from the mirror and staggered to her feet. But she could feel Agatha there, hovering, just waiting to reclaim her life and her family. Her heart rocketed inside her chest; and her pulse skipped, jumped, then settled into a steady but too-rapid pace.

Still battling dizziness, Shelby sank onto the foot of the bed and held on as if her life depended on it. And maybe it did.

All her life she'd longed for a place to belong. Now she'd found one, but nothing had changed. She could lose it at any moment.

Somehow having experienced the sense of belonging only made the pain worse. Before, she'd endured a kind of wistful ache, now the thought of going back to the loneliness hurt as if someone had slashed her with the broad edge of a sword.

If she returned to her own time, all these people would be dead. Zacharias, Meg, Colin—even Mordechai and Andrew. How would she get through each day knowing that Zacharias was gone, or that those two energetic little hellions had become old men whose lives had ended? If she went back now, there'd be no hope. No chance of ever seeing Mordechai and Andrew again or of ever spending another moment in Zacharias's arms.

Like someone drawn to the scene of a horrible accident, her eyes strayed back to the mirror. Her image hadn't faded. If anything, it seemed even stronger. "Please don't come back yet," she whispered around the lump in her throat. "Don't make me leave."

The blue eyes widened, and Shelby felt that same dizziness that had once pulled her through time begin to swirl around her again. Without thinking, she ran to the door and hurried out into the corridor. She wanted to get away from that mirror, away from the fate it decreed for her.

Maybe she was making a mistake to run away from it. Maybe her effort would be wasted. Maybe she couldn't outrun the pull of the mirror. But she had to try.

Clinging to the bannister, she started down the stairs. To her immense relief, the dizziness began to fade when she reached the landing. Sobbing with relief, she sat on the window seat and leaned her head against the glass. She lifted her hand and traced the outline of Winterhill, barely visible beneath the bright moon, with her fingertips.

But she knew now that it was only a matter of time.

Exhausted and disillusioned, Zacharias climbed the stairs toward the nursery. He'd tried all day to keep his mind on business and forget, even for a time, the encounter that faced him. Soon—very soon—he'd have to tell Agatha about Patricia's child. But not yet.

No matter which solution he chose, someone would be hurt. He couldn't bear the idea of hurting Agatha further, couldn't imagine his life without her, but he'd never be able to look himself in the mirror again if he turned his back on his child.

He wiped his face with his hand and stretched his neck to work out the knots of tension that had been there all day. Just now, he wanted to spend some time with the twins. If anything could clear his mind, hearing their laughter would do it.

Reaching the third-floor landing, he started down the corridor. But just as he made to step into the nursery, the sound of his mother's voice caught him up short.

"Do you know who she is?"

"A friend of Papa's." Mordechai sounded nervous. Almost frightened.

Zacharias ducked out of sight, certain without being told that his mother was talking about Agatha. Curiosity made him hover there.

"A friend?" His mother sounded relieved. "Nothing more?"

"No, Grandmama."

"Good. Excellent. It's very important that you two do not befriend her."

Zacharias clenched his fists in anger and forced himself to listen further.

Andrew protested his grandmother's warning. "But we like her. And Papa says—"

"You mustn't like her," Victoria interrupted sharply.

"Agatha is nice," Mordechai argued. "She likes us."

"She doesn't like you." Agitation made his mother's voice louder. "And you mustn't listen to your father when he tells you to be nice to her. His brain has been addled."

Anger surged through Zacharias like a prairie fire. Though he'd long realized how bitter she was, he could scarcely believe she'd stoop this low. Again, he forced himself to hold his place and his tongue.

"What's 'addled' mean?" Andrew's voice, this time, filled with confusion.

"Touched," his mother explained. "His mind has been weakened, much like what happens when a lady spends time in the sun."

"Is Papa ill?" Mordechai sounded worried.

"I think perhaps he is," Victoria said, "but he isn't aware of it. So we mustn't let him know that we've had this discussion."

Zacharias had heard enough. He would not tolerate her putting such a burden on their tiny shoulders. To purposely frighten them and then warn them not to seek comfort? Never in his life had Zacharias wanted to strike a woman—not even when Agatha had been at her worst—but listening to his mother purposely frightening the boys made him wish she were a man for just ten minutes.

"But if Papa is ill," Andrew said slowly, "shouldn't we take care of him?" He broke off when Zacharias stepped into the doorway and glanced from him to his grandmother in confusion.

"I couldn't help overhearing your conversation," Zacharias said, fighting to keep his voice low so he wouldn't frighten the boys further. "It was interesting, if not quite accurate."

Mordechai dropped his wooden soldier and ran to him. Andrew still held back. Zacharias lifted Mordechai into his arms without taking his gaze from his mother's face. "Your grandmama is only teasing you, boys. My brain has not been addled, nor am I ill."

"Teasing?" Mordechai looked at his grandmother, then back at Zacharias. "But why?"

"Because she knows how important it is for you to like Agatha."

His mother shot to her feet. "Stop it this instant, Zacharias. I will not allow you to influence these poor children."

"I might give you the same warning, Mother."

Her face reddened and her nostrils flared. "I have only their best interests at heart."

"On the contrary." Zacharias tried to keep the anger from his voice, but only because he had no wish to frighten his sons. "I'm quite certain you're only concerned with your own best interests."

"You are being insolent."

"And you are being vicious and hateful." Zacharias forced himself to take a steadying breath, kissed Mordechai lightly on the cheek, then set him on the floor.

"We shall continue to see Agatha," he assured his children, who both looked confused and a little frightened. "And we shall hear no more from Grandmama on the subject."

"I warn you, Zacharias—"

"No, Mother. *I* warn *you.* You shall say nothing more to the boys about Agatha." He stepped away from the door and motioned her toward it. "You and I shall continue this conversation elsewhere."

He couldn't remember a time in his life when he'd been this angry. The day Agatha had refused his repeated apologies and forced him out of Summervale came close, but even that hadn't been as bad. Agatha had been stiff-necked and haughty, and she'd insisted that he remove himself and the boys from her presence, but she hadn't purposely tried to hurt someone else. And not for want of the opportunity.

She could have made trouble for Patricia. She could have exposed the entire truth to the light of day. Instead, she'd simply turned away from him. And she'd kept the truth quiet for five long years.

His mother, on the other hand, was methodically trying to destroy another human being. And that he wouldn't tolerate.

Now, he followed her down the stairs and led her into the library, where he shut the door firmly between them and the rest of the world. "I warned you once," he said before she could try to take over. "This is twice. I shan't give you a third chance. If I hear so much as a whisper from you about Agatha, you shall not spend another night under my roof."

His mother glared at him, angrier than he'd ever seen her. Angrier than the day he'd announced his intention to marry Agatha. Angrier than the day his father had lost a veritable fortune on a horse race. Angrier, even, than the day he'd told her the truth about the breakup of his marriage.

"You are behaving like a fool," she warned. "You will destroy everything."

"I'll destroy *nothing*." His voice rose but he made no effort to soften it. "You are the one who wants to destroy, Mother. You always have. And I warn you for the last time, I won't tolerate it under my roof."

She stood for a moment, her chest heaving with anger. Before his eyes, she transformed into someone weak and tearful. "I'm only trying to protect you, Zacharias."

He marveled at her acting skills, and shuddered to think how often he'd been taken in by them. "I almost wish I could believe you, Mother. Unfortunately, I've seen you in action too often." He ignored the pathetic slump of her shoulders and went on. "I want to make sure you understand me. I will not have you talking to the twins about Agatha. I will not tolerate your interference in my marriage—"

"And *I* will not be spoken to this way." His mother abandoned the pitiful pose the instant she realized it wasn't working. She opened the door and stood in the doorway, in one of the most majestical poses Zacharias had ever seen. "I am still your mother, Zacharias, whether you like it or not. And I insist that you show me the respect I deserve."

"For the first time in my life, I'm showing you *exactly* the respect you deserve," he assured her an instant before the door crashed shut between them.

Still seething, Victoria climbed the stairs quickly. She couldn't believe the way Zacharias had spoken to her. She couldn't believe the lack of respect, the blatant hostility.

And why?

She'd done nothing wrong. Obviously *that woman* was having more influence on him than she'd thought.

She brushed past a chambermaid in the hallway, so upset she barely heard the girl's mumbled apology, then ordered a second maid from her bedroom, and slammed the door behind her. Only then did she let down her guard.

She was worried. Terribly, terribly worried. If Agatha

got her clutches into Zacharias again, all her efforts would be in vain. All her hard work would be for naught.

Why couldn't Zacharias see how right she was? Why couldn't he understand how wrong Agatha was for him? He was, she thought sadly, too much like his father. Too stubborn for his own good. And far too softhearted.

Well, Victoria hadn't let Hugh's bleeding heart stop her from doing what she knew was right. And she wouldn't let Zacharias's, either. One way or another, she'd put a stop to this madness.

Chapter 14

ZACHARIAS LEANED BACK on the grass and watched the boys playing with Jada on the edge of the pond. Beside him, Agatha sat stiff as a board on the marble bench. She'd kept her eyes riveted on the boys constantly since she arrived that afternoon—almost as if she didn't want to look at Zacharias. Almost as if she knew.

Scowling slightly, Zacharias wondered if that were possible. No, he assured himself quickly. She couldn't know. Who would have told her? Patricia? The very thought made him laugh. His mother? He could no more imagine his mother willingly speaking to Agatha than he could pigs suddenly taking flight.

Still, the last time he saw Agatha, she'd been flirtatious and coy. She'd behaved as if putting their marriage back together was the most important thing in the world to her. Today she seemed remote, distant, and preoccupied. *Something* had brought about the change in her.

He wondered if she'd gotten back a piece of her memory, if she was beginning to remember why she hated him. Each sidelong glance, every gentle sigh sent chills of foreboding up his spine.

Giving himself a stern mental shake, he reminded himself that it was possible something else had affected her mood. Something totally unrelated to himself. He wondered if perhaps he should try to broach the subject, then decided he'd be wiser to leave her alone.

It might be that she was simply more irritable than usual. Zacharias had noted when they shared the same roof that she became more moody at a particular time of the month, and he suspected that might be the case today. He didn't pretend to understand the workings of the female mind, but he knew when to keep his mouth shut.

Plucking a blade of grass, he stole another peek at her. A light breeze had pulled a lock of hair loose and tossed it across her face. He had to force himself not to brush it back from her cheek. Their relationship still teetered on a very thin ledge, and he couldn't relax enough to make physical overtures. Those would have to come from her—if they ever did.

When she turned her eyes toward him, he quickly shifted his gaze to the cloudless sky and observed, "It's a beautiful day today, isn't it?"

"Yes, it is."

"Just right. Not too hot, not too cool." He busied himself rolling up his shirtsleeves and waited for her response.

"Yes." Her voice sounded flat and lifeless, but she watched the boys with such obvious wistfulness, he reassured himself again that she hadn't reverted to her old ways.

He shifted his weight onto his elbow. "Would you like to take a stroll around the pond?"

She skimmed a glance across his face, then turned away again. "No thank you. I'm fine here."

Nodding slowly, he contented himself with watching the twins. She let the silence stretch between them for a moment or two, then let out a heavy sigh.

Maybe it *would* be wiser to leave her to her thoughts, but her strange mood had him jumping out of his skin.

"You seem different today," he said casually. "Is something wrong?"

"Wrong?" Her gaze shot to his again. "Why do you ask that?"

"Only because you're quieter than usual." He rolled a blade of grass between his thumb and forefinger. "You haven't had any of your memory return, have you?"

She shook her head quickly, but the slight narrowing of her lips made him wonder if her answer was completely honest.

"You'd tell me if you did remember anything, wouldn't you?"

She didn't speak for a long moment. So long, he started to get nervous. "Yes," she said at last. "Of course I would."

Well, that was a relief. To lose her now, after knowing her this way, would be even more painful than the first time. He shifted up onto his elbow again. "Then what is it that has you looking so sad?"

She seemed to argue with herself for a moment, then came to a decision and turned her gaze full on him. "Isn't there something *you'd* like to tell *me*?"

"Tell you?" He sat up and brushed the grass from his lap, all the while thinking furiously. He could honestly answer "no" to that. He didn't *want* to tell her anything.

But she knew. She *must* know. The look in her eyes said she did. And the lump of disquiet that dropped into the pit of his stomach confirmed it.

"There is one small matter I would like to discuss with you," he said hesitantly. "But I thought I'd wait until we were alone." He stole a quick glance at her, noted the slight coloring of her cheeks, and felt his heart sink.

"Maybe you should tell me now. The twins are too far away to hear."

She'd paved the way for him, but he still couldn't make himself step onto that rocky path. He'd been down it before and he knew how treacherous it was.

When he didn't speak, she frowned slightly. "Okay.

If you won't tell me, then let me ask you something. Is Patricia Starling pregnant?"

The blood left his face and his heart stopped beating for one long, agonizing moment. He had to force himself to speak. "Yes."

He steeled himself for anger, for hatred, for the sharp sting of her tongue. Instead, she let out a shaky breath and tears filled her eyes. "I see."

Drawing together the tattered edges of his courage, he stood. "No, Agatha, I don't believe you do. Patricia is with child, and the child is mine. But it happened before . . . before the change in you. Long before you ever suggested the possibility of a reconciliation. I haven't been with her in months."

Her eyes dragged slowly across his face, but she said nothing.

Anger would have been far easier for him to deal with than the immeasurable sadness he saw on her face. He could have railed against hostility, defended himself hotly against accusations, and justified himself a thousand ways if she'd given vent to her spleen as she usually did. But her sadness left him without a single defense.

"And the twins? Are they her children, too?" Her voice came so softly, it was scarcely more than a whisper and the breeze nearly carried it away.

He forced himself to breathe, to speak the truth, though the pain of it was sharper than any he'd ever felt. "Yes."

"Why didn't you tell me?"

He mopped his face with his palm. "Because I lost you the first time, and I couldn't bear the thought of losing you again."

"So you lied." She stood slowly to face him. "And what now? Will you divorce me so you can marry her?"

"I don't want to do that." He battled the urge to touch her, to hold her. It would have been a selfish act, and he'd caused too much pain from selfishness already. "I love *you*."

"How can you say that when you don't care enough to tell me the truth?"

"The truth," he argued, "would have served no purpose."

"The truth always serves a purpose." She flicked an unreadable glance at him. "Always. The truth might hurt, but lies hurt far worse."

She didn't understand. Maybe she couldn't understand his need to give his sons a future. After all, she had no children of her own. But if they had any hope of a future together, she had to accept that this was one compromise he would not make. "I would do anything—tell any lie, hide any secret, if doing so protected someone I love."

A faint pink stained her cheeks. "Can a lie ever protect someone?"

"Indeed it can. The only lie I've ever told—the only *real* lie—protects those I love most dearly." When she looked as if she might argue, he held up a hand to stop her. "Do you know what life would be like for Mordechai and Andrew if the truth were ever revealed? The stamp of illegitimacy would destroy their lives and crumble their futures as surely as if the earth shook beneath their feet."

She swept another glance over him. "Maybe. But they also need to know who their mother is. There is nothing in this world more important than that—not even fortune." She went on before he could frame an response. "If I'd known the truth, I would never have tried to take her place. I'd have stepped aside and let you put your real family together."

His mind raced, trying furiously to come up with a compelling argument that would convince her not to step aside now. "*You* are my family," he said at last. "And so are they. They've grown to love you—"

"And I love them." Tears pooled in her eyes and spilled onto her cheeks. "But I still have no right to keep them from their real mother."

"You have *every* right." Agitation made his movements jerky, his voice harsh. "You are my wife. It's you I love, not Patricia."

"And I love you, Zacharias. More than I ever imagined I could ever love anyone."

That gave him hope, made him more determined than ever to make her understand. "Then how can you turn your back on everything we could have together? If you truly love the twins, how can you turn away from them again? What kind of love is that?"

Pain flashed across her face and made him wish he could take back the last question. "A far more honest love than one that would let me think I gave birth to them and then abandoned them. More honest than letting me feel guilty for being a horrible mother."

"I was wrong to lie to you," he admitted, taking a step toward her, "but you must understand why I did it."

"I do understand." She moved away from him again. "I understand that you want to give the twins the best of everything, but all your money and houses and prestige is *nothing* if you don't give them honesty." She glanced at the twins with such longing, he thought her heart would break—and his along with it. "Give them the truth, Zacharias, if nothing else."

Before he could stop her, she started across the lawn toward the arbor. Frustrated beyond measure, cut to the quick, more angry with himself than he'd ever been, he could only stand by helplessly and watch her.

What now? Shelby wondered as she paced the length of her bedroom. She'd forced herself to walk away from Zacharias, but she couldn't stop the tears that had been falling steadily ever since. He'd lied to her. And though she understood his reasons, though she wanted to forgive him and go on, she couldn't let selfishness cloud her judgment.

This wasn't her life. This wasn't about Shelby Miller or her heart. It was about the future. About Zacharias, Patricia, the twins—and the new child on its way.

But oh! How it hurt to realize how wrong she'd been.

How desperately she wished he could understand what the boys truly needed.

Hating herself for failing, she stopped in front of the mirror and studied Agatha's reflection. She hadn't been able to save Agatha's marriage or her life, but she had sent Zacharias to Patricia's waiting arms. She had provided the twins with a mother. She'd rewritten history.

So, now what?

Would she go back to her own life, or live out the few remaining days of Agatha's alone? She'd grown so used to this body, this reflection, these dark eyes and thick brown hair, she could scarcely remember what her own looked like.

If she did return to her own time, what would she find there? Maybe Agatha was busy making a mess of *her* life. Except there was nothing to make a mess of. She had no family to destroy, no husband to lose, no children to hurt, no parents to alienate. She had nothing. Not in her own life, not in this one.

She stalked to the window and stared out at the gardens below just as a tall man in an unrecognizable livery descended the front steps, mounted a horse, and rode off down the lane. It was so odd to see a visitor at Summervale, curiosity immediately took the place of self-pity.

Racing across the room, she threw open the door and ran down the stairs to the entry where she met Meg holding a small white envelope in one hand and wearing a look of utter bemusement.

"Who was that?"

"Someone from Grand Oaks." Meg held out the envelope almost as if she were sleepwalking.

"Grand Oaks?"

"Orville and Lydia Englund's estate." Meg dropped her hands to her side and waited, but she was obviously curious about the contents of the envelope.

Shelby knew what it was, but her hands still trembled as she broke the seal and pulled out the single sheet. "It's an invitation to Lydia's ball."

"Lord above." Meg clasped both hands to her mouth and rolled her eyes heavenward. "I never thought I'd see this day again. You've done it, madame. You've made your way back in to society."

"Yes." But what a hollow victory. Shelby lowered the invitation to her side. "I've managed to secure one invitation."

"One invitation from Lydia Englund," Meg pointed out. "If Mrs. Englund wants you at her ball, other invitations will soon follow. You can count on that. Now . . ." Meg tapped her finger against her chin thoughtfully. "What will you wear?"

Shelby shook her head quickly. "I'm not going."

"Not going?" Meg stared at her as if she'd lost her mind. "Why ever not? This is what you've been working for."

"It's what I *was* working for. But things have changed."

Meg eyed her suspiciously. "What *things*?"

"Things." Shelby sat on the bottom step and confided, "I've recently learned that Patricia Starling is the twins' mother."

Meg scowled at her, but she didn't seem even slightly surprised.

And the realization dawned quickly. "You knew, didn't you?"

Meg nodded, but she looked miserable. "I knew."

"And *you* didn't tell me, either?" The sting of Meg's betrayal ran almost as deep as Zacharias's. Shelby shot to her feet again. "How could you keep something like *that* a secret? How could you let me believe that *I* was their mother? That I'd abandoned them?"

"You *should* be their mother," Meg said firmly.

"But I'm not." Shelby kneaded her forehead with her fingertips. "I'm not. Patricia Starling is. And it's not right to keep the truth from the twins."

Meg's eyes narrowed. "You can't mean that you think they should be told. That their illegitimacy be exposed."

"I think they deserve to know who their mother is. I

think they deserve to know their mother's love."

Meg let out a derisive laugh. "A mother's love? From Patricia Starling? You don't remember what she's like, do you?"

"Does it matter? She's their mother—"

"And you're Zacharias's wife."

"Not for long." The words fell between them like pebbles dropped into a deep well.

Meg's mouth fell open. "You'll step aside and let Mrs. Starling sink her claws into Zacharias? You'll let her manipulate him through those poor children?"

"He belongs with her," Shelby said firmly. "And so do the twins."

"He belongs with you." Meg's voice rose with each word. "Patricia Starling would be a horrible mother to those sweet boys. She cares nothing for them."

"You don't know that."

"I do know," Meg insisted. "For five long years you've cooped yourself up in this house and let the world think the worst of you for turning your back on your own children. Meanwhile, the woman who *really* abandoned them dances around town with a glowing reputation and behaves like the belle of the ball."

Shelby opened her mouth to argue, then stopped and tilted her head to look at Meg. "Say that again."

"Being noble is one thing, but you've carried it too far. Patricia Starling is the one who's turned her back on those children, not you. She's in that house at least three times a week and yet she never spends a moment with them. Now, I ask you, what kind of mother is that?"

"Maybe she's just concerned about keeping the truth hidden."

"And maybe she's more concerned with dancing and winning gentlemen's hearts than with anything of substance." Meg's face puckered with disapproval. "If she wanted to see those boys, she could. There's nothing stopping her. Nobody else would ever have to know. But Jada tells me that she has never once set foot in that nursery."

"Yes, but—" Shelby broke off and kneaded her forehead again. "But she's their *mother*. They need her, and I have no right to take her place."

"You can toss me out on my ear for saying this," Meg said firmly, "but deciding what's right and what's wrong isn't that easy. At least, it never has been for me. If it was that easy, I daresay scarcely a soul alive would ever do wrong."

Miraculously, the weight began to lift from Shelby's heart. She studied the invitation for a long moment, arguing with herself, weighing the pros and cons, trying not to let her feelings for Zacharias cloud her judgment.

"If you'll pardon me for saying so," Meg blurted after watching her with obvious impatience, "it's time you started listening to your heart once in a while. You've let your head rule you for far too long."

"But what if I do the wrong thing?"

"You might," Meg conceded. "But isn't there an equal chance you'll do the right thing? If I'd listened only to my head, I'd never have given Colin the time of day. And I certainly wouldn't have stayed here with you these past five years." She took Shelby's hand in hers and squeezed it gently. "You didn't ask for my advice, but I'm giving it anyway. Take the risk. See where your heart takes you. Stop looking at the world as if everything is all one way or the other. It isn't. Maybe you *didn't* give birth to those boys, but they belong with you."

Shelby wanted to believe that, but she couldn't. "There's one more thing you don't know," she said. "Patricia is pregnant again."

"Another child?" Meg's brows knit, the edges of her mouth curved into a deep frown. "Just now?"

"Yes. So, you see—"

"What I *see*," Meg interrupted, propping her hands on her hips, "is that it's an amazing coincidence that another child would turn up just as Zacharias realizes he's in love with you. And if you don't see that, you're looking at this entire situation with your eyes shut."

Shelby began to tremble so badly she had to sit on the step to steady herself. "You think it's a trick?"

"I think it's a lie," Meg said. "A dirty lie cooked up between Patricia and Victoria together."

Shelby stared at her, unable to speak, scarcely able to think. Of course. *Of course.* Victoria would go to any length to keep Agatha and Zacharias apart. Concocting a story like this certainly wouldn't be beneath her. She knew how deeply Zacharias loved his children. She knew he'd do anything to protect them, to make their lives better.

"So?" Meg demanded. "What are you going to do about it? Are you going to sit here on the stairs and let that woman waltz away with your husband, or are you going to fight for what's yours?"

Shelby smiled slowly. She met Meg's gaze steadily, drew a deep breath, and stood to face her. "I'm going to fight."

Zacharias paced the sitting room at Summervale, waiting for Agatha to join him. Why had she sent for him? What did she want of him? He hoped for the best. He feared the worst.

Scowling, he glanced at the mantel clock and heaved a deep sigh. She'd kept him waiting for nearly fifteen minutes already, and if she didn't come soon, he was likely to jump out of his skin.

What could be keeping her?

He paced to the window and frowned out at the gardens. He could see Colin pulling weeds along the path and Meg talking to him. He heard Colin's quick laugh. Meg's almost girlish smile. They had a fine love. A deep and abiding love that had stood the test of time. Zacharias would give anything to know the joy of it.

"Zacharias?"

He'd been so engrossed in his thoughts, he hadn't heard Agatha come in. At the sound of her voice, he spun around to face her. She wore a simple gown of sapphire blue that flattered her immensely and showed off her figure from the waist up in such a way that warmed his blood.

He couldn't lose her now. Not *now*. And he wouldn't. Not while there was a breath left in his body. Whatever she had to say, she'd have to hear him out first.

But he could scarcely manage to say, "You wanted to see me?"

"Yes." She motioned for him to sit and, amazingly, sat close enough for him to catch her scent each time she moved. "I've been thinking about our situation."

"As have I," he assured her.

"I've thought a lot about our marriage, about the twins, about this new child—"

"Before you say anything," he interrupted, "let me speak, please. You have every right to be angry with me. Every right to turn me away for good. But I realize now that if there's any chance at all for us, it will be through the truth."

She lifted those incredible brown eyes to his. "Thank you."

"Don't thank me yet." He scrubbed his face with his hand. "I love you, Agatha. I've always loved you, but I love you more now than I ever did in the past. No matter how it might appear to you after you hear what I have to say, I need you to believe that."

She nodded slowly. "All right."

"The children love you, too. Remember that."

She glanced at her fingers and took a deep breath. "I love them, too."

"Yes, I know. That's what makes this so damned difficult to say."

Agatha lifted her gaze again and tilted her head to one side in that endearing way she had of late. "What is it you're trying to tell me, Zacharias?"

"I'm trying to tell you why our marriage broke up."

She looked for a moment as if she might stop him, then bit her bottom lip and nodded slowly. "All right."

"You don't remember, of course, but I was in love with you before our marriage. We knew each other only slightly before the war. You were too young to catch my notice. But from the moment I came home from the war and saw you, I knew you were the only woman I'd ever love. You embodied everything *I'd* been fighting for. Charm, grace, and beauty."

To his surprise, tears glimmered in her eyes. "I think that's the most beautiful thing anyone's ever said to me."

Her words touched him, and he smiled for the first time since he'd made his decision to come clean. "We married quickly, and I suppose we both had expectations of the other that we soon realized the other couldn't or wouldn't live up to. I thought you would be as warm and charming in private as you seemed to be in public. And you thought I'd be equally gallant. Neither of us were. The marriage grew strained."

"Because I didn't welcome you in our marriage bed."

"That's what I told myself." Too agitated to sit still, he shot to his feet and began to pace. "Or maybe the fault was mine because I wasn't willing to give you time to grow accustomed to that side of our relationship."

"Maybe we were both at fault."

Zacharias turned to face her. She'd never expressed a sentiment like that before, and her willingness to take part of the blame soothed him. "Perhaps. But I take full responsibility for what happened next. In frustration, I turned to Patricia. My mother had long expected me to marry her, but I wasn't interested once I found you. When things began to sour between us, I started wondering if my mother was right. And Patricia was only too willing to convince me she was."

"And so you began your affair." Again, there was no note of accusation. In fact, it seemed as if she was helping him with his confession.

"Yes. There was a time, before the war, when I thought I might marry Patricia. My mother certainly wanted me to, and she spent the entire war assuring her that I'd return and marry her. When I didn't . . ." He lifted his shoulders in a helpless shrug.

Agatha stepped in to help again. "She turned to someone else."

"Yes." He mopped his face again and sent her a weak smile. "Her husband died shortly after their marriage, so she was lonely and more than willing to listen to me pour out my frustrations about our marriage. I didn't turn to her intending to start an affair, but one thing led to another, and before I really knew what I was doing, there we were."

This time Agatha didn't help. But neither did she look as if she'd like to kill him. He took heart in that.

"Of course, you began to suspect, and it hurt you deeply. Things between us became even more strained. Occasionally, even with the affair, you and I would . . ." His voice trailed off as he searched for the right way to say what came next.

"Make love?"

He stared at her in disbelief. "Yes. But only occasionally. I needed an heir—or so I convinced myself. It seems I was a master at justifying my actions."

"We all do that," she said softly. "I'm sure I justified a few things, too."

Another piece of apprehension fell away. "Perhaps. You conceived twice, and both times lost the child. Dr. Mensing warned you about having another, and with that last enticement for continuing our relationship out of the way, our marriage fell completely apart. In hindsight, if I'd ended my relationship with Patricia and been a decent and loving husband to you, I think we could have patched things up between us. But your disappointment over not being able to have children was difficult for me to deal with. And I convinced myself that I had every right to do what I was doing."

Again, that soft smile curved her lips, and again she surprised him. "Just as I convinced myself I had every right to be cool and aloof."

"After several months," he said, "Patricia informed me that she was with child. She was unhappy, to say the least. She was a widow with a reputation to protect."

"Just as she is now."

He nodded miserably. "She wanted to end the pregnancy, but that idea frightened me. She assured me that many women took drastic measures like that, but I was afraid she'd die. Or maybe it's more accurate to say that I was afraid she'd be successful and rid herself of my child."

"It would have been a great risk," Agatha agreed.

"I told myself it was my only chance to have children and came up with a plan that would not only protect Patricia's reputation, but give me the heir I so desperately wanted. She left town and gave birth, not to one baby, but to two. I had them brought to me and, in my pomposity, presented them to you as a fait accompli."

"I didn't know about them before that?"

"No. I kept it from you, and no one else but one of Patricia's maids knew." He let out a heavy sigh. "Since you'd already withdrawn from society, I knew we could easily pass them off as our children. So I came to you, foolishly expecting you to welcome my bastard children into your home and raise them as your own."

Agatha's face changed suddenly, and she showed the first sign of anger. "Don't call them that," she warned. "Don't *ever* call them that again. Mordechai and Andrew are not to blame for what happened. You, Patricia, and I are the guilty parties."

He took a step backward, shocked to the core not by her defense of the children, but by her acceptance of part of the blame. "Those were your words," he told her gently. "Not mine."

Her anger faded as suddenly as it appeared. "Then I apologize."

That shocked him nearly as much as her anger. Maybe even more. "As do I, Agatha. As do I."

"It seems we both have much to apologize for."

"Indeed, we do." Suddenly exhausted, he sat in a wing chair and gripped the armrests. "You demanded that I leave and take the children with me. After much arguing, I managed to convince you not to reveal the truth about the childrens' birth and in exchange, I left you with Summervale and promised never to darken your door again. We continued that way for a long time."

"Five years."

He nodded. "Until you lost your memory. When I realized what happened, I told myself I had every right to keep the truth from you. But I was wrong. My wounded pride made me behave like an ass." He rubbed his forehead with his fingertips. "For what it's worth, I'm deeply sorry. I've brought unbelievable heartache upon you out of nothing more noble than selfishness."

"Yes," she said with a smile, "but it seems I've brought unbelievable heartache upon you out of self-righteousness."

"And now, with history about to repeat itself, I can't blame you for wanting to send me away again. . . ."

Her smile widened even further. "No, Zacharias. I don't want to do that."

His heart lurched and his pulse raced. He couldn't believe his ears. "You don't?"

"No." She reached across the space between them and put her hand over his. Her touch warmed him to the deepest part of himself. "I love you, Zacharias. And I love the children. If Patricia truly doesn't want to be their mother—"

"She doesn't want to be their mother," he assured her, "although she would dearly love to be my wife."

"So I hear." Agatha squeezed his hand gently and held his gaze. "Unfortunately for her, you already have one."

He turned his hand over and held hers tightly. "But what about this new child?"

She tilted her head and sent him a sly smile. "Are you certain there is a new child? Or does the timing strike you as a bit too convenient?"

Zacharias could only stare at her in stunned silence for what felt like forever. "It's possible," he managed at long last, "and I want to believe that more than I've ever wanted anything. But what if she's telling the truth?"

"If she's telling the truth, we'll deal with it. If she's

not, I'll bet you a million dollars she suffers a miscarriage after you tell her that we're not divorcing." At his hopeful smile, she went on. "We've let pride stand in our way far too long, Zacharias. I think it's about time we put it aside and concentrated on what's best for Mordechai and Andrew—and for us."

He was quite certain his heart would leap out of his chest, but he couldn't ignore one last obstacle to their future. "Can I be sure that you won't change your mind when your memory returns?"

"As sure as I can be." Her gaze flickered away. "But if that happens, Zacharias, please remember that as I am now, at this moment, I love you with all my heart."

It was a strange way to put it, but he didn't care. He crushed her to him and covered her mouth with his own. Fire raged inside him and he couldn't seem to catch his breath. She wrapped her arms around his neck and gave herself to the kiss with more passion than he'd ever known.

He touched her lips with his tongue and groaned with pleasure when she opened hers to welcome him. All the years of hurt, all the angry words, all the distrust faded to nothing.

They could face anything, as long as they were together.

Chapter 15

SHELBY STOOD AGAINST one wall and watched the crowded dance floor. Gowns of satin, silk, and brocade swirled endlessly in front of her. Music drifted from the orchestra loft, punctuated by laughter and conversation.

So far, so good. She'd done her best to ignore the curious stares and whispered speculation behind raised fans. She'd done her best not to care, to keep her smile pasted in place, to keep her chin up and her shoulders back.

Zacharias had been wonderfully attentive all evening, but seeing Patricia Starling for the first time and realizing how incredibly lovely she was made all the feelings of inadequacy that had plagued her since childhood come rushing back.

Shelby would have felt much more confident if Patricia had been a snaggle-toothed, knotty-haired woman with three eyes instead of a porcelain doll. Every once in a while, when she saw Patricia swirl past in the arms of a partner, or when she heard her laugh tinkling clear as a bell, she wondered if Zacharias would really be able to resist her.

Trying to put her doubts aside, needing a moment to pull herself together, Shelby dodged behind a potted plant. To her dismay, instead of the solitude she longed for, she found herself face-to-face with the one woman she least wanted to see.

Patricia Starling.

She was even more beautiful close up—cute little button nose, big blue eyes, perfect wheat-colored hair piled high on her head and cascading in ringlets to her smooth shoulders. She had straight, even teeth; and breasts rose out of her neckline like silicone implants.

Even in Agatha's body, Shelby felt like a runner-up.

Patricia seemed almost as surprised at the encounter as Shelby, but she recovered quickly and sent her a doe-eyed look. "Good evening, Agatha."

"Patricia."

"How lovely to see you again."

Shelby believed that like she believed in the Easter Bunny, but she did her best to smile. "Thank you."

Patricia flicked open her fan and waved it slowly in front of her perfect face. "You and Zacharias are creating quite a stir this evening."

Shelby forced herself not to look away, even though looking into Patricia's face made her think of Zacharias making love to that woman, which was a mental image she didn't want. She tried to ignore her sudden flare of jealousy. "I'm sure we must be. But I'm equally certain people will soon get used to the idea that our marriage is on firm ground."

"Is it?"

"Yes." *No thanks to you.*

Patricia let her gaze travel over the couples swirling together on the dance floor. "Then perhaps they will get used to it—in time."

Even her voice was perfect. Not too high, not too low, not breathless or childish. Shelby said a silent prayer of gratitude that she didn't have to face this woman in her own medusa-haired body. "No doubt some new scandal will come along to divert their attention."

Patricia didn't acknowledge by so much as a faint blush that she might easily provide that scandal. "I'm sure you're right," she said, letting her gaze travel the length of Shelby as if she saw something distasteful. "Still, I suppose they'll all be abuzz with it for a little while. And you really can't blame them. You have been rather . . . aloof for the past few years."

"Yes." Shelby flicked open her fan and used it to stir the rancid air between them. "But that's all changed now."

"How nice. At least for as long as Zacharias remains at your side. I'm sure Victoria is thrilled by your reconciliation."

Shelby had never been good at insincere conversation. Patricia was obviously a master. Her air of confidence and her apparent certainty that she would walk away with Zacharias made Shelby livid. "Whether or not Victoria approves isn't something I worry about."

"Perhaps you should. She can be a formidable opponent. When she decides she wants something, she'll do whatever it takes to get it."

"Maybe," Shelby said slowly, "but I am equally determined to keep my family together."

"Perhaps the choice won't be yours to make," Patricia suggested.

Shelby forced a chilly smile. "Then I consider myself fortunate that Zacharias is equally determined not to let anyone come between us."

Patricia looked out over the dance floor, found Zacharias deep in conversation with a group of men, and betrayed her first sign of agitation. "You seem quite assured that you're headed for a fairy-tale ending."

"I'm well aware that there's no such thing," Shelby assured her. "But I also know that trust and honesty are as essential as love to make a marriage work. And, since Zacharias has been completely honest with me about the obstacles in our way, I am assured that we'll be able to face them together."

Patricia lifted her chin almost imperceptibly, but she

gave no other sign that Shelby's words had found their mark. "I'm well aware of how you feel about honesty, Agatha. You've made yourself quite clear in the past."

"Maybe I once believed in secrets," Shelby said firmly, "but no longer. Now, I'd like nothing more than to have them all exposed to the light of day."

Patricia's gaze flicked over her rapidly. "You would expose everything?" She laughed coldly. "Somehow I find that hard to believe."

"Would you like to try me?" Shelby's hands trembled with anger, but she refused to back down. "Maybe we could persuade Dr. Mensing to confirm or deny the most recent threat to Zacharias's peace of mind."

Patricia's demeanor faltered, but only for a moment. "I'm sure Dr. Mensing would be happy to offer his opinion about your mental stability."

"That wasn't the threat I had in mind." Shelby took a step toward her, so angry she could have chewed nails and spit them out again, but she forced her voice lower. "I'm not going to roll over and play dead this time, Patricia. I'm not going to run away while you and Victoria try to destroy my family. And I'm certainly not going to let you waltz into Andrew and Mordechai's lives and pretend to love them just so you can share Zacharias's bed without fear for your reputation."

With a confidence she didn't feel, she turned her back on Patricia and rejoined the others. Only after she'd put some distance between them did she acknowledge the trembling of her limbs, the numbness in her knees and legs.

She'd thrown down the gauntlet. She'd issued a declaration of war. And she had a sick feeling she wouldn't have to wait long to find out how the enemy would respond.

Shelby took Zacharias's hand to alight from the carriage and let it linger there. After her conversation with Patricia, the rest of the evening had gone perfectly. The scent of magnolias and jasmine filled the air. The silence of the night was unbroken by anything but the soft clip-clop of the horse's hooves as his driver led the carriage a discreet few feet away.

Zacharias put an arm around her waist and led her toward the front door. "Did you enjoy yourself?"

"Mm-hm." Shelby leaned against his shoulder and smiled up at him. "So much it was positively wicked. Did you?"

He grinned at her. "Holding you in my arms as we danced and showing you off to all those old buzzards was the most fun I've had in ages."

Shelby's heart turned over and a slow warmth crept through her. "For me, too."

Zacharias slowed his step and turned her to face him. "You are so incredibly beautiful. Have I told you that lately?"

Shelby laughed softly. "Not in the last ten minutes."

"Then I've been amiss." He wrapped both arms around her and pulled her close. "You are incredibly beautiful. Breathtakingly beautiful." As if to prove it, he lowered his lips to hers and stole her next breath.

The moonlight, the scent of him so close, the feel of his arms around her, were all too much. Shelby melted against him and surrendered herself to the kiss. It wasn't smart, she told herself, but she couldn't deny herself the pleasure.

Zacharias tightened his embrace and worked magic on her lips, her body, her soul. She felt so right snuggled here against his chest, wrapped in his arms, and she gave herself to the moment. She didn't care about the future. She only knew that at this moment she belonged right here.

He ended the kiss, but he didn't release her. Instead, he trailed kisses up her cheek, pressed his lips to her temple, and whispered against her skin. "Agatha." It was little more than a sigh, but it brought Shelby back to her senses with a resounding crash.

Agatha.

She'd never imagined that she could fall in love with

someone who belonged to another. Never in her wildest dreams. She had no right to his kiss, his embrace, his love. But it was so hard to turn away. "I should go up to bed. It's getting late."

Zacharias pulled her into his arms again and nuzzled her cheek softly. "I could go with you."

Every cell in her body screamed for her to say yes. Every inch of her heart longed to take his hand and run up the stairs. And some convoluted piece of logic told her she wouldn't be wrong to do it. After all, this was Agatha's body. There would be nothing wrong with Agatha making love to her husband.

Except that Agatha wasn't here and Shelby knew that making love to Zacharias would be much more than a joining of bodies; it would be a sharing of souls. And for that reason, she couldn't say yes.

She forced herself to resist the almost overwhelming physical need. She didn't want to leave him without hope and lose him for Agatha completely. "Soon," she promised.

"But not tonight?" His breath tickled her ear and sent another coil of desire spiraling through her.

"I think we should wait a few days longer."

This time he stepped away. "Why? I love you, Agatha. And you love me, don't you?"

"More than you can imagine."

"Then why? We *are* married, you know."

Shelby thought frantically for a way to hold him at arm's length. What could she possibly say that wouldn't ruin everything? If only . . .

She bit her lip and held back a smile. There was one way that would probably make him have second thoughts. "It would be . . . inconvenient tonight." She sent him a wide-eyed look that she hoped conveyed the rest that a woman of the 1800s would never say. Or at least she didn't *think* one would say. Maybe the women were more open about their monthly cycles than the history books indicated. "If you can be patient for another three or four days, I'm sure I'll be back to normal by then."

Zacharias looked confused for a second, then his eyes widened slightly and a flush climbed his cheeks. "Oh, yes. I see. Of course." He walked toward the wicker chair and snagged up his hat. "Yes."

Shelby tried not to laugh at his obvious discomfort, but really, men were so silly about something that was perfectly natural. Even in her own time, with television and magazine ads hitting them in the face all day, some men still got embarrassed when women discussed *that* subject.

Zacharias brushed another kiss to her forehead. "If you promise I won't have to wait long, I'll content myself with this." He trailed his lips to her mouth again. "And this."

Shelby's resolve nearly disintegrated at the silky touch of his tongue against her lips and the heavenly brush of his fingertips against her breasts.

Just as she was about to toss principles to the wind, he released her and opened the door. "Until tomorrow?"

The evening breeze teased her feverish skin. The moonlight traced his outline and made her long to run after him and tell him she'd changed her mind. Instead, she nodded mutely and watched him walk away. But she knew this night would be one of the longest of her life.

Meg stood at the bottom of the stairs, waiting, forcing herself not to run to the window to see what was going on outside. Agatha and Zacharias had been out there for an awfully long time, and Meg just hoped that meant things were progressing as they should.

Everything was in readiness. She'd put fresh sheets on Agatha's bed, filled the room with candles and flowers. She'd even laid out Agatha's most provocative nightgown, but if things went according to plan, Agatha wouldn't need it.

She waited a few minutes longer, but when they still

didn't come inside, curiosity got the best of her. She
crossed to the door, leaned her ear against it, and
strained to hear voices. She couldn't hear anything at
all. Moving to the window, she nudged back the curtain
just far enough to see outside.

When she saw Agatha and Zacharias locked in an embrace so passionate it nearly took *her* breath away, it
was all Meg could do not to cheer aloud. Grinning, she
hurried back toward the stairs and waited.

It seemed to take forever for the door to open, but
when it did, Meg put on a serious, noncommittal expression. It would never do for them to think she'd been
spying on them.

To her dismay, Agatha came in alone and she heard
the unmistakable sound of a carriage driving away.
Stunned, Meg took Agatha's wrap and followed her up
the stairs. "Where is he?"

"On his way home."

"Why?"

"Because it's late and I need to go to bed."

Meg scowled at the door. "What's wrong with him?
He should have found it impossible to leave you."

"He wanted to come in with me," Agatha said, trailing
her fingers along the bannister. "I sent him away."

Meg stopped with one foot poised to hit the landing.
"You did *what*?"

"I sent him away." Agatha laughed at the look on her
face. "Oh, don't worry, Meg. I haven't ruined anything."

"You *hope* you haven't." Meg shook her head in disbelief and wished she could shake some sense into the
missus. "After everything you've done to win him over,
what good do you think will come from turning him
away?"

"Believe me," Agatha said, "it really was necessary."
Agatha sent her an unreadable glance. "It's my time."

Meg warned herself not to overstep her bounds, but
really! If anyone knew the truth about *that*, Meg certainly did. "Even during the worst of times you've never

lied to me before. And I don't understand why you'd start now."

Agatha's smile evaporated and her eyes rounded. "I'm sorry, Meg. I forget that you know as much about me as I do."

"I know enough to know it isn't your time," Meg said sharply. "And I'll bet Zacharias knows it, too. You've used *that* excuse often enough in the past."

"I have?" Agatha let out a weighty sigh and cast a glance behind her. "Great. Then, maybe I have ruined everything."

Her obvious distress made Meg feel marginally better. "So, why did you send him away?"

Agatha's shoulders sagged and her step slowed. "I had to, Meg. Believe me."

"You didn't *have* to do any such thing." Meg straightened the shawl over her arm. "You haven't been leading him on, have you? Making him think you'll change your mind about the private areas of your marriage when you have no intention of following through?"

"No. Of course not. At least not intentionally."

"Then why?"

Agatha moved to the window seat and sat down on it with a thump. "Oh, Meg, I'm so confused. I don't know what I'm doing."

Meg could have told her that. But she refrained. "Then send Colin to intercept him before he gets home. Get him back here and put your marriage back on track while you still can."

"I can't." Agatha's eyes filled with tears. She wiped them away with her fingertips and sighed again. "I can't."

"I don't know why not. He's your husband, isn't he?"

"That's the problem." Agatha turned her watery eyes on Meg. "Oh, Meg, I so desperately need someone to talk to. Someone I can confide in."

"I'm here, madame. You've always confided in me." And that was true, Meg assured herself, at least as much as Agatha ever confided in anyone.

"If I tell you something, something completely un-believable, will you think I'm crazy?"

"Of course not."

Agatha patted the window seat beside her. "Then sit here with me and let me try."

Meg's irritation faded a bit more. Though she was un-comfortable sitting beside Agatha, she did as she was bid. The child obviously needed her help, and Meg was will-ing to do whatever it took to set things right again. "What is it, dear heart? What's wrong?"

The childhood endearment seemed to touch Agatha deeply. The tears ran a little faster and she shuddered with those still unshed. "I warn you, Meg, it *sounds* crazy."

"Don't you worry about how it sounds. I've heard just about everything after a lifetime with Colin, so just get it off your chest."

"You haven't heard anything like this," Agatha warned. She took a long, deep breath, shot a glance at Meg, and blurted, "The truth is, I'm not really Agatha."

Lord above. Meg gripped the edge of the window seat to steady herself. Not really Agatha? The missus really *had* lost her mind.

"You don't believe me."

"Of course I do," Meg said quickly, suddenly terrified of saying the wrong thing and setting her off. "Of course I do."

"No, you don't. You think I'm crazy, and I don't blame you. I told you it sounds demented."

"Well, now, madame," Meg said, struggling to keep a smile in place and a soothing note in her voice. "If you aren't Agatha, who are you?"

"My name is Shelby Miller, but I'm *in* Agatha's body. That's why you can't tell."

"In her body?" Meg said a hasty prayer and resisted the urge to stand up and put some distance between her and the missus.

"Yes. I'm from the turn of the century—the *next* cen-tury. I was zapped here one day while I was trying to figure out how to save the twin houses from being demolished."

"Zapped." The word squeaked out around the nugget of fear clogging Meg's throat.

"Yes, zapped. Or dropped. Or . . . I don't know, Meg. I don't know how I got here. All I know is, here I am. And I'm supposed to fix something here, but I don't know what. At first, I thought I was here to mend the rift between Agatha and Zacharias. Then, I thought I was here to be the twins' mother. Now, I don't know what to think."

"*I* think the excitement of the evening has been a bit too much for you." Meg started to stand, but Agatha clutched her hand and pulled her back to her seat.

"It's not the excitement of the evening. Think about it, Meg. You said yourself how differently I've been behaving lately."

"Yes, of course. You have, indeed. And if that's what you think—"

"I'm not making this up."

Her eyes looked so clear and bright, Meg wondered for a moment if there might be some truth to the story. She gave herself a mental shake. Nonsense. She was ill, that's what she was. Not a visitor from some other century—some other millennium. "I think we should get you up to bed. You'll feel better in the morning."

"No!" Agatha pulled away sharply. "Meg, look at me. Look straight into my eyes. Do I look the same to you?"

Meg wasn't at all certain what she was supposed to say. She glanced up the stairs, wishing she hadn't sent Colin ahead to bed.

"Please, Meg?"

Hesitantly, Meg did as she was told.

"Can you see a difference?"

Meg nodded. She saw a difference, all right, but she was suddenly fearful about what kind of difference it was.

Agatha shot to her feet. "I know I look like Agatha. I know that I sound like Agatha. But I'm *not* Agatha.

But how can I expect you to believe me?" She paced to the other end of the landing and back again. "What's something I couldn't possibly know if I was Agatha?" She tapped her finger against the side of her cheek as she walked, and her agitation made Meg more nervous than ever.

"Perhaps a good night's sleep . . . ," Meg suggested softly. If she could just get the poor mad thing upstairs to bed without upsetting her, she'd wake Colin and send him to Winterhill for Zacharias. Surely he'd know what to do.

Agatha stopped pacing and wheeled around to face her. "I don't want a good night's sleep. I want to convince you that I'm telling the truth."

Meg kept her voice gentle and soothing. "But I already believe you."

Agatha scowled so hard, a ridge formed above the bridge of her nose. "Oh, stop it, Meg. You think I'm totally off my rocker, and I can't say I blame you. But it's true. My name is Shelby Miller. I was born in 1971. I work at Winterhill as a caretaker." She scratched her head and swore softly—which was nearly enough by itself to convince Meg she was telling the truth—then went on talking gibberish and frightening Meg half to death.

She told about women wearing mens' trousers instead of proper dresses, about machines that carried people through the air and others that moved them about on the roads without horses. She made up nonsense about politics, about literature, about inventions, about wars and fashion and a hundred other things Meg couldn't even begin to follow.

It was enough to boggle Meg's mind and scare the devil out of her at the same time. She certainly *sounded* convincing, and if Meg hadn't known better, if she hadn't had a level head and kept her wits about her, she might even have started to believed her.

At long last, Agatha gave up and sat on the window

seat again. She looked so defeated, Meg's heart went out to her. "I can't convince you, can I?"

"You must admit," Meg said carefully, "it sounds a bit far-fetched."

"I know it does." Agatha kneaded her forehead then moved her hand to the back of her neck. "That's why I haven't said anything until now."

"Can I offer some advice, madame?"

"Please."

"Go upstairs to rest. By tomorrow, you'll be fine again—I'm sure of it." That wasn't completely true. Meg wasn't sure of anything. "You've been under quite a strain these past few weeks, what with your memory loss—"

"I didn't lose my memory," Agatha interrupted. "I made that up to excuse all the things I don't know about Agatha's life."

"Of course you did." Meg put an arm around her shoulder and tried to lead her up the remaining stairs. "So, you'll rest tonight, and tomorrow you can begin again. You'll get your life with Zacharias back in order and everything will be just fine."

"I can't get my life with Zacharias back in order," she argued mildly. "I can't make love to him because he's not my husband. But he thinks he is, and I have to pretend that he is until Agatha and I switch places again—if we ever do."

Meg patted her shoulder gently, soothingly, but she kept her moving up the stairs. "Put it all out of your mind for tonight. If you still believe it tomorrow, we'll talk about it then."

"You're patronizing me," Agatha said with a frown.

"I'm taking care of you, just as I've always done." Just as she always would. It was a pity, but Meg finally had to concede defeat. Victoria Logan was right, the horrid old bat. Agatha wasn't sane.

Not by a long shot.

Chapter 16

"SO THE EVENING went well."

Zacharias lit a cigar and smoked silently for a minute or two in the comfortable leather chair. He watched the smoke drifting lazily toward the ceiling, listened to the muted conversation buzzing around him, and pointedly ignored Philip's question.

"It went well," Philip went on, "yet you went back to Winterhill to your own bed."

Zacharias flicked ash into the ceramic tray at his elbow. "I told you, the evening was an unqualified success. I couldn't have asked for anything more."

Philip pointed accusingly with his cigar. "I can read you like a book, my friend. I know you better than anyone does. *Something* went wrong last night. Now what was it? Patricia? Your mother? What?"

Zacharias took another long drag from the cigar and shook his head slowly as he exhaled. "My mother was a paragon of virtue. Patricia didn't make a scene. Agatha was a model wife. I'm telling you, Philip, the evening went splendidly."

"Then why are you here with me today instead of moving your things back over to Summervale?"

Zacharias took another slow drag from his cigar. "I'm not ready to move back to Summervale yet. Agatha and I are taking our reconciliation slowly."

Philip's brows knit. "Is that your choice, or hers?"

"We made the decision together." The lie didn't come easily, but Zacharias wasn't about to admit, even to Philip, that she'd rebuffed him again, or that she'd used the same excuse she'd used so many times—far too many times for it to be true—during the early stages of their marriage.

"I see," Philip said, nodding skeptically. "And you expect me to believe that."

Zacharias wondered why he'd never noticed his friend's cynical nature before. Or at least why it had never irritated him as it did today. "Why not? It's true."

"Because I know you, remember?" Philip propped his cigar in an ashtray and glanced around to make sure they couldn't be overheard. "This is *me* you're talking to, Zacharias. If you didn't spend the night at Summervale, it wasn't your idea."

"Your opinion of me is hardly flattering," Zacharias said, his tone purposefully brittle. "I am perfectly capable of spending spend time with a beautiful woman without expecting the evening to end in the bedroom."

"Of course you are." Philip sent him a superior smile. "Especially when the woman is your wife and the very issue at stake *is* the bedroom."

The observation hit a bit too close to the mark for comfort. But pride kept Zacharias from admitting it. "What is it you want from me? Would you be satisfied if I confessed that my wife turned me away at the door?"

Philip's smile faded. "Did she?"

Zacharias didn't answer, but apparently his silence was answer enough.

Philip picked up his cigar again and studied it thoughtfully. "I see. And did her sending you away make you change your mind about reconciling?"

Had Philip sounded even slightly condescending, Zacharias would have refused to answer. But the worry in his eyes and the genuine concern in his voice unlocked something inside. "No." He smoked for a second or two, then stubbed out his cigar and leaned forward with his arms on his thighs. "The outcome might have been the same, but she seemed completely different. She was as eager as I was, Philip. I swear she was. She's never been so responsive. But when I suggested that I accompany her upstairs, she pulled away and made an excuse to send me home. Maybe I'm being foolish, but I could swear she was as disappointed as I was."

"And now you're more determined than ever to win her over."

"Exactly." Zacharias leaned back in his seat and shook his head. "Though maybe it's a fool's errand."

"And maybe not." Philip turned his cigar over and over in the ashtray. "You say she pulled away when you suggested that you accompany her upstairs?"

Zacharias nodded.

"And before that she was responsive?"

"Very."

Philip's scowl deepened. "Tell me, Zach, how did you win her the first time?"

Zacharias wagged a hand in the air. "I wooed her, just as any man would."

"Well, then . . . ?" Philip raised his eyebrows expectantly.

It took a moment for his meaning to sink in, but when it did, Zacharias scowled thoughtfully. "Are you suggesting that I woo her again?"

"I think it might be preferable to the way you've been behaving. Good Lord, man, what do you expect? She is a woman, after all. Women like pretty things. They like to be wooed. And if you want the outcome I think you do, it seems to me you might try a softer method than suggesting you join her in her bedroom."

Zacharias growled in irritation, but he grudgingly admitted to himself that Philip might have a point.

Philip grinned at him. "In the business world, the direct method is best. With women, it's not the one I'd recommend."

"I'll not play games," Zacharias warned.

"Soft words and poetry isn't a game, it's a strategy." Philip lowered his voice even further. "And if you want Agatha in your bed again, I suggest you consider it."

"I'll not start lying to her again."

"Hell, man, I'm not suggesting that you *lie*. I'm simply suggesting that you make the suggestion more palatable."

"And suggesting that the idea of sharing a bed with me is so unpalatable I need to resort to treachery in order to lure my own wife there?"

"To me, the idea of sharing a bed with you is very distasteful, but it might not be to her."

Zacharias sent him a dark scowl. "Your jokes aren't helping, Philip."

"Neither is your foul mood. Honestly, Zacharias, take the poor woman some flowers. Write her of your heart's desire. Tell her how much she means to you. Women need to hear that kind of thing."

Zacharias supposed there was some truth in that. He loosened his cravat and shook his head. "It seems odd that I'd be reduced to wooing my own wife. . . ."

"As I understand it, man, that's what we'll spend the rest of our lives doing. But you've had a taste of the alternative. Can you honestly say you'd prefer to spend the rest of your life alone at Winterhill—with your mother?"

The suggestion left Zacharias cold. He held up both hands to stop Philip from saying more. "You've made your point, and much as I hate to admit it, it's a good one." He let the idea grow on him for a minute or two, then laughed softly. "I'll do it. I'll woo her again." But as Philip turned to find a waiter who could bring him some wine, Zacharias wondered if it could possibly be that easy.

Would Agatha respond to pretty words, or would she merely turn up her nose? His pride had taken a beating at her hands once before, and he had no desire to leave himself open to another wound. If Agatha hadn't changed so dramatically, he wouldn't even consider wooing her.

But she was different. He loved her as he'd never thought it possible to love any woman. And the thought of spending the rest of his life without her left him colder than the fear of possible rejection.

So, he'd try to woo her again. He just hoped he hadn't forgotten how.

Candlelight danced across the desktop, bathing the blank sheets of paper at Zacharias's elbow in shadow. Outside, a stiff wind blew against the house, rattling the windows and souring his disposition. The twins had been asleep for hours. His mother had long ago climbed the stairs to her rooms, and he'd sent Abraham and the other servants to bed. There was no reason for everyone to go without sleep.

Besides, he didn't want or need an audience to this particular failure. Swearing in frustration, he crumpled his most recent effort into a ball and tossed it at the wastebasket on the floor. It landed, as so many of the others had, several inches away on the floor.

He'd been at this for hours already, and so far every word he'd penned sounded either trite, foolish, childish, or lecherous. Just how *did* one go about writing a love letter? What did one say?

Had it been any other woman, Zacharias could probably have managed a decent letter. But this was Agatha. Agatha. The woman who'd rejected him soundly, who'd once destroyed nearly every ounce of confidence he had.

Rubbing his eyes, he pushed away from the desk and began to pace. His cravat lay abandoned on a chair atop his coat. His boots lay on their sides on the floor. Now, as he strode past the window, he rolled up his shirt-sleeves and thought.

The task shouldn't be this difficult. He had only to list Agatha's fine qualities, expound a bit on her beauty, declare his love, and be done with it. But the right words seemed to hover just out of his reach, and as the night pressed on his mind seemed encased in fog.

Pushing aside the curtain, he stared at the blackness of the night. The clock on the mantel chimed one o'clock and prompted a yawn that brought tears to his eyes. He dashed them away and tried to knead a knot from the muscles in his neck.

The truth was, he felt like a fool. His feelings for Agatha ran deeper than he had words to express, and the last thing he wanted was for her to think him ridiculous. Or too pushy. Or disgusting.

How could he tell her that the change in her made him love her more completely than he'd ever loved anyone? How could he express the wonder he felt each time he looked into her eyes? How could he say those things without insulting the woman she'd once been?

Perhaps a love letter wasn't the answer. Perhaps he should concentrate on another method of wooing her. But what? Not flowers. The old Agatha would have thrown them back in his face. Not jewelry. He'd tried that once before and failed miserably. Certainly not music. His singing voice made dogs howl.

He battled another yawn and started to turn away from the window, but the sudden flare of a light through the trees caught his attention and rooted him to the spot. The glow came from the top floor at Summervale, and he wondered if Agatha was having as much trouble sleeping as he was.

He imagined her standing on the top level, looking out the window toward Winterhill. He could almost see her wearing nothing more than her dressing gown and her thin nightgown, her thick, dark hair cascading to her shoulders and beyond. He could almost smell the scent of the lavender she'd worn at the ball and feel the touch of her hand. If he closed his eyes, he could have imagined himself kissing her, holding her, touching her.

He shook himself soundly. To imagine any of those things would be tantamount to self-inflicted torture. He'd be a fool to think of the day when he could make love to her again, to imagine the soft touch of her hands on his body, to dream of the sensation of his skin touching hers, the soft light of pleasure in her eyes and the whimper of ecstacy coming from her throat. . . .

Need, stronger than any he'd ever felt, tore through him. Desire, more powerful than he could remember, filled him. Yearning so overwhelming he could scarcely breathe racked him.

He stood that way for a moment, watching the light and indulging in his silent, horrible battle, then slowly lowered the curtain back into place, ran his hand across his face, and let out a ragged breath.

He glanced at the writing desk, at the crumpled paper on the floor surrounding it, at the pen and ink waiting for him. Maybe he didn't know what to say, but if there was any possibility that he could win Agatha's heart through words, he'd figure it out if it took the rest of his life.

Two full days had passed without word from Zacharias, and Shelby had grown so nervous she didn't care what anyone thought of her. Two long, tortuous days with her body and her mind going through misery, reliving every look, every touch, every kiss, every smile. Two agonizing days while Meg watched her suspiciously, just waiting for another sign of madness.

Anything could have happened since she saw Zacharias last. Patricia could have retaliated for the way Shelby had talked to her at the ball. Victoria could have concocted another scheme. One of the twins might have been taken ill. Zacharias might have changed his mind. Dr. Mensing might even be preparing commitment papers for her.

She couldn't stay cooped up inside Summervale, or she *would* go mad. She couldn't sit here for one more second, twiddling her thumbs and waiting for Zacharias to call on her. But she couldn't sneak past Meg's vigilant eye to call on him.

Still, she needed to do something. Something that would ground her and help get her thoughts in order. Something that would help push aside the longing and the regret at having sent Zacharias away.

She could almost hear Jon's voice taunting her from the "real" world—the world that grew less real to her every day. *You can't rewrite history, Shelby.*

Oh, but she could. She had. And it had been frighteningly easy.

She dressed quickly in one of the simple cotton gowns she'd had Meg alter so she could wear it without the corset, slipped into an old pair of slippers she didn't mind ruining, and hurried downstairs. She found the old straw bonnet she used to protect Agatha's skin from the sun and hurried out into the garden.

Working in the soil had always calmed her, and today was no exception. The earth felt warm and rich beneath her fingers, and she soon lost herself in the simple pleasure of working with nature. The sun caressed her shoulders through the fabric of her gown and she gave in to the urge to feel the sun on her face, her legs, and arms.

Tossing aside the bonnet, she hiked the skirt to her knees, loosened the pins in her hair, and shook it loose. She tilted her face to the sun and closed her eyes. Immediately, all her worries rushed in to disturb her again.

Had she been wrong to turn Zacharias away? Had she lost him forever? Could she win him back? What if she seduced him?

A delicious shiver shook her, but she forced it away. No matter how much she loved him, she couldn't make love to him without telling him the truth first. She'd pulled the truth from him—grudgingly at times—and she'd hate herself if she tricked him. Worse, *he'd* hate her once he learned who she really was. And she couldn't delude herself into believing he wouldn't. The truth always worked its way to the surface. Always.

Guilt for hiding it from him this long doused the gentle flames of desire that warmed her. She hated deceit. She believed in truth. But she'd spent nearly a month

lying to the man she loved. Looking him in the face,
kissing him, letting him open his heart to her and lying.

How sympathetic was *that*?

She had to tell him. The trouble was, she didn't know
how. She'd nearly frightened Meg to death with her confession. What would Zacharias think if she blurted out
her story? He'd probably give in to his mother's demands and put her in an institution. Or divorce her and
run back to safe, sane, devious Patricia.

That thought brought her up short. Was she any *less*
devious than Patricia? No, she realized with a rush of
guilt. Not one bit less. Zacharias was surrounded by
women who'd lie to him for their own ends. She had no
right to pass judgment on Patricia or Victoria when she
was doing the same thing to him. She couldn't say she
loved him out of one side of her mouth and lie to him
out of the other.

She didn't know how long she sat that way before she
heard footsteps crunching in the gravel. Her eyes flew
open and she blinked rapidly, trying to adjust to the sudden, bright glare.

"Agatha?"

She recognized Zacharias's voice before she could see
more than his shadow, and her heart flipped over in her
chest. As her eyesight adjusted, she could tell his gaze
was riveted on her bare legs but she couldn't read the
expression on his face.

She tossed her skirt back into place and scrambled to
her feet quickly, embarrassed that he should find her
looking so disheveled.

He averted his gaze quickly and studied the clumps
of weeds and dirt she'd tossed onto the path. "You're
busy, I see."

"I was just pulling a few weeds—nothing earth-
shattering." She made a vain attempt to do something
with her hair.

To her surprise, he reached out and stayed her hand.
"Leave it. I like it that way."

Her heart lurched into overdrive at the touch of his

hand and her knees threatened to fold and land her right back on the ground when she looked into his clear blue eyes.

She lowered her hand slowly, wishing he'd pull her into his arms and take her breath away, sweep her from her feet and carry her upstairs, make her his and remove this paralyzing doubt from her mind.

But he did none of those things. He dropped his hand and toyed with a sheet of paper he held in his other hand. "I . . ." He broke off uncertainly, averted his gaze quickly, and tried again. "I've seen a light upstairs the last two nights. Have you been having trouble sleeping?"

"Some. But why have you been awake so late?"

"I've had business to attend to." His gaze flitted across her face, then away again.

"At one in the morning? Is something wrong?"

"No." He shifted his weight and sent her a halfhearted smile. I was taking care of some correspondence."

"For the sawmill?"

"Yes. . . ." Again that uncertain gaze caught hers. "No. Not exactly."

She waited for him to go on, but he didn't. His hair caught the sunlight and invited her fingers to lace through it. "It must have been important to keep you up so late."

"It was."

Again Shelby waited. Again he clammed up. She brushed a lock of hair back from her shoulder and turned away to make him less uncomfortable. "And what brings you to Summervale this morning?"

He smiled nervously. "I thought it would be a good idea for us to spend some time together."

Her heart gave a little skip, but she tried not to show her elation. "Oh? Well, you're welcome to help with the weeding if you'd like."

Zacharias scowled at the pile of weeds on the path. "Why isn't Colin doing this? You don't need to dirty your hands or get calluses—"

"Colin doesn't even know I'm out here," Shelby interrupted. "Besides, I love working in the gardens."

"Oh?" One of his eyebrows winged upward. "When did you take up gardening?"

Too late, Shelby realized she'd made a mistake. She tried to backpedal. "That's not exactly what I meant. I meant that I've wanted to *begin* gardening." Shelby zeroed in on another weed and gave it a yank. "It looks soothing," she said as the roots rained soft dirt down onto her lap.

"And is it?"

"Very."

Zacharias nodded slowly. "I'm glad you're enjoying it." He took a step or two away, then turned back to face her. "Would you stop that?"

"Stop?" Shelby halted with her hand around another weed's neck. "Why?"

"I'd like to talk . . . about us."

She took an unsteady breath and wiped her hands on her skirt. "We do need to talk. There's something I need to tell you. . . . It's about the other night. I'd like to explain why I sent you away."

"I'm not upset about the other night," Zacharias assured her.

Now that Shelby had started, she wouldn't let herself stop. "It's just that," she said again, then rushed on before she could change her mind. "I haven't been myself lately."

"You are different," Zacharias agreed, "and I like the change in you. It suits you. It suits *me*. And that's what I came to tell you."

She shook her head quickly. "I mean I *really* haven't been myself." She took his hand and led him toward the stone bench a few feet away. He followed her willingly, even if he did seem a little bemused. "I need to explain."

He touched her cheek lightly and sent a wave of despair mixed with longing through her. "Whatever it is, Agatha, don't say it."

"But I have to."

"No, you don't." He cupped her face with his hand

and ran his thumb across her lip. "Let me tell you why I'm here."

She was sorely tempted, but she couldn't chicken out now. If she did, she might never tell him. "This is important," she insisted.

"So is what I have to say."

"But—"

His brows knit and his eyes clouded. "Dammit, woman, will you be quiet? You're making it damned difficult to woo you."

He couldn't have stopped her better if he'd bound and gagged her, but horror, not joy, brought tears to her eyes.

"Now what's wrong? What did I say?" Zacharias shot to his feet and paced an agitated step away. "I *told* Philip I was no good at this—"

"No. You're very good. You're here to woo me?"

Zacharias dropped to the bench beside her again. "It occurred to me that perhaps I've been a trifle . . . uncouth . . . in my efforts to show you how I feel."

"Uncouth? No, Zacharias, you've been wonderful—"

He cut her off with another quick scowl. "Will you *please* let me say what I've come to say? I've rehearsed for two days, and you're making me forget the finer points."

He looked so serious, so distressed, she clamped her mouth shut.

Apparently satisfied, he spoke again. "I told you I was taking care of correspondence, and I was. I wrote this"—he pulled a letter from his pocket and held it out to her—"for you."

"What is it?"

"For hell's sake, Agatha, if you'd just read it you'd know that it's a love letter."

"A love letter?" She took it quickly and clutched it tightly.

"Now what's wrong?"

"Nothing. It's just so . . . sweet."

"Sweet?" He snorted as if she'd accused him of something horrible. "It's not *sweet*. I just thought I should tell you how I feel about you, that's all."

She started to open the envelope, but he stayed her hand as he had earlier. "Don't open it now."

"Why not?"

"Because . . ." He waved his hand and tried to look annoyed, but she could see uneasiness lurking just beneath the surface. "Because you should read it when you're alone."

She smiled softly, so touched by his obvious discomfort, by his sudden shyness, she thought her heart would burst. He was so different from the angry, scowling, bitter man she'd met her first day in Summervale, it took her breath away.

He pulled back and deepened his scowl. "What are you smiling at?"

"You seem ill at ease."

"And you find that amusing?"

Shelby wiped the smile from her face, but not from her heart. "No, not amusing. Endearing."

Zacharias met her gaze again, but he seemed a little less rigid. "Endearing?"

"Very."

"Endearing enough to earn a kiss?"

"Or two."

"Endearing enough to—" He broke off and shook his head as if trying to rid himself of an unwelcome thought. "Two. And perhaps I should claim them now, before you read my feeble efforts and discover how inept I am at the gentle art of courtship."

She went willingly into his arms and tilted her head back for his kiss. She put every ounce of love she felt into the moment, knowing that when she confessed the truth to him, he might not want anything to do with her. And, foolishly perhaps, deciding to wait just a little longer before she had to watch the light in his eyes fade.

It wasn't smart. Shelby knew that. It might even be dangerous. She knew that, too. But one kiss in the garden had turned into a dozen and wiped away reason. She clutched his hand while he led her through the foyer, and followed him quickly up the stairs.

When Meg poked her head out of a doorway, Zacharias motioned for her not to worry. "Mrs. Logan and I need some time alone, Meg. See that we're not disturbed."

Meg's bright smile left no doubt that she suspected the reason for the "visit" but Shelby didn't even care about that. She only knew that she wanted Zacharias as she'd never wanted any man before.

Once they reached her bedroom, Zacharias kicked the door shut and pulled her to him. She went to him eagerly, melting against him and lifting her mouth with an impatience he matched.

He groaned softly when their lips met and tightened his arms around her. She couldn't breathe, couldn't think, couldn't feel anything at the same time she was overwhelmed with sensation. Her breasts tingled and her skin felt as if someone had ignited a fire beneath her.

Zacharias ran his hands along her back to her bottom and cupped it gently. But there he stopped and pulled away to look at her. "Are you sure about this? I don't want to rush you."

Shelby nodded and ran her fingers along his shoulders, delighting in the shiver her touch tore from him. "I've never been more sure of anything in my life," she whispered.

"Good." A fire burned in his eyes and his hands started moving again. "From now on, let's have nothing between us. No secrets, no lies, no half-truths."

Shelby closed her eyes and willed the nagging voice to go away. She didn't want to destroy this moment. But she'd destroy everything if she promised truth now and lied again.

Chapter 17

NEAR TEARS, SHELBY opened her eyes again just as he bent his mouth to hers once more. "Before we do this, there's one thing I need to tell you."

"Later."

It had been a long time since any man had looked at her with such hunger, and every instinct shouted for her to agree. If she made love to him now, at least she'd have the memory to cherish if she had to spend the rest of her life without him.

But she didn't want to remember him making love to Agatha. She had to know he was making love to *her*.

She gave herself a mental shake and followed it with a quick shake of her head. "No," she whispered. "I have to tell you now. Then, if you still want me . . ."

He tilted his head to study her. "*If* I still want you? This must be some news. I can't imagine anything that would change my mind right now."

Shelby clenched her hands tightly and forced herself to put some distance between them. "This might sound crazy. In fact, I'm *sure* it sounds crazy." She turned to face him again and took a fortifying breath, then blurted it out before she could change her mind. "I'm not ˌ.ga-tha."

"You're—" Zacharias stared at her for a second, then threw back his head and laughed. "All right. If it suits you to pretend we're strangers, I suppose I don't mind."

"I'm serious, Zacharias. This isn't some kind of kinky sex game. I'm not Agatha. I just happen to be stuck inside her body."

"I'd very much like to join you," he said, grinning wickedly.

"Will you be serious for a minute?" Shelby caught him with both hands just before he pulled her back into his embrace.

He scowled at her. "All right, then, you little minx. Who are you?"

"My name is Shelby Miller, and I'm from the future. Somehow—don't ask me how because I can't explain it—I was transported through time and dropped into Agatha's body."

One eyebrow quirked. "Through time."

"Yes. I was working as caretaker at Winterhill and when I found out they were planning to tear down the twin houses, I came to Summervale and started looking for Agatha's journals. Something happened with the heat and the mirror and the next thing I knew, I was here."

Zacharias sent her a skeptical look. "From the future."

"Yes." Shelby ran her fingers through her hair and let out a sigh of relief. Not because he believed her but because she'd actually managed to tell him. Even that took a weight off her shoulders. "In real life, I'm five foot seven and I have shoulder-length curly blond hair."

"Is that right?" His eyes narrowed slightly. "And what has become of Agatha?"

"I don't know for certain, but I'd guess she's living my life. I've seen her a couple of times in the mirror, and I keep expecting to change places again, but so far I'm still here."

Zacharias rubbed his chin thoughtfully. "And when did this miracle take place?"

"The day I told you that I'd lost my memory."

"Ahhh." He nodded as if everything made perfect sense. "And why didn't you tell me about this at the time?"

"Because you weren't exactly on speaking terms with Agatha." Shelby sent him a sheepish smile. "And because I figured I'd been brought here to fix your relationship with her."

Zacharias rubbed his chin again, adjusted the waist of his trousers, ran his hand along the back of his neck. "And so you have," he said after a long pause.

"Maybe. I'm not so certain anymore. Everyone in my time believes Agatha was crazy, and that she deserted you and her children to live here as a recluse. Nobody knows the truth."

"Indeed? Well, that's good. I never have wanted my children's unsavory past revealed."

"I know. And now that I understand everything that happened, I'm not so sure *why* I'm here. All I know is that somewhere in the process of trying to get you and Agatha back together, I fell in love with you, myself."

His eyes softened slightly. "And I with you. But if, as you say, you're not Agatha—"

"I'm not. I only wish I could prove it to you."

"No more than I wish it," he muttered almost too low for Shelby to hear.

"Do you hate me for not telling you sooner?"

He worked up a smile and met her gaze again. "Hate you? No, Ag—What was your name again?"

"Shelby."

He nodded again, slowly. "I don't hate you . . . Shelby. But I think perhaps this isn't the best time to . . . to . . ." He waved a hand toward the bed.

She hadn't expected any other reaction, but that didn't stop the pain of rejection. She had no right to ask him to believe her or even to trust her, but that didn't take away the searing pain in her heart. She had to give him time to adjust to the bombshell she'd just dropped, but that didn't give her hope.

"No," she whispered around the lump in her throat. "No, it isn't. I understand." And she did—logically.

But her heart didn't understand anything at all and her soul felt as if someone had rent it in two.

Her tears nearly did him in, but Zacharias contrived to remain strong. And he struggled not to show how much the news had devastated him. He'd almost convinced himself that she wasn't crazy—in spite of his mother's dour warnings, in spite of Agatha's odd behavior, in spite of everything.

Until now.

Now, he had to admit that she'd lost her mind. And this was far worse than anything else she'd ever done. A traveler through time? Some blond woman named Shelby Miller from the future? His heart ached just thinking about how confused Agatha's poor mind had become.

He put an arm around her shoulders and pulled her to him. Knowing that she'd lost her mind did nothing to change the love he felt for her. But it hurt. Oh, Lord, it hurt. He'd had such dreams of their future together. He'd counted on putting their family together the way it always should have been. Now, it seemed, his mother was right.

He couldn't allow her to stay in Summervale if she was this demented. He couldn't put the twins in that kind of danger. And she must be a danger. If she wasn't now, she soon would be. Look how deeply disturbed she was already.

She turned her tearstained face up to his. "I'm sorry, Zacharias. I should have told you weeks ago."

"It doesn't matter," he assured her. And in truth it didn't. In fact, he was glad she hadn't told him. At least he'd had this time to love her before he had to send her away.

With her heart breaking, Shelby watched Zacharias drive away in his carriage. Though it hurt worse than anything she'd ever experienced, she knew she'd done the right thing. She wondered how he would have reacted if she'd waited until after they had made love to tell him the truth. It would have been even worse.

She heard the bedroom door open behind her and shut with a bang. "You told him, didn't you?"

Shelby nodded without taking her eyes from the empty drive. "I had to, Meg. I couldn't deceive him."

Meg came to stand behind her. "I know you believe it, but what you told me is impossible." She pulled Shelby around to face her. "Do you understand? Impossible." She spoke slowly and loudly, as if she thought Shelby had lost her mind and her hearing at the same time.

"I'm not crazy, Meg. I really am from the future."

"Agatha . . ." Meg let out a heavy sigh. "Perhaps it would be wise not to repeat that where others can hear— especially Victoria."

"Yes. Victoria." Just the thought of her made Shelby sick. "You don't think Zacharias will tell her, do you?"

"I don't know. He loves you with all his heart, but he looked terribly worried when he left here. And this may be what finally convinces him to follow his mother's advice."

"And lock me away?"

"Yes." Meg rubbed her arms gently. "Please, Agatha, for your own sake, don't tell anyone else."

Shelby nodded slowly. "If only I could think of some way to convince you both. But telling you about the future won't help. How would you know I'm not making it up?"

Meg shook her head. "Don't worry about it now, dear. I think a lie down would be the best thing for you."

"I don't want to lie down." Shelby caught her reflection in the glass and scowled at it. "I *want* to find some way to convince you and Zacharias that I'm not crazy."

"After you rest. You'll feel better afterward, I'm sure."

Shelby pulled away from her. "I'm not crazy, Meg. I'm in complete control of my faculties. Ulysses S. Grant is president of the United States, and Rutherford B. Hayes will be the next one. In just a few years, Mark Twain—or Samuel Clemens as you know him—is going to publish a book called *The Adventures of Tom Sawyer* based on his boyhood adventures here in Hannibal. He's going to write a sequel, and they'll become great pieces of American literature. He'll be one of America's most beloved literary figures."

"Sam Clemens?" Meg laughed aloud. "Oh, Agatha, really! Couldn't you choose someone a little more believable? Great literary figure, indeed."

"It's true, Meg. What do I have to do to convince you?"

"Tell me what the weather will be tomorrow."

"Hot and humid," Shelby said sarcastically. "I'm not clairvoyant, Meg, I'm from the future. I only know the big historical events."

"Well, then," Meg kept her voice annoyingly gentle and soothing as if she was speaking to a child. "Tell me about some big historical event."

Shelby thought furiously, trying to remember something, anything, about Missouri, or more specifically, about Hannibal, but nothing came to mind. "What do you want to know about? The sinking of the *Titanic*? That doesn't happen for about forty years. World War One doesn't start until 1917, I think." She ran one trembling hand along the back of her neck. "I don't *know* what to say to convince you, but you have to believe me, Meg. You have to."

Meg's gaze never faltered, her expression never changed, but something in her eyes seemed to shift. "You're serious, aren't you?"

"I've never been more serious in my life. Remember when I first changed? *Remember?* I didn't recognize you. I didn't remember anything about my parents. I didn't even know who Zacharias was at first because I'd only seen a couple of old pictures of him in history books. And I'm here because, according to those same books, Agatha dies in just a few days. But she's not supposed to, Meg. I know she's not. And I'm here to stop it from happening. I'm here to save her life, only I've fallen in love with Zacharias and I've completely lost my heart to the twins, and you and Colin are like the parents I never had when I was growing up, and I don't *want* to give her life back to her. I want to stay."

Meg didn't say anything for what felt like forever. She let her gaze roam Shelby's face and linger on her eyes. And then, slowly, shaking her head and smiling grimly, she finally broke her silence. "And so you shall, Shelby Miller. If I have anything to say about it, that is. Though I hope heaven will help us both if you aren't who you say you are."

Agatha was crazy.

No doubt about it, she'd gone stark, raving mad. The words echoed in time to Zacharias's footsteps as he paced the floor of his study. And yet, even that didn't change the way he felt about her.

So what was he going to do about it? He still hated the idea of divorcing her—perhaps even more now that he realized how ill she truly was. And the thought of staying married to her and putting the twins in danger made him break out in a cold sweat.

There must be *something* he could do to help her. Maybe Dr. Mensing would have a suggestion. He shook that thought away quickly. If he told Mensing about this latest delusion of hers, the doctor would commit her to an asylum faster than Zacharias could blink. Worse, the entire town would know, and there'd be nothing he could do to salvage her reputation.

But why did he care about the reputation of a mad-woman?

He stopped by the window and stared at the row of trees, at the turrets of Summervale visible over their tops. Could it be that he believed her?

No.

A visitor from the future? Unbelievable. A strange woman inside Agatha's body? Outrageous.

Still, it *would* explain the sudden changes in her. It would explain why she'd suddenly become warm and caring and lighthearted. It would explain why she'd taken such an interest in the twins, why she'd suddenly decided she wanted to be their mother, why she'd suddenly become so passionate whenever he kissed her.

Yes, it would explain a lot. Except that it was absolutely impossible, inconceivable, and absurd. A far more logical explanation was simple insanity. But how could an insane person be kinder, warmer, and more loving than a person in full possession of all their faculties?

A dull ache started behind his eyes and moved to his temples. He rubbed them, gently at first, then more vigorously, as if he could rub away his confusion, as if he could make this whole thing make sense.

"Sir? Begging your pardon, but Mrs. Starling is here. She wishes to speak with you."

Zacharias wheeled around to face Abraham. "Patricia?" Not *now*. He didn't want to see her. Didn't want to see anyone.

He considered asking Abraham to tell her he wasn't at home, but why postpone the inevitable? It was another problem he had to deal with. Another problem that wouldn't go away if he ignored it.

Squaring his shoulders and running a hand across his waistcoat, he nodded. "Show her in, Abraham."

He settled himself near the bookshelves and tried not to look irritated by the interruption. Patricia swept in a moment later, dressed to the nines, her hair piled in coils atop her head, a sweet scent emanating from her, her cheeks rosy, her lips darkened with something that looked suspiciously like lip rouge.

Zacharias's heart sank. If she'd come looking like that, she must want something—and he had a pretty good idea what that something was. Still, he gave his best effort to looking, if not pleased to see her, at least not *dis*pleased.

She waited for Abraham to leave them alone, then

smiled up at him from beneath her lashes. "Thank you for seeing me, Zacharias."

All of the usual responses he could have made sounded false, so he said only, "Of course. What can I do for you?"

She toyed with the string on her fringed bag for a moment, then slanted a glance at the closed door behind her. "May we walk outside? I'd like to speak with you privately."

Where his mother couldn't listen, no doubt. "Of course. In the gardens?"

"That would be lovely."

Fighting apprehension, he motioned her toward the glass doors that led to the terrace. Neither of them spoke until they'd descended the stone steps and put some distance between them and the house.

Patricia made an innocuous comment about the weather. Zacharias responded in kind. She queried him about the Hastings's ball the following week. He gave her a noncommittal reply. She stopped to sniff a flower. He waited with mounting impatience.

Finally, after what felt like forever, she got to the point of her visit.

"I've come to ask what you intend to do about our child."

Zacharias didn't answer immediately. He didn't know what to do or say. On the one hand, Agatha was clearly troubled. On the other, troubled or not, he was deeply in love with her. Still, what did his personal feelings matter when his sons needed a mother? What did his happiness matter when so much was at stake? Didn't he owe his children stability? Didn't they deserve a life without the taint of insanity?

Patricia moved a little closer. "Zacharias, please. Don't shut me out. I've given this so much thought, and it was so difficult for me to come to you this way."

"Yes," he said slowly, forcing a thin smile, "I'm sure it was." He extended his arm, and she slipped her hand beneath it. "You've given me much happiness over the years."

She lifted her gaze to meet his again. "No more than you've given me."

"And you've given me the most incredible gift of all—two healthy, fine sons."

Her eyes clouded. "Perhaps three."

"Perhaps." He slowed and looked deeply into her eyes. "Perhaps. But I can't give you what you're asking in return. Whether it's foolish or wise, I love Agatha."

"I'm not asking that you love me," Patricia protested. "I love you enough for both of us."

He patted her hand gently. "Sadly, my dear, that isn't possible. Trust me. I speak from experience."

"But—"

He cut her off, hoping to spare her further embarrassment. "Our relationship was wrong, Patricia. Wrong. No matter what justifications I used to excuse it, it was wrong. And it's simply not possible to start with a wrong and make it right. Even if Agatha and I don't end up together, you and I cannot make something good and right out of something that began in the shadows."

Tears filled her eyes and made him feel like an incredible jerk. "How can you say that? I love you, Zacharias. Is love wrong?"

"A love based on lies and deceit? Yes." He stopped walking again and took her gently by the shoulders. "I don't blame you, Patricia. I blame myself. I dragged you into this and allowed myself to exploit your kindness for my own selfish reasons."

Patricia wiped away a tear and frowned. "Your nobility is admirable, but let's at least be honest with each other now. You didn't use me or exploit me. I was a willing party. That's why you came to me." She smiled up at him, a semblance of the sultry smiles that had once set his blood boiling. "For that matter, I am still. And we do have the children to think about."

Zacharias stopped walking. "Let's not kid ourselves about that, either. You didn't want the twins when you found yourself inconvenienced with them. If you had, they'd be with you now. You turned them over to me anxiously, and you've not concerned yourself with them in the past five years."

"I've changed. Didn't I join you at the pond the other day?"

He shook his head without taking his eyes from hers. "No, Patricia, you haven't changed."

"Agatha turned them away," she argued. "Why will you believe that she's changed, but you won't believe I have?"

"Agatha has proved herself. She has asked about the twins, spent time with them, listened to them, hugged them, cared for them. When did you last do any of those things?"

"I can start."

"Why would you want to?"

"Because they're my children."

"They've always been your children, Patricia, yet you only make this offer when *our* future is threatened."

Her cheeks paled, her eyes seemed to lose color. "Isn't she doing the same thing?"

He smiled slowly, remembering. "Actually, no. She was quite willing to step aside and grant me a divorce so the twins could be with you."

A quick, pleased smile curved Patricia's lips and the color returned to her face. "Then, there's nothing to worry about."

"She offered," Zacharias said, "and I refused."

"You *refused*?"

"I refused. It seems that we have a situation reminiscent of King Solomon on our hands, don't we? Only in this case, the real mother is more concerned with herself than with her children."

"How can you say that? You know how concerned I've always been with the twins."

"Concerned about getting them out of your way." He stepped away from her and clasped his hands behind his back to prevent her from taking his arm again. Her touch

chilled him to the bone. "I'm aware that you've been
discussing sending them to school—"

"Of course. But only because it would be the best
thing for them. They need discipline."

"They need love."

"They need structure."

"They need security." He glanced back at Winterhill,
and smiled softly. "And laughter."

"And you think Agatha can give them that?"

"I know she can."

Patricia's face hardened. "If you try to keep my children from me, I'll fight you. The truth will be exposed.
Everyone will know—"

"The truth." He slanted a glance toward Summervale.
"Perhaps it *is* time for the truth to be told."

Patricia's face flamed. "You'd do that to me? What
about the child I carry now?"

"I'll make you the same offer I made with the twins.
If you truly want the child, I'll not attempt to separate
you from it. I'll see to its financial needs—and yours,
of course—once Dr. Mensing verifies that there's a child
to consider. And if you don't want it, I'll bring it home
with me and raise it with Mordechai and Andrew."

Not surprisingly, she didn't move past his reference
to the doctor. "You ask me to submit to something so
vile as an examination to verify that I'm telling you the
truth?"

"If you want my assistance."

"Never. I refuse. I—I—"

"That's certainly your right," he said evenly. "However, without proof, I'm afraid I can't overlook the star-
tling coincidence that you suddenly find yourself with
child at this precise moment. I'm finding it difficult to
ignore the very real possibility that you and my mother
cooked up this scheme together in order to force my
hand."

The blood rushed from her face and she darted such
a quick, worried glance at the house, he knew Agatha—
Shelby—had been right. When he realized that he'd

started to believe in her incredible tale of traveling through time, he took another step away from Patricia and sketched a bow. "I've told you what I'm willing to do, Patricia. Now the choice is yours. I assume you'll let me know your decision, once you've made it."

She stared at him for a long, breathless time, then picked up her skirts and pushed past him. He watched her go with mixed emotions, then tilted back his head and let the sun play across his face.

Perhaps *he* was the one who'd lost his mind, but he did believe Shelby. Listing her virtues for Patricia had been the clincher. Agatha would never have put the twins' needs before her own. Not in a million years.

He couldn't understand how it happened, he wasn't certain he wanted to understand. But somehow, he'd fallen in love with a stranger—who just happened to be inhabiting his wife's body.

Shelby stepped back into the shadow of a tree and tried to catch her breath. Zacharias and Patricia had looked so comfortable together, so intimate, her head began to swim. And when Patricia walked away and Zacharias gave in to a moment of such pure joy Shelby could feel it across the distance, the ground tilted so precariously beneath her feet, she *knew* she was about to be sick.

She couldn't decide whether to step out from her hiding place and let him know that she'd seen them together or rush back to Summervale and pretend she'd never left it. It didn't matter that she'd told him something that sounded so farfetched she had trouble believing it herself. It didn't matter that *any* man would have reacted with stunned disbelief and maybe even a little fear to such news.

Rational or not, she hated knowing that Zacharias still didn't believe her, and she hated *him* for rushing straight back to Patricia's waiting arms. It said something about his character.

She pushed away from the tree and smoothed her skirts carefully. But anger turned to fear, to worry, to self-blame. Then her emotions ran the gamut again. She wanted Zacharias to believe her. She wanted to know he loved *her*, not Agatha.

But maybe she'd destroyed everything by confessing the truth. Maybe he'd never fall in love with Agatha now. And if he did, there was still the threat of being whisked back to her own time.

If she let Zacharias think she was crazy, would Agatha die in a few days? If she did nothing, would Agatha live? Or would she die anyway? And just exactly where would Shelby be at the time?

Too many questions darted through her head. Too many possibilities tore at her. Too many things could go wrong. Maybe they already had.

Shelby started back toward Summervale, but she paid no attention to the ground in front of her and nearly lost her balance several times on buried rocks and roots sticking up through the soil.

Maybe Patricia and Zacharias *were* supposed to be together. Maybe that's why Shelby had come back. She stumbled again and caught herself as she fell, scraping the palms of her hands. But she didn't even notice the pain.

There were so many possibilities, but one kept coming back to her. Maybe she'd created this mess by holding on to Agatha's life for too long. Maybe it was time to let Agatha come back, reclaim her life, her husband, the twins, her home, and her friends. Maybe Shelby was making everything worse by selfishly longing to stay.

Or maybe she was destined to remain here and die as Agatha in just a few days.

Chapter 18

ZACHARIAS PACED THE length of his dressing room, muttering under his breath, trying to make sense of the strange phenomenon that had brought Shelby to him. Surely, there must be some way to keep her here. Surely, fate wouldn't be so unkind as to snatch her away from him now.

Would it?

He tossed back a brandy and scowled at the walls around him. Fate had never been kind to him, he didn't know why he expected this time to be any different. It had saddled him with a mother who wanted to control everyone and everything in her path, with a wife who couldn't love, and a future he didn't want.

Even as he paced the floor, he could feel the certainty of the future Shelby had shared with him pulling him, dragging him away from Hannibal, from the twin houses, from the life he'd always led.

He wanted to live, to experience, to feel, to explore, not merely to exist. Yet if he lost Shelby now, he would merely exist for the rest of his life. He wouldn't love again. He wouldn't want to even try.

With trembling hands, he poured another brandy and

sent it chasing after the first. But even that fire couldn't warm him. Everything inside felt as if it had turned to stone.

A knock on his door interrupted his melancholy. He was sorely tempted to ignore it, but what if Shelby or the twins needed him? Scowling darkly, he threw open the door, hoping to find Abraham standing there but knowing even before he looked into her eyes that he'd have to deal with his mother.

"I'm glad you're here," she said before he could offer an excuse and send her on her way. "There are matters we must settle."

"Not now, Mother."

"Yes, now. This has gone far enough. Too far. I will not allow you to carry on this way any longer."

He could feel the brandy stirring his temper, but he made no effort to control it. "If you're talking about Agatha, save your breath. There's nothing you can say that I want to hear."

"Nevertheless, you will listen. She's leading you about like a fool, Zacharias."

"I don't agree."

"That's because you're too confused to think clearly. That's obvious to anyone who knows you."

"You're entitled to your opinion, of course, but you're not entitled to voice it inside this house."

"I *will* voice it, and you will listen."

"No, Mother, I will not." He turned his back on her. "Now, if you'll excuse me—"

"I will *not* excuse you." She pushed past him into the room, a fortress of black silk. "You behaved abominably to Patricia the other day. She came to me in tears. This must stop, Zacharias. There is no other acceptable solution. Dr. Mensing is on his way here to settle Agatha in a home where she will be comfortable."

Fury blinded him and wiped away every iota of duty he'd ever felt toward his mother. It took every bit of self-control he had to keep his hands clenched at his side. "You've gone too far, Mother. Even for you. Agatha is not crazy, and I'll not let Mensing lay one finger on her."

"Oh, Zacharias, *please*." His mother's face hardened. "You're destroying your life, and you cannot expect me to stand by and watch."

"You only believe I'm destroying my life because I've stopped letting you control it. I warn you, if you try to harm Agatha—"

"I'm not trying to hurt her," his mother snapped. "I'm trying to protect her from herself."

"Don't!" He held up both hands to ward off her excuses. "Don't try to justify your bitterness and hatred as caring. You don't care for anyone but yourself."

"How can you say that?" She put one hand to her breast as if he'd wounded her. "You know how much I love you."

"No, Mother, I do not. You manipulate. You control. You dominate. But you do not love."

She blinked rapidly and a finger of guilt tickled him. "I *do* love you, Zacharias. I only want the best for you." A tear spilled onto her cheek and she drew a ragged breath.

But Zacharias wouldn't let himself fall for her tricks again. "You've done everything you could to break up my marriage to Agatha, but I won't tolerate it any longer. If you care anything at all for me, you'll leave Agatha alone. You'll accept my decision to put my marriage back together and bite your tongue in the future. Because if you force me to choose between you and the woman I love, I warn you the contest will be short. My future is with Agatha. My happiness is in her hands."

"You weren't happy with her before. You weren't happy when she locked her bedroom door on you, or when she turned your children away."

"No," he admitted reluctantly, "but Agatha has changed."

"Changed? She's worse than ever. She's crazy, Zacharias."

"I love her."

"Love." Victoria laughed bitterly. "You place too much value on such a fleeting commodity."

"It doesn't have to be fleeting," Zacharias said, his shoulders sagging with the weight of her resentment on them. "Haven't you ever loved anyone?"

"Of course I have. I love you. I love the twins. That's why I want to be sure you make the right choices. Why I try to help you make intelligent decisions. You'll do the same thing for your children. Every parent does. What kind of mother would I be if I let you rush into a situation that I *knew* would hurt you?"

He wanted to argue that he wouldn't get hurt again, but he couldn't. He knew nothing about what brought Shelby here, nothing about what might whisk her away again. "Perhaps," he said, the anger suddenly gone from his voice, "there are times when all you *can* do is stand back and watch. I don't want to live my life making decisions based only on intellect. Once in a while, there are choices that require nothing but heart."

"And this is one of them, I suppose."

"Yes, it is."

"She's not the right sort of woman for you," she warned, but her anger had evaporated as well.

"She is exactly right for me," he assured her. "Whether love proves to be fleeting or not, at least I'll have this moment. Don't try to take it from me. Agatha isn't a vicious woman, Mother. She never was." He paced a few steps away and rubbed the back of his neck. "Whatever pain we've suffered, I'm the one to blame. Not Agatha."

His mother stood there, stiff as a board for a moment or two. "You can't truly love her," she said, but it was less a command than a question.

"I do."

"And you believe you can be happy with her in spite of everything?"

"I do," he said again. He would be happy as long as Shelby stayed.

His mother studied him for a long time. He could see

the different emotions crossing her face, he could see her arguing with herself, torn between wanting him to be happy and her desperate need to cling to her own vision for him.

Finally, after what felt like forever, her shoulders unbent slightly and an almost imperceptible softening crossed her face. "If she makes you unhappy again, I'll never forgive her."

Zacharias could live with that. He grinned suddenly and put his arms around his mother in a gesture so spontaneous, he knew it caught her off-guard. But it had been too long since they'd shared anything but anger. She tolerated his embrace for a heartbeat, then pushed him away.

"Release me, Zacharias. You're mussing my gown."

He stepped away and grinned at her. "Of course, Mother. But I feel it only fair to warn you, I'm not the man I used to be. You may have to suffer an occasional embrace from me."

She tried desperately to maintain her scowl, but a corner of her mouth twitched and he could have sworn he saw a faint sparkle in her eye. She straightened her bodice, gave her skirts twitch, and turned back toward the door. But there she stopped and glanced over her shoulder at him.

"I daresay I could get used to it—occasionally."

Shelby clung to every moment she had with Agatha's family. The calendar had finally reached the day she'd been dreading. By midnight, she'd either be dead or back in the future. She tried not to show her dismay. She didn't want to upset Zacharias or the twins. But every smile tore another piece from her heart, every laugh made her eyes sting with unshed tears, every touch made her ache for tomorrow.

As if he could sense her mood, Mordechai climbed onto her lap and wrapped his arms around her neck. "Don't be sad, Mama."

"I'm not sad," she assured him quickly and forced a

smile to prove it. "I'm just amazed at how big and strong both my boys are."

She could feel Zacharias watching her, so she turned a teasing smile on him, as well.

He leaned back on the grass and surveyed them all as if he were king of the castle. "I received an invitation to a barbecue at the Keller place next week. Will you come with me?"

Shelby nodded. "Of course. If I can."

"Of course you can."

"I mean . . ." She scooted Mordechai away gently. "If I'm still here, I'd love to."

"You'll be here," Zacharias said firmly. "I won't allow you to leave."

"Unfortunately, even you may not be able to control that."

He scowled as if she'd insulted him deeply. "I won't allow it, my love. Whatever it takes to keep you here, exactly as you are, I'll do it."

"Zacharias—"

"You think I'm foolish, don't you?"

"Foolish?" She smiled gently. "Never that. But maybe just a little too confident about something we know nothing about."

"Then I'll learn. I've made up my mind to keep you here, and I shall."

She put a hand on his shoulder and brushed her lips to the top of his head. "Let's not spoil the day with talk about the future. Let's just enjoy this moment while we have it."

His eyes sparkled and she knew exactly where his thoughts had gone. "I'd love to discuss the future, Mrs. Logan. Just how long are you going to make me wait to seal this union of ours?"

"Soon," she promised, and she hoped with all her heart she'd still be here tomorrow so she could keep it. "In the meantime, let's make sure we each have some beautiful memories to carry with us—just in case simply being stubborn doesn't work."

"Stubborn?" Zacharias's eyes twinkled. "You're calling *me* stubborn?"

"Actually . . . yes."

"Look, Mama." Andrew bounded between them clutching a bouquet of flowers in his tiny fist. "These are for you."

In spite of all her efforts, Shelby's eyes filled with tears. She ducked her head to keep Zacharias from noticing, and pressed a kiss to the top of Andrew's golden head.

Andrew scowled up at her. "Why are you crying? Don't you like them?"

"Oh, Andrew, of course I love them." She inhaled greedily, wondering how many of these memories she could take with her. "They're the most beautiful flowers I've ever seen."

Mordechai scowled. "Not as beautiful as mine."

"Did you pick me some flowers, too?"

His tiny scowl deepened. "Not yet. But I'm gonna." Wheeling around so quickly he nearly fell over, he raced toward the gardens. Andrew, outraged, tore off after him.

Zacharias chuckled softly, moved onto the bench beside her and wrapped an arm around her shoulders. "They love you, you know."

"And I love them." Shelby forced away the tears and smiled up at him. "And you."

He kissed her then, and his tenderness nearly tore her heart in two. When he lifted his head again, he held her gaze. "It's going to be all right, Shelby. We belong together. Believe me. I won't let you go."

She would have given almost anything to believe him. But she knew this would be their last kiss, the last time she'd look into his eyes, the last time she'd feel his arms around her. By tomorrow morning, it would all be over. She just hoped God would give her the strength to hold on until then.

• • •

Meg followed Agatha—she couldn't think of her by any other name—up the stairs, worried about the mood she seemed to be in. She tried to lighten the moment with chatter, but Agatha seemed distracted. Distant. Almost as if she wasn't here any longer.

"Colin tells me the rose garden is nearly finished," she said, hoping that would spark some interest.

Agatha smiled, but there was no joy in it as there had been yesterday. "That's nice. I'm glad. The gardens will help make these houses a showplace."

"He wondered if you want to give him some ideas about the azaleas."

"I'm sure he knows what to do. He's wonderful in the gardens, Meg. Please make sure he knows I thought so."

"For heaven's sake," Meg protested. "What's gotten into you? You sound so gloomy." She bobbed her head firmly. "You'll tell him yourself in the morning."

Agatha looked away as if she were trying to hide something. "Of course. But if I don't, you'll tell him, won't you?"

Meg's spine tingled. She didn't like this mood, not one bit. "Now, why would you not tell him? Your ideas for the gardens have made them so lovely, he's strutting around like a rooster most of the time."

She expected Agatha to laugh. Instead, she smiled sadly.

Another tingle raced up Meg's spine to the back of her neck. "You can tell him yourself, as I said." She waited while Agatha opened her bedroom door, then made to follow her inside.

But the missus blocked her way. "I think I'd like some time alone, if you don't mind, Meg."

Meg didn't like the sound of that at all. It wasn't like the missus as she'd been lately. Before, yes. But not this past month. She tried to think of a clever way to refuse, but she couldn't think of anything that wouldn't sound cheeky. "Of course. You'll ring if you need me later?"

"Yes." Agatha started to turn away, then stopped herself. "Thank you, Meg. I want you to know how much I appreciate everything you've done for me in the past month."

"La," Meg said, trying to sound cheerful. "It's been a pleasure, madame. I can say that without hesitation."

"And Colin, too. He's a very fine man."

"He's a stubborn old mule," Meg said, "but I'm glad to have him."

Agatha's slight smile disappeared completely. "You should be. Love isn't easy to find."

"No, it isn't. But you've found it for yourself."

"Yes." Agatha's lip trembled. She pulled it between her teeth, took a deep breath, and released it again. "But it's not mine to keep, Meg."

"Sure it is." The chills racing up Meg's spine grew stronger. "All it takes is a bit of work and some patience. But Zacharias loves you and he's proved that he's willing to compromise. And you can't ask for a better quality in a man."

"I'm lucky, aren't I?" Agatha said, turning a glance toward Winterhill though she couldn't see it from here at her door. "To know real love, even for a little while, is a priceless gift."

Meg's nerves twitched. She had second thoughts about leaving Agatha alone. "Let me at least turn down your bed—"

"No." The word dropped between them quickly, forcefully, and sent a shard of foreboding through Meg. Agatha managed another smile, but it didn't fool Meg. "You've done enough. You're tired. I'll be fine."

The door closed between them, leaving Meg cold all through. It was almost as if Shelby had been saying good-bye. But Meg didn't want her to leave.

Though it seemed disloyal to think so, Meg liked having Shelby here in Agatha's place. Summervale had come alive since she arrived. So had Zacharias. And those tiny boys—those tiny, innocent, boys—finally knew the love of a mother.

Not that she didn't care for Agatha, Meg assured herself as she hurried down the corridor. She did. She always had. But Agatha had her problems, no doubt about that. And she wasn't good for those babies or for Zacharias.

She rushed down the stairs, and into the kitchen, thinking again about the look on Agatha's face, the sadness in her eyes, the finality of her tone. She didn't know quite what to do, but she had to do something.

If Shelby was planning to leave, Meg had to stop her. But her arguments wouldn't be persuasive enough. She couldn't offer the missus any compelling reason to stay. The only one who could do that was Zacharias.

Grabbing her shawl as she pushed out into the night, she began shouting for Colin before her foot even hit the dirt.

He came out of the stables slowly, as if his feet were stuck in cold molasses. "What is it, woman? You're shouting loud enough to wake the dead."

"Take the horse," she managed as she gasped to catch her breath. "Hurry to Winterhill and fetch back Zacharias."

"At this time of night?" Colin reared back and stared at her. "Ye've gone daft, woman."

"The missus is in trouble," she shouted, shoving him toward the stables again. "I don't care what time of night it is, Zacharias must come. He's the only one who can stop her."

"Stop her?" Colin glanced at the house. "Stop her from what?"

"From leaving, you old fool. Now git. Don't stand here yapping at me while she slips away." When Colin still didn't move, she added, "If she leaves, the real Agatha will come back."

That got his feet moving. He ran back into the stables, saddled a horse for himself, and pulled himself into the saddle. "Stay with her, Meg. Don't let her do it."

"I'll do my best." She slapped the horse's flank to set it in motion, then turned back to the house and ran across the hard-packed earth. Her heart threatened to burst from her chest, but she didn't slow down.

She tossed her shawl across a kitchen chair and raced back up the stairs as quickly as her legs would carry her. Her knees buckled and she nearly lost her footing just past the landing, but she ran on. She prayed frantically as she climbed—for Agatha, for Shelby, for Zacharias and the twins.

Maybe it was wrong to want Shelby to stay in Agatha's place. Maybe she was wicked for trying to prevent them from switching back. But she couldn't bear to see the life seep out of this house again, couldn't face more years as the past five had been, couldn't think about what having Agatha back would do to those lively little boys.

When she reached the second floor, she hurried to the corner bedroom and knocked.

No answer.

She knocked again, louder this time.

Silence.

She pounded, frantic. "Agatha? Madame? Open the door."

Nothing. Not even a footstep.

Her heart thudded ominously in her chest. A huge lump of fear blocked her throat. "Shelby!" She raised her voice and turned the knob. "Open this door immediately."

But only silence answered her.

Zacharias sat bolt upright in bed, startled by noises coming from the drive in front of the house. Not just noises. Voices. Agitated ones, at that.

He fumbled for a match, struck it, and lit the lamp beside his bed, then stumbled across the floor and checked the clock on the mantel. His eyes, still blurred from sleep, refused to focus. He settled the lamp on the mantel, rubbed his eyes, and checked again.

Who on God's green earth would be making such a

racket at one o'clock in the morning? There must be trouble somewhere, he realized slowly.

Suddenly nervous, he grabbed the lamp again, scorching his thumb in the process, and hurried out of the room and down the stairs. He could hear Abraham arguing with someone, and as he drew closer, he had the sick feeling he recognized the second voice, as well.

Colin? His stomach lurched when he realized something must be wrong with Shelby. He couldn't imagine Colin creating a disturbance under any other circumstances.

Worried now, he tore across the foyer and reached for the door.

"Zacharias? What is the matter?"

He wheeled about to face his mother, who'd come to the landing in her thin silk wrapper. "I don't know, Mother. I'm on my way to find out."

"Well, for heaven's sake, make them quiet down or they'll wake the children."

Waking the children was the last thing Zacharias was worried about, but he didn't see the need to bring his mother up-to-date on his concerns. He nodded quickly and stepped onto the porch.

Colin noticed him immediately and pushed past Abraham to get to him. "Meg sent me for you, Zacharias. She says you're to come quickly."

"I'm sorry, sir," Abraham began.

Zacharias motioned for him to be quiet. "What is it, Colin?"

"Its Agatha. Something's dreadfully wrong."

Zacharias shouted for someone to saddle his horse, but Colin motioned him toward the mount he'd brought from Summervale. "Take mine. There's no time to spare."

Numb with worry, Zacharias mounted the horse, speaking to Colin as he did. "Dammit, man! What is it? Is she ill?"

"Worse." Colin came to stand behind him as he

wheeled the horse around. "Meg thinks she's trying to leave."

Zacharias's heart dropped and icy fingers of dread curled around it. Without taking time to say another word, he spurred the horse and rode hard toward Summervale. Clouds hid the moon and bathed the road in shadow, but Zacharias didn't slow the mount. He knew the road well, and he just prayed he'd find nothing in his path tonight.

His heart hammered as if he, not the horse, was making the run that seemed interminably long. He knew exactly what Colin meant, and he couldn't bear the thought of losing her. How could she think of leaving? How could she bear to throw away everything they'd finally found together?

Anger churned with hopelessness in his stomach and he spurred the mount even faster. The sound of insects filled the night and made the long ride seem even more ominous. He tried to tell himself she couldn't just decide to leave, but in truth, he knew nothing of the miracle that had brought her to him, and he feared that she might be able to force her departure. If so, he just prayed he'd reach her in time.

At long last, the road to Summervale rose up in front of him. He sawed on the reins to steer the horse toward the house. There, he leapt from his mount even before it came to a complete stop, tossed the reins toward the hitching post, and tore up the front steps onto the porte cochere.

With his heart thundering, he took the grand staircase three steps at a time and found Meg outside Agatha's bedroom. Her pale face and tearstained eyes send a chill straight through him.

"She's locked the door," Meg said when she saw him. "I can't get her to open it."

Zacharias motioned her away and kicked near the lock using all the strength he could muster. The door creaked but didn't give way, and he cursed himself for insisting on the best materials when the house was being built.

He kicked again and again and threw his weight against the door with his shoulder, but the door held. He could hear Meg crying softly, but he couldn't give in to the despair that tore the breath from his lungs and screamed through his veins.

He backed up to the bannister and charged at the door, hitting it squarely with his shoulder and ignoring the pain that shot through him when he hit. But it held fast.

"Open the door, Shelby!" he shouted as he backed away to try again. "Dammit, woman, open the door."

Fear and frustration drove him on. "Downstairs," he ordered Meg. "Get the sword from above the mantel in the library. Be quick! We can't lose her."

Meg raced away, and Zacharias tried twice more to break the lock before she returned dragging the heavy sword behind her. Yanking it from her, he worked the steel blade beneath one of the hinges. Praying that he wouldn't snap the blade, he threw his weight against it. The wood gave way with a satisfying crack. He repeated the process twice more and the door fell open at long last.

He tore inside, with Meg only a step behind. But he was too late. Shelby's limp, lifeless form lay on the floor in front of the dressing table.

Chapter 19

SHELBY OPENED HER eyes slowly, aware only of the pounding in her head and a burning sensation in every muscle in her body. Musty air stung her nostrils and dust filled her mouth and eyes. She closed her eyes quickly and tried to stand, but she was too weak even to lift her arm.

Groaning softly, she lay there until something skittered across the floor near her head. At once more fully alert, she opened her eyes again.

Where was she?

Inside somewhere, she realized. She couldn't see the sky. Shadows filled the corners, and only a little sunlight spilled into the room through the chinks in the boards covering the windows. Even that tiny bit of light hurt her eyes and made the hammering in her head worse.

She let out a deep sigh and gingerly put her arm over her eyes to block the light. Silence surrounded her, broken only by something stirring softly near her head. She tried moving her legs, but the effort left her breathless and sent a jagged searing pain through her back.

Where was she?

In spite of the pain, her legs seemed curiously free.

No yards of fabric covering them, and even in this state she could tell she wore no corset. In a rush everything came back to her. She dropped her arm and looked around carefully.

Summervale. Summervale of the future. She'd done it. But she wished with all her heart she hadn't.

Hot tears filled her eyes and spilled onto her cheeks. "Zacharias," she whispered to the empty room. "Oh, my love, what have I done?"

She curled into a ball and lay there for what felt like forever, sobbing until the muscles in her stomach protested and her throat was raw and sore. Until she had no more tears to shed and exhaustion left her even weaker than she'd been before. Until her head felt as if it would explode and she couldn't breathe.

Then, with no other recourse, she got to her knees and pulled herself to her feet using the chipped, listing dressing table to help her.

Nothing had changed, she realized with despair. Summervale was still deserted. And she'd lost her will to try to save it—along with everything else.

Slowly, carefully, she made her way through the room and out into the corridor. How much time had passed? Was it the same day? Had she been lying here a month? No, surely not, or she'd be dead of starvation and water deprivation.

Had anyone noticed her absence? Or had only a few minutes passed? She descended the staircase, wincing at the effort, holding her head with each jarring movement. The huge, gaping hole where her heart had been ached as if someone had wrenched her soul from her body. But she had to keep moving.

When she reached the first floor, she crossed carefully on rotting floorboards to the door and stepped outside into the fading afternoon sunlight. She took several deep breaths, battled the urge to cry again, and started toward Winterhill.

How long would it be before Evan sold the house? Or had he already? How long before demolition began?

How long before she was forced to leave? How long before she was denied even that small connection to Zacharias and the twins?

Her head throbbed with every step. Her arms and back twinged and her legs threatened to buckle beneath her. Insects tormented her, but she didn't even have the energy to swat them away.

After what felt like forever, she reached Winterhill's gardens. They looked empty. Lifeless. But she knew that was only because Zacharias and the twins weren't there to give them life.

A wave of dizziness made her reach for the stone bench where she always sat in the mornings, but it wasn't there. Confused, she rubbed her forehead and glanced around. The gardens looked different, but she couldn't say why. Had roses always filled that bed? Had the Japanese Maple always been there on the curve of the path? She couldn't remember.

She forced herself to keep moving toward Winterhill, toward her bed where she could rest and regain her strength. She wouldn't sleep. She wondered if she'd ever really sleep again. But she needed rest so she could think and plan. After all, she had an entire lonely life to face.

The denim of her jeans chafed at her legs. She felt oddly naked without her corset and dressed only in a thin T-shirt. She wondered how long it would take to get used to dressing this way again. How long before the memories would began to fade and the pain to subside?

Battling another wave of dizziness, she climbed the front steps of Winterhill and turned the knob to open the door. To her surprise, the door didn't open.

She tried again, half convinced she was simply too weak to open it. But the knob refused to turn and she realized slowly that it was locked. Maybe she *had* spent longer than an afternoon in Summervale. Maybe Evan had already changed the locks. Maybe the house had already been sold.

In that case, what would she do? Where would she go?

Jon, she thought with a wave of relief. Jon would give her a place to stay. But she didn't have the strength to walk into town. She'd have to beg whoever lived here to let her use their telephone.

She knocked, then leaned her head against the door frame and waited. *Please*, she begged silently, *let someone be home.*

To her immense relief, she heard footsteps approaching, and a moment later the door opened. But when she looked at the person who filled the door, her knees buckled and she had to clutch the wood to hold herself upright.

She stared straight into a pair of blue eyes, took in the wildly curling hair, and gaped at the ski-jump nose.

"Agatha?"

The eyes that had once been hers widened in shock and she heard her own voice a second before everything faded to black.

"Is there any change?"

Zacharias glanced up at Meg and shook his head. Shadows stretched across the room. The air hung heavy around him. Perspiration soaked his shirt and trickled down his temples onto his cheeks. But he made no move to check it.

"She's the same," he said.

Meg tried to keep her voice chipper—for his sake, Zacharias knew. "Ah, well, at least she's no worse." She removed the cool rag from Agatha's forehead and replaced it with a fresh one, glancing at him from the corner of her eye as she worked. "You look tired."

"I am," he admitted. "I don't remember ever being this exhausted."

"You should rest."

He shook his head quickly. Not while Shelby's life hung in the balance. "I can't leave her." His voice came out curt and he tried to soften it with a thin smile. "I need to be with her, Meg."

"I know, but you'll do her no good if you make yourself ill in the process."

"I won't make myself ill," he insisted. "And I won't leave her. I need to be here in case she wakes up."

Meg set aside the bowl and came to stand beside him. Her face was tight with worry, her eyes dark. "You've been here for two days, sir."

"And I'll be here another twenty, if that's what it takes." He ran his fingers through his hair and added, "I appreciate your concern, Meg, but you don't understand."

"I understand more than you think." She slanted a glance at Shelby. "Have you considered that when she does wake up—*if* she wakes up—"

He cut her off angrily. "You'll not talk like that, Meg. Not where she can hear you. Not where *I* can hear you."

"Of course not, sir." Meg looked contrite. "But have you stopped to think that she may not be the woman you love when she wakes?"

"You mean, she might be Agatha?" Zacharias massaged the muscles in his neck and nodded slowly. "Of course I have, Meg." He turned his gaze back to the face he loved and said again, "Of course I have. But it doesn't matter. If Shelby comes back to me, I'll spend the rest of my life making her the happiest woman in the world. And if Agatha returns, I'll do exactly the same thing."

Meg scowled, her confusion deepening. "You've changed your mind about Agatha, then?"

"No." He sighed heavily. "But if Agatha returns, at least that will mean that Shelby is alive somewhere. And I'll show my gratitude by devoting my life to making my wife—whoever she is—happy. If I can do that, maybe Shelby will be happy in her own life."

Meg averted her gaze, and Zacharias knew she didn't hold out much hope of either woman returning. But he refused to give in to the despair that hovered on the edges of his consciousness. He simply would not allow either of them to die.

He lit another candle and nodded toward the door. "Go, Meg. Fix Colin his supper. No doubt he's hungry."

"He has no appetite, either," she said with a tight frown. "He's as worried as we are."

"He's a good man," Zacharias said. "No matter what happens, your future is secure. I promise you that."

Tears pooled in Meg's eyes. She dashed them away as if they made her angry. "Do you think we care about that now?"

"No more than I do," Zacharias said with a smile. "But I need to express my gratitude in some way."

She put a hand on his shoulder and gave it a gentle squeeze. "And we appreciate it, sir. We truly do. I shouldn't have snapped at you—"

He waved away her apology. "We're all upset, Meg. Thank God we have each other to cling to." He stole another glance at the inert form on the bed and felt some of his optimism slip. She looked so weak, so pale, so near death it frightened him beyond words. "Is there nothing else we can do?"

"Nothing that I know of, sir. I've exhausted all my remedies. Short of calling in Dr. Mensing, all we can do is wait."

He dropped into the wing chair again and covered his face with his hands. And, as he'd done a thousand times in the past two days, he pleaded with God to keep both women alive. When he'd finished, he lifted his gaze to Meg's again. "Am I wrong to keep the doctor away from her?"

"I don't know." Meg crossed to the bed and felt Agatha's forehead tenderly. "I don't know what more the doctor could do for her. And if she seems no better, at least she's no worse."

That, at least, was something to be grateful for. Zacharias leaned forward and took the limp hand in his. It was cool to the touch, but he could still feel the weak pulse in her wrist. "We'll wait awhile longer. But if she shows signs of weakening, we'll summon the doctor without delay."

He just hoped he wasn't making a mistake.

"I'm not going back there."

Shelby watched, fascinated, while the body she'd lived in for twenty-eight years paced in front of the fireplace. Strangely, she didn't think of it as *her* body anymore. She'd grown quite comfortable in Agatha's during the past month.

She took a bracing sip of tea and set her cup aside. "Zacharias is ready to work out your marriage," she argued, "and the twins need a mother."

Agatha shook her head. "I'm not going back."

"But Zacharias—"

"Has Patricia Starling."

"But he loves you," she said softly.

Agatha glared at her. "Love? He wouldn't know the meaning of the word."

"But he does," Shelby insisted. "He's worked through so much. He's ended his relationship with Patricia. All that remains is for you to take your place at his side again."

Agatha raked a cool blue glance over her. "You have been busy, haven't you?"

Shelby nodded slowly. "I know that's why we changed places, Agatha. So that history would change."

"Perhaps." Agatha sat on the settee across from her. "Perhaps the Logan family's history will change, but nothing you can do will change the way society was back then."

"That's true, but—"

"And I have no wish to return to it." Agatha dropped her hands onto her knees and held Shelby's gaze steadily. "You've had a taste of it. Can you honestly say you prefer the stifled mores of that time to the freedom you have here?"

"Freedom's a relative word, don't you think?"

"Exactly." Agatha crossed her legs and smiled.

"When Zacharias began his affair with Patricia, I was crushed. I had tried so hard to be everything he wanted me to be. I'd nearly died trying to give him children."

"I know."

"And he repaid that by running to the bed of another woman." Agatha laughed. "You see? I can *say* that here. Back then, I wasn't even supposed to *think* it."

"Times are different," Shelby admitted, "but—"

"I was expected to ignore his little fling. To turn a blind eye and smile sweetly. To accept him back into *my* bed without even raising an eyebrow. And when I didn't, all hell broke loose." She laughed again. "God, it's wonderful to be able to speak my mind without having someone collapse in a faint."

"But you spoke your mind then," Shelby argued mildly.

"Yes, and had the entire county convinced I was crazy because of it."

Shelby couldn't argue with that. She thought furiously, trying to come up with a convincing argument. If she had to stay here, in Agatha's body, her life would be even *less* connected than it was before. "But he's changed. He's ready to be your husband."

"Good for him. May he spend the rest of his life miserable and alone. Then maybe he'll know what I felt like as his wife."

Shelby battled an immense sadness. "Can't you forgive him?"

"No."

"But the twins—"

"Are none of my concern."

Sighing softly, Shelby rubbed her forehead. "They need you, Agatha."

"They don't need me," Agatha said firmly. "They need their mother."

"Patricia doesn't want them. She'd make a horrible mother."

"Yes, she would." Agatha's smile evaporated. "But

they'll have to get along without me, because I'm not going back."

Shelby stood, then immediately regretted it. Her head swam and her knees buckled. Carefully, she lowered herself back to the settee. "I don't understand how you can turn your back on your family. I'd have given anything to have one."

"Family is a headache," Agatha insisted. "I quite enjoy being you, having no connections to anyone or anything, no one to expect anything of me, no one to be disappointed if I don't behave the way they want me to, no one to disapprove of me." She paused for a moment and let her gaze travel across Shelby's face. "If you're so fond of them, why don't you go back?"

Shelby took a deep breath and voiced aloud the fear that rampaged through her. "I'm not certain I can."

"Nonsense. You made it back here, didn't you?"

"Yes," Shelby said slowly, "but have you read the history books? This is the date of your death. I'm not sure there's anything for me to go back to."

"My death?" Agatha pulled back as if Shelby had slapped her. "Don't be ridiculous. According to the books I've read, I lived to a ripe old age, even though I was a miserable old woman."

Shelby's heart skipped a beat, then began to race. "You didn't die?"

"Of course not." Agatha stood quickly and crossed the room, returning a moment later with a thick volume Shelby recognized from her own research. "Look."

Shelby took the book but her hands trembled so violently, she could hardly turn the pages. Had she really managed to change the course of history?

Agatha noticed her struggle and sat beside her, turning the pages quickly and pulling back her hands when she found the chapter on the Logan family. The pictures Shelby recognized were still there, but there were others, as well. Zacharias as an old man, still tall, still proud, but his hair shot through with silver and a great, drooping moustache adorning his mouth.

On the following page, a picture of Agatha, well into her sixties, still stern and disapproving, her face a map of wrinkles and her eyes still hard as stone. But Shelby didn't care. That the picture existed at all gave her great hope.

She glanced up at Agatha, her heart thudding dangerously. "This is different than it used to be. According to the history I read, you died June 30, 1871."

"Obviously, your presence in the past changed that."

Shelby touched the picture gingerly, then noticed one beside it of Zacharias and Patricia together. Her stomach lurched and tears filled her eyes. She traced Zacharias's face with her fingertips and whispered, "But they end up together."

Agatha glanced at her, her eyes narrowed, her lips pursed in contemplation. "Do I detect a note of sadness when you say that?"

Shelby hadn't meant to give herself away. She blinked away the tears and tried to look unconcerned. "Only because I don't think they'll be happy together."

"They wouldn't be," Agatha predicted. "Patricia is an odious woman. But could it be because *you* have feelings for Zacharias?"

Shelby opened her mouth to deny it, but the lie wouldn't come. She nodded miserably and closed the book. "I'm sorry, Agatha. I know it's wrong—"

"Wrong?" She laughed as if she'd never heard anything so amusing. "Why? Because of me? Believe me, any feelings I had for Zacharias died long ago."

"But—"

"But nothing," Agatha insisted. "I'm perfectly happy here in this life of yours. I can go anywhere, do anything, *say* anything I want. I have no ties to hold me, no social mores to chain me. I've never been so free."

"Yes, but—"

"You, on the other hand, seem happier in the life I've deserted." She met Shelby's gaze again. "Am I right?"

Shelby nodded slowly.

"Well, then, if you actually want my life—though

God only knows why you would—and if you actually want Zacharias—though I can't imagine why you should—then have them both, with my blessing."

Shelby couldn't believe she'd heard right. "But—"

Agatha waved her silent again, then covered Shelby's hands with hers. "I believe I was meant for this life of yours," she said, and the urgency in her voice left no doubt she meant it. "And, apparently, you were meant for mine."

Shelby still couldn't believe Agatha was giving her permission to return to the past and make a life with her husband. "But if his infidelity hurt you as much as you say it did—"

Again, Agatha cut her off. "It did, at the time. But I've had time to think, as well. Zacharias's affair with Patricia hurt me, but not because I was so terribly in love with him. I married him simply because that's what one *does* in that dreadful time. I had no real interest in marriage. I had no desire to share my life or my bed with any man. But to remain single—by choice—was simply not acceptable. And to remain single because no one wanted you . . ." She broke off with a shake of her head and a thin laugh. "Well, you see, though I didn't love him or want him, I wanted even less to be a spinster."

Hope turned from a flicker into a flame. "Then you truly don't mind that I've grown to love him?"

"Truly." Agatha's smile softened. "I don't love him. I never loved him. And if I'm honest with myself, I'll admit that I probably drove him to Patricia Starling's bed. He isn't really a bad sort, I suppose. In fact, he's really quite softhearted. I suppose my obvious distaste for his lovemaking probably hurt him."

Shelby's heart threatened to beat right out of her chest. "For what it's worth," she said softly, "he is sorry."

Agatha waved away the apology as if Zacharias had made it himself. "I'm sure he is. But that doesn't mean I want to return to him. Nor would it be fair for me to do so. He deserves to be loved, Shelby. And if you love him—and it certainly appears that you do—by all means, return."

Overcome with gratitude, Shelby threw her arms around Agatha's stiff neck and hugged her. Agatha remained unyielding for only a moment, then softened and returned her embrace. "Go," she whispered. "Make him happy as I never could. Fill that horrid old house with joy."

Zacharias had spent so many hours pleading with God, his knees hurt. He'd gone so many hours without anything but the most shallow sleep, his eyes felt as if someone had filled them with hot coals. He'd shed so many tears, his throat felt raw.

But he didn't stop praying. He didn't get up off his knees. He refused to give up hope. *It doesn't matter which woman comes back to me,* he insisted silently. *Just keep them both alive.*

Perhaps losing Shelby now was the price he had to pay for his weakness. Perhaps he'd brought this all on himself. But he couldn't bear to think that Shelby and Agatha would have to pay for his mistakes. *If you must take someone,* he bargained, *take me. But let them live.*

His eyes filled with tears again, which was surprising given that he'd already shed so many as he held vigil at Shelby's bedside. He dashed the moisture from his eyes and lay his head on the bed beside her hand.

Though he refused to voice aloud the despair that filled him, hope dwindled a little more with every passing hour. She'd grown so weak. She looked so frail. How could she hope to survive this?

Perhaps he was making a mistake by keeping Dr. Mensing away. Perhaps—

A featherlight touch brought him out of his reverie. He glanced quickly at Shelby, but her hand lay in exactly the same position as it had for the eternity he'd sat vigil beside her.

Slowly, gingerly, he pushed to his feet. His knees had

been locked in that position so long, he had trouble straightening, but he was determined to save her. And if that meant he had to bring in Dr. Mensing, that's exactly what he'd do. If he had to spend the rest of his life fighting to prove that she wasn't insane, he'd do it and gladly—as long as he knew Shelby was alive somewhere.

He took a step toward the door, but a sound, soft as a baby's sigh, brought him back around again. Again, he studied the face of the woman he loved, searched it for some sign of recovery. But again, he found nothing.

He turned away again, but this time an unmistakable groan halted his step. He hadn't imagined *that*.

Rushing back to her bedside, he sat on the edge of the mattress and gripped her hand. "Shelby? Agatha?"

To his immense relief, she groaned again. He held the hand tenderly and rubbed it in hopes of stirring the blood a little. He leaned forward and readjusted the cool compress on her forehead just as her eyes fluttered.

His throat dried, his hands went numb. He leaned closer and whispered her name. "Agatha?"

Another soft groan, another flutter of the eyelids, and he found himself staring into her wide brown eyes. She looked startled, disoriented. He couldn't tell which woman was in there, but at this moment, he didn't care.

"Agatha?"

Her eyes closed again, but only for a heartbeat. She sighed softly and groaned again as if she was in great pain and it tore through him, as well. She blinked again, rapidly, as if she was having trouble focusing.

"Agatha?"

She shifted her gaze to his face, but her expression didn't soften. Yes, he thought with a pang he couldn't stop, Agatha. He squared his shoulders and reminded himself of the bargain he'd made. If Agatha returned to him, that meant Shelby was alive somewhere. And that was all that mattered.

That was *all* that mattered.

He put a hand on her forehead. "Are you in pain?"

She turned her face away and let her gaze travel around the room. "Am I dreaming?"

"No. You've been ill. Terribly ill." He swallowed around the lump in his throat and tried to tamp down the horrible pain of loss that filled him.

She let her gaze rest on the dressing table. Her eyes narrowed slightly. She took a deep breath, then shifted her gaze back to his face again. "Zacharias?"

"Yes. I've been here the entire time you were ill, and I won't leave you now—unless you want me to go."

Her eyes fluttered shut again and she let out a soft sigh. "Zacharias. It's really you?"

"Yes."

She tried to lift her hand, but she was too weak. It fell back to her side and her eyes remained closed.

Terrified, he checked her pulse but it seemed stronger than it had for a long time. Her breathing steadied, slowed, and sounded as if she were sleeping instead of hovering on the brink of death.

For now, Zacharias told himself, he'd have to content himself with that. Though it appeared she might be out of death's grip, he couldn't make himself give up the vigil he'd maintained at her bedside. And he tried to prepare himself to spend the rest of his life with the wrong woman, though he realized now that it had been easier to say than it might be to do. Still, he reminded himself again and again as he knelt there, gripping Agatha's hand, that he could live with anything if it meant Shelby was alive somewhere.

She'd be happy, he had no doubt. She'd meet a man and fall deeply in love. And, in time, her memories of him would fade. But he knew without doubt that his memories would never die.

Some time later—he had no idea how long—Agatha stirred again. "Zacharias?"

He lifted his head and looked at her, hoping he didn't look distraught or disappointed. "Yes, Agatha. I'm still here."

She crooked her finger and beckoned him closer.

He stood quickly and leaned across her on the bed. "How are you feeling?"

"Like hell."

His heart leapt at her profanity, but he couldn't let himself get his hopes up. "Rest awhile," he said gently. "I'll have Meg bring some broth."

"Broth?" She scowled at him. "I don't want broth."

"It will help strengthen you," he argued.

"I don't want broth," she said again, her voice a little stronger this time. She studied his face for what felt like forever, then her lips curved into a smile. "You're really here, aren't you?"

"Yes, dear."

"Dear?" She let out a weak laugh and touched his cheek. "Sit beside me."

Hope flickered again. "Shall I change the compress on your forehead?"

Her fingers traveled to the cloth and lingered there for a moment. Shaking her head, she pulled the cloth away and tossed it to the floor. "I'm not dreaming, am I?"

"No."

Her hands traveled to his face again and traced the outline of his cheek. "Did you miss me?"

"Very much."

A satisfied smile curved her lips, but Zacharias still couldn't tell which woman she was. "Good," she said after a lengthy pause in which she seemed to gain more strength. "What day is it?"

"July first."

"Then I made it."

"Made it?"

"I didn't die."

"No, though we worried you might for a while."

She sighed softly. "Good," she said again. He started to stand, intent upon calling Meg, but she grabbed his hand and pulled him back to the bed with a surprising amount of strength. "I don't want Meg," she said as if she'd read his mind. "Not until you kiss me."

"Kiss you?" He sounded like a dolt, but his heart

thundered in his chest. "*Kiss* you?" He'd never heard sweeter words in his life.

"Please."

"Agatha?"

She shook her head slowly and grinned at him.

"Shelby." The name felt like a prayer on his lips. Relief rushed through him with such force he was glad he *wasn't* standing. "Is it really you?"

Her expression grew mischievous. "If you really doubt it, why don't you kiss me and find out?"

Still hesitant, he leaned forward and brushed a kiss to her temple.

She scowled at him, then laughed softly and threw her arms around his neck and pulled him closer. "Not like that. Like this." And without giving him a chance to think, she locked her lips onto his, opened her mouth beneath his, and touched her tongue to his lips.

Groaning deep in his throat, he wrapped his arms around her and crushed her to him. He kissed her until he thought his heart would cease to function, until his lungs refused to draw breath, until his head swam with need. Even after he ended the kiss, he couldn't make himself release her.

"I'm back," she said, stealing another kiss. "I'm back forever."

"Are you certain?"

"Yes."

"But Agatha—"

"Is perfectly happy where she is."

"Then she won't return?"

"Nope." She grinned at him. "You'd better get used to me, because it looks like I'm going to be here for a long time."

He ran his hands along her sides, her back, cupped her face gently, and ran a thumb across her lips. "And will you spend the rest of your life with me? As my wife?"

"In every sense of the word?"

"Every damn one of them," he said, laughing with joy.

She grinned again and rested one hand on his chest. "I thought you'd never ask."

Epilogue

"IF YOU'LL ALL step this way..." Jon Davenport stood to one side of the grand staircase and waited while the members of his tour group climbed to the landing. When he was certain they were all together, he motioned for the chatter to cease and swept open the curtains behind the window seat. This was, and always had been, his favorite part of the tour.

Gasps arose from the crowd when they saw Winterhill towering on the next hill. "As you can see," he said with a satisfied smile, "the two houses are virtually identical. The only differences you'll find are inside. Winterhill is furnished in a style that's slightly less ornate than Summervale's."

An elderly woman stepped toward the window, then looked back at him. "Isn't it unusual to have two identical houses so close together?"

"Yes, it is." Jon made himself comfortable on the window seat. "And the story of how it came about is fascinating. Zacharias and Agatha Logan, the original owners of Summervale, had a rough marriage in the beginning and for a time, after Agatha learned that Zacharias was unfaithful to her, they separated.

"Zacharias built Winterhill and even lived there with his sons for a brief time—about five years, according to the records. But something happened to bring them back together again. Agatha's journals are remarkably detailed, but only after that period in their lives."

"She forgave him." He recognized that voice, of course, and turned to smile at Shelby, who descended the stairs to join them. She smiled at several of the women in the group. "But don't worry. She didn't give in until after he saw the error of his ways."

"They reunited," Jon explained, casting another glance at Winterhill, "and spent the rest of their lives together here in Summervale where they were, by all accounts, inseparable."

"Zacharias died when he was in his seventies," Shelby said. "And Agatha died shortly afterward. Upon their deaths, each of Zacharias's sons inherited one of the houses. Their descendants live in the houses to this day. Their two youngest children—both daughters—married and lived nearby, and Agatha was never happier than when she was surrounded by her children and grandchildren."

A young woman sighed. "How romantic."

A woman in her forties scowled out the window. "You said Zacharias's sons, but they were Agatha's children, too."

"Actually no," Jon said, "they weren't. The boys, Mordechai and Andrew, were both sons of Zacharias's mistress, but Agatha raised them as her own."

The woman turned a warning glance on the balding man who stood behind her. "She must have been a paragon. That's more than I'd do."

"She was an incredible woman," Jon assured her. "Their marriage was a real example of forgiveness in action."

Shelby took over, as she always did at this point in the tour. "If you'll follow me upstairs, I'll show you Agatha's pride and joy—the ballroom. According to her journals, she and Zacharias entertained often. She loved having people around all the time . . ."

Her voice trailed away as the group rounded the stairs and started up to the third floor.

Jon turned back to close the curtains, letting his gaze linger once more on Winterhill before he closed them completely, then he climbed the stairs and stood beneath his favorite portrait of Zacharias and Agatha.

He'd always thought there was something familiar about her. Something in the eyes . . .

He stared up at the portrait for a moment, imagining what kind of woman she might have been. She looked high-spirited and mischievous, but most of all, she looked happy.

"Ah, Zacharias, old boy," he said to the empty corridor. "You were a lucky, lucky man to be loved so completely." Then he turned resolutely away from the portrait and followed the tour group toward the ballroom.